Bridge

Quest

**A GameLit Adventure Series
(BRIDGE QUEST Book 1)**

pdmac

Bridge Quest is a work of fiction. Though actual locations may be mentioned, they are used in a fictitious manner and the events and occurrences were created/invented in the mind and imagination of the author, except for the inclusion of actual historical fact. Similarities of characters or names used within for any person – past, present, or future – are coincidental except where actual historical characters are purposely interwoven. The actions, thoughts, and dialogue of the historical characters featured in this story are fictional and not meant to reflect actual personalities and behavior.

Published by Trimble Hollow Press, Acworth, Georgia

ISBN: 978-1-946495-15-0

Cover design by Trimble Hollow Concepts
Cover art by James Esquivel

for Terri Lynn
my Soulmate and Best Friend

Marbeck

Abeloft

Westhaven

Durness

Hulgard

Tal Olca

Hillfurt

Berismo

Misted
Isle

Contents

Chapter 1

Karl sat on the end of the examination table, his knees dangling over the side, wondering why hospital dressing gowns were always open in the back. Any time he had to go use the bathroom, he was sure he was mooning everyone.

The door to the room opened and Dr. Bryant came in. He was a trim older man with wavy salt and pepper hair, and the bedside manner of a mortician.

"Well," he said, sliding out a wheeled stool and easing down before flipping the computer screen around so that Karl could see the internal image of his stomach area. "Let's approach this from a bad news good news perspective. First, the bad news. You have stage four intestinal cancer." He pointed to a thin shaded area close to a small spot on the image.

Karl's heart went to his throat.

Dr. Bryant saw the look and held up a hand. "Remember. I said there was good news."

"What's the good news?" Karl asked, his voice raw, staring at the MRI image.

"The good news is that while we don't have a cure for it yet, we do anticipate finding a cure in the future."

Karl's face hardened. "How the hell is that good news?"

"Let me finish," he soothed. "While medicine is developing a cure, there is a new science called immersion technology that will allow you to live a somewhat normal productive life without the angst or pain of a terminal illness."

"Immersion technology," Karl repeated.

"Yes. It's a new development in the field of medicine and technology. I could try to explain it to you, but there's someone more qualified who can provide an explanation and answer your questions. His name is Doctor Josef Heinrich of Immersion Technology Labs. Listen to him fully before you write him off as some sort of quack. You're not the first person to undergo what they offer."

"What is it they offer?"

Dr. Bryant smiled. "I'll let him explain it. Once you're finished with him, we can talk about what's best for your future. Stay right here. I'll be back in a moment."

He was out the door before Karl had a chance to reply. Two minutes later, Bryant returned, followed by a young man who Karl swore was still in high school. The man carried an expensive Bottega leather attaché case.

"This is Dr. Heinrich of ITL," Bryant said by way of introduction. Heinrich was a baby-faced gentleman with long soft brown hair held back in a ponytail.

"I'm twenty-five," Heinrich said with a grin, his voice smooth and melodious.

"Pardon?" Karl frowned.

"I said I'm twenty-five. I can see by the look on your face that you're about to ask me if my mother knows where I am. I get that a lot. But don't let appearances fool you. I completed a Ph.D. in micro cellular electronic interface before I was twenty-two."

"That's nice," Karl replied for lack of anything intelligent to say.

Heinrich chuckled then continued. "Dr. Bryant has briefed me of your situation and I believe we can work through this unfortunate situation in such a way that will more than make up for the… um, unusual approach. However, before we get started, you need to understand that everything I'm about to tell you is classified in accordance with the Industrial Classifications Act. Once you agree to the terms of the non-disclosure agreement, you are legally bound to protect and secure any and all information relating to this discussion and any further discussions, actions, information, disclosures and knowledge of the ITL mission within the constraints of this project."

"What project?" Karl frowned.

Ignoring him, Heinrich opened the attaché case and pulled out a sheath of papers. "Do you agree to keep this conversation and all subsequent conversations and information secret?"

Karl's frown deepened, for Heinrich reminded him of the last time he received a security clearance when he was in the Army. He had been selected for a special project and was awarded an equivalent clearance far above Top Secret. The man who briefed him on the responsibilities of the clearance had been a humorless man with a cold handshake.

Though Heinrich appeared nothing like the man, why did this seem so familiar? Realizing that Heinrich was waiting for his response, he shrugged. *What the hell do I have to lose? I'll be dead soon enough.*

"Yeah, sure," Karl answered. "I agree."

"Excellent." Heinrich smiled and relaxed, handing a few papers to Karl. "This isn't quite like when you were in the Army," he assured him. "The NDA is really quite simple. You agree to never mention what I am about to tell you, unless authorized by a duly designated ITL official. Take your time and read through your responsibilities." He leaned back and turned to Bryant. "Might there be some coffee available?"

"Of course," Bryant answered with a fawning smile, jumping up. "It's one of those module machines. Any particular flavor?"

"Just good old regular black coffee, thanks."

Karl finished reading the NDA before Bryant returned with a ceramic mug of steaming coffee. "Seems pretty straight forward."

"We like to keep things simple and in terms anyone can understand." He handed him a pen. "Just put your initials at the bottom of each page and sign and date it at the end."

Doing as instructed, Karl handed the papers back, watching Heinrich nonchalantly slide them into the folder and the folder back into the attaché case. Then it occurred to him. "How did you know I was in the Army?"

"We always research our prospective clients. Some are more suited to our services than others. We've found that an initial environmental adjustment always occurs. Some are better able to handle the shock of an artificial world." Taking a sip of coffee, Heinrich smiled in satisfaction. "Good coffee." Holding the cup in his hand, he narrowed his focus on Karl.

"So, let's begin with a general approach. Aside from the muscle and tissue of the human body, we are comprised of electronic impulses, a sort of unique wired system that's self-sustaining. Without the electronics in the human body, all the muscles and tissues would be useless. As long as the electronic circuit is functioning, the body works fine. If anything affects or interrupts the circuit, obvious problems occur. Do you follow me so far?"

"Yes," Karl said, wondering what electronics had to do with his cancer.

"Good. You see, essentially, as long as the electronic circuit is whole and functioning properly, it doesn't really matter what the externals are doing. You could lose an arm, for example, and the circuit adapts to the shortened system, but still functions as a complete system. So what happens if or when the system shuts down? You die. That's the reason old people die. Just like your house or car, things wear out. You have to replace various parts in order to maintain the system. If you replaced the worn parts sooner, old folks would live longer. But I digress."

Karl shifted a confused glance at Dr. Bryant who held up a hand telling him to wait.

"My point here," Heinrich said, "is that electrons don't really wear out. What happens when diseases occur is that they inhibit the body's electronics. If we can remove the disease from the system, or," he paused, "the system from the disease, we can focus our efforts on the disease. You follow me?"

"Not really," Karl objected. "I have, what sounds like, terminal cancer, which means I'm going to die very soon. Dr. Bryant here said that there was a new thing called immersion technology that would allow me to live a 'somewhat normal productive life,' whatever that means. Then you come in here talking electrons and circuits and systems and I haven't a clue to the connection. Does that answer your question?"

"Perhaps I can help," Bryant soothed. "What immersion technology does is take your life's soul or energy, your electronics, and places them into another system so that in the meantime, medicine can work on finding a cure to the disease."

"Very good, doctor," Heinrich chimed in. "The key difference is that you'll be very much alive, just in a different system."

Karl shot a half-lidded stare at Heinrich then back to Bryant. "I'm just a slow-witted country boy. How about we cut to the chase and explain what happens."

Bryant chuckled. "Hardly," he said, looking at Heinrich then back to Karl. "Heinrich already knows that you're a professor in Nordic studies at the university. And if I remember correctly, also a martial arts expert." He purposely held back that they knew of Karl's covert military past. After all, no sense blurting something in public that Karl had assumed few knew about.

"Which has little to do with why I'm here," Karl pointed out. "So let's get back to the simple explanation."

"As you wish," Heinrich smiled. "What we propose is to remove your body's electronics and place them into a separate self-contained system where you will function as a normal everyday human being, but within the context of a unique world." Noting his explanation seemed to have made little progress, he said, "Are you a gamer?"

"A what?"

"A gamer, like in role playing games, an RPG kind of guy."

"No. Never saw the sense to them. Besides, I don't have the time to veg in front of a computer and play games."

"Pity. Besides missing out on a world of incredible imaginations, it would make it easier to explain. Let me put it like this. What we are going to do, with your consent, is to place you inside a role playing game."

Karl's eyes fluttered as he processed the statement. "You're serious. You're going to somehow place me inside some computer game?"

"Exactly."

Karl turned to stare at Bryant who seemed quite complacent about the absurd idea then redirected his attention back to Heinrich. "Let me see if I understand. You're going to somehow take my whatever you want to call it and place it in a computer."

"That's correct. The idea is not as farfetched as you think. Remember, we're all simply a higher form of cyborg, to use an analogy."

"What happens to my body?"

"Your body is cryogenically frozen so that the tissues do not decompose and the disease is momentarily stunted in place."

"Then when you find a cure, my uh, electronics are placed back into my body and I'm back to normal and the disease cured."

"Exactly," Heinrich grinned. "You do understand."

Karl frowned in pensive thought as he sorted out the whole concept. "You said I would continue to live a somewhat normal productive life. How and where?"

"Immersion Technologies has developed an RPG game we call Bridge Quest –"

"Bridge quest," Karl repeated, raising an eyebrow.

"It's not as silly as it sounds. The gaming world has some of the finest computer minds in the world, not to mention some of the best story development. Besides, from our perspective, why reinvent the wheel? We recruited some of the best gaming brains and put together an incredible world, specifically designed for individuals in your situation."

"How... how does it work? I mean, am I aware of my surroundings?"

"Not only are you aware of your world, you live it and experience it like you do right now. You feel pain, heartache, love and so many other emotions. You won't know the difference between now and your new world, except for one significant difference."

"Oh?" Karl said, suddenly alert.

"The world we've created is different than what you are used to. The world we created is one of heroes and villains and challenges, excitement and love and adventure all within a fantasy world so much better than what passes for modern existence. Once you experience it, you'll wonder why you haven't been a gamer your whole life."

"Enough with the advertisement," Karl said, smiling with only his lips. "How is it possible?"

"Remember what I said about electronics?"

Karl held up a hand to stop him. "OK. I get it. We're all a bunch of electronic circuits running around. How is it possible to get my existence into a computer?"

"It's rather complex, but it has to do with converting your body's electronic configuration into recognizable and useable components then inputting them through an interface into a database. You'd be surprised at the amount of data the human brain stores and the way the brain retrieves information. Needless to say, the storage requirement for one individual is rather significant. Thank God for nanotechnology."

"How many have done this before me?"

"Ah," Heinrich smiled, "a wise question. If you decide to participate, you would be number thirty six."

"Thirty six," he repeated, surprised. "How many have returned to their original bodies?"

"None yet," Heinrich admitted. "The cures are still progressing. We won't bring them back until we are one hundred percent sure they will be cured when they return."

"How come I've never heard of you?" he asked, surprised at the number.

"Remember what I said about security? We're off the grid for now. At the moment, we've no results to report yet. We're waiting until we have at least 100 subjects before we report, though we may lower that depending on returnees' success."

"So this is all just experimental. You're not really sure it will work."

Heinrich leveled his gaze at him. "Nothing in this world is for sure, just like you getting cancer. I don't mean to be harsh, but everyone wants a fool-proof guarantee. Life isn't like that. What I *am* offering though, is a chance to live far longer than you could expect under the present circumstances. The choice is yours. If you say 'no,' I simply go down the list to the next suitable individual. I lose nothing. You, on the other hand…"

Karl's frown turned into a glare then softened. "Point taken. So tell me, how does this all work? I mean, if I say 'yes,' what happens next?"

"After you sign all the requisite forms, you will be taken to the ITL transfer center where a technician will explain the world's fundamentals and rules. After that, it's just a matter of placing you into the game, which is the fastest part of the whole affair."

Karl turned to Bryant. "You're sure of the diagnosis?"

Bryant grimaced as though affronted. "Of course I'm sure. I didn't arrive at this conclusion willy nilly."

"How long do I have?"

Bryant hesitated. "Three months, maybe six at the most."

Karl's shoulders slumped and he swore the pain in his stomach swelled. He knew Bryant was right, for all the treatment he was undergoing, his pain was only getting worse.

"OK," he sighed. "I'll do it."

"A wise choice," Heinrich said, "I brought the paperwork with me, so we can get that out of the way here. Why don't you get dressed and we'll finish up in the doctors' conference room. One of our gaming technicians is waiting there for us."

"Pretty sure of ourselves, were we?" Karl smiled.

"Yes," Heinrich replied with a smug grin.

Karl walked into the conference room where Heinrich and another young man sat at the far end of an oval table. Heinrich leaned back in the chair and waved Karl to a seat to his right.

"This is Hans," he said, introducing a young man who appeared to be the same age as Heinrich. Hans had a cherub face with short thick blond hair done up in stiff spikes.

Karl nodded his greeting. *Heinrich and Hans... Is the German connection coincidence?*

"Let's get the paperwork done so Hans can explain how the game works." Heinrich pulled out a thick folder crammed with legal documents.

"Damn," Karl uttered. "This is like taking out a mortgage."

"It's pretty close," Hans replied with an affable grin.

Almost forty-five minutes later, his hand tired from signing papers ranging from the various forms of his legal name to the promise not to inform, tell, relate, or communicate in any way unless specifically authorized and yada yada, the last page was signed.

"Now," Heinrich announced as he neatly tapped and stacked the pages on the table, "Hans will explain the game. Feel free to ask as many questions as you want. We want you to be comfortable knowing what to expect."

"The game is called Bridge Quest," Hans began. "Think of this as any other sort of RPG game."

"He's never played before," Heinrich interrupted.

Hans regarded Karl with overt suspicion bordering on disbelief. "You've *never* played before?"

"I know," Karl sniffed. "A real shocker, isn't it. I can only imagine your utter amazement when I tell you I don't have a tattoo either."

Heinrich burst a laugh and shook his head at Hans. "I told you he was perfect."

Hans blinked at the realization he was again going to have to start at the beginning, muttering under his breath, "You would think that just one time one of them had a clue." With a resigned sigh, he opened the folder in front of him and unfolded a map, spreading it out on the table and twisting it around so Karl could see it.

"This is the world of Bridge Quest. It comprises a planet made up of islands. The object is to complete the various quests on all the islands. There is only one way to get to each island, and that is via a bridge that connects one island to another, hence the name, Bridge Quest. However, there is only one bridge between islands. There is no other way to go from one island to the next. Also, once you leave an island, you cannot go back. In other words, all the bridges are one way only."

"Why?"

"That's so players, what individuals like you are called, don't stagnate in one spot. The object is to make life an adventure, a continuous adventure. Staying in one spot defeats the whole purpose of the game."

"Suppose someone, a player, likes where they are and wants to stay?" Karl asked while looking at the map.

"I suppose they could, but it would get boring after a while."

"So I'm interacting with other players?"

"Yes and no," Hans replied, wearing a pained expression as he realized this was going to take far longer than he wanted. "Yes, you do interact with other players, but there are also nonplaying characters, called NPCs. They are characters introduced into the game to help you along with your quest. In many games, the NPCs tend to be linear and provide you with information when asked, and that's all they do. In this game, NPCs are every bit as human as you are. Though they are computer generated, they have emotions and feelings and everything else, just like you."

"Do they feel pain?" Karl asked.

"Yes," Hans replied. "In fact, it will be difficult to tell the difference between a player and an NPC, but not impossible."

"OK. So I'm in the game and I'm on my quest," Karl began before Hans stopped him.

"Not so fast. There are a few things to accomplish before that. First is choosing your avatar."

"Huh?"

"Your avatar, your persona," Hans explained. "You choose what you want to look like."

"What's wrong with the way I look now?"

"It doesn't work that way," Hans fussed.

"Let's just say," Heinrich intervened, "that most folks prefer to have another persona. It allows them to engage their creative imaginations. For example, you can choose to be a human, an elf, a dwarf and a number of other characters."

"An elf?" Karl snickered.

"Yes, an elf," Hans stiffly replied. "You can even be a Halfling or some other race."

"What's a Halfling?"

"They're somewhat similar to humans, but half their size," Hans curtly answered then caught himself. "The first thing you choose is your race." He pulled out a page from the folder and slid it in front of Karl. "You'll see the major categories listed there from humans to dragonborn to elf and others. So right now, you get to choose what race you want to be."

"I've been a human my whole life," Karl chuckled. "I think I'll stay human."

"Human it is." Hans checked the block on another piece of paper. "Now you choose a class and then further refine from there. You can choose to be a warrior, a magician, a rogue, or a cleric."

Karl examined the list and the various subcategories. Two immediately caught his eye.

Paladin: The Paladin is a brave and powerful fighter, motivated by the cause of justice and a devotion to a deity or higher being. He has additional gifts with healing, white magic, and combating undead, demons, and other dark supernatural creatures. However, his adherence to his cause/deity may impose behavioral limits and should he stray or transgress those rules of conduct, his abilities may be weakened.

Warlord: This warrior is a tactical master. He is the grand strategist when leading armies against a foe. He is equally forceful whether in the front lines or commanding from his headquarters. His charisma translates into protective auras that enhance and increase the fighting effectiveness of himself and his army. Though not as individually powerful as a berserker, for example, his charisma and genius are enough to sway the battle in his favor.

"I think I'll choose Paladin," he announced. "He seems the more interesting, though I do like the warlord's strategic talents."

"So I'll put you down as 'Paladin'?" Hans said.

"Yes."

Hans checked the box 'Paladin' on the selections page. "Now comes some of the other finer points of the game. The first is your gear. As a level 1 Paladin, you have armor consisting of scale mail –"

"Wait a minute," Karl interrupted. "I've changed my mind. I want to be a Viking instead."

"A Viking?"

"Yeah. It says here," he read, "that the Viking is a combination of the barbarian, swashbuckler, and paladin. When it comes to combat, he is fearless and ruthless, having greater than normal physical strength compared to other warriors. Though he can invoke berserker rage, he prefers agility, speed, cunning and daring to brute force, yet is not above extravagant theatrics. The ancient gods and magic play an important role in the Viking's daily life and he can invoke the supernatural powers when necessary. Magic is a natural part of life to a Viking." He looked up at Hans. "I'll be a Viking."

Wadding up the paper, Hans pulled another selections page from the folder. "Class, human, character, Viking," he said, checking the boxes. "You do realize the Viking starts off with far less gear."

"Easier to keep track of," Karl shrugged.

"You have a choice of weapon from a broadsword, falchion or a claymore."

Karl thought for a moment then decided, "Make it a broadsword. I prefer a double edge and the true claymore is a little longer than I like."

"Then you have a choice of shield or buckler."

"Hmm," Karl mumbled. "A buckler is good for close combat, but doesn't really help against arrows, whereas a shield is good for overall protection, but can be cumbersome." An epiphany burst and he narrowed his gaze at Hans. "Is this a combat game, like some sort of dystopian drama where I'm expected to fight to survive? If so, I want guns and ammo and hand grenades and things like that."

"It's not like that, Karl" Heinrich explained. "In this world, there are no modern weapons. Think of Bridge Quest as set in medieval times with the addition of magic and fairytale qualities."

"Seems an odd choice," Karl replied. "Why not simply make it like today's environment? It'd be a lot simpler."

"Like I said before, why reinvent the wheel. The RPG world is a highly developed universe. Why attempt to develop a completely new game when we could take the best from what already exists?"

An unhappy thought suddenly occurred. "What's the chance of me getting killed?"

"That's a very real possibility," Hans said.

Karl sat back. "This is absurd. You throw people into a game where the result is the same had they not played at all. What's the point?"

"It's not like that," Hans placated. "If you are unlucky enough to be killed –"

"Unlucky is right," Karl retorted.

"Let me finish. If you are unlucky enough to be killed, you respawn."

"Respawn," Karl repeated with a concentrated frown.

"Respawn – you come back to life again. You see, in the game, you can't die. Well, you can, but it's not permanent. You come back again to your bind spot."

"Bind spot?"

Hans looked helplessly at Heinrich who understood the technician's frustration. This would go a lot quicker had Karl the rudiments of gaming. Unfortunately, even pro gamers had to start somewhere. Part of him wanted to hand him a manual and be done with it. Instead, he patiently smiled at his coworker.

"Let's go back to the beginning, shall we?" He turned to Karl. "You have an idea of the world you'll be living in. It's a fantastic world in both the sense of adventure as well as design. We've developed this world to be exciting, better than the real world you're temporarily leaving. Our hopes are that once you are part of Bridge Quest, you'll never want to come back. That said, there are some essential rules and guides we want you to know to help you deal with the various aspects of the game. However, we cannot answer every variable as it would consume valuable time. The best thing we can do right now is give you the basics and get you into the game. Does that make sense?"

"I suppose," Karl replied without conviction.

"Let Hans finish the essentials and then I can answer any questions you might have."

"Fine."

"We ended at choosing between a buckler or a shield," Hans said.

"Buckler."

Hans checked the box. "Now comes the part where we discuss your initial skill levels. Every player begins at Level 1. As your skills improve and you complete quests, your levels increase. The greater your level, the more powerful you are. The highest level a player can reach is 100. So, for instance, if two players were to fight each other and one was a level 10 and the other a level 1, which one do you think has the advantage?"

"Level 10."

"That's right. Now suppose the level 1 player had a magic potion that allowed him to freeze-in-place a level 10 opponent who would have the advantage now?"

"It depends," Karl replied, "on the weapon the level 1 player had and if the potion lasted long enough for him to continue attacking the level 10 player until he killed him."

Hans smiled with satisfaction. "Now you understand. It's not necessarily the strongest who can win a fight at any given time. You have lots of other things you can use. But there are restrictions as to what and when you can use certain spells, potions, or weapons. If I understood correctly, you study martial arts."

"That's correct."

"What level are you?"

"Fifth degree black belt."

"OK, good. When you were a white belt, could you use a Bo staff correctly?"

"No," Karl answered with an understanding nod. "I needed training and experience."

"Exactly. The same applies here. Thus, beginning characters are awarded points in a number of basic skills. As your experience grows, the number of skills and the points per skill increase. For example, here is the listing for the basic skills of a Viking." He twisted a page around and slid it across the table to Karl.

Strength: 10 points
Speech: 8 points
Magic: 4 points (locked)
Health: 10 points
Mana: 10 points
Combat: 12 points

"What's mana?" Karl asked, reading the list.

"Mana and magic are interrelated," Hans replied, "though not necessarily interchangeable. Think of mana as the power to use special abilities or spells. Different abilities use difference amounts of mana. For example, if you want to cast a certain spell, it would require a certain amount of mana to cast it. Based upon how much mana you have determines how many or how powerful a spell you can cast. If your mana points drop to zero, what happens?"

"I can't cast a spell," Karl answered.

"Exactly."

"So once my mana goes to zero I can never cast a spell again?"

"No," Hans explained. "Your mana regenerates based upon time and your character. Certain characters' mana regenerates faster, druids for instance. So, for example, when you check your stats, you'll see a set of numbers displayed as a value, such as '35/70.' The second number represents the max amount of mana you can have. The first number is the current amount of mana available. Understand?"

"I think so," Karl said. "What about speech?"

"That's the ability of other languages and decoding."

"Decoding?"

"Say you have a magic document written in code," Hans explained. "Certain levels of speech help decode it."

Karl reread the list. "OK. I got it."

"As you play the game, you'll want to keep track of where you are as well as determining other players and characters levels. In the game, you can call up a screen by simply pretending there is a screen in front of you. All you have to do is concentrate on the idea of a computer screen and one will pop up for you. Think of it like VR and its touch technology. When you call up your screen, all the screens of every other character immediately become visible. To get rid of the screens, simply press the off button at the bottom of the screen. Here's a picture of what it looks like." He slid another page with a screen graphic on it across the table.

Karl studied it then glanced up at Heinrich. "I'm surprised you still use paper when all this could have been done on a laptop."

"It's all a question of legality," Heinrich replied. "We need your signature, in person."

"I understand that, but why not have a laptop here with the game on it so I can see how it looks?"

"It wouldn't be the same," Heinrich smiled indulgently, "even in holographic form. It would give you a basic idea, but it would be nothing like the world of Bridge Quest with its sounds and smells and vibrancy."

"I have just a few more items to review and then you can ask questions to your heart's content," Hans interrupted.

Gaining Karl's attention, he continued. "Along the way on your quests, you will gain weapons, potions, scrolls, coins and other items. You need a means to store these. You have two options. For potions, scrolls, jewels, coins and other small items, you have a belt with ten pockets. Each pocket holds an unlimited amount of items. While this might be unrealistic, we decided for sake of ease to leave it. However, just because you can store all sorts of things doesn't mean you should. For example, whenever a character is killed his possessions are up for grabs unless he can get back to his death spot in time to claim his stuff."

"I don't understand," Karl frowned.

"It's called your bind spot. Whenever a character is killed, he respawns back at his bind spot. So, for example, if your bind spot is in a tavern, anytime you respawn, you will reappear in the tavern. You can change your bind spot whenever you want, so it behooves you to pay attention."

"Suppose my bind spot is in an island I just left?"

"Good question," Hans said, pleased that Karl was beginning to understand. "Your bind spot will automatically move to the end of the bridge on the next island should you forget to move it. But back to my point, if your bind spot is too far away from your death spot, it's possible you can lose everything you had on you, including your belt. You will be unable to store any items until you get another belt."

"How do I do that?"

"There are certain NPCs who can provide you with a belt, but it comes with strings attached."

"I don't understand," Karl said, his frustration showing.

"For example, Hans placated, "suppose you are killed and you respawn. You're buck-naked by the way. You need a belt. A NPC offers you a belt in exchange for completing a quest. You get the belt, but you are obligated to complete the quest. If you don't, you lose everything and the belt along with it."

"Suppose I get killed again and have to respawn?"

Hans nodded knowingly. "It behooves you not to get killed, which by the way, respawning is exceedingly painful. Not something you want to experience if you can help it. And that reminds me, in addition to your belt, you have a small bag always with you. Think of this bag like a genie's bottle. You can store all sorts of weapons and armor in it, but it's small enough to hardly be noticed. And again, while this is unrealistic, it's done for the sake of the game. The same rules of respawning apply to the bag as the belt."

Hans continued his explanations for the next two hours, finally stopping when he saw that Karl was beginning to grow tired.

"I think we've covered quite a bit of ground today," he cheerfully said.

Heinrich indulgently smiled then turned to Karl. "You've signed all the necessary forms. Now it's merely a question of when do you want to insert. My advice is the sooner the better."

Karl yawned and rubbed his eyes. Lately he noticed that he tired easily and had chalked it up to fighting a bug or not getting enough sleep. Now that he was in the grip of cancer gave understanding to his change in health. Dr. Bryant's prognosis rattled around inside his brain. He had maybe six months to live. Why wait? All he had to do was get his affairs in order and how long could that take? His will left what little he had to the kids. The divorce last year gave new meaning to the idea of starting over.

He then had a perverse pleasurable thought and smiled at the sweet revenge of coming back when Judy was old and grey and wrinkled. Wouldn't that be just perfect. A scenario played out with him swinging by the retirement village to talk about the kids who now looked older than he did.

Awareness crept in and he realized they were waiting for an answer.

"Sorry," he sheepishly said. "How about as soon as possible?"

"Excellent," Heinrich grinned, slapping the table. "Let's get this show on the road."

Chapter 2

Karl lay on the table wired to electrodes and IVs and other machines, both medical and analytical. Doctors, nurses, computer technicians and other support staff hovering around him mostly ignored him as they were too busy with their respective responsibilities to worry about the patient until the time came for his cross-over.

The anesthesiologist, a pretty blond woman in her early 30s, leaned down and smiled sweetly at him. "We're just about ready. I'm going to give you some relaxing juice. When you wake up, you'll be on your new adventure."

His heart racing in nervous apprehension, he nodded and felt a warm sensation as she pushed the drugs into his system.

"He's under," she announced. "Give him another twenty seconds and you're good to go."

Twenty seconds later, the lab technician at the control board placed a hand on the conversion switch and began a count down. "Ten... nine... eight... seven... six... five... four... three...two... one... zero."

As he flicked the switch, the team of medical and technical personnel froze in place as they focused their attention on the numerous screens and beeping machines.

The heart monitor was the first to register complaints when the pulse dropped to danger levels. Yet no one reacted with concern. It was when the monitor flat-lined that they left their posts and crowded around a young man at the game terminal.

"He's in," he proclaimed with gusto. "All systems normal. We've got another one in the game." He pumped his fist for added emphasis.

An audible sigh of relief filled the room as the tempo slowed to a relaxed routine.

"Get the body down to deep freeze," Hans commanded. "We'll decide what to do with it later."

The first thing Karl noted was the mist and he shivered at the unexpected change in temperature. That there was a mist was logical as this island was called the Misted Isle. They told him the mist usually lifted by mid-morning. Right now, it was thick and heavy, hiding anything a few feet away.

He did a quick assessment, noting that he had physically changed. He had been lean and strong before. Now he was muscular and taller... with blond hair that came to his shoulders. His left hand held a buckler and in his right hand was his broadsword. The question now was where was he and what was he supposed to do? They told him he'd find out as the game progressed.

Lifting his hand with the sword still in it, he pressed a finger in the air, calling up his stats screen. Locating the map icon, he pressed it and found the little red flag indicating his location.

The island was in the shape of a curved hand with the extended fingers as the starting promontory. The bridge to the next island was on the opposite thumb side of the island. What lay between was a series of rivers, forests, mountains and bogs.

He felt his stomach grumble and knew he had to eat. It had been more than a day since his last meal. Studying the map, he saw he was close to a town called Marbeck. All he had to do now was orient the map and be on his way, which was impossible as the mist obscured everything.

Sword and buckler at the ready, Karl slowly and cautiously made his way in the mist, discovering that he was on a well-traveled dirt road, which seemed odd as the map had him at the very edge of the island. He was even more surprised when he nearly bumped into a large medieval looking gate of dark wood and iron hinges. Exploring to his left and right, he learned that the walls surrounding the gate were made of smooth drab-grey granite. How high they rose was another matter as all he could feel when he tapped his sword as high as he could reach was stone.

Returning to the gate, he probed the solid wooden gates and after a minute of searching for an entry, gave up, banged on the door and called out.

"Hullo. Anyone there?"

When no reply came, he pounded on the door with the pommel of his sword.

"Hullo. Anyone home?"

He was about to pound again when a small sliding window scraped open and a pair of irritated grey eyes stared out.

"Whaddaya want?" the voice demanded. It was a man's voice, hoarse with age.

"I'm a traveler looking for a place to eat and rest."

"Go away. Come back when the mist is gone. Won't open the gate until then," he grumbled then slid the window closed.

"How long is that?" He banged on the gate again, causing the window to jerk open.

"I said go away. Gates won't open 'til the mist goes away."

"How long is that?"

"How should I know? Do I look like a damned weather wizard?"

"What place it this?"

The eyes glowered at him for a moment. "Marbeck, ya damned fool. Now go away."

Again the window slammed shut.

Acknowledging that at least he knew where he was and accepting that he wasn't gaining entry until the mist cleared, Karl walked over to the side and sat down, leaning against the stone wall, his sword across his knees. He then focused his senses, penetrating into the surrounding mist. He heard the pounding of the surf and wondered how high above the ocean the town lay and whether the view from the walls was invigorating.

And then he wondered who and how they were able to make this so lifelike. He placed his hand against the stone wall and felt the cold solid resistance of hard rock. It felt real, just like this mist felt real. Was it his imagination dreaming this? Was he in some sort of suspended state where they fed him dreams and situations making him believe it was all real? If only he could have talked to someone who had been in the game and returned. Then he'd know for sure.

He didn't know how long it was, but his legs were beginning to ache and he stretched them out, noticing that the mist seemed brighter and parts of it began to dissipate enough so that he could make out more of the walls as well as the close cropped vegetation edging the road to his front.

When a bright sun and a broad expanse of blue sky replaced the evaporating mist, Karl again found himself wondering how they created this world that seemed just too real. Pushing himself to standing, he was surprised to discover that the town was almost on the edge of a cliff that dropped precipitously down to the sea. The road he walked began or ended, depending on one's destination, at the town's gates. He was admiring the view when he heard movement on the other side of the gates followed by the groaning of the heavy doors as they swept inward.

A crotchety older man with an awkward gait came limping out, took one look at Karl and folded his arms.

"So yer the one wantin' to come in 'fore it's time. Well c'mon. We're open now." He turned around and hobbled back through the gates, standing to the side as a merchant drove a wagon filled with pots and pans, and small bits of furniture through the wide opening. "Welcome to Marbeck."

A screen popped up in front of Karl's face.

Marbeck: also Maradhur, a town at the edge of the Shrouded Forest. Marbeck (original name Maradhur) was built by the Nevlings, a mixed race of elves and men during the middle kingdom as a trading center and outpost. During the Ocean Wars, the town suffered numerous attacks, changing hands at least a dozen times before finding itself forgotten as the Wars moved on to other islands. Populated by a mixture of races, humans carved out significant portions of the forest for farming and livestock. However, the Ocean War disrupted many kingdoms, forcing migrations of various tribes and clans to other islands to escape the devastation of the War. With the subsequent arrival of the forest gnolls of Normuncrof and the growth of the surrounding forest, Marbeck was left to fend for itself, a forgotten outpost. It is a tight community, welcoming anyone who wishes to become part of a town too tough to die.

Pressing the 'X' icon to close the screen, Karl stood to the side and watched as more carts passed by, some driven by men, some by dwarves. Karl stood in fascination, returning a smile when he caught the eye of a merchant. Once the last cart passed through he walked up to the man.

"Why did I have to wait until the mist cleared?"

"Gnolls," came the reply.

"Gnolls?"

"Yup. It's obvious yer new 'round here, otherwise ya wouldn't have showed up like ya did."

"Gnolls are pretty dangerous?"

The man cocked an eyebrow and stared up at him. "You funnin' me? Say, how'd you get here anyway?"

"Long story," he replied.

"See any gnolls along the way?"

"Didn't see a single one," Karl answered, which was the truth. "Know a good place to get something to eat?"

"Yup. The Crab's Claw's got the best seafood. If'n ya want steak, Preston's Porterhouse got no equal. An if ya want good home cookin', aside from my own missus, the Widow's Pantry is the best."

Karl deliberated between the steakhouse and the home cooking place. "Between the Porterhouse and the Widow's Pantry, which would you choose?"

"I like my cookin' with a touch of home in it, so I'd choose the Widow's place. Mind you, she's a mite peculiar, but the cookin's the best and the ale ain't bad neither."

"How do I find it?"

The man lifted an age spotted arm and pointed. "Straight on down the main street here. Can't miss it. It'll be on yer left. If'n ya get to the other side o'town, ya gone too far." He slapped his leg and snorted a laugh.

"Thanks," Karl smiled, thinking the man reminded him of his father who had a penchant for telling lame jokes.

"Say," the man said, narrowing his gaze and giving Karl the once over. "You're one o' those new folks that shows up outta the blue, ain't you."

"Guilty as charged," Karl replied, unsure of how to address the issue of total immersion.

The man stared hard at him for an uncomfortable moment then grinned. "Well. Good luck."

"Thank you." With a finger to his forehead as a wave, Karl ambled away, taking in the town.

Marbeck looked to be an ancient place with a high stone wall that circumnavigated the entire town. Human guards in simple Spangenhelm helmets and carrying crossbows manned the walls, though they seemed to spend most of their time looking wistfully at the bustling activity in the town. The main thoroughfare, bordered on both sides by one long open air market, ran through the center of the town. Merchants, divided into sections by merchandise, hawked their wares in loud raucous voices. The food market contained vegetables, fish, freshly butchered meats, bakers selling hot mince pies, and the overlapping pungent aroma of spices.

Karl chuckled thinking of the marketing wisdom in placing the food market first. Any traveler coming into the town would be sorely tempted to part with coin, especially the still warm bread. His growling stomach demanded food, but he suppressed the need as he marveled at the complexity of the supposedly simple town. No attention to detail was missing. Even the people were unique, distinct and he thought of how long it took to design this place, let alone the rest of the world.

"You look like a man who could use a meat pie," a voice called out, piercing his musings.

Karl glanced over to a plump baker who held up a tray with small individual meat pies still steaming. The bouquet made Karl's mouth water.

Despite the overwhelming desire to satisfy his hunger, Karl knew he needed to manage his meager resources and the cost of a pie plus the cost of an ale would be more here than from in a tavern.

"No thank you," he politely replied.

"Aw go on. Try one. It's free." The baker's eyes glistened with anticipation.

"Free?" How could he refuse when the price was right? As he reached for the pie, his character screen popped up, flashing a warning.

Caution. Baker Chesel is known to put salvia, a hallucinogenic plant, into his pies. Only accept food from reputable vendors.

Karl's hand jerked back. "Uh, that's OK. Thanks."

The baker's overt anticipation abruptly vanished and his head snapped to seek out other shoppers, ignoring Karl who stood rooted before the merchant's table.

"If you're not gonna try a pie, move along. I got a business to run."

Startled at the man's brusque manner, Karl meandered away pausing when he heard the baker's voice enticing another individual. Turning, he saw a tall elf, a long bow in one hand, reaching for a pie then pause as the elf received the same message.

"Whoa," the elf exclaimed. "Sweet." Accepting the pie, he bit into it and sighed with contentment. By the time he finished the pie, the elf was giddy, flapping his arms. "Look. I'm flying."

Once he started 'flying' around the street, two stout guards arrived, lifted him up by his armpits and hauled him off.

"Very smart of you not to accept the pie," a woman's voice complimented.

He turned to gape at a human sorceress of stunning beauty. Her long flowing raven hair was secured by a single leather strand circling her forehead. Her face was oval and angular, yet smooth, with piercing emerald green eyes that danced with humor. She wore a tight leather bodice accentuating her more than ample cleavage. Her narrow midriff was bare, revealing a toned stomach. A hip-hugging leather skirt ended in the middle of her thighs. Below that, calf-high leather boots gripped her muscular legs. She held a staff with a dragon's head carved on the top.

Watching his expression, she laughed. "You're new here."

"How can you tell?" he replied, taking a deep breath to collect himself.

"Your expression. You're wandering around here like it's your first time to Disney World, awed and overwhelmed."

Karl chuckled. "Am I that obvious?"

"Yes," she replied with a captivating smile then held out a hand. "My name's Annabeth."

"Karl," he answered, shaking her hand. "Are you a player?"

"Yes. I assume you are too." When he nodded, she continued, "When I first came here, I thought it would be easy to tell the difference between us and NPCs. Where you headed?"

The question caught him off guard. "Uh, to the Widow's Pantry to get something to eat."

"Good choice. I could use something to eat. Mind if I join you?"

Good God of course not. "Yes. I'd like that."

"That's how I can tell the difference, you know," she said as they headed past the numerous vendor stalls.

"The difference?"

"Between NPCs and us. I'm beautiful. I know that. That's why I chose this avatar."

"So you're saying you aren't so, um, impressive in real life?" Though Karl watched where he was going, he couldn't help but cast repeated glances at her.

"Hell no. I'm a plain Jane in real life. Everything about me is average: average height, average shoe size, average IQ. You name it; I'm the poster child for average. To make up for it, I exercised my butt off. I have a great body, but with an average face and average personality, too average for most guys to give a second glance. I'm not butt ugly mind you," she quickly added. "I mean, I look good dressed up. But how do you compete with those women who are beautiful as soon as they roll out of bed?"

"I wouldn't know," he shrugged.

"Of course not. You're a man. You don't have to look good. You can be 80 years old and still be sexy. Women? We're expected to be sexy until the time gravity starts taking advantage of our age and then no one wants to see us naked. It's just not fair."

"I suppose not," he responded, wondering if she had a point to all this. "You were saying about the difference between us and NPCs?"

"I'm getting there," she said. "The point is that when you saw me, your mouth slacked open and I could see the lust in your eyes."

Karl suddenly felt awkward. "That obvious, huh?"

"I don't say it like it's a bad thing. In fact, I like it. But the point is that while NPCs will respond in the same way, there's a difference. It's hard to explain. If I were to flash my boobs at you, I would get an honest reaction. With an NPC I would get an expected reaction. You see the difference?"

"Not really," he replied, silently praying she would conduct the experiment.

She shifted her eyes at him and laughed. "I know where your mind just went, you bad boy. Maybe later."

Karl reddened and changed the subject though latching on to the 'Maybe later' remark. "How long have you been here?"

"A little over a month," she said, stopping before a four story building wedged against its two neighbors. A small carved sign adorned the front, 'Widow's Pantry.' The windows to the side of the door were shuttered tight. In contrast, the windows on the second floor were wide open. Annabeth pulled the door open and led the way in.

Inside the Widow's Pantry was a noisy affair filled with elves, dwarves, monks, mages and rogues, all clamoring, laughing, swilling ale and generally keeping the serving girls bustling. As soon as Annabeth stepped in, a voice called out above the din.

"It's Annabeth. C'mon over here."

Karl's eyes slowly adjusted to the dim room as Annabeth weaved around tables, patting friends on the shoulders and high-fiving others before arriving at a table with two dwarves and a lady ranger.

"Who's your friend?" The lady ranger slyly smiled, letting her eyes slowly roam his body.

Karl had the distinct feeling that she was undressing him and it made him feel self-conscious. He guessed he ought to be offended, but, like Annabeth, the woman was beautiful with thick auburn hair that came to her shoulders. She was dressed somewhat similar to Annabeth in leather bodice, the difference being she wore leggings and a cape, with the hood pushed back.

"His name's Karl and he's just arrived."

"Just arrived?" a dwarf exclaimed, yanking out a chair. "Sit down. Join us." He waved a hand to catch a serving girl's attention then called out, "An ale for my friend here."

"And something to eat?" Karl said.

"And something to eat," the dwarf loudly repeated.

Annabeth slid out a chair and sat next to the ranger with Karl on her left next to the dwarf.

"This is Raquel," she said, introducing the ranger. "Next to her is Conrad and next to you is Wendell."

Wendell peered intently at Karl then chuckled. "What's-a-matter? Never seen a dwarf before?"

"You two could be twins," he replied, shifting his gaze back and forth.

"Yeah," Conrad sighed. "We know. Wish they would've said something like, 'someone already looks like that.' I coulda chosen to look like someone else."

"There ya go again," Wendell huffed. "This is a perfect set up. We work this right and we'll never get caught."

"How ya figure that?" Conrad said, rolling his eyes. "I know, I know. One of us is seen while the other one steals what we need. That only works when no one knows who we are."

Ignoring him, Wendell turned to Karl. "So what's it like?"

"What's what like?"

"The outside. What's it like?"

"How long you been here?" Karl frowned.

"What's the date?"

"Seventeenth of August."

"What year?"

"2032."

Wendell's lips moved as he silently calculated. "Been in here for almost a year."

"A year?" Karl sputtered. "And you're still on the Misted Isle?"

Wendell shot a guilty look at Raquel then at Conrad.

"Wendell's not sure he wants to leave here," Raquel answered for him. "He and Conrad have been refining their skills —"

"With little success," Conrad complained. "I arrived six months ago and when I saw him, I nearly fainted. But then I saw the advantage of looking like someone else.

"The problem is that the two of them are well known in town here, so after the third time of getting caught and tossed in the jail, they decided to call it quits for a while, especially when the burgomaster threatened to toss them over the wall and never let them come back in." She smiled affectionately at them.

"How long have you two been here?" Karl asked, looking at the two women.

"A month," Raquel replied with a seductive smile.

A serving girl in a low-scooped peasant blouse deposited the ale and a bowl of stew in front of Karl.

"How much?" he asked, turning to gaze up at her. She was probably in her early twenties, with long blond hair and Nordic skin and features. She was also quite attractive. Not as beautiful perhaps as Annabeth and Raquel, but certainly a close second.

"Is this your first meal here in Marbeck?" she asked, her voice warm and buoyant.

"Yes it is."

"Then it's on the house," she beamed. "Missus Scully does that for all the newbies who have their first meal here."

"Thank you."

"You're welcome," she sweetly replied, laying a tender hand on his shoulder, a move at once innocent yet subtly sensual.

As she sashayed away, Karl looked around the room noting all the women were more than good looking, regardless of status. All except the cooks and Missus Sully whose wrinkled face wore a perpetual scowl.

"You noticed it too," Raquel observed.

"Why?"

"Why not?" Conrad leered.

Raquel shook her head in patient indulgence. "It's like a thematic meme. All the serving girls have to be babes. As far as the players, who'd want to choose to be ugly?" Eyebrows raised, she grinned at Conrad.

"How can you all afford to stay here for so long?" Karl asked, tallying up his own meager resources.

"We go out on daily hunts," Raquel replied. "There's a bounty on gnolls."

"And there's an unlimited supply," Annabeth added.

The serving girl returned and refilled his stein of ale. "With Missus Scully's compliments."

"Thank you." Karl caught Missus Scully's attention and lifted his ale in appreciation, receiving a quick smile and nod in return. He turned his attention back to Raquel. "You were saying?"

"Whenever we run low on funds, we go kill a few gnolls to replenish our accounts," Raquel explained then glanced around the room. "Everyone does it."

Shoveling in a mouthful of stew, Karl turned to look around the room. "Are they all players?"

"Every one of them," Conrad confirmed.

"There has to be almost twenty-five players in here," he said, dumbfounded.

"Nineteen to be exact," Wendell answered.

"But there are more than nineteen players in the game," Karl pointed out.

"Some spend their time at other taverns," he replied.

"And others decided to try Baker Chesel's pie," Annabeth grinned, "and they hang out in prison for a while until they figure out they need to bribe the guards to get out."

Karl glanced around the table. "Has anyone ever left Marbeck?"

"I only know of three," Annabeth replied, staring into her half-filled ale mug.

Karl looked at Wendell, who squirmed before saying, "I've met a few more."

"What happened to them?"

"Don't know," Wendell answered with a shrug. "They never came back here."

"As far as we can assume," Raquel replied, "they crossed the bridge."

Karl finished his stew and pushed the bowl away. "I still don't understand why you all are still here."

"It's comfortable and you can level up without too much stress," Annabeth replied.

"Yeah," Raquel agreed. "Annabeth and I are Level 3 while these two clowns are still Level 2. All you have to do is kill a few gnolls and you can start raising your levels and your stats."

"What about quests?" Karl asked, peering at her over the rim of his mug.

"Yeah, well, there is that," she evasively answered.

Karl's brow furrowed and he glanced around the table. "So you all are content to spend the next however many years in Marbeck, killing gnolls and drinking ale in the Widow's Pantry?"

"Easy for you to say," Conrad scoffed. "You just got here."

"No offense intended," Karl said. "How many of you were gamers before you came here?"

"None of us," Raquel answered for the group. "In fact," she ticked her head indicating the room's occupants, "as far as I can tell, no one in here has ever been a gamer. We're all literal newbies."

Karl blinked at the revelation and gave voice to his thoughts. "Why would they do that?"

"Who knows?" she shrugged. "Maybe they figure a true gamer would be at the end before they had a chance to find the cure. Throwing us ignorant children into a complex game sort of makes sense. Do you know how many bridges we have to cross to get to the end?"

"No."

"Neither does anyone else. The way I figure it, they can keep adding bridges so that the gifted among us will always have a challenge. Though it sort of puts it in the category of insanity. You know, doing the same thing over and over and expecting different results. Only here, it's the continual search for the last bridge."

"Wow," Wendell commented, impressed. "That's deep."

Karl too was impressed. Not only was Raquel gorgeous, she was smart. "So, in all your battles with the gnolls, have you ever been killed?"

Raquel, Annabeth, and Wendell shook their heads while Conrad assumed a look of guilt.

"What was it like?"

"It damn hurts," he snapped. "Picture getting hit by a bus at full speed, a bus with flailing knives that slice you while it hits you.

"So you do feel pain," Karl observed.

"Unimaginable pain," he shot back. "I don't recommend it, even knowing I can respawn."

"So where was your bind spot?"

"Right here in this room."

Wendell barked a loud laugh. "My God you shoulda seen him. One minute I'm eating a late dinner and the next minute I see dwarf-boy here materializing… buck naked."

"Naked?"

"Yeah." Wendell started laughing again. "So here he is, standing in the middle of the room when he suddenly realizes where he is. His hands leap down to cover up his little tallywacker, which he only really needed a pinky to cover –"

"You shut up," Conrad snarled.

"But if you two are exactly alike," Annabeth interrupted with an innocent smile, holding up a pinky and gazing at Wendell.

"Yeah," Conrad sneered, "Mister Big-mouth. At least I had the balls to try and fight, unlike the coward you are who ran screaming like a little girl once the battle started."

"That's a lie," Wendell bellowed, rising out of his chair.

"Will you two either shut up or take it outside," Raquel huffed then turned to Karl. "I swear these two are worse than little kid brothers sometimes."

"Well he started it," Conrad grumbled.

"See what I mean?" she said, rolling her eyes.

Karl turned to Conrad. "Did you lose everything?"

"Yes. Fortunately it wasn't much, but I still had to start over. That's when these two," he nodded at Raquel and Annabeth, "stepped in and helped me get back on my feet."

"We were glad to do it," Raquel said with a sisterly smile. "After all, we're all in this together." She looked back at Karl. "So. What are your plans?"

Karl thought for a moment, taking a sip of ale. "I suppose I ought to get myself organized and get a feel of the place, leveling up as much as I can before I head out."

"You intend to cross the bridge?" Conrad asked.

"That's the plan."

"Why?"

"While you got a great hustle going on here, I know I would get bored and need to move on. So I might as well prepare for the move."

Raquel and Annabeth exchanged a glance and a nod.

"We can help you," Raquel offered, "in exchange…"

"Exchange for what?" Karl asked, curious.

"We go with you."

"You're leaving?" Wendell blurted in shock.

"No, don't leave," Conrad begged.

"Sorry boys," Raquel shrugged. "Now that we've found ourselves another competent warrior, it's time to go."

"How do you know he's competent?" Conrad argued.

Raquel turned to Karl. "What did you do in real life?"

"I was a martial arts instructor," he replied, purposely leaving out the university professor part. After all, he had an image to maintain.

"Damn," Wendell uttered, dazzled.

"What level were you?" Conrad asked.

"I was midway thought my 6th degree black belt."

"Double damn," Wendell mumbled, awed.

"I knew it the minute I saw him," Annabeth boasted. "The way he carried himself, he was more than just a newbie in a gorgeous body."

Though liking the compliment, Karl felt a bit awkward, as though eavesdropping on a private conversation, even if it was about him.

Raquel studied her for a brief moment then gave her a sly grin. "Did you promise to show him your tits?"

"It worked, didn't it," she replied with a confident smile.

"Now you're going to have to follow through." Shifting her attention to Karl, she passed her tongue over her lips in a sensual lick. "I might have to join her."

"Can I watch?" Conrad perked up.

"Perhaps another time, dear," she replied with a maternal smile, patting his arm.

Karl smirked, though unsure what to make of it all. His first hope was for the two women to immediately make good on the tease, yet he felt awkward like it was simply a game for them. The second hope was to figure out how to proceed. They told him he had to accomplish a quest in order to cross the bridge, but they never told him what the quest was, or how to go about finding out what it was. His thoughts were interrupted when Raquel snapped her fingers at him.

"You were gone there for a moment," she said.

"Sorry. Just thinking about how to move forward from here."

"I believe we said that in exchange for helping you get started, we would join up as a team. There's a greater chance of success in a team."

"Besides," Annabeth added. "You'd have two knock-out babes as your partners. One thing I forgot to mention is that in this world, there are no STDs and players can't get pregnant."

Karl smirked and nodded. "Yes. I would love to be a team with you two."

His personal screen popped up.

Congratulations: You've joined a team. You've added team building to your skills.

Just as Karl closed the screen, Conrad stiffly demanded, "What about us?" He threw an arm around Wendell.

"I thought you two wanted to stay here," Karl explained.

"Maybe we do and maybe we don't," he retorted. "At least we'd like to have the chance of deciding for ourselves."

"By all means," Karl readily agreed. "Think about it. By the way, what special skills do you have?"

"We're rogues," Wendell replied as explanation.

"Yes, I know, but if you're level 2 rogues, what are your skills? What can you add to the group? These two are easy," he said, indicating the two women. "One's a warrior, a fighter, the other's a sorceress working to be a powerful sorceress. When it comes to battle, I know I can depend on them to fight, and fight well."

Annabeth shot a smug look at Raquel. "Told you."

"Told her what?" Wendell sourly demanded.

"Told her that I would find the right person to lead this group."

"So now he's the damned leader?" Conrad snapped. "What the hell? He's been here for what, five minutes maybe, and now he's the leader?"

"Slow down Conrad," Raquel coldly replied, "and pull your head out of your ass and think about it. What did you do before you came here?"

When he didn't respond, instead choosing to glare at her, she answered for him. "You were an accountant. And you Wendell?" she continued, turning her hard gaze at him. "You were a restaurant manager. Annabeth here was in retail and I was a marketing guru. Out of all of us, Viking boy here," she arced a thumb at Karl, "is the only one with true combat experience. You don't come to a gunfight armed with a computer." She sat back, her polemic finished.

"Just because he's a martial arts expert, how do you know he's got combat experience?" Wendell countered.

"Trust me. I can spot it a mile away."

Conrad shifted his chair to study the Viking. "You ever been in the military?"

Karl was silent for a moment before admitting, "Yes."

"Ha," Raquel chortled. "Told you."

"Combat?"

"Yes."

"Where?" Wendell chimed in.

"South America."

Conrad pondered for only a moment before his eyes widened and he exclaimed, "The Tiwanaku War."

"Yes."

"Who were you with and what did you do?"

"I was with the Widow-makers and that's all I'll say."

"Triple damn," Wendell uttered. "You ever get wounded?

"Four times," he replied, frowning. "Can we get back to the present time, here and now?"

Raquel studied him with newfound curiosity and respect, though tinged with concern. The exploits of the Widow-makers made international news. "I'm surprised they put you into the game."

"That part of my life is sealed away, private and classified. I'd like to keep it that way."

"Works for me," Annabeth brightly interjected. "You two still have a problem with him being the leader?"

"Nope." Conrad shook his head and gulped his ale.

"And nope," Wendell added, still in awe.

"Why me?" Karl asked looking at Annabeth and Raquel. "Both of you have more experience in this world than I do."

"Call it a hunch," Raquel smiled at him. "You OK with assuming leadership?"

Karl debated the idea. One of the reasons he left the military was the responsibility for others' lives. One wrong choice and good people get killed. Even good choices could result in good people dying. When he left too many friends on the battlefield, he knew it was time to move on. Was this different? Fortunately respawning could ameliorate bad choices.

"OK. I accept on the condition that I expect to be obeyed at all times, unconditionally. Once a decision is made, we all accept it like it was our own decision. Further, we're a team and that means we leave no one behind. Agreed?"

"Agreed," came the unanimous responses.

"The no-man-left-behind mantra might be hard to maintain," Raquel pointed out, "especially if one of our bind spots is miles away from where we are and we have to move on."

"Good point. If that happens, you're on your own until you can get to the rendezvous point. I won't jeopardize the group for one person's safety. If you can't make it in time, Xin Loi."

"Sin Loi?" Conrad repeated?

"It's Vietnamese," Karl replied. "It literally means 'excuse me' or 'pardon me.' Translated into GI, it means, 'It sucks to be you.'"

"Oh," he quietly said, fully expecting him to be the one on his own. Maybe staying in Marbeck wasn't such a bad idea. He slid his eyes to cast a surreptitious glance at Wendell who gawked at Karl in obvious hero worship.

"We all in agreement?" Karl asked, already assuming control.

Again they nodded and expressed their willingness.

"OK. Right now we're five, with two possible 'not coming.'" He held up a hand to stop Conrad's objection. "I'm not condemning you. I'm merely stating the obvious. We need a backup plan if you two decide to stay here. Five's a good sized group. Big enough to handle most situations, but not too big to be unmanageable. Three of us are warriors, but we need other skills besides warriors."

"Like rogues for instance?" Raquel pointedly said.

"Exactly," Karl replied.

Conrad and Wendell turned to each other and as if on cue, Conrad let out an exasperated sigh. "Aw hell, we're comin'."

"Excellent," Karl grinned. "Now we need two more."

"Two more?" Annabeth repeated. "I thought you said five was enough."

"Seven is better," Karl explained. "We need more diverse talent, like a mage and a monk or cleric."

"A monk?" Conrad spat. "What do we want some religious nut with us, always telling us what evil sinners we are?"

"A mage I can understand," Raquel said. "But like Conrad says, why do we need a monk?"

"I'm not saying it has to be a monk," Karl relied. "We don't know what to expect in the future. I believe it would be wise to find someone who could provide skills that the rest of us don't have, someone who can fit in with this group, the essential part being a team member. It doesn't mean we have to start with someone here in Marbeck. If no one is suitable, we wait until we find the right person."

Annabeth shrugged and grinned. "Makes sense to me. I'm feeling pretty good about the future already."

Conrad nodded agreement then smiled a saintly grin. "So now that the business part of the meeting is down, what about flashing those beautiful boobs at me?"

Annabeth stood up and stretched then leaned over and looked Conrad straight in the eye. "If I did, it would only end up giving you wet dreams."

Standing outside the city gate, Karl listened as Raquel explained their method.

"Gnolls tend to be nocturnal. We've got another hour or two before nightfall. That gives us a chance to set up an ambush. What we've noticed is that gnolls travel in the same direction in the same spot all the time unless something disturbs the pattern. So once we conduct an ambush, we can do it again two more times before they change their patterns. Tonight's ambush is day two so it will be easy."

The other three stood close by, scanning the area.

"Tell him about the mist," Annabeth said.

"The mist arrives every night at midnight. It's so thick that you can't see two feet in front of you. That means we need to conduct our ambush and hightail it back here before midnight. Otherwise, it's a painful night of trying to evade gnolls and other things that go bump in the night, and they are unforgiving creatures if they catch you."

"Has anyone not made it back in time?"

"You'll notice we're the only ones out right now," Conrad grimly chuckled.

"Just about everyone you saw in the Widow's place made the mistake of not listening to the sound advice of their betters," Wendell added. "So intent of getting leveled up, they forgot the first rule of self-preservation."

"Which is?" Karl asked.

"Don't do stupid stuff," Wendell answered.

"Sound advice. So, where and how do you set up your ambush?"

"It's not far from here," Raquel said, leading the way.

The road leading out from the gate went along the side of the city wall, essentially acting as a border between the wall and the precipice that fell down to the sea below. A none-too-sturdy wooden fence lined the side by the sea.

Curious, Karl started to take a detour to look over the edge when Conrad stopped him.

"I wouldn't do that if I was you. I think the fence is there more for decoration than a barrier. I saw one townie get too close and disappear over the edge. It's a long fall to the rocky bottom."

"Advice accepted," Karl said with a nod of thanks.

Once around the corner, Karl noticed the land spread out into farm fields dotted with numerous cottages. Smoke curled from the chimneys of every home.

"I thought it was dangerous to live outside the city walls," Karl remarked.

"It is," Annabeth replied. "Every cottage you see here is a solid building with iron doors that are tightly locked once night falls. No one gets in or out once the door is closed. Doesn't matter who you are or what's going on."

"Some of the players who were caught outside in the mist," Raquel added, "made their way to a home only to be refused admittance and left outside to the attacks of the gnolls and killed. In a way, I understand it. Why sacrifice your family for some fool too stupid to heed warnings. On the other hand, if I was one of the 'too stupid' people, I'd certainly hold a grudge against the house than refused me sanctuary."

"That's why you'll see some animosity between the players and the farmers," Annabeth explained. "Those who have been killed and respawned want nothing to do with the farmers and vice versa. The problems happen when a player discovers the family who refused him sanctuary is now selling fruits and vegetables in the merchants' area. A couple of players felt it was their right to exact vengeance. They're now locked away in prison with little hope of release."

"Their own damned fault," Conrad said, offering no sympathy. "Think about it though, to spend the rest of your days chained inside a foul smelling dungeon, until someone discovers your cure and you get sent back."

"Or you escape," Wendell added.

"Doesn't sound like fun," Karl blandly commented.

The road leading away from the city was lined on both sides with a low stone wall about waist high. Outside one cottage, a farmer was putting away his scythe and rakes when he saw the group approaching. Pausing, he stared at them with unfriendly eyes until he recognized Raquel and Annabeth.

"Ah," he smiled. "Good evening to you, gnoll-hunters. Out for another cleansing."

"Yes, my friend," Raquel answered with a wave and a warm smile. "We'll be setting up down the road a piece. Hopefully the noise won't bother you and your family."

"A gnoll's death cries are a welcome sound," the farmer asserted. "I see you've brought a Viking with you. Hopefully you will kill many of them tonight."

"We'll do our best."

"Good hunting to you, my friends. Be sure to stop by my stand in the city. I sell the best apples around."

"We will," Raquel answered with a friendly wave.

Ten minutes later, she stopped at an intersection and announced, "We're here."

"Here?" Karl said, aghast, for 'here' was in the middle of a wide expanse of smaller field sections all bordered by the low stone wall. There were no trees to hide behind, no buildings to hunker down in, nothing to provide protection.

"I know it may look crazy, but trust me. We've been doing this for a month now. We know their patterns and what to expect."

"But... but," Karl hesitated, growing doubt with the chances of their success.

Raquel placed a gentle hand on his arm. "I know you're a proven warrior, but I ask you to trust me. If you know a better way or place, I'm willing to listen."

Karl stared at her, immediately realizing he was clueless as to how things went around here. Back in the real world this would have been a stupid place to set up an ambush. But this wasn't the real world.

"Sorry. We'll do it your way."

Raquel lifted her head and took stock of the wind direction. "Gnolls have a heightened sense of smell, like bloodhounds," she explained to Karl. "We need to ensure we're downwind."

She positioned the two dwarves on the opposite side of the road then sent Annabeth a little farther down and across the road. She then led Karl a short ways up to hide behind the opposite wall.

"You and I will be the confronting force while the others will attack from the rear."

"How will we know when they come through?" he asked, trying to figure out how they would signal when they couldn't even see each other.

"You'll see. By the time they come through, the moon will be full and it will be almost like daylight."

"Until midnight," Karl added.

41

"Exactly. One more thing," she said, her voice low. "The gnolls patrolling out here are usually Level 3 with an occasional Level 4 along. They are strong and tough fighters. We will have surprise on our side, but be warned, they are tough. A simple sword thrust through the heart will not kill them. You have to make sure you eliminate all their life points. You're gonna have to just about cut off their heads to finish them off."

"Appreciate the head's up."

Karl and Raquel hunkered down behind the stone wall and waited. Just like Raquel said, by the time night had fallen, a brilliant moon had risen and flooded the land with brilliant moonlight. They waited patiently until they heard an owl's hoot and Karl knew it was Annabeth signaling their quarry was on the way.

What surprised Karl was that he swore he could hear voices and then realized what he heard was an argument. He strained to listen and understand but all he heard were modulated grunts and low whines until one of the voices spoke, his voice low and raspy.

"I ain't understood a word you said fer the past half hour. Speak common tongue."

"You don't understand because you ain't smart enough to understand."

"You sayin' I'm stupid?"

"I'm ain't saying it. You are."

"Will you two shut up," another voice snapped. "It's no wonder we never catch anything with you two yapping all the time. I ain't had human meat in more'n a month. You two keep it up and I might just find out what gnoll tastes like."

"He said I was stupid," the first gnoll complained.

"Well you are," the second snorted.

"I've a mind to show you how stupid I am," the first gnoll snarled.

The third gnoll let out an exasperated 'Not again,' as the sounds of a scuffle ensued.

"Now," Raquel commanded and leaped out from behind the wall.

Karl followed and was immediately surprised at how large they were, far larger than he had imagined and his marvelous plan of a crushing hit and run suddenly didn't seem such a good one, and the vision of a tall half-man, half hyena was a bit disconcerting. However, with the one gnoll watching his two companions wail on each other, Karl attacked, leaping high and swinging his blade so hard that it nearly decapitated the gnoll who wavered and turned, weakly struggling to lift his arm.

Debilitating head wound: the gnoll has sustained 16 points damage

Karl wasted no time and thrust his sword into the gnoll's heart.

Death wound delivered: the gnoll has sustained 8 damage points and is eliminated.
Congratulations: You've defeated a Level 3 opponent.
You've received: 6 Strength points.
You've received: 4 Health points.
You've received: 6 Mana points.
You've received: 8 Combat points.
You've received: Experience.
Reward: Battleax: Common, Damage: 8-15, Durability: 85/100.

Irritated at the inopportune distraction, Karl jammed his thumb on the 'X' icon and his screen disappeared and he focused his attention on the other gnolls who were now aware of their imminent danger, for they were now fighting for their lives against the five players. Deciding they had the situation under control, he did a quick sweep of the area, determining there were no more gnolls.

By the time he returned, the remaining gnolls were dead.

Raquel looked at him with questioning eyes.

"Nothing else around," he replied.

"Of course not," she responded.

"How do you know?"

"They only travel in small groups," she explained, relaxing then bent down to cut off the left ear of one of the gnolls while Annabeth did the same to the other.

"What are you doing?" Karl questioned.

"We can't just say we killed some gnolls when we go back. We have to have evidence, a left ear. For each gnoll we kill, we are paid five gold, which we split among us."

Without a word, Karl returned to the gnoll he killed and sliced off the left ear.

"Don't forget to check them for coins and things," Raquel reminded to him, "and keep their weapons, too. If you don't want them, there are those in town who will pay handsomely for them.

Karl bent down and rifled through the creature's pockets, pulling out coins and a small vial then picked up the battle ax. It was then he realized that the main gate to the city was closed tight and wouldn't open until tomorrow morning, that none of the houses around here would offer them sanctuary, and in an hour or two a thick mist would descend, leaving them in dire straits.

"Now what?" he asked, hiding his apprehension.

"We head back home," Annabeth cheerily answered.

"But the gate is locked," he pointed out.

"The *front* gate is locked," she replied. "The back door is always open to adventurers. You'll see."

"Stand back," Raquel warned.

Karl stepped back in time to avoid the fizzle and pop as the bodies of the gnolls disappeared.

"It's not that it's dangerous," Raquel said. "It's like sticking your finger in an electric socket. It won't kill you, but it'll remind you not to do it again. Ready?"

"And no more gnoll patrols will appear?" Karl asked.

"They will after the mist descends," Annabeth answered. "They always send out one patrol during the moonlight to scout the area. Then they wait for the mist to come and use their sense of smell to track down victims."

"And how'd you figure that out?" Wendell challenged.

"I know how to read," she lightly replied. "You should try it."

"Too damned much to figure out," he grumbled.

As they headed back, their trophies and spoils in hand, Karl glanced down at Conrad. "You've been awfully quiet."

"Being out here in the dark like this always weirds me out. I'd rather be in a tavern somewhere safe, drinking and chasing skirts."

"A commendable preference," Karl admitted. As they silently walked back to the city, Karl's screen popped up.

Strength: 16 points
Speech: 8 points
Magic: 4 points (locked)
Health: 14 points
Mana: 16 points
Combat: 20 points
You've received: Experience

"How do you turn these damn things off?" he fussed, jabbing his finger at the 'X' icon causing the screen to disappear. "The stupid screen popped up in the middle of the ambush."

"They're there to keep track of your progress," Annabeth explained.

"Jumping up in front of my face when I'm in the middle of a fight is not helping me keep track of my progress. Thank God I wasn't fighting more than one gnoll at a time."

"The notifications usually wait until the appropriate time," she said, "though I do agree that they can be pretty annoying."

"Still don't see the sense to them," he grumbled, wondering if being in charge was such a good idea. Yes, he had combat experience, but this world was so unlike what he was used to. Raquel seemed to have been the leader of the group before he arrived. Why was she so willing to yield that role?

He could make out the city in the distance and wondered where the back door might be when Raquel made an abrupt turn and headed towards a cottage in the middle of a small farm plot. Pushing the door open, she marched across the floor to the fireplace, reaching a hand inside the hearth. A moment later, the entire fireplace swung open, revealing a dimly lit set of stone stairs set in a descending spiral.

"Watch your step," she cautioned, reaching into her bag and withdrawing a thin vial that she shook, causing a green glow to emerge. "Last one through, be sure to close the fireplace." Single file, they followed her into the gap. As Wendell was last, he pulled a metal lever by the gap and the fireplace scraped shut.

Holding up the weak light, she led the way to the bottom of the stairs, which ended at a thick iron barred door. She knocked twice on the door then three times then twice again, repeating the pattern.

The door slid to the side and they faced a towering corpulent man standing behind an iron portcullis. A meat cleaver rested on his shoulder. He wore leggings and a butcher's apron spattered with dried blood. A single torch placed in a wall sconce provided dim flickering light.

"Good evening, Lady Ranger," the man said, placing the meat cleaver against the wall. Reaching down, he grunted and lifted the portcullis high enough for the group to walk through. Except for the two dwarves, the others had to bend over, careful not to scrape against the pointed ends of the bars.

"Was it a good hunting?" The man lowered the portcullis and pulled a lever on the wall to close the door.

"We took out three," Raquel replied, "an entire patrol."

"Excellent," he nodded with a grim smile. Taking the torch, he motioned for them to follow him down the short hallway, carved out of the rock.

The hallway dead-ended into another hallway and they followed the man, turning left. From then on, it was turns and twists into other hallways before finally emerging into a wide room where a sleepy merchant sat behind a table. A ledger, ink well and feather pen, and two small boxes were neatly arranged on top. Wall sconces jammed with torches circled the room, giving it more than ample light.

The merchant looked up, recognized Raquel and smiled. "Good evening, Lady Ranger. I trust your venture tonight was profitable."

"Up late, aren't you, Sigurt?" she grinned.

"It was my turn tonight," he sighed. "I'm glad you're back so I can get you paid and go back home to bed. So what're the damages?"

"Three dead," she replied, placing the ears on the table.

"Ah," he grinned with satisfaction, "three less to worry about." He collected the ears and placed them in one box then opened the other, a money box, and counted out fifteen gold coins, stacking them in plies of five coins. Scooping them up, he deposited the coins into Raquel's waiting hand.

"Ya know," he said. "Whenever you go out on a mission, you and your team always come back with no scrapes or bruises. Other teams go out and they come back with one or two of them missing and the others bleeding and hurt with maybe one ear among them. You? You always wipe out the entire patrol." He glanced down at the ledger. "I also can't help but notice that of all the gnolls killed, you are responsible for almost 90% of the kills."

Raquel shrugged. "We have a good team."

Karl noted the response. It wasn't '*I*' have a good team.' Small wonder the others trusted her. She was a gifted leader and a team player.

"Yes, you do," Sigurt agreed, regarding Karl with a favorable nod. "I see you have a new member."

"This is Karl," Raquel said. "He just arrived today."

"Glad to have you here in Marbeck, Viking Karl." Sigurt yawned and rubbed his eyes then turned his attention to the silent giant. "We're done here, Maurice. You can show them the way out."

"I know the way," Raquel said, leaving Maurice and Sigurt to close shop.

Halfway down the hall, Karl chuckled. "The giant's name is Maurice?"

"Yes," Annabeth grinned. "He's a butcher. Has a vendor spot in butcher's row. He's honest as the day is long. He's also one mean-ass drunk when he's had too much, so

I'd watch myself if ever you happen to be in the same tavern when he's out on the town."

"Speaking of mean-ass drunk," Conrad piped up. "I could use a drink myself."

"Patience, Grasshopper," Annabeth intoned. "We need to divide tonight's spoils first."

"Where do we do that?" Karl asked.

"Back in my bedroom at the tavern," Raquel answered. "We pool our take and divide it fair and square. We all put in what we got tonight." She shot a stare at Conrad.

"Why you looking at me?" he complained.

"No reason," she blandly replied.

Despite his best efforts to keep track of their path, Karl gave up after a while and simply followed where he was led. They emerged into an empty room with a single door opposite them. Opening the door, Raquel led them outside where the mist was beginning to claim the night.

"Follow me," she commanded then expertly led them through the streets and alleys of Marbeck.

Five minutes later, they stood outside the door of the Widow's Pantry.

"That reminds me," Karl said. "I still need a place to stay."

"I'm sure she still has rooms available," Raquel said. "Most of the players stay here."

Karl frowned as he sized up the outside.

Raquel saw his doubt. "The tavern goes back a ways and besides, the rooms aren't all that big."

"The price is good though," Annabeth added. "She'll give you a deal for long term lodging."

"I don't know how long we'll be staying," Karl mused. "Perhaps I'll do week to week."

"How long before we... uh..." Conrad said, his apprehension obvious.

"Move on?" Annabeth finished for him. "That's a good question. Captain Viking?" she flashed Karl a sweet smile.

"Not until we've all leveled up as high as we can," he explained. "We need to be in the best form we can be before we move on."

Conrad relaxed and pointed to the door. "Ale?"

Raquel's room was on the third floor. Like she said, it was small with a single bed, a wash stand with pitcher and basin, and a small chest of drawers.

It didn't take long to divide the spoils. Karl was pleased to have the extra cash and immediately went downstairs to pay for a room, which ended up on the fourth floor. Debating whether to get some sleep or share an ale with the team, he opted for the ale and descended the three sets of stairs and entered the main room of the tavern, finding the others at the table. Wendell saw him and waved him over.

Karl caught the eye of a pretty brunette serving girl. Miming tapping ale into a mug, he pointed to himself then the table, receiving a nod and a smile of understanding. As the girl sauntered away, he slid a chair out and plopped down.

"So where's she put you?" Annabeth asked.

"In the nose bleed section in the back."

"What room number?"

"444."

"Easy to remember."

The serving girl approached, her hips swaying seductively. Placing the ale on the table, she winked at him."

"Here you are, sir." She locked her gaze on him and demurely smiled.

"Thank you," he said, smiling back at her, tipping an extra copper coin.

She bent over at the hips to scoop up the coins, letting the low cut peasant blouse pull away from her chest, giving him a lingering view of her firm breasts. She laughed when she caught Conrad leaning far over to catch a glimpse.

With another wink at Karl, she twirled around and sauntered away.

"She wants you," Conrad said with obvious frustration. "Why can't I find someone like that?"

"Aren't there other dwarf women available?" Karl asked.

"It ain't the same," Conrad moaned. "I like 'em tall and curvy in all the right places."

Karl was about to ask why he decided to be a dwarf when a tall elf approached, giving Karl a haughty stare.

"You think you're something, now that you're hanging around with these clowns."

Conversations stopped and the room grew oppressively quiet as the others watched the exchange.

"You think you're hot stuff because you went out on a patrol and now come here to brag about your prowess, you Level 1 Viking. You know what I think? I think you're nothing more than an overgrown coward."

There was an overt sucking in of breaths as those in the room waited to see Karl's response.

Karl looked up at the elf then turned his head to both sides as if looking to see if there was someone behind him, before staring intently at the elf. "Oh wow, you've mistaken me for someone who gives a shit what you think." He picked up his mug and took a slow sip.

The elf stiffened and has face hardened, especially when he heard the laughter behind him.

"Back off Simon," Raquel warned. "He killed a gnoll by himself in two blows tonight. Can you make the same claim?"

"I've killed some gnolls," he defiantly replied.

"What?" Raquel sniffed in disdain. "Two maybe, total in your whole time here and that was with a group helping you, and one of your team was killed in the process." She leaned back to give the room a passing glance. "Everyone knows that. Isn't that right, Alex?"

Another elf, nursing an ale while brooding in the corner, looked up at the mention of his name. "Yeah. That is right. What of it?"

Raquel turned back to Simon. "Why don't you tell us why Alex no longer wants to go out on patrols with you instead of coming over here and acting like something special?"

Simon curled a lip and snarled, "I'd watch your back if I were you."

"That's what I'd expect coming from you," she shot back. "You're the kind that would shoot someone in the back. You hear that everybody," she called out. "Simon here has no qualms about taking out another player, and he's not afraid to hide and shoot you in the back."

"You shut up, you damned slut," he threatened, bowing up like he was getting ready to strike.

"Back off, elf-boy," Karl growled, looking up at him with cold steel eyes.

"Or what?" Simon challenged. He grimaced when he heard Wendell start laughing. "What's so damned funny?"

"You," Wendell replied shaking his head. "You know nothing about the man and you're all over here like you're some sort of warrior god. What are you in real life again? Oh, that's right, you're a toll collector on some interstate in Missouri. You ever hear of the Tiwanaku War?"

"Yeah?"

Wendell jerked a thumb at Karl. "Meet one of the Widow-makers."

A strained hush settled on the room as Simon's arrogance vanished and he swallowed hard. "Really?"

"Why should it matter?" Karl replied, his hard gaze remaining. "We're all in this game together. We can either work together or go our separate ways. If you want adulation, I suggest you do something to earn it. Now if you don't mind, our team here would like to enjoy an ale together. I'd say it was a rough night, but quite honestly, killing three gnolls happened so fast, we didn't even break a sweat." He took another sip and tuned his attention to Raquel.

The noise in the room returned to the normal cacophony leaving Simon awkwardly standing next to Karl's table. Hoping no one noticed anymore, he quietly slunk away to his room.

"What was that all about?" Karl asked.

"That's Simon," Annabeth answered. "He wants to be the leader, so he was here trying to assert his dominance. While some willingly follow him, those like us here, ignore him and hope he'll go away."

"I expect we'll be doing that first," Conrad said.

"So what's the plan for tomorrow?" Wendell asked.

Karl looked at Raquel. "We have maybe one more opportunity with the patrol in the same place tomorrow night?"

"Yes."

"Then we hit them again tomorrow night, and as often as we can these next two weeks. We'll need experience working as a team." He saw Raquel raise an eyebrow. "You four already are a team," he explained. "I'm new, remember? And any other we accept will have to train to be part of a team that thinks like one."

"Tomorrow then," Annabeth announced, holding up her mug.

"Tomorrow," the others replied, clinking their mugs.

Back in his room, Karl arranged his weapons close to the bed and was unbuttoning his shirt when a knock on the door interrupted him. Frowning, he ambled over and opened the door to reveal the serving girl who had given him so much attention. In one hand, she held a cutting board with a loaf of bread and a small block of cheese. In the other was a cold bottle of ale.

"I noticed you hadn't eaten much today," she said with a shy smile. "I thought you might like something before you go to bed."

Karl was tired and wanted nothing more than to go to sleep. Yet here was this gorgeous woman apparently wanting to join him in bed. Part of him said, 'What's wrong with you? Open the stinkin' door and let her in.' Another part said to be careful. It was the 'be careful' part that won. Besides, it wasn't like it would never happen again.

"What's your name?"

"Kylie."

"Kylie. That's a pretty name." He fought back a yawn. "You're very kind and thoughtful, but I think tonight I'd just like to get some sleep." He gave her his best winning smile, wanting to let her down without ruining further chances.

"Are you sure?" she said, deflated.

"Yes, I'm sure. May I take a raincheck on that?"

Her mood flipped and she dipped her head. "Of course. Another night then."

"Thank you."

Closing and barring the door, Karl fell into a deep and restful slumber.

During the next week, Karl and the team went out every evening and eliminated the gnoll patrol. They also added two new members, a druid and a cleric, both recent additions to the game. The druid was a pretty woman named Lana, with strawberry blond hair, emerald green eyes and a captivating smile. The cleric was a quiet reflective man named Brad who immersed himself into his character in true Stanislavski method. Yet his wit was dry and quick and he was not averse to telling the occasional bawdy joke.

By the end of the second week, word had leaked and the group found themselves inundated with requests to join.

"What are we gonna do?" Wendell moaned, seated across the table from Karl who had just thanked a woman elf huntress for her interest. "Everyone wants to join."

"Almost everyone," Conrad countered, ticking his head in Simon's direction, watching him trying to sway players to his leadership.

"Here is what we'll do," Karl answered looking at each of them in turn. "We take anyone who wants to go with us."

"That'll be a nightmare," Conrad complained. "Too many of them are still Level 1's and 2's."

"Let him finish," Brad said, but not unkindly.

"Thank you, Father Brad," Karl said with a grin and a gentle tease. He had come to like the quiet man. "The seven of us are the core team. If we find someone who is a genuine fit, great... otherwise, we proceed on the foundation that we are the core. We continue our training and operations as always, taking along those who can cope. But, we do not make accommodations for those who cannot keep up. As the cliché goes, we're only as good as our weakest link."

He was interrupted by a dwarf who wanted to join. After politely listening, he sent the dwarf away with the belief he was joining the group.

"Like I was saying," Karl continued. "We here are all Level 3's. The way I see it, there's little likelihood of us increasing our levels the longer we stay here. It's time to move on."

"I was afraid you were going to say that," Conrad sighed.

Ignoring him, Karl said, "We move out in one week. That will give us time for gather supplies and send out long range recon patrols. Each of us needs to make sure we have all the potions, elixirs, and whatever that we can afford and carry. Same holds true for weapons. Questions?"

"Yeah," Wendell said. "Where we going?"

"Pull up your maps, everyone," Karl commanded then opened his personal screen, pressing the map icon and using his thumb and finger to stretch it wider. "We're here at Marbeck, at the northern point of the island. We want to head down and around to the bridge at the point. How far that is, is anyone's guess as there are no keys providing distance. However, note the terrain. The shortest distance to the bridge takes us over mountains. Therefore, we'll work the coastal roads and plains to get to the bridge."

"We still have to do a quest," Lana reminded him.

"I know. If any of you have a clue as to what it is, sing out."

"So what do we do with all the tagalongs?" Conrad asked.

"We shed them along the way," Karl answered. "I know it sounds harsh, but there it is. We still have to make it past the forest surrounding Marbeck, and the gnolls, and the mist. My guess is that we'll lose half of them before we make it past the forest."

"Don't remind them of their bind spot," Brad suggested. "If they are killed, they'll likely come back here, too far away for them to catch up."

"My thoughts exactly," Karl complimented. "I'll have a route mapped out by tonight and will show it to you in the morning."

There was a sudden burst of excitement at a table close to the door and they turned to watch as a paladin's body began to glow then sizzle like a steak on a grill and then disappear with an audible pop.

"My God," a voice cried out in shock. "He's gone."

Voices rose, overlapping in questions and wonder. What Karl could figure out, sifting through all the noise, was that the paladin's name was Drew, that he had suffered from an autoimmune disease, and that he had been in the game for over a year. The consensus was that a cure had been found for Drew and he had gone home.

Once the version of Drew's disappearance as a result of a cure was accepted, the interest in leaving Marbeck waned. Folks didn't want to jeopardize the developers not finding them. That eliminated ten hopefuls from joining Karl's group. Yet another ten remained, ignoring Simon's protestations, leaving him with four or five loyal followers, all elves.

"What the hell did you do?" Marc demanded, storming into the cubicle on the Designers' Floor of ITL. He glared down at the young man who had pulled off the headphones when he felt a presence looming behind him.

"I pulled a player out of the game," Jackson retorted, curling a lip at the pompous bastard whose sucking up to those above him was so obvious that everyone called him 'trailer hitch lips.'

"But he doesn't have a cure yet. Who gave you authority to do that?" Marc folded his arms and stared imperiously at him.

"None of your damn business who gave me authority," Jackson tartly replied. "Why don't you go back to your cubicle where you belong and leave the gaming operation to those who actually know what they're doing."

Marc bristled and his jaw clenched. Spinning around, he marched off, returning moments later with their direct supervisor, an attractive languorous woman in her early 30's.

Jabbing an accusing finger at Jackson, he exclaimed, "He pulled a player out of the game."

"Yes, I know," she replied, frowning at him. "I told him to do that."

"You did?" he blurted. "But why? Now all the players are going to think that they found a cure for him."

"Exactly," she said.

"But... but... if they all think he's been cured, they're never going to leave Marbeck."

"That's the point, isn't it," she answered. "But the bigger issue here is that Drew was beginning to infect the other players with his whining and his constant harping that he wanted to be in another game. I'm sure you noticed that, didn't you." It wasn't a question.

"Well... uh, yeah, I did, but I thought that he'd get over it and move on."

"How long would you have left him there?" she challenged.

"I... uh..."

"Exactly my point," she drawled. "I'm sure you've noticed that with Drew's vanishing, the folks flocking to Karl's banner have suddenly found excuses for not going with him."

"But what about Drew?" Marc awkwardly asked. "There isn't a cure for him."

Barely suppressing a grin, Lisa narrowed her focus on him. "Trust me. He'll be fine."

Marc's mouth gaped open. "But he's going to die as soon as he's placed back in his body."

Lisa gave him a maternal glance. "Why don't you let us worry about that and go on about your own work." Turning her attention to Marc, she said, "Keep me apprised of your progress."

"Yes, Mam," he replied with a triumphant smile. "Oh, one more thing, Lisa. Karl finds the popups irritating. We're treating this game like all others, that players obsess over individual points and track leveling progress on a frequent basis. Karl still hasn't checked his stats. What's the down side of eliminating his popups? It's not like he ever checks them. Besides, it would make the game even more realistic without the constant reminder that it *is* a game. "

She knitted her brow and slowly nodded. "Give me a paper on it with the pros and cons and your recommendations."

"Yes, Mam."

She was halfway down the corridor between the cubicles when the epiphany hit Marc. "You're putting Drew into another game."

Shaking his head, Jackson rolled his eyes. "Duh. By the way, hotshot, what game are you immersing into?"

Taken aback by the question, Marc stiffened with self-righteousness, giving him a condescending stare. "I'm immersing into Legendary Hero."

"Figures," Jackson snickered, "an MMORPG, though I do have to admit the graphics are killer awesome. Still," he chuckled, "never took you for a risk taker. Figured you go into some corporate game like Chairman of the Board or something equally boring."

"Well that shows how much you know," he sniffed. "And what about you? What game are you going into?"

Jackson broke into a wide grin and his eyes twinkled. "Harem Quest."

"Harem Quest" Marc scoffed with a disapproving frown. "You're going to spend the rest of your life pursuing sex."

"Yup," Jackson triumphantly replied. "And as soon as I can get the kinks out of Bridge Quest, I'm outta here."

"You're pathetic," Marc sniffed in disdain.

"Look who's talking?" Jackson shot back. "You're gonna spend the rest of your miserable life getting stomped on by better players than you. You're gonna end up a lackey for some two-bit Don Quixote wannabe, carrying his satchel full of wasted dreams. In fact, I'm gonna start calling you Sancho. Now don't you have work you have to do, instead of bothering me, Sancho?"

His nostrils flaring, Marc whirled around and stomped off, his mind racing as to how he could get Jackson immersed into an S&M game.

Chapter 3

Karl had admonished the group to tell no one when they were leaving, so when the time came, it was just another day as seventeen humans, elves and dwarves assembled outside the main gate as the sun burned off the morning's mist.

Karl gathered them to the side to give last minute instructions. Looking over the assembled group, he couldn't help but notice a subtle separation: Raquel and the core team stood apart from the rest.

"You all know what we're about to do," he said. "It's not going to be easy. You'll notice that we had a much larger group before Drew's disappearance. Those who chose to stay believe that their cures will happen very soon and they prefer to stay here. I can understand their reasoning. It's safe. But it also assumes an answer we don't know for sure is true. That said, if anyone else wants to stay here, do it now. It's not going to bother me or anyone else who has made the decision to go. It would be far better for all involved that you go now than regret your decision two days from now when we're fighting gnolls and who knows what else."

He folded his arms and waited, silently watching the faces of those who had chosen to stand with him. Then he observed two women elves share a look. One shook her head and picked up her gear.

"I can't," she said with a guilty sigh. "I'm just not ready."

"It's OK, Sara," Karl soothed. "We all understand. Go in peace."

There were tears in her eyes. "I'm just not ready," she repeated.

The other woman elf picked up her gear and edged closer to Sara. She said nothing, but her intentions were clear.

"That's fine, Jessica," Karl said with a comforting smile. "Like I said, it's better you make the choice now than two days from now." He caught the eyes of the others. "You all need to be one hundred percent certain."

When no one else moved, he stepped to the side and let Sara and Jessica slip past and back through the gate.

"Anyone else?" Karl challenged. "This is the last call. Go now." He waited then placed his hands on his hips. "Alright. A few final things to remember. One, we travel in silence. This isn't a stroll in the park. We all know there's danger out there. We need to listen to every sound, noise, or bump in the night. That means we pay attention. Second, we travel until an hour before nightfall then dig in. That means we prepare a perimeter defense. We've all been through this, but now it's time to put it into practice. Third, we wait for no one. If you can't keep up, you're on your own. I know that sounds harsh, but everyone has a responsibility to the group and that means keeping up.

"What about that 'no man left behind' stuff?" Ross, a human Ranger, challenged.

"There's a difference between being hurt and needing help," Karl intoned, peering intently at Ross, "and being unequal to the task. If you can't keep up, you don't belong with the group and you jeopardize the entire group. Any other questions?"

When none came, he said, "OK. Let's see who we have left." Scanning the group, he counted seven humans, four dwarves, and three elves, already arranged into three teams.

The first team, Team Alpha, consisted of Sakura, an attractive human assassin dressed in black: Bruno, a tall elf who decided he'd rather be a thief than one of the traditional archetypes: Sharyn, an elven paladin; Jill, a dwarf druid: and Wendell. The second team, Team Bravo, was composed of Dieter, a hulking barbarian of enormous size: Carole, an elf lore-keeper; Ross, a handsome human ranger; Kendra, another dwarf healer; and Conrad. The remaining team had Raquel, Annabeth, Lana, Brad and himself.

For the most part, Karl was pleased with the mix though he hadn't a clue what to do with Carole. What exactly was an elven lore-keeper and how was that going to help them when they ran into trouble? Still, she was here, ready to be part of the group, even if she was a little ditzy.

"OK. Listen up. Order of march is Raquel and Annabeth out on point, Conrad and Wendell rear security. I'll be in the middle. Brad and Lana, I want you close to me. That leaves two teams of four each. Team Alpha is between me and the point team, with Bravo team between me and rear security. Take note of who is close to you. Ready? Let's move out. And keep your distance. Don't bunch up. Be far enough away to still see the person in front of you, but close enough to render assistance if necessary."

Raquel and Annabeth led the group around the city walls then headed west through the farm fields then into the thick forest and along the coast line. Karl noted that the day was like every other day so far, sunny, clear skies and warm. A sea-scented breeze blew in from the ocean, reminding him of his other life when he was healthy and whole, when a day at the beach was a welcomed respite from the job.

Though the forest was thick with tall trees and overlapping branches, shafts of sunlight penetrated the canopy, illuminating the forest floor and providing more than enough light to guide them. Raquel and Annabeth kept a moderate pace and the group made good time, the initial fears of the unknown fading in the relaxed ambiance of the day.

It was mid-afternoon when the two women on point jerked to a halt. Annabeth scampered back.

"There's a house up ahead. It looks deserted."

Karl motioned for Sakura, the Alpha team leader, to come to him. Sakura was a Level 3 assassin, with short black hair and dressed in a tight black body suit that accentuated her athletic body.

"Take your team and scout around the house and the surrounding area. We'll come up behind you."

Sakura nodded and silently collected her team.

By the time she had scouted the surrounding forest, Karl had the rest of the group arrayed in a perimeter around the house.

Though the stone home looked deserted, it was not dilapidated or in disrepair. It was a small house, with two fireplaces. A small yard consisting of low cut grass and flowers surrounded the house. The thatched roof looked to be well tended and trimmed. It looked like the quintessential fairytale house set in an enchanted forest, which caused Karl to shake his head and wonder why the developers placed this house here. Sakura materialized and hunkered down next to Karl, causing him to startle at her sudden appearance.

"There's a well-worn path leading from the house deeper into the forest," she said. "We followed the path for a ways, but didn't want to get too far away. We didn't find any other trails or paths."

"Then I guess we better find out if anyone is inside. You come with me." Turning to Raquel, he said, "Pass along the word to stay in place. You're in charge, should anything happen to me."

As Raquel passed along the mission via hand-signs, Karl and Sakura stood and approached the home, finally standing at the front door. Karl looked once around, shrugged then knocked. When he heard no response, he knocked again then tried the door, which opened easily.

The inside of the home was tidy and organized with a rough-hewn table in the center surrounded by four wooden chairs. A fireplace was tucked in one corner with a cooking pot dangling from a cooking iron. Shelves filled with leather bound books lined the walls. A trestle table layered with scrolls and large papers sat against a side wall. Another door faced them on the opposite wall.

"Check it out while I see what else is here," he said then watched and marveled at her silence and grace as she slipped through the door.

He walked over to the trestle table and rummaged through the various papers. The larger flat ones were maps and he twisted them around to study the lines and features. It was the second map that startled him for it showed the city of Marbeck with the surrounding farmland, and then pinpointed the gnoll strongholds when his screen popped up.

Congratulations: You've discovered the Maps of Dairnach Forest. These will help you safely navigate the forest. Caution. Sometimes the trees seem to move.

He again startled when he realized that Sakura was standing beside him.

"I hate it when you do that," he fussed then grinned at her impish smile.

"It's just a bedroom," she reported, "one bed big enough for one person, chest of drawers and a wardrobe. I checked the chest and wardrobe. Nothing in either. One thing I did notice though was the remnants of thick spider webs. Someone's obviously gone to a lot of trouble to clean the place."

"Look at this," he said, dipping his head at the map.

Sakura bent her head to study it then uttered a surprised, yet quiet, gush. "This map shows the route all the way to Abeloft, along with the gnoll positions." She looked up at him. "Wonder who lives here."

"Hopefully we'll find out. Get everyone together. We'll stay inside here tonight."

Watching her slip out the door, he returned his attention to the maps and then the scrolls. He picked up a scroll and unfurled it.

Congratulations: You've received a scroll of weapons enchantment. It increases your weapon's damage by 10%. A level 3 mage or sorcerer is required to enact the enchantment. Enchantment enacted for one battle only.

Sighing at the unsolicited message, he thumbed the 'X' on the screen and wondered if the occasional informational message might not be helpful in the long run. Still, there had to be a better way than appearing all of a sudden. He slipped the scroll into his belt and shuffled through the rest of the scrolls, none of which he could read, deciding that Lana probably could make more sense of them. He was leaning on the table, studying the maps when the rest of the group silently filed in through the door and dropped their gear.

They stood in the main room, waiting for him to finish. Standing up, he nodded with satisfaction.

"We stay here tonight. Find a spot to settle down. You can talk, but quietly. We need to hear what's going on outside. Raquel and Lana," he said, catching their attention. "I need you here."

While the rest of the group found places to get comfortable, Conrad and Wendell stretched out in a corner, propped against the wall. Conrad pulled out a long stemmed pipe and filled the bowl, offering the tobacco pouch to Wendell who gladly tapped the cut tobacco leaves into the bowl of his own pipe. Before long, the sweet aroma of chocolate permeated the room.

Brad walked over to stand above them, shaking his head. "That is just so wrong," he complained with a grin. "I haven't had a good piece of chocolate since I was a kid."

"If you have a pipe, I'd be glad to share some," Conrad offered.

"I don't smoke," he replied. "And anyway, I'd rather have the chocolate."

"Can't help you there, but this is the next best thing. Tastes the same and doesn't fill you up."

"You poor dwarf," Brad commiserated. "Nothing tastes like chocolate."

Karl flashed them an indulgent smile then returned to the maps and scrolls. "Lana, I need you to go through these and see what we can use." He filled her hands with eight scrolls, each one loosely bound with ribbons of different colors.

As she went off to peruse the scrolls, Karl and Raquel focused their attention on the maps. He showed her the screen message.

"So what does the warning mean? Sometimes the trees seem to move."

"I don't know. I guess we'll find out."

Karl glanced at her out of the corner of his eyes. "You're like a caged animal," he said, turning to gaze at her fidgeting.

"I can't help it," she replied. "I'm a ranger. Being cooped up in small places like this makes me uncomfortable. I can't see beyond the walls of the room."

Karl looked out the window. "We got maybe an hour of daylight left. You wanna take a patrol out?"

"Yes," she replied without hesitation.

"Pick who you want and scout to the southwest. Be back before night falls."

"Thanks."

Raquel found Sakura and Annabeth and the three women went out to scout the area.

Finished with the scrolls, Lana came over. "These are all enchantment scrolls for weapons, armor, jewelry and things like that. Some of them require a level 5 or higher mage to unlock."

"Anything you can use?"

"Not me specifically. I can help with some of the lower tier enchantments."

"Good," he said, pulling out the scroll he had sequestered. "Here's one more."

Unrolling it, she read the contents and rolled it back up. "I've found two more that increase battle damage 15%."

"How many do we have like that?"

"We have four that we can use, all concerning weapons enchantment. Two more are for armor, one's for jewelry and one is for flying," she added with a puzzled smile, "but you have to be a level 12 to use it."

"Can you enact the enchantment for the weapons scrolls?"

"Yes."

"Good. When Raquel and the others get back, use two scrolls for her and Dieter, one for me, and save the last one. Make it a 15% one."

"OK."

Karl went to the front door and stepped out, taking note of the position of the house and the time of day. Poking his head back in, he looked around for the Bravo team leader and found Dieter staring out the window on the opposite wall.

Dieter was a seven foot tall imposing barbarian whose weapon of choice was a double-edged battle ax. His shoulder length blond hair was secured by a thin brown leather headband and a plain twisted iron torc adorned his neck. He wore a sleeveless leather jerkin and leather leggings revealing massively muscular arms and legs. His thick leather boots, laced with thin leather strips, came up to just below his knees.

"Dieter," Karl called out.

"Yes, Boss?" Dieter replied, his piercing azure blue eyes sparkling with the excitement of adventure.

"How about taking Bravo team and scout west for a bit?"

"Roger that," he happily nodded then motioned for the rest of his team to move out.

Karl stood at the door and watched them stealthily slip among the trees. The aroma of chocolate catching his attention, he turned to the two dwarves amiably chatting in low conversation. Grinning at them he commented, "You'll make pipe smokers out of us all. If I had a pipe, I'd be tempted to join you."

"Easily remedied," Conrad said. With a flourish, he produced another long stemmed pipe.

"How many of those things do you have?" Karl asked, walking up.

"More than enough for those who wish to partake." Conrad filled the bowl and handed it to Karl then struck a match to light the tobacco.

The tobacco had a mild flavor, but a strong aroma and the smell of chocolate permeated the house. Karl stepped back outside to wait for the patrols to return. The first to arrive was Raquel and company. Karl frowned when he saw only Raquel and Annabeth.

"Where's Sakura?" he asked then looked to his left to see her standing next to him. "How do you do that?"

"I'm an assassin," she replied with a nonchalant shrug. "I'm not supposed to be seen."

"We found nothing," Raquel reported. "The road leading away from the house goes on for a while, forest on both sides. There are numerous trails that crisscross in the woods. We followed a number of them with no result. It's too quiet out here, if you ask me."

"I agree," he nodded. "Dieter's out scouting the area to the west." He looked up at the darkening sky. "He should be back any moment now."

Annabeth looked beyond his shoulder and saw the towering barbarian lumbering towards them. "Well?"

"Nothing," he answered. "It's too quiet around here. There ought to be night sounds or something."

"Let's get back inside," Karl said. Once inside, he ordered, "Close and lock all the shutters. Light a torch." Then, with a puzzled frown, he walked over to the fireplace, peered inside the pot then down at the hearth. Reaching into the pot, he felt the smooth interior.

"What's up?" Annabeth asked, walking up to stand beside him.

"This whole set up," he answered. "Look." He pointed to the fireplace and cooking pot. "This pot looks like it's never been used. Also, where's the wood for the fireplace? There are two pieces of charred wood in the hearth, but look at them then look at the fireplace. There's no soot marks, and the charred wood looks like it was placed there. I don't think anyone really lives here."

"What about the road?" Raquel pointed out. "It looks like someone uses it."

"I don't know," Karl said, shaking his head then turning to the group. "OK folks. We're somewhat secure in here. I want a rotating watch. At least two people awake at all times. There are fifteen of us. Team leaders, designate a rotation. The rest of us will fill in where you need."

Once the watch was set, conversations dwindled and they drifted off to sleep. Karl peeked into the bedroom and smiled to see the mattress on the floor with three dwarves sleeping sideways across it. He tiptoed amongst the stretched out bodies, ensuring all were getting some sleep before he found a spot and stretched out on the floor.

He was tired, but his mind wouldn't let him sleep. The chocolate aroma had dissipated, replaced with subtle bouquet of flowers, the smell intensifying to a cloying level. His body began to feel the heaviness of a body before it settles into deep sleep. It was the tug on his boot that startled him and caused him to sit up.

There, in the dim rippling light of the torch stuck in the wall, his groggy brain tried to focus on the small black bodies scurrying around the room. Another yank on his foot caused him to look down as a spider, the size of a small poodle, lifted his leg to wrap a sticky silk around his ankles.

Without thinking, though still drowsy, he lifted his sword and thrust at the black body, piercing it and causing it to shriek out in a high-pitched squeal, black gooey blood pouring out onto the floor, the odor foul and retching.

The screech jolted him awake and he yelled as he sliced through the webbing. Rapidly assessing the scene, he saw dozens of spiders working their webbing on the others. One body was already being hauled up the chimney.

Leaping up, sword in hand, he grabbed the torch and attacked, stabbing and slicing and waving the torch around. Suddenly he felt another by his side, and he twisted his head to see Sakura, stiletto blades in hand, stabbing and cutting.

The cacophony of spider shrieks pierced the drug induced slumber and shook the others awake. A few of them struggled to free their hands and arms which had been wrapped in spider silk. Others, not yet bound, sliced through their bonds and freed those wrapped up then attacked, forcing the spiders to back up towards the chimney where only the web-wrapped head of their victim now showed.

Unable to escape up the chimney and cornered by the players, the spiders swarmed forward in an attempt to get to the front door. Recognizing their assault objective, Conrad and Wendell spread themselves across the door and swung their hammers, smashing and crushing the spiders.

Unfortunately, by the time the last spider was dispatched, the body was up the chimney. Karl raced to the door and yanked it open only to discover that mist enveloped the land. Any effort in rescuing the poor player in the chimney would endanger the rest of the group. With a growl of frustration, he closed and barred the door.

"Who did we lose?" he asked, taking a head count.

"Jill the dwarf," Dieter grimly answered.

"No!" Conrad and Wendell cried in unison. Jill and Kendra were female dwarves and the objects of their growing attention. Jill's departure meant the two friends were now vying for the lone lady dwarf.

"There's nothing we can do about it," Karl responded. "She'll respawn in Marbeck, which reminds me. We need to change our bind spots, but I do not recommend changing it to here." He then turned to Dieter and Sakura. "Who had watch?"

"Carole and Jill," Sakura replied.

Karl turned a questioning eye upon Carole who awkwardly shrugged. "I don't know what happened. Jill and I were near the front door, quietly talking, and the next thing I remember there were spiders everywhere. But I do remember there was this smell, like some sort of flower and I said something to Jill about it. Then all of a sudden we were fighting spiders."

"Some kind of sleep inducing drug?" Sakura offered.

Karl remembered the sweet bouquet and nodded. "Most likely. That means we need to be doubly aware. Break up the table and chairs to use as firewood. I want a fire in that fireplace."

Dieter smashed the table with the flat of his ax then ripped apart the chairs. Piling the debris into the fireplace, he turned to Annabeth. "Got anything to start a fire?"

Annabeth blinked for a moment then accessed her skills chart. "I do. I have a spark skill." Pointing her finger at the pile of broken furniture, she uttered, "Spark." A crack of energy flicked from her finger onto the wood, which burst into flames. With a loopy grin, she looked down at her finger then back to Dieter who replied with a chuckle and a nod.

The stench of the dead spiders was overpowering and Karl snatched one up by the legs, unbarred the door and tossed it out. Needing no urging, the others did the same thing, occasionally stabbing a not-quite-dead-yet spider before tossing them out the door. After the last spider was disposed of, Karl again barred the door.

Though the spiders were gone, the stink remained.

"I can't breathe," Wendell complained.

Karl assessed the likelihood of anyone getting sleep with the fetid miasma. "Open a window and the door. Whoever has a pipe, now would be a good time to light up."

Congratulations: You have defeated the Spiders of Ravnar.

You've received: Experience.

You've received: Leadership +4 points.

You've received: Sleeping potion resistance +2 points.

"Damn it," Karl muttered, punching the screen off.

Despite the open door and windows, it took over an hour for the chocolate aroma to overwhelm the spider odor. By then, they realized there was little floor space that was not sticky with spider blood.

"How am I supposed to sleep?" Conrad moaned as the door and widows were closed. "This stuff is all over the place."

"Do your best," Karl said. "And that goes for everyone else. Find a spot and get some sleep. Same schedule for the watch."

Karl slept little that night, reminding him of the days when he was in the military and an hour or two of sleep was enough to carry out a mission. That worked fine for a couple of days, but by the end of a week, his body crashed and he slept hard. But his mind was too active and the adrenaline was still pumping through his veins. He envied those folks who could go fall asleep anywhere under any conditions.

His was sitting in the corner, head on his forearms, resting on his knees when he woke. Daylight rimmed the window facing the sea. Looking around, others were still asleep except for the two on watch. Standing, he stretched then worked his way towards the door, stepping over bodies. Quietly unbarring and opening the door, he gazed out and could see the hazy forms of trees in the morning mist, knowing it would burn off quickly now.

Turning, he looked at the two on watch. "Go ahead and get everyone up. It's time to move out."

It wasn't long before they were all outside, munching on jerky or coming back from a visit to the woods to relieve themselves. By the time the mist burned off in the morning, they were itching to be on their way.

Karl consulted his personal screen map and compared it to the maps found in the house. He kneeled and spread one map on the ground. The two team leaders along with Raquel, Annabeth, and Sakura kneeled around the map.

"As far as I can tell," he said, "we should reach Abeloft today." Using his finger, he traced the road between the house and the town. "We'll rest up for a day or two, restock supplies then move on. Gnoll positions are here, here and here." He placed a finger at each spot ensuring they saw the places were close to the road. "Gnolls are nocturnal, so we shouldn't have any problems. However, let's not assume. Same order of march, unless you two need a break," he said, addressing Raquel and Annabeth.

"We're fine," they replied.

Collecting up the maps, Karl circled his finger in the air then pointed down the road. Raquel and Annabeth took point again and the group moved out.

It was late afternoon when the two women on point called a halt. Karl came forward and looked to where Annabeth pointed. The forest was clearing to an edge and he could see a large walled town in the distance. It looked much like Marbeck. Pulling up his screen, he read the blurb about Abeloft.

Abeloft: also Abetolft, a town on the coastal region midway between Marbeck and Hulgard. Once a significant trading center due do proximity to a deep water port, the town fell into decline as a result of the Ocean Wars and the destruction of the port. Abeloft (original name Abetolft) was built by the Nevlings, a mixed race of elves and men during the middle kingdom as a trading center and outpost. During the Ocean Wars, the town suffered numerous attacks, changing hands at least a dozen times before finding itself forgotten as the Wars moved on to other islands...

Karl scanned the rest of it for it sounded the same as Marbeck. Looking around at the rest of the group, he nodded and motioned for them to proceed, but be cautious.

The lay of the land looked familiar as did the city walls and main gate, and Karl swore the developers had simply transplanted Marbeck to here. As they drew close to the gate, traffic increased. Most noticeable were farmers' carts, drawn by slow oxen. Having sold their produce and purchased needed supplies, they were headed home.

Yet there was a difference as the group approached the gate. The farmers and other pedestrians regarded the newcomers with surprise and curiosity. One farmer's curiosity got the better of him and he drew back on the reins to halt his wagon.

"Where'd ya all come from?"

"From Marbeck," Raquel replied.

"Marbeck?" he repeated, his jaw dropping. "Honest?"

"Yes, honest," she smiled.

He stared at her, as though waiting for the punchline.

"Is that a problem?" she asked.

"Other than ain't' no one come from there since long afore I was born." He then peered intently at her and at the others who came up to listen, his head titling back when Dieter stood next to his wagon. "Hot damn. We ain't ever had yer kind here. Wait'll I tell the missus. C'mon," he exclaimed, wheeling his wagon around. "We gotta let them know yer here."

They waited for him to turn the wagon around then followed behind. Once within hailing distance of the gate guards, the farmer called out, "They're here. They're here. Go tell the burgomaster. They're here."

The two gate guards had already sized up the visitors and had sent a runner to alert the town's leadership. As the group entered the gate, the burgomaster, a plump little man wearing the medallion of office suspended from a chain around his neck, bustled up, three aldermen following on his heels.

"Welcome, welcome," he expansively greeted them. "Welcome to our little slice of heaven. Will you be staying long?" he asked with a hopeful smile.

"Long enough to rest and get some supplies," Karl answered.

"Yes, yes, of course," he said, his smile a permanent fixture. "We have numerous outstanding establishments to meet your every need. You'll be wanting a place to stay, no doubt."

"Yes," Karl replied with a smile, wondering why this man was being so obsequious.

"Excellent, excellent," he grinned, bobbing his head. "We have all sorts to choose from, from the simple lodging for those preferring the simple taste, to those with exquisite furnishings and the finest food. Which do you prefer?"

"Good food and a soft bed," Conrad loudly observed.

"Quite right, quite right," the burgomaster readily agreed, causing Karl to wonder if the man always spoke in pairs. Snapping his head around to gaze at the aldermen, the burgomaster lowered his voice and asked, "Where should we send these fine folks?"

The three aldermen were actually two men and a woman who did their best to hide looks of guilt as they pretended to ponder and offer suggestions until one said, "Humphrey's Haven," upon which the other two agreed with unbridled enthusiasm.

"Of course, of course," the burgomaster said flipping a hand. "Why didn't I think of that?" Turning to Karl, he grinned most ingratiatingly. "Humphrey's Haven has heavenly..." he paused and giggled. "Listen to me. I'm just too full of alliteration. But, to the point, Humphrey's Haven has everything you need, and at good prices too."

"Sounds good," Karl said, amused with this strange little man. Before he could ask how to find it, the burgomaster pointed down the main street.

"Straight on through the city. Go around the square and keep going straight. Humphrey's Haven is on your left just past the square. Once again, welcome to Abeloft." Spinning around he flapped his hands at the aldermen, shooshing them away. "Come, come. Let's let these good people get settled."

Karl watched the aldermen skitter away, the burgomaster herding them like a mother hen. Chuckling, he looked over his shoulder and said, "Let's go find Humphrey."

Finding Humphrey's Haven was easy. It was the walk there that caused them to feel self-conscious for as they made their way past the numerous busy shops and vendor stalls, crowds parted while merchants and customers paused their transactions and emerged out into the street to silently stare at the visitors. Dieter seemed to receive a disproportionate share of looks, all of them impressed and pleased with his size.

The murmuring started as soon as they passed, and followed them like a ripple. By the time they arrived at the tavern, a sizeable crowd had grown and tailed along behind them, stopping when Karl and company stopped at the tavern's door.

Karl turned and saw the wonder and excitement in their eyes, and the unmasked adoration for Dieter. "Thank you for escorting us here," Karl spoke. "You all have a great rest of the day."

Walking into the tavern, Raquel leaned in to Karl and whispered, "What the hell was that all about?"

"Haven't a clue."

Humphrey's Haven was laid out like the Widow's Pantry in Marbeck. Even the serving girls looked the same. Humphrey, the proprietor, was a bald rotund man whose apparent passion was food and wine. His wide grin as they entered told Karl that they were expected.

"Welcome, my friends. Please come in," Humphrey enthused. "Pick a place, find a seat. Sit, sit. I'll bring you the finest food and ale in Abeloft."

There were few patrons in the tavern, yet their faces reflected the same fervor as those outside. With practiced ease, Annabeth and Raquel headed for the corner table, Conrad and Wendell tagging along. Karl stood back to allow everyone to get settled before ambling over to the seat Raquel had saved for him.

In short order, Humphrey and his serving girls were hauling out plates filled with fresh bread, cheeses, steaming meats, and mugs brimming with cold ale. And just as quickly, the noise in the room rose as more patrons filled the tavern, prompting retelling tales of spiders and gnolls.

A serving girl in a low-scooped peasant blouse deposited another ale in front of Karl.

"How much?" he asked, turning to gaze up at her. Like the girl in Marbeck, she was probably in her early twenties, with long blond hair and Nordic skin and features, and the usual quite attractive and buxom.

"This is all part of the room price," she relied, her voice warm and pleasant. "You *are* staying aren't you?"

"Yes."

"Then this is included."

"All the ale I can drink?" he teased.

"Uh, no," she smiled. "The first one is included. After that, it's added to your bill."

"Thank you."

"You're welcome," she sweetly replied, laying a tender hand on his shoulder, a move more than subtly sensual.

As she sashayed away, Karl looked around the room and wondered if all the taverns in the game looked the same, and all the tavern girls looked the same. If so, he'd have to figure out a way to notify the developers to expand the characters.

Humphrey came over to the table, wiping his hands on his apron. "I count fourteen of you," he smiled a toothy grin. "How long will you be staying?"

Karl shifted a glance between Raquel and Annabeth who both held up two fingers.

"Two nights."

"It's one silver and ten coppers per night, food included, one ale per meal. Anything more is extra, including the girls, so please treat them well. I'll have your room assignments in a few minutes. How's the food?"

"Excellent," Karl acknowledged.

"Thank you."

As Humphrey waddled away, the serving girl approached, her hips swaying seductively. Placing the ale on the table, she winked at him.

"Here you are, sir." She locked her gaze on him and demurely smiled.

"But I haven't finished this one yet," he said with a smile, holding up his mug.

"This one's on me."

"That's very kind of you," he said, smiling back at her and placing five copper coins on the table. "In appreciation for your thoughtfulness."

She bent over at the hips to slowly and deliberately scoop up the coins, allowing the low cut peasant blouse to dip away from her chest, fully exposing her firm breasts. She smirked when she saw Conrad nearly fall out of his chair, vainly leaning over to catch a glimpse. Giving him a wink, she paused long enough to allow him a lingering view before sauntering away.

"Just damn," Conrad moaned. "Why doesn't anything like that happen to me?"

"Because you're a goofy dwarf," Raquel smirked, though staring at Karl.

Humphrey came back before Conrad had time to think of a snappy reply. "Here are the rooms for you and your friends," he said handing Karl a list with names, room numbers, and a handful of keys with number tags on them. "Please remind them that when they go out to leave the key at the desk there."

"Will do," he replied, suddenly feeling tired.

Annabeth plucked the list out of his hands and read through the names and locations then handed it to Raquel. "I'm room 315." She stood and stretched then held out her hand for the key. "I need a nice hot bath."

"Need someone to scrub your back?" Conrad chirped.

Annabeth flashed him a patronizing smile. "Remember what I said about wet dreams?" Turning to Karl, she asked, "What're we doing tomorrow?"

"Take the day off. Relax," he answered.

"I like that." She looked down at Raquel. "You coming?"

Raquel nodded then finished her ale in one long gulp. "I'm in room 316," she said, glancing down at the tag on the key.

"So where'd he put you?" Annabeth asked Karl.

Looking down at the list, Karl shook his head. "Weird. I'm in 444 again."

"It does make it easy to remember," she said. "I was in 315 in Marbeck."

"You don't find that strange?" Karl wondered.

"Not really," she shrugged. "That way I don't have to keep track of different rooms in different towns. If I get the same room in the next town, I'll know the developers are either keeping track of me or are lazy enough to keep things simple."

He smiled at her and paused to watch the two beautiful women saunter to the door leading to the stairs to the various floors. Still distracted by the vision of them naked in the bath, he shook his head and handed out the rest of the keys.

Deciding that he too would like a bath, he caught the eye of the pretty blond serving girl.

Making a beeline for him, she stopped so close that he could feel her body heat. "Yes, sir?"

"I'd like a bath, please, nice and hot."

"Of course," she smiled with pleasure. "I'll arrange for a tub in your room. Give me a few minutes, please."

As the girl sashayed away, he leaned back and inhaled the overlapping aromas of ale, baked bread, and sizzling meat. Thinking back to when he arrived in the game, standing outside the gates to Marbeck and the subsequent times out on patrols killing gnolls, followed by long enjoyable meals in the tavern and romping sessions with Kylie in his and her bedrooms, he was hard-pressed to think of when he had had more fun. And the flip side was that even if he was killed, he wouldn't die. He'd simply respawn back in Marbeck. What was the downside?

The downside was that once he crossed the bridge, this island and the NPCs in it were lost to him forever. He admitted that he had developed a fondness for Kylie, one that could have grown into something more. But he knew he was leaving and purposely held his emotions in check.

And then there were Raquel and Annabeth… and Sakura, and Lana, players that could move along with him. But were they interested in something romantic, especially if one of them had to respawn so far away that there was little likelihood of them ever being together again?

Of all the women PCs, he was attracted most to Raquel and Annabeth. But was it wise to get involved with subordinates, if he was the supposed leader? He was in the midst of his musings when the serving girl came back.

"Your bath is ready, sir." she sweetly announced.

"What's your name?"

"Elena."

"Elena," he repeated. "Thank you, Elena."

Taking the mug of ale with him, he followed Elena up the stairs to his room, which was now steaming from the hot water in a portable wooden tub that was placed in the middle of the floor. Dipping his finger in the water, he sighed with pleasure at the thought of lounging in a hot tub, with a beautiful woman scrubbing his back… and other things.

Placing his belt and gear on the floor by the bed, he turned to see Elena watching him, an expectant smile curling the corners of her lips.

"Why are you staring at me like that?" he asked.

"I've never seen a Viking before."

"Never?" he frowned. "Surely there have been other… uh, people like me come through here."

"Never," she replied. "I've never seen dwarves or elves or people like that giant man."

He noted the dreamy expression and wondered why she decided to come here instead of being with Dieter. "My guess is that he's probably figuring out how to get a bath. With his size, it's hard to accommodate him. Perhaps you might want to see if he needs some help."

"That's OK," she hastily replied. "I'm here to serve you."

"I'm sure Dieter could use some help. I'm fine. Really. He's in room 205."

"Are you sure?"

"Yes, I'm sure."

"I can check on you later if you like."

"There's no need. Hopefully I'll be sound asleep after the bath. I think Dieter is the one who could use a little help."

"Thank you." She dipped a curtsy and slipped out the door.

Sighing with disappointment, he unbuttoned his jerkin and hung it on a wall peg by the bed. He was in the process of unbuttoning his pants when he heard the door open.

"I'm fine, thank you," he said over his shoulder.

"I know you are."

He stood up when he recognized the voice. His hands still on the first button of his pants, he turned to see Annabeth, barefoot and dressed in a silk robe, standing in the doorway. Her long raven hair fell past her shoulders and draped over her breasts.

Closing the door, she slid the locking bolt home and turned around. Smiling impishly at him, she said, "We tossed a coin and I won."

"We?"

"Raquel and I. I won, so I get you tonight. She gets you tomorrow night."

Karl swallowed hard, staring at how the silk wrapped and folded to her body.

"Remember when I said about flashing my boobs at you?"

"Yes."

She opened her robe, revealing she was completely naked. Her breasts were large and almost unnaturally firm. She watched as his eyes traveled down to her toned stomach and shapely thighs.

"You see?" she charmingly laughed. "That's the difference. I'm getting an honest reaction."

Letting the robe slip to the floor, she stepped into the tub. "Ooh. My goodness. It's hot. Well?" She titled her head and raised her eyebrows. "Are you just going to stand there or are you going to join me?"

Karl unbuttoned the rest of the buttons and slipped the pants off and tossed them on the bed then turned to face her.

"Yes," she leered, letting her gaze take in the tall Viking. "Now that's what I'm talking about."

Karl was at breakfast with Annabeth when Raquel pushed through the door leading to the upstairs rooms. Seeing them, she smiled and waved and walked over, sliding out a chair.

"I slept so soundly last night," she happily sighed. "How about you two?"

Karl suddenly felt exposed, especially when Annabeth replied, "We slept great, though the bed's a little small for two people."

"I wonder if I should ask for a large mattress tonight," Raquel mused, as though Karl wasn't there.

"I should have thought of that," Annabeth bemoaned then grinned. "Next time I will."

Before Karl had a chance to ask if he had any say in the matter, a grim faced Sakura pushed through the door and marched over to the table.

"I can't find Carole anywhere. I went by her room to check on her and all of her things are there, but she isn't."

"Have you asked Humphrey or his girls if they've seen her?"

"Yes," she answered with frustration, "and I can't get a satisfactory answer."

Cocking an eyebrow, Karl stood and motioned for Humphrey to come over.

"Yes, sir?" the chubby proprietor grinned.

"Have you seen an elf dressed as a mage this morning?"

"I believe she went with the burgomaster's friends early this morning," he replied, his smile lessening.

"Where did they go?"

"Uh, well, you see," he cough then cleared his throat. "It's just that I'm not exactly sure, if you take my meaning."

"No I don't," Karl replied with a cold hard stare.

The door to the tavern opened and the burgomaster, followed by the aldermen, came in. Seeing Karl and Humphrey in discussion, he bustled over.

"Good morning, good morning." He greeted them with a broad smile. "Did we have a good night's rest?"

"Where's our team member?" Karl asked, getting directly to the point.

"Well, ah, yes, her," the burgomaster hemmed and hawed, twisting his fingers. "You see, it's a matter of your presence here and when you said you were leaving. It simply wasn't convenient for us to have you leave so soon, especially with all that's going on. You understand."

"No, I don't understand," he replied, folding his arms.

"You don't?" the burgomaster replied, surprised.

"Of course not. Where is she?"

"Well, you see, she's, uh, she's safe, rest assured, but hidden away."

Karl's lips tightened. "Why?"

"Because we need your help and we needed leverage to make you stay."

"What kind of help?" Raquel asked.

The burgomaster cast a helpless glance at the aldermen who motioned for him to continue. "You see," he began. "We need your help."

"You've said that already," Karl intoned.

"Yes, yes I did, didn't I. Well, it's like this." He took a deep breath and then in a monotone rush, exclaimed, "Once a month a band of orcs comes here and demands to be fed. They threaten to tear down the city walls unless we feed them. The last time was a month ago. We had no food to give them, so instead of tearing down the walls, they tore down the house of one of the farming families and carted them off to be slaves, the entire brood, husband, mother, and six kids. Then they ate all their cattle. Then they came back to the gate and said that was just a warning and that they'd be back day after tomorrow. If we didn't give them enough food, they would tear the city apart and kill everyone in it. Then you showed up and now we're saved because you all are big and strong and clever. You can save us. You will help us, won't you?"

Quest Alert: Save the town from orcs
Reward: Unlimited access to supplies, scrolls, potions, and weapons currently in the town
Do you accept this quest? Yes   No

"What happens if we don't accept?" Karl asked, frowning as he reread the alert.

There was a pregnant pause before an alderman hesitantly replied, "Then we sacrifice your friend to the orcs."

"That would be a terrible mistake on your part," Karl warned. "If you think orcs are bad, you haven't seen us operate."

The burgomaster's eyes bolted wide as he abruptly realized Karl and company were already inside the city walls. His nervousness increased when Dieter entered the tavern, followed by the rest of the company who slowly made their way across the room and arrayed themselves behind Karl.

"You have two minutes before we tear this city apart to find her," Karl threatened, "starting now." He placed a hand on the pommel of his sword.

Before the burgomaster had a chance to response, an alderman was out the door.

"What's going on?" Dieter asked.

"They've kidnapped Carole,' Karl explained, "and will release her in exchange for us taking care of some orcs."

Dieter stood to full height, towering over everyone in the room. "That was stupid."

"Yes, yes," the burgomaster replied, his hands fidgeting. "I can see that now."

"A minute and a half left," Raquel intoned.

"Please," the burgomaster whined, his hands patting the air. "Please. She'll be returned safely. I promise."

Ignoring him, Karl turned to Raquel. "Your thoughts?"

"Once we get Carole back, I think we might want to consider his proposition."

"I agree," Annabeth added

"How many orcs were there?" Karl asked the burgomaster.

"Three," he answered with a mix of hope and apprehension.

Karl activated his screen and scrolled through the listings of characters and pulled up 'orc.'

Orcs are obnoxious, aggressive, cold-blooded, and arrogant. They are bullies by nature and only respect raw strength and power. Their arrogance makes them believe they are entitled to anything they want, unless another stronger than they can stop them from taking it. Prone to laziness, they avoid anything associated with 'work' unless it pertains to the battlefield. This attitude stems from the belief that the strong have a right to impose their will upon the weak, much like Nietzsche's Ubermensch. The weak are nothing more than tools to be used. They take slaves from other races and would enslave their own kind if given the opportunity. Orc men brutalize orc women, children, elders, the infirm and any other too feeble to fight back. Deformed babies are killed upon birth. With the understanding that no one likes orcs, they have developed a culture that has a stoic indifference to pain, yet replete with vicious tempers, and a hair-trigger willingness to commit acts of atrocity and vengeance against anyone who dares oppose them.

Orcs are powerfully built and typically stand a few inches taller than the average human. Females are slightly smaller. Though seemingly of equal size to humans, they are differentiated by greater muscle mass, broader shoulders, and thick muscular hips that give them the recognizable lurching gait. They typically have dull green skin though orcs of a rust color are not unusual. An orc's hair is coarse and dark, black being the prominent color. Orcs have beady red eyes, and protruding, tusklike teeth. Orcs prefer wearing vivid colors such as blood red and mustard yellow. Orcs consider battle scars marks of distinction. As they are fond of tattoos, they will incorporate these scars into a form of body art.

"One minute left," Raquel announced.

Karl skipped the parts about orc society, religion and relations, and was about to jump down to the stats chart when a paragraph caught his eye.

Orcs view dwarves and elves with an odd mix of overt hatred, resentment, and caution. Though orcs respect strength and power, they cannot fathom why these two races of inferior strength have kept orcs at bay for countless ages. As such, they never miss an opportunity to torment a dwarf or elf who falls into their hands. However, when it comes to full-scale battle, they proceed with caution unless certain of the outcome. Orcs view humans as weaklings who, like sheep, blindly follow. However, even sheep can produce an obstinate ram. Thus, while they happily kill and/or oppress humans too weak to fend for themselves, they always keep one eye open for that human who will not back down.

He then dropped down to the combat stats.

Orcs are proficient with all simple weapons preferring those that cause the most damage in the least time, such as the falchion or the double axe. They like to attack from concealment and are proficient in setting up ambushes. Orcs will obey the rules of war (e.g., honoring a truce) only as long as it is convenient for them.

- *+4 Strength, -2 Intelligence, -2 Wisdom, -2 Charisma.*
- *Night vision: strong out to 50 feet.*
- *Light Sensitivity: Orcs prefer operating at night, in overcast conditions, or in the predawn hours. Bright sunlight affects their ability to wage combat. The same holds true within the radius of a daylight spell.*
- *Languages: Common, Orc. Additional languages: Dwarven, Gnoll, and Goblin, though these languages are not as prevalent.*
- *Favored Class: Berserker/barbarian*

Raquel was about to say, "Thirty seconds left," when the door opened and Carole came in. She was an attractive elf despite looking like she had just awoken. Her hair was wild and she walked with a list.

"What's wrong with her?" Karl demanded.

"She's been drugged," Brad snarled.

"It was the only way we could get her," the burgomaster bemoaned.

Karl snapped his head around to look at Humphrey who avoided his eyes and pretended to wipe the bar counter clean.

As Carole flopped down into a chair, Karl's anger rose then dissipated. Carole was back safe, there was no sense in elevating the issue. He stared at Humphrey until the man met his gaze.

"Bring her some food. Good food."

"Of course, sir." Humphrey leaped to the opportunity to make amends, silently rehearsing how he would explain that the burgomaster and aldermen made him do it.

"You all can go now," Karl commanded. "I'll let you know what our decision is."

"But, but," the burgomaster moaned. "The orcs will be back the day after tomorrow."

"Go." Karl folded his arms, intimating he brooked no further discussion.

Crestfallen, the burgomaster and aldermen moped out of the tavern, slowly closing the door behind them.

Humphrey emerged with a plate of fried eggs, warm bread, sliced pork and a cold ale, setting them down with a great flourish in front of Carole.

"I had no choice," he apologized. "They made me do it. Said they would ruin my business if I didn't do what they wanted." Nodding at Carole, he said, "It's sleeping potion. She'll be back to normal in an hour or two."

"We understand," Karl answered with a tone that said he bore him no ill will. "Just be sure you notify the rest of us the next time you drug one of us."

"Absolutely," he said, breathing a sigh of relief. "Will you help us?"

"We'll see. How about you give us a chance to talk about it?"

"Oh. Sorry." Humphrey hustled back into the kitchen.

Karl looked at Carole who sat staring at the eggs. "You OK?"

"Sure," she said, giving him a loopy smile. "I'd kill for some coffee."

"Wouldn't we all," Brad chuckled. "Talk about gross negligence in game development."

Karl looked around at the assembled group. "You heard what's going on. The way I see it, though their methods were stupid, they did us a favor."

"How ya figure that?" Conrad asked.

"As near as I can figure it, to get off this island, we have to accomplish at least one quest. Here we have a quest handed to us. There are three orcs and fourteen of us. I'm sure we can handle three orcs. If you look at the quest, once we accomplish it, anything in the city is ours. So. I'm looking for input. Pros and cons."

"The only con I see is that we stay here another day or so," Raquel answered. "What's the big deal in that? We could stay here a week and it wouldn't matter in the overall scheme of things."

Dieter grunted agreement as did most everyone else.

"Any other cons?" Karl asked.

"Just one," Conrad said. "I hate to be a party pooper, but suppose one or more of us gets killed?"

"OK?" Annabeth challenged. "Suppose that does happen? What's your point?"

"If one or more of us gets killed, it's back to Marbeck to start all over again."

"Just change your bind spot to here," Sakura answered, stating the obvious.

Conrad's mouth slacked open then closed as he realized he had forgotten a key part of the game. "Doh. Sorry. I take back all I said."

"No problem." Karl smiled kindly at him. "Conrad brings up a good point. None of us are gamers. We are going to forget things on occasion, like bind spots. If we're going to succeed together, we need to remember that we succeed or fail as a team. Everyone, right now, change your bind spot to here."

"How about our bedrooms," Conrad suggested. "That way when you return buck naked, you won't be standing here in the middle of the tavern."

"Good idea," Wendell grinned.

"Everyone needs to accept the quest," Raquel pointed out.

A minute later, bind spots changed and the quest accepted, Karl called out, "Humphrey."

The proprietor burst out the kitchen with a wide smile, having eavesdropped on the proceedings from the kitchen. "I should send someone to get the burgomaster."

"And anyone else who might be helpful."

"Of course. How about an ale, on the house?"

It was late in the afternoon as Karl, Raquel, Annabeth, Dieter and Sakura sat at the table in the tavern.

"OK," Karl said. "What do we know so far?"

"There's three of them," Annabeth said with a grin.

"They came at the end of the day," Dieter added.

"Two of them carry battle axes," Sakura said. "The third has a falchion. They wear some armor, but we're not exactly sure where."

"They're all Level 4," Raquel stated. "Don't know their health stats. Wish the townies would have paid attention to that."

"What else?" Karl asked. When no one could think of anything, he said, "They don't move as quickly as we do. However, their fighting strength is enough to make up for the slower speed. They came here with no other security, out in the open. They assumed the town would again cower before their demands. They stood before the gate, fully exposed. They're over-confident. They always use the same route of approach. Not only are they over-confident, they're careless. We need to attack them where and when they least expect it."

Impressed, Dieter asked, "Where should that be, Boss?"

"Along the road leading to the city," Karl answered. "The fences are just like those at Marbeck and provide enough cover."

"That's gonna be a little harder for me, Boss," Dieter said, with concern.

"I know," he smiled. "We save you for the right time. Now here's the plan."

In the dwindling afternoon, two days later, the company was positioned on both sides of the road about 400 meters away the city. Karl and Raquel were at one end of the ambush, farthest away from the city, with Annabeth and her team on one side behind the stone wall and Sakura and her team opposite. Dieter, Brad and Lana were at the edge of the city wall, waiting for the ambush to start. Conrad was with Annabeth and Wendell was with Sakura.

Daylight was just beginning to fade when the sounds of orcs in conversation rolled out of the forest.

"Shut yer face, Fezgul. Yer a damned liar."

"The hell I am, Grac. Yer the one sez he's so fearsome."

"Will you two just shut up. What're we gonna do if they don't got any food?"

"Yer the one said we was gonna tear the place apart," Fezgul said. "Ain't that so, Grac? Weren't Borc who said it?"

"Yup. Though the cows was good the last time we was here."

"An' anyway, how come we always come here at the same time?" Fezgul demanded.

"'Cause it's easy pickins," Borc tartly replied. "I get tired of the wife jabbin' all the time, even after I smack her down. She's a stubborn one, I'll tell you that. I give her credit for not backin' down. That's why I married her."

"Like we care," Grac sneered. "What about no food? How're we gonna make them pay?"

"I got an idea," Borc replied. "We'll just start lootin' the farms. When they sez they got no food, we won't say a word. It' scare the shit out of 'em."

They walked in silence for a bit and were halfway into the ambush when Borc stopped and sniffed. "I smell dwarf... and elf."

Karl and Raquel rolled out from their hiding spot.

"How can you smell anything other than your own stench," Karl taunted, noting the size of the three creatures. The middle orc carried a falchion while the other two wielded battleaxes.

The orcs whirled around in unison. Whatever fear they had immediately vanished.

"Looky there," the orc in the middle spoke. He was about the same height as Karl, but much broader. Two large teeth protruded from the under-bite of his jaw. He sneered as he readied his falchion. "The humans finally got a spine."

"Now," Karl commanded and the two sides of the ambush rose and leaped over the wall to surround the orcs.

The sudden increase in humans, elves, and dwarves aroused no concern in the orcs. The middle orc looked at those surrounding them and spat. "I knew I smelled elf and dwarf. They stink enough to make me puke." He shifted a quick glance at his two companions. "Grac back. Fezgul right. Attack."

The orcs launched a surprise attack on Sakura's team who fell back with the sudden onslaught. Fearing the orcs were trying to break through and run, Karl leaped into the fray, ducking a swinging blow from a battle ax and delivering a slicing cut at the knees, hoping to immobilize the orc.

Yet the battle was a foregone conclusion. Fourteen humans, dwarves, and elves against three orcs was a lopsided battle, even before Dieter had a chance to inflame his berserker rage. By the time the giant arrived on the scene with Brad and Lana in tow, three orcs lay dead and pierced with multiple arrows. Raquel was nonchalantly yanking arrows out of the corpses and cleaning the tips before placing them back in her quiver.

"They'll want proof," Karl observed. "Cut off the left ears." He looked up at a disappointed Dieter. "Sorry, big guy. Next time we'll figure out a way for you to get first licks."

Congratulations: You have completed the Quest - save the town from orcs.

Reward: Unlimited access to supplies, scrolls, potions, and weapons currently in the town.

Reward: Reputation. You and your company have increased your reputation: +2 points.

Karl ignored the alert, instead pressing the 'X' icon to make it disappear.

When they arrived back at the gate, half the city was there to greet them, their jubilation overflowing with even Conrad and Wendell reveling in the adoration and plentiful kisses of the relieved citizens. The burgomaster strode up, the aldermen tailing behind with their airs of self-importance, and waved his arms for the crowd to settle down. After repeated attempts, he gave up and motioned the victorious company back into the safety of the city walls.

Karl stopped him and in a grand display of theatrics, flourished high the three mutilated ears of the dead orcs, causing the crowd to erupt even louder.

When they finally arrived back at the tavern, the company was more than ready to be rid of the fawning masses, all except Conrad and Wendell who would have remained outside absorbing all the kisses they could take had not Dieter dragged them both inside and barred the door.

As the group flopped down in the chairs, serving girls, carrying trays of steins brimming with ale circulated among the tables, depositing a mug before each individual.

"It's on the house. Help yourselves," Humphrey called out as he backed out of the kitchen, carrying a tray laden with steaming steaks and pork chops and placed it on an empty table. One of the cooks followed with a tray filled with bread hot from the oven and another tray with numerous cheeses.

Needing no urging, they pushed themselves up to partake. All except Karl, who remained seated, remembering the rule of the leader that troops were fed first before he got something to eat.

To his surprise, both Annabeth and Raque brought back a plate for him. They arrived at the same time, looked at each other and laughed, placing both plates in front of him.

"Enjoy," Raquel said, sitting to his right. "It's not every day you get two beautiful women serving you food."

"I can't recall that *ever* happening," he replied, sipping his ale.

Midway through the feast, the burgomaster and alderman came traipsing in through the kitchen door.

"My dear Karl the Viking," he grandiloquently began with an exaggerated bow. "You have rid the city of our oppressors. In return for such bravery, gallantry... uh – "

"Skill," an alderman whispered.

"And skill," the burgomaster said, thankful for the prompt, "we are your obedient servants. The city opens its arms to satisfy all your needs."

"Thank you," Karl politely replied.

"How may we serve you?"

"Haven't really thought about it," Karl answered. "Our attention was focused on eliminating the threat to the city."

"Quite right, quite right," he acknowledged then added a subtle, "um, how long do you plan on staying?"

"We're beginning to like it here," he deadpanned. "Not more than a couple of months."

The burgomaster swallowed hard and he smiled with only his lips as he struggled to calculate the cost to the city. "Um, no doubt you're all anxious to prepare for your next adventure and I'm sure you're all anticipating the next thrill of battle and all that. Uh..." he looked to his aldermen for help but their blank faces told him he was on his own.

Licking his lips, he did his best to smile before giving the aldermen a curt wave to follow him. "We'll just leave you to celebrate your victory."

"I'll have a list of items we'll need from you the day after tomorrow," Karl said, his face impassive.

The burgomaster relaxed as his hopes rose with the expectation that they would be leaving very soon. "Yes, yes, that would be fine."

Once the burgomaster and aldermen left the tavern, Dieter stood and stretched. "What's the plan, Boss?"

"We take tomorrow to scour the town identifying things we need or can use, like weapons upgrades or magic potions. Take your time. Identify what you want and let me know. I'll put together our list and give it to him the day after tomorrow. In the meantime, enjoy the excellent food and ale and other things." He smiled at Dieter when Elena sidled up to him and slipped an arm through his.

"Speaking of which," Raquel said, looking at him then at Annabeth. "I believe it's my turn tonight."

"And mine again tomorrow night," Annabeth brightly replied, "and then yours the next night and so on."

"Don't I get a vote?" Karl asked.

Raquel patted his hand. "If you're too tired…"

"I didn't say that," he quickly replied.

She smiled smugly at him. "I didn't think so."

"You're not complaining are you?" Annabeth sweetly asked.

"Not in the least," Karl answered, hoping his strength could match their stamina.

"Good," Raquel said, standing up. "C'mon then lover boy. A different kind of adventure and excitement awaits you." She led him through the doors to the upstairs rooms.

"I think I shoulda been a Viking," Conrad wistfully said, watching the beautiful ranger lead her quarry to her bedroom.

"And miss out on all the kissing this afternoon?" Wendell scoffed.

"Kissing might be good enough for you, but I need more to get me satisfied." Standing, he cast a lustful glance at Kendra who was talking with Brad.

He had yet to take a step when Wendell popped up and downed the rest of his ale in one gulp. "Wait for me."

It was early morning when Karl awoke. Through the open window, dawn's light was struggling to pierce the thick gray of the morning's mist. Nestled next to him in a bed barely wide enough for one, the gorgeous Raquel lay on her side, her soft breathing telling him she was sound asleep.

Placing a hand behind his head, he smiled at the previous evening's bedtime frolic. Physically, Raquel looked a lot like Annabeth: large firm breasts, narrow waist, narrow hips, curvaceous legs...and a ravenous appetite. By the time they were 'finished,' he was wondering whether he'd ever be able to walk again. That he was awake now more than surprised him.

Though physically similar, Raquel and Annabeth were very different personalities and it had him curious what they were like in real life. He already knew a little about Annabeth from their first encounter. Annabeth was refreshingly honest and pretty much said what she thought, but did it in such a way that she had the gift to tell someone to go to hell and he'd look forward to the trip. And her personality was outgoing and charming. Yet Karl sensed there was an underlying need for validation.

Annabeth was loquacious compared to Raquel. It's not that Raquel didn't like to talk; it's just that she tended to choose her words more carefully as if sorting out the meaning and ramifications of what she was about to say. There was a quiet intensity in Raquel that simmered just below the surface. It was as though she was struggling to keep herself in check, that if she let her emotions run rampant, she would lose herself.

He had felt her intensity last night. The power of her lovemaking was electric.

That thought caused him to smile. Electric. Was sex just a series of electrical impulses? How boring to think of it that way. It's like the moon and the stars. Once science took control, all the romance went away.

He didn't want to live that way. Though he was thankful that science gave him an extended life, he did not want science defining his passions.

Raquel rolled over, blinking her eyes. "Why are you awake?" Her voice was soft and warm.

"I have no idea," he sighed.

"Was last night not enough?"

"My God," he gushed. "It was wonderful."

She raised her head to look over his chest and out the window. "It's still the middle of the night. Go back to sleep."

"I'll do my best," he smiled, kissing her forehead.

She snuggled against him, feeling the warmth of his body. Resting an arm across his chest, she closed her eyes and soon settled into the shallow breathing of sleep.

Still, sleep eluded Karl and he pondered his future. Why wasn't he content to stay in Marbeck like so many others? Yes, the gamers told him the object was to get to the last island. Yet they never did answer how many islands there were, even when he asked them point blank.

"So how many islands are there in the game?"

"Weeeell," the developer replied in one long drawn out syllable. "We're still working on that."

She was a young woman who couldn't have been more than sixteen years old, with wild blond hair and purple eyes and a body that most men lusted after. Sixteen. Would that make her a young woman or a girl? She certainly wasn't a girl in the traditional sense of the word. So, here she was, a young woman who was already in the corporate world as a high level game designer, a genius who oozed self-confidence… and it showed.

At sixteen, he had been awkward and clumsy and worried about zits. The difference between her and him at sixteen was painfully obvious.

"So how many islands are there now?" he had repeated.

"For now, there are ten, but that will change as we continue developing," she answered with a hint of sympathy.

He felt suddenly exposed as though he were some old man in the final days of his life, vainly clinging to any hope or chimera that promised reprieve. The thought angered him. Yes, he was old enough to be her father, but *not* her grandfather, and it was damned unfair of life to deal him this card. He was in the prime of his life… at least he had been.

"How long does it take to go from one island to the next?" he asked, genuinely interested while wanting to determine how long he was likely to be in the game.

"It depends," she said, "on how good a gamer you are. Each succeeding island is more difficult and the quests take longer."

"Suppose you're not a gamer?"

She stared at him with a look of pity mixed with condescension. "Then it will take you a lot longer."

Karl shifted to get comfortable, careful not to disturb Raquel. If he was honest with himself, on so many levels this gaming life was certainly far more interesting than his former real life. Where else could he be a tall and handsome Viking lying next to a beautiful ranger?

So that begged the original question. Why not just stay here and enjoy the perks of two lovely ladies and the occasional ambush on orcs? It was certainly safer.

Intrinsically he knew the answer. It wasn't a question of growing boredom. It was something like the old Chinese proverb: 'Do not fear going forward slowly. Fear only to stand still.' Staying here in Abeloft would be standing still. He knew himself and he knew that he craved change and challenge, both of which he missed when he left the military and went into academia. Once again, he regretted his decision to leave the military, though at the time it seemed to make the most sense. From the time he graduated high school, all he had known was the military. His career found him working with the CIA, NSA, and other acronyms no one would ever hear of. Along the way, he completed a Bachelor and Master degree in Nordic studies, which had absolutely nothing to do with his career but was something he enjoyed.

So what changed?

As his career progressed, he found himself desk-bound more often than not and he chaffed at being surrounded by four walls. He missed the cloak and dagger, the insertion into enemy territory, the thrill of immediate danger. It was time to make a change. Unfortunately, academia was the wrong change.

Raquel stirred and snuggled closer, causing him to wonder if his getting cancer was a blessing in disguise. He felt her stir again and looked down to see her eyes open.

Kissing his chest, she twisted her head to look up at him. "I wonder how early they start serving breakfast?"

"I don't know."

"Doesn't matter. I think we need to take a bath."

"Do I smell that bad?" he asked, suddenly aware of his manly aroma.

"I said 'we'," she replied with a wink and flicking her eyebrows. When he still looked confused, she added, "The tub is big enough for two."

Even with the shared bath, Karl and Raquel were the first ones down for breakfast. A yawning Humphrey butted the kitchen door open and carried over a tray containing a small basket with hot rolls, plates with sausages, butter, jam and two cold ales.

"Did we sleep well?" Humphrey smiled.

"Very," Karl replied with a warm smile at Raquel.

The upstairs door opened and Annabeth bounded in, looking refreshed and chipper. She scooted a chair out by Raquel and plopped down. Reaching for a sausage, she nibbled on one end and grinned at Karl then turned to Raquel.

"Told you he was good," she merrily confided. "I'm thinking of exploring all the positions in the Kama Sutra."

"Hopefully not in one night," Raquel deadpanned.

"No, just the first fifty, then spread out the rest the next couple of times."

"You do realize I *am* sitting here," Karl intoned.

"Don't mind us," Annabeth cheerfully replied. "Pass the butter, please."

Midway through breakfast and the numerous ways Annabeth pondered having sex with Karl, to include a night time skinny dip in the ocean, the upstairs door opened and Dieter emerged, Elena right behind him, her hand in his. Casting a sheepish glance at the three already at the table, he slid a chair out and sat as Elena kissed him on the cheek and went to the kitchen.

Dieter noted the three staring at him, smiling. "What can I say?" he shrugged.

"You don't have to say anything," Annabeth sweetly answered, patting his hand. "You have the right to enjoy yourself just like we all do. She seems like a real sweet girl."

"The question is," Karl said, "how are you going to feel and what are you going to do when we have to leave tomorrow?"

Dieter paused and stared down at the plate before him. "I was wondering if we could take her with us."

"What an interesting idea," Annabeth mused aloud.

"She's a serving girl," Karl sharply pointed out. "And you'd be distracted by worrying about her."

"You worry about us," Annabeth countered, nodding at Raquel and herself.

"It's different. You two are players, a sorceress and a ranger. I don't have to worry about you. You can take care of yourselves."

"You mean you don't worry about us?" She pretended to pout.

"Stop it," he half-smiled. "It's not the same. How would she contribute to the company?"

"She can cook," Dieter stubbornly replied, "and bake."

"That could come in handy," Annabeth agreed, "especially when there are no towns around."

"I think," Raquel spoke up, "the question is whether it's allowed, in the game I mean. Can an NPC just go wandering off with a player?"

There was a lengthy pause as they realized she had a valid point. Karl searched his memory for any indication or rule that an NPC had the same sort of freewill a player had.

"If I understand it," he said, "NPCs are placed in towns, places, and situations to help or hinder a player."

"Players respawn," Raquel added. "I think NPCs do too, but it's different."

"So if Elena went with us or was killed," Annabeth reasoned, "either way she would no longer be part of the game."

"But that would only hold true for us," Dieter said, "here and now. Elena is part of the town, right now. If someone else entered the game after we did, even if she came with us, she would still be here when the next player came along, because it would be a new game for him."

"Whoa," Annabeth marveled. "That's deep."

"How can she be in two places at once?" Karl argued.

"It wouldn't be her," Raquel thought out loud. "I mean, it would be her, but it would be her doppelganger. The old Elena would be with us, and the new Elena would be here when the new player came along."

"That's even deeper," Annabeth said in reverent tones.

"Then what would happen when the two Elena's met?" Karl asked. "Suppose we had to retrace our steps back here? And anyway, are you saying that once we leave here a new Elena magically appears to take the old Elena's place?"

"I don't know what I'm saying," Raquel shrugged. "All I know is that when my son plays RPGs, he can kill an NPC on his way to a quest. A friend of his does the same quest a day later and kills the same NPC."

Silence thudded upon those at the table as the others tuned into a single word she had said.

"You have a son?" Karl said, suddenly feeling guilty.

"And a daughter," she said with a pained sigh, irritated that she had let slip that part of her life.

"You never told me," Karl said.

"You never asked."

"Touché," Annabeth chimed in.

"I have three boys," Dieter softly announced. "They live with their mother. We divorced a few years ago, long before I was diagnosed with... my illness."

Annabeth glanced around the table. "Sometimes I forget that all of us are here because we are terminally ill. For my part, I've been given a new lease on life and I'm going to take advantage of it. I've been given a gorgeous body and a sorceress' skills. I'm going to enjoy this life to the fullest. Already I'm having more fun than I ever did in real life. The only thing we truly have to worry about is respawning." She cast a meaningful glance at Karl. "I don't even have to worry about getting pregnant."

Turning back to the others, she added, "That's why I choose to see my glass as half-full. Just look at the fun we've had so far, killing gnolls and humongous spiders, and ambushing orcs... and other things." She wiggled her eyebrows at Karl. "I tell you, it's only gonna get better."

"Thank you Miss Sunshine," Conrad laughed as he pushed through the upstairs door. "Any chance of flashing those gorgeous girls of yours?"

"Remember what I said last time?" she reprimanded him with a grin.

"Yeah, yeah. Can't blame a guy for tryin'. What's everyone doing down here so early in the morning? Mist hasn't even burned off yet."

"It's called breakfast," Annabeth explained. "You eat it after you wake up in the morning. You remember."

"Ha ha," he replied, stone-faced.

The upstairs door opened again and Sakura, Brad, and three more entered, greeting Karl and the others with a wave as they headed for another table, their conversation continuing.

Karl noticed Annabeth lean over and whisper something to Raquel.

"You have him tonight," Raquel reminded her.

"Oh alright," she sighed with a smile. "Mind if I tag along?"

"Of course not. I'd like that."

"Where're we going?" Karl asked.

"Shopping," Raquel replied with a mischievous grin.

In the warm sunshine of the early afternoon, Karl, Raquel and Annabeth sat at a table outside a pub and watched the city's people go about their business. Many recognized the orc-killing warriors and greeted them with plaudits and smiles.

"Wonder why they didn't think to add coffee as part of this game?" Annabeth observed, watching a woman marching down the street, a young urchin in each hand.

"Where'd that come from?" Karl chuckled.

"I just thought it'd be nice to have an espresso right this moment... and a Danish."

"Welcome to medieval Europe," Raquel said.

Karl studied Raquel for a bit. "Tell me about your children."

"Yeah," Annabeth joined in, leaning forward.

Raquel was irritated at first, but then relaxed. "Not much to tell. My son is fourteen and my daughter is eleven."

"And your husband?" Karl asked.

Raquel paused, taking a sip of ale as she chose her words. "We were never married. We had that idiotic belief that as long as two people loved each other we didn't need to be married in the normal sense of the word. We were 'married' because we supposedly loved each other. Common-law is what they call it."

"You sound unhappy," Karl said.

"I am. Even though we thought of ourselves as husband and wife, merely living together does not constitute a marriage, especially a legal marriage or a common-law marriage. After five years of living together and giving birth to two children, he informed me one morning over coffee that he felt confined and needed more space, that I was too demanding, too restricting. He moved out and I haven't seen him since. Neither have the children. I learned later he was living with another woman in Idaho."

"So you had to raise your kids by yourself," Annabeth said. "Lemme guess, and with no support from him."

"Bingo."

"Where are the kids now?" Karl asked.

"With my sister," she replied, a lump in her throat. "She's a good woman with two kids of her own. Thankfully she's in a stable marriage." She turned to look down the street, her eyes misted. "I hope I can get back before they forget all about me."

"You're their mother," Karl comforted, placing a hand on hers. "I doubt they could ever forget you."

"Thank you," she replied with a weak smile. "All things considered, I think Annabeth has the right outlook. Life for us is here and now. We need to make the most of it." As if suddenly understanding her place, she brightened. "I need to live life to the fullest, have adventures, excitement, so when I do go back, just think of the stories I can tell my kids."

"See?" Annabeth softly spoke. "I told you you'd find an answer." She glanced around the busy street then back to her ale. "Now if they could come up with some coffee, I'd say life was perfect."

Karl and company were in the tavern, enjoying a late meal while sharing their finds of the days and planning the morrow's departure when the burgomaster and aldermen came in. Karl was about to call out his thanks for the city's support when he noticed the burgomaster's look – a mixture of awkward embarrassment and anxiety.

Seeing Karl, the burgomaster made a beeline for him, the aldermen in single file behind him. The room went silent to hear what he had to say.

Swallowing, he tapped his fingertips together. "Ah, they're back."

"Who's back?" Karl replied with a frown and a smile.

"The orcs. They're back."

"That's impossible," Karl affirmed. "We killed them yesterday. You have their ears."

"Yes, yes, I know. But, you see, they're back. They're standing outside the gate demanding we feed them."

"That's impossible," he repeated, bolting out of his chair. "Show me. Wait." He turned to the others. "Get your weapons, but keep them hidden until I tell you."

Quest Alert: Save the town from orcs - again
Reward: Unlimited access to supplies, scrolls, potions, and weapons currently in the town
Do you accept this quest? Yes   No

With a snarl, Karl smacked the 'Yes' icon. "Damned nuisance." When the rest returned, fully armed, the burgomaster led the way to the walls above the city gates.

As they made their way up the stairs, Dieter touched Karl on the elbow. "If there are orcs, I'd like a chance at them this time."

"Fair enough. Stay out of sight for the moment."

"Thanks, Boss."

Karl and the rest of the company lined up behind the battlements and much to their surprise and chagrin, saw the three orcs standing outside the gate. The orc in the middle carried a falchion while the other two wielded battleaxes. They looked to be the same ones from last night, although Karl wasn't quite sure how to differentiate orcs other than their clothing, for all orcs looked the same.

"Bah," the middle orc spat. "I knew I smelled dwarf and elf."

"You don't smell so good either, cupcake," Conrad shot back.

The orc's bravado wavered slightly when he saw the Viking flanked by a ranger and a sorceress. "This don't change a thing. Give us food or we destroy this place."

"Food?" Karl called down. "Of course. I'll make sure they give you plenty of food. What would you like? Mutton? Bread? How about ale?"

"Mutton?" The orc on the left eyes lit up. "Yes. Mutton... and ale. Lots of ale."

"Of course." Karl turned to the burgomaster whose stunned face told him the poor man was trying to figure out how to explain to the city that not only were the orcs back, Karl was demanding they be fed. In a voice loud enough for the orcs to hear, he announced, "My good burgomaster, a feast for our guests outside."

"But... but," the burgomaster stuttered, horrified.

Karl suavely pushed him aside and called down to the orcs. "Give us a few minutes. Make yourselves comfortable. How about an ale while you're waiting?"

"Yes," the orcs on the flanks said at once.

"No tricks," the middle orc growled.

"Tricks? Of course not. My friends and I are simply passing through. We'll be on our way back north tomorrow."

Stepping away from wall and out of view, he gathered the group, beckoning the burgomaster closer.

"I need two volunteers to act as a distraction by taking the ale out to them."

Everyone raised a hand, which surprised and pleased him. He pointed to Ross and Carole.

"OK. You two will carry the ale out." He switched his attention to Annabeth holding her staff. "What can you do with that?"

"I can do both a fire bolt and an ice bolt."

"Good." He turned to the mage. "Lana? What do you have?"

"I can do a mind confusion spell."

"OK everyone, here's the plan. As soon as Ross and Carole are halfway to the orcs, Annabeth will hit the middle orc with a fire bolt then hit the orc on the right with an ice bolt. At the same time, Lana will cast her confusion spell on the orc on the left. Dieter will lead the rest of us in the attack. Myself and Raquel will be in reserve. Questions?"

"You want Lana and me up here?" Annabeth asked.

"Yes. Sorry. I should have been more explicit. Up here gives you better line of fire. Any other questions?"

When no one said anything, Karl turned to Dieter. "Go ahead and organize your attack."

"Thanks, Boss," he replied, pleased with the responsibility.

While Dieter briefed the attack force, Karl turned his attention to the burgomaster. "Get me three mugs and a pitcher of ale."

"Yes, yes," he responded, excitement and relief in his eyes.

As the burgomaster headed back down the stone steps to fetch the ale, Karl leaned over the battlement. "It'll be just a minute more, gentlemen," he cheerfully called down to the orcs. "We're looking for ale mugs large enough to hold your ale."

"Just bring a damned pitcher," the orc on the left impatiently stated.

"Ah. Good idea. Why didn't I think of that?" He suppressed a smirk when he saw the anticipation of the two orcs on the flanks. The middle orc still appeared wary. Disappearing from view, he turned to the group. "Get ready."

Within a few minutes, all were in position and waiting. The burgomaster and aldermen bustled up with the ale and mugs, a small crowd of citizens following. Handing the pitcher and mugs to Ross and Carole, he stood there, hands on his hips as if to say he had done his part; now it was up to Karl to fix the problem.

"You might want to take cover in case the orcs break through," he counseled.

The burgomaster's smug confidence vanished and he spun around to shoosh everyone away. Yet few would leave, instead wanting to crowd the battlements to watch the show. With a helpless shrug, he turned back to Karl.

"If you want this done right, keep them out of our way," Karl warned then led the way up to the battlement.

He gazed down at the impatient orcs and called out. "Are you ready?"

"We been ready," the middle orc snapped.

Though smiling at the orcs, he whispered to Annabeth and Lana, "Hit them when their attention is diverted when the gate door opens." Then in a loud voice for all to hear, he called out, "OK. Go ahead and bring out the ale."

The gate door opened and Ross, carrying the ale pitcher, stepped out first. In unison, the orcs dropped their gaze and focused their attention on the door. No sooner had their heads dropped that Annabeth thrust her staff at the middle orc, sending out a burst of fire that ignited his skin and clothing, and sent him dancing and flapping his arms in spasmodic terror.

At the same time, Lana swirled her hands and pushed out a confusion spell that hit the orc on the left whose rapt attention on the pitcher was abruptly interrupted and he dumbly stood there, watching his mate roll around on the ground as the fire continued consuming his clothing and flesh.

By this time, the orc on the right was encased in a thin layer of ice, his eyes locked in frozen horror as he watched a human giant emerge, a large double headed battle axe gripped in his right hand. More humans, elves and dwarves spilled out behind him.

The crowds on the battlements roared their glee as Dieter swung his axe and decapitated the orc frozen in ice. The confusion spell was just starting to weaken in the other orc when Conrad, Wendell, and Sharyn, a high elf, made quick work of him, killing him where he stood.

Sakura and the others calmly walked over to the final orc, kneeling on the ground, his charred and bubbled flesh split to expose the sinews and muscles of his frame. He looked up at them, defiant to the last, reaching for a weapon too far away. Sakura walked behind him, grabbed what was left of his hair and jerked his head back as she sliced his throat.

Another roar erupted as the company sliced off the left ears, collected what little the orcs had, and headed back through the gate

Congratulations: You have completed the Quest - save the town from orcs, again.

Reward: Unlimited access to supplies, scrolls, potions, and weapons currently in the town.

Reward: Reputation. You and your company have increased your reputation: +2 points.

"Damn it all," Karl snapped and slapped the 'X' closing the notification. "Just stop."

As they walked through the fawning crowd, Conrad and Wendell lagging behind to enjoy the hugs and kisses of the fairer ladies of the city, Karl's brow furrowed as he thought through the scenario. He turned to the burgomaster who paraded beside him, soaking up the applause.

"I thought you said the orcs only come once a month."

"They do," he replied, grinning and waving at the crowds lining the street.

"Then why did they come back today?"

"I haven't the faintest idea," he answered, his attention on the adulation of the crowds. "Yes, yes. Thank you. All in a day's work. Just keeping your safety and welfare top priorities."

Karl cast a side glance at him, rolling his eyes at the consummate politician, taking credit for the work of others.

Yet the inconsistency of the orcs returning caused him to be cautious. Once the crowds went home and the company was back at the tavern, he waited for everyone to sit before standing.

"Let's review our attack. I estimate it took all of thirty seconds to wipe out three orcs. It was brilliantly executed. The only problem I see is that Dieter got to decapitate only one orc."

"You shoulda seen the look on that orc's face when Tiny here swung that battle axe," Conrad chortled.

"Tiny?" Dieter frowned.

"It's a nickname, a term of endearment," Conrad explained. "And think how funny it would be when we tell some enemy they need to back off, otherwise we'll sic Tiny on 'em."

Dieter saw the humor and the genuine affection and respect of the rest of the company, yet wasn't sure he wanted the appellation. He'd wait and see how he felt.

Karl let the chuckles subside then continued. "What today showed us is that we need to make use of everyone's special skills. I'll be the first to admit that I tend to approach things from the old school mentality of swords and bows and arrows. I forget we have the power of magic. You can see by the results that Annabeth and Lana proved very critical to our success. What that means is that I, and everyone else, need to know your strengths and weaknesses, and what special powers and skills you have. What that also means is that we're staying here an additional day."

He smiled when he saw Dieter's obvious pleasure for that meant another night here with Elena.

"One more thing," he said. "Something's not right about the orcs. According to the burgomaster, the orcs only showed up once a month. This is two days in a row that we fought them, and I swear they were the same ones."

"I thought so too," Brad agreed. "They certainly looked familiar, too familiar."

"So," Karl continued, "We wait another day or two to make sure we won't be impeded when we move on. Oh yeah, one more 'one more thing.' We completed another quest here which means we are again entitled to whatever we want. Take tomorrow to go through your stuff and make sure you have what you really want. Then take advantage of the free gifts. Otherwise, see you all tomorrow." Karl sat down and found himself between Annabeth and Raquel.

"What did you decide about Elena?" Raquel asked.

"I haven't," he answered. "Your thoughts?"

"Seems to me that your concern about NPCs respawning was answered tonight," she pointed out.

"If they were the same ones," Karl countered. "Truth is, I can't tell the difference between orcs. And though the clothing was familiar, it doesn't mean that two orcs won't dress the same."

"But three orcs dressing the same?" Annabeth said.

"Yeah, I know."

"What's you real concern?" Raquel asked.

"The same as it was before. Dieter's attention is divided. Instead of focusing on the primary mission, he'll be worried about her and it may cost him or someone else a life."

Raquel nodded in understanding. "While I agree with your reasoning, I think as long as someone can pull their own weight, we may want to reconsider."

"So when Conrad and Wendell find someone and all the others decided they want to have a lover or two or more along, pretty soon we have camp followers. Do we really want to deal with that?"

"You have two lovers," Annabeth smiled.

"Like I said before, you two are different. You're a ranger and a sorceress, with skills and powers. You can take care of yourselves. The same can't be said for NPCs."

"We don't know that for sure," Raquel quietly observed.

Karl cocked an eyebrow. "Did Dieter put you two up to this?"

"No," Annabeth asserted. "We're just looking out for the welfare of our friends."

"In the final analysis," Raquel added. "What's the problem with taking her with us? If his attention is diverted and one of us dies, we respawn. It's not like we're gone forever."

Karl was silent as he absorbed their arguments. "There's still one little detail you both are forgetting. First, can an NPC leave the island? And second, suppose Elena can leave the island. We know that once we leave the island we can't return. If Elena dies, will she come back here and be lost to Dieter forever."

"You said one little detail," Annabeth teased. "That's more than one."

"What's the difference?" Raquel argued. "He leaves her here; she's lost to him forever. She dies on another island; she's lost to him forever. Why not let her go with him so he can at least enjoy her for the time he can?"

"I'm not sure that's a heartache I want to deal with," he soberly replied.

"I understand," Raquel softly answered, placing a hand on his. "But it's his heartache, not yours. He's a big boy. Let him deal with it."

Karl let out a soft exhale. "I suppose you're right."

"You're too used to everything being permanent," Annabeth counselled. "You were a soldier once. When a person got killed, that was it. Here, it's different. It's like we have eternal life."

"As long as someone doesn't pull the plug," he chuckled.

"Speaking of pulling a plug," Annabeth commented flicking her eyebrows. "I think it's time you and I adjourn to my boudoir, said the spider to the fly."

"That sounds ominous," he laughed. He cast a glance at Raquel who masked a fleeting look of disappointment, telling him he would probably have to make a decision soon. And therein was the problem – could he tell one of them that he preferred the other? And was that such a smart idea? Would it cause problems within the company? Deciding that no decision was his present decision, he followed Annabeth upstairs.

"You look lonely," Brad said with a smile, pulling a chair out and sitting.

"Not anymore," she smiled back. Though she liked Brad as a friend, there was nothing more, despite his attempts with subtle hints.

"It has to be hard seeing them walk off, knowing where they're going and what they'll be doing."

Raquel looked at the door and shrugged. "Not really. She's my closest friend and I like seeing her happy."

"Even at your expense?" he raised an eyebrow in doubt.

"How is it my expense?" she countered. "I'll have him tomorrow and it will be at her 'expense,' according to you. Yet it is an arrangement that works just fine among three consenting adults who have made a mature decision. Why does that bother you? Or as a cleric are you trying to impose some sort of religious persuasion on me?"

"Hardly," he smiled, defeated. "Just making conversation."

Her glance wandered over to the table by the hearth where Conrad and Wendell were giving Kendra their amorous attentions. She smiled seeing the three dwarves interact, wondering if Kendra would seek the same arrangement that she had with Annabeth and Karl.

"Is this a private conversation?" Dieter said, sliding out a chair. His massive frame dwarfed the chair as he sat down. He wiggled a little to get comfortable. "Thank God these things are sturdy." He placed his ale mug to the side.

Sensing Dieter desired to talk privately to Raquel, Brad stood. "Think I'll call it a night."

"G'night Brad," Raquel replied with a nondescript smile.

Dieter merely jiggled his fingers and watched the cleric push through the upstairs door. "He still dogging you?"

"Yeah," she shrugged. "No big deal."

"I heard you and Annabeth talking to Karl about me and Elena." He stared intently at her.

"What did you hear?"

"Not much. Just our names. He still against me taking her?"

"He's worried about you and what would happen if something happened to her." She lifted her ale mug and stared into it, noting it was empty.

"Want another one?" Dieter asked.

"Not sure yet. Depends which part of me wins out – the part that says, 'go to bed' or the part that says, 'go ahead and have another.' And then there's that part that says, 'one more ale and you'll be making more visits to the bathroom during the night so you might as well stop now.'"

Dieter grinned then returned to the matter at heart. "So? Did he decide anything?"

"I think he might be leaning towards letting her come." She watched him visibly relax then warned, "But don't quote me. I'm sure you've thought the whole thing through, right?"

"What do you mean?"

"How do we know that she can cross the bridge with us, or even leave here for that matter? She's an NPC."

Dieter paused before answering and took a sip of ale. "I know where you're going with this and on the face of it, it does seem absurd. I've fallen for a fictional character in a role playing game, placed there for no other purpose than to serve ale and be a temptation to players. Yes, it makes no sense. But then I ask myself two things. First, how did they make her so real, down to the emotional depths of a human being? She laughs, she cries, she gets hurt both physically and emotionally. She loves. I swear she's more human than I am."

Raquel responded with a sympathetic smile. "And the second thing?"

"She's nothing more than a series of electrical impulses, programed to behave like a human being. But then, according to ITL, I'm nothing more than a series of electrical impulses and have been programmed to behave based upon my life experiences and conditioning. So what's the real difference?"

"You're a player and she's an NPC." She looked over at a serving girl standing by the ale counter. "Maybe I will have another one." She raised her finger and caught the girl's attention.

"Why can't she be a player?"

"Because she's never been human," Raquel replied, pointing out the obvious. "When they discover your cure, you go back to a body of blood and guts. Her? She was a product of someone's imagination and given a role in a game. She has nowhere else to go."

"They could if they wanted to," he grumbled.

Raquel waited until the serving girl placed the ale on the table and scurried off to help another patron.

"If they wanted to what?"

"They could put her into a body," he answered, "sort of like taking organs from someone who's just died. Instead of harvesting organs, they could put her electronic signature into the woman who died... just like they do to us."

"But we're not dead," she began then caught herself.

Dieter gazed at her. "See? Even *you* know that our bodies, though cryogenically frozen, are dead. If they can bring us back to life, why can't they to that to NPCs?"

"They'll need bodies," she replied then realized that cloning could provide all the bodies they would ever need. Her imagination then surged as she thought about genetically engineering humans via RPGs, but her brain couldn't wrap around why someone would want to do that, especially with the feeding and nurturing requirements under present conditions.

Dieter watched her as she worked though the various scenarios, her placid face morphing to shock.

"My God," she muttered, shaking her head. "I never thought about all the possibilities."

"Those are just some of the possibilities, I've been pondering. Try this one on for size. Suppose they find a cure and decide not to bring me back? What's to stop them? Remember the fine print on the contract we signed? We agreed to be immersed for as long as they deemed appropriate, which means they could disposed of my body and I'd never know about it."

Raquel blinked as she stared back at him. "You're just full of good news tonight."

"Living here and now in this world, we tend to forget there's a *real* world outside the walls of this game. I think Karl is too caught up in the here and now. And by the way, what happens to our little group if they find his cure and he suddenly disappears?"

"Then someone else takes charge," she answered, unconcerned. "It's no different than if we were at war. A leader dies and the next in line takes over."

"Unless there's a coup."

"What are you saying?" She cocked an eyebrow, giving him a stern stare.

Dieter chuckled and held up his hands. "Slow down girl. I'm a loyal subordinate. I admire and respect the man and will do as I'm told. I merely point out the possibilities."

Raquel studied him for a bit. "I think you picked the wrong character. You should have been a philosopher."

"That character wasn't available," he replied. "The closest thing was a cleric and I'm too much an agnostic to be devoted to some mythical god or goddess. Besides, the zealots would probably have me burned at the stake for questioning everything."

Grinning, Raquel noticed Elena standing by the ale counter, her expression a mixture of rapt devotion to Dieter and suppressed possessiveness that he was spending so much time with another woman.

"I think a certain serving girl needs your attention," she said, looking past his shoulder.

Dieter turned his head, saw her and beckoned her. "When are you off?" he asked as she glided up.

"Now," came the direct reply.

"Then I think it's time we said good night," he announced, standing.

Hand in hand, they walked to the upstairs door. Just before stepping through, Elena turned to give Raquel a pitying smile.

When Karl awoke at the same time as the previous morning, his first thought was *I can't keep doing this. I'm gonna need a good night's sleep sometime soon.*

Annabeth lay next to him, her long raven hair framing her silk smooth face. She slept the repose of a woman finally at peace. Only once during the night did he have to hold her and comfort her, waiting until the nightmares subsided. He wondered what dark visions encumbered her thoughts, but she could never remember them in the morning and he was loath to resurrect the occurrences. As far as he knew, she was unaware of her restless sleep, though the bad dreams did seem to be lessening.

Her shallow breaths reminded him to let her sleep. *At least one of us ought to be rested.* Silently slipping out from under the covers, he dressed, quietly opened the door and slid out then headed to his room.

This part of the tavern where the lodgers stayed was quiet except for the sound of his feet as he padded his way down the hall and up the stairs to open the door to his room. To his surprise, someone was sleeping in his bed, someone with thick auburn hair. She rolled over when he approached.

"What are you doing here?" he asked with a warm smile.

"My room just seemed too lonely," Raquel replied. "I can feel your presence here. You don't mind do you?"

Sitting on the edge of the bed, he stroked her cheek. "Of course not."

She looked past his shoulder towards the door. "Where's Annabeth?"

"Still asleep."

"Why are you up?"

"I'm awake."

"You look tired," she soothed, noting the bags under his eyes.

"She has nightmares."

"I know."

"You do?"

"Before you came, we shared a room. Poor girl doesn't even know she's having them. You want me to leave so you can get some sleep?"

"No, that's OK."

"Then why don't you join me?" She lifted the covers enough to expose her nakedness.

Karl thought for a moment. "Is that within the rules?"

"It's your room, your bed, your rules," she replied.

Needing no urging, he pulled off his clothes and slipped in beside her, feeling the warmth of her body. Snuggling close, she kissed his chest and rested her head in the crook of his shoulder. His breathing settled and he relaxed and was soon asleep, leaving her to smile with contentment that she had made the right choice.

On the floor below, Annabeth rolled over and sensed she was alone. Groggily looking around the room, she saw his clothes were gone and assumed he had either gone back to his room or went downstairs to get something to eat. Either way, she thought as she gazed out the window, it was too early to get up.

When Annabeth bounced through the upstairs door to the tavern, most of the company was already there having breakfast. She saw Karl and Raquel at their usual table and strode over, giving Karl a full kiss on the lips and Raquel a kiss on the cheek.

"Good morning you two." She plopped down next to Karl. "Any coffee yet?"

"Only in your dreams," Raquel sighed. "I wonder if there's a way to get word to the developers. Why shouldn't there be coffee in our world? Has anyone asked Humphrey?"

"Humphrey," Annabeth called out.

The kitchen door opened and the chubby man emerged, smiling cheerfully. "Yes?"

"Any coffee?"

"Coffee?" he repeated. "I don't know what that is."

"It's the elixir of life," Carole chimed in, "the secret to eternal happiness."

Humphrey's eyes blinked wide. "It is? Where can I find this coffee?"

"We were hoping you might know," Annabeth sighed.

"What does it look like?"

"It's a dark brown liquid that's normally served hot," Carole explained, "though some do drink it cold. I prefer it hot, with cream."

"Hazelnut cream," Annabeth crooned.

"Yes," Carole agreed, rising to the vision, "hazelnut cream."

"What is hazelnut cream?" Humphrey asked.

"It's a potion you add to coffee that makes it taste even better," Annabeth answered.

"Where can I find this hazelnut cream?" Humphrey had his own visions and those were of making a bundle of money with this coffee potion. He wondered if coffee was as much in demand as ale.

"Alas," Annabeth dramatically sighed, "we have been unable to find it. However, if we ever do, we'll make sure you are amply supplied. With coffee, you could rule the world."

Karl laughed at Humphrey's incredulous look, knowing they had just pumped up the man with false expectations. "In the meantime," Karl said, "I'll take another sweet roll and some cider." Turning to Annabeth, he grinned and shook his head at her. "You are so bad. The poor man is going to dream about coffee the rest of his life."

"Maybe someone will come up with something similar. Who knows?"

"Speaking of which, what other talents do you have?" Karl asked.

"Wow," Annabeth grinned. "That was a non sequitur. Coffee to sorceress. I'm sure there's a connection there somewhere. But to answer your question, I have a number of talents. Like you saw last night, I can toss out fire and ice and I can also do lightning. But at my present Level 3, I still have a ways to go. I can also do magic, spells and enchantments. As you can tell from my lack of combat skills, I'm not too good with weapons though I can invest them with magic. But, like I said, I'm still only a level 3. As I level up, I imagine my power with spells, et cetera will increase."

"So that's why you weren't so keen on being in the front line of battle," Karl acknowledged. "It makes sense now."

"Part of my problem is forgetting I have powers. My first instinct is to react like I would in real life. I see a spider and I grab something to kill it."

"Don't we all," Raquel agreed, remembering the spiders of Ravnar.

Karl and company were back in the tavern in the early evening. Except for Karl, everyone else chatted about the day and the latest finds. It was when the door to the tavern opened and the burgomaster hustled in, again followed by the aldermen, Karl knew his fears were realized.

"They're back," the burgomaster groaned. "I don't understand it. They shouldn't be here, not yet." He clutched his hands in front of his chest.

"No worries, mate," Karl answered. "We got this. OK, folks, listen up. Three orcs. You know the drill.

Their ales were still cold when they arrived back in the tavern. Karl shook his head and looked at the much relieved burgomaster.

"I don't know how much longer we can keep doing this," he stated. "That's nine orcs we've killed. We've pretty much collected everything we need. There's not much more you all can give us as a reward."

The burgomaster's eyes widened in worry. "You won't leave us here defenseless, will you?"

"We'll stay for as long as the problem exists, but at some point we're going to have to move on."

"Just a little longer, please," he begged.

"I already said we would say longer, but you all will need to think of something that will make it worth our while to stay." Karl couldn't help but notice sudden worry explode across the burgomaster and aldermen's faces, causing him to wonder what they had in the city that they might be hiding.

The rest of the evening proceeded like the night before, except that Karl spent the night with Raquel. And just like the previous mornings, he was awake at dawn.

Feeling Raquel's relaxed breathing, he slipped an arm out from beneath her head, dressed, and made the trek up the stairs to his room. Opening the door, his shoulders slumped when he saw the long raven haired woman snuggled in his bed. She had awoken when he entered. Without a word, she held open the covers, revealing her exquisite nakedness.

Slipping his clothes off, Karl joined her in bed, wondering if perhaps he ought to rent another room and not tell anyone. That way he might get some sleep.

The big news the next day was the arrival of a female dwarf named Tina, much to the elation of Conrad and Wendell. Even Kendra was pleased to have her as it would take the pressure off her.

Yet, Tina looked rode hard and put up wet. The company gathered around her as she related her story.

"What happened?" Conrad asked, scooting his chair close to her.

"I was with a group. There were seven of us. Simon was the leader."

"Simon?" Conrad moaned. "A tall elf?"

"Yes. You know him?"

"Sadly, yes. Most everyone here knows him."

"So what happened," Wendell encouraged, giving Conrad an irritated glance for hogging the woman's attention.

"Well, things were going fine until we stayed at a house in a clearing."

"Spiders," a voice intoned.

"Yes," she answered. "How did you know?"

"We stayed there too," Conrad comforted.

"What happened?" Wendell politely asked, again grimacing at Conrad.

"Well, we settled in for the night. Someone found some maps showing the way here, so we all agreed to strike out for Abeloft in the morning. During the night, I hear this awful scream and wake up to realize that the spiders are attacking us."

"What about security?" Karl asked.

"Simon said we didn't need any because we were safe in the house." She shook her head at the memory, while the others exchanges looks that expressed their thanks that Karl had the forethought to take appropriate measures.

"Then what?" Wendell asked.

"Well, like I said, the scream woke me up and I see these huge spiders everywhere. One was even down at my ankles trying to enmesh me. I grabbed my hammer and started swinging. I smashed the spider at my ankles then took to smashing as many of them as I could. They saw me and backed away. But by then two of our team were gone, one was in the process of being sucked up the chimney and the other three fled out into the mist and night. I took a torch and started burning cobwebs and dead spiders. My God the stink was enough to make me want to puke and rush outside, but I knew the gnolls would get me. So I stayed awake the rest of the night. In the morning when the mist burned off, I waited around a little longer to see if anyone was close by. But around midday, I couldn't wait any longer so I took off on my own. I sure am glad to see you."

"So Simon and the others?" Conrad asked.

"Dead as far as I can figure."

"Sucks to be him," Wendell snickered.

"How long have you all been here?" Tina asked.

"Couple of days," Conrad replied. "How come we haven't seen you before, like when we were in Marbeck?"

"I only arrived three days ago," she explained.

"And you already decided to move on?" Wendell said, impressed.

"Yeah," she sheepishly smiled. "They told me that we were supposed to go on quests and cross bridges to the next islands. So I figured that's what I should do."

"How'd you end up with Simon?" Conrad asked.

Tina gave him a lame shrug. "He was the only one who had any gumption of leaving. I couldn't believe how many were content to stay there and just drink and gossip. I lasted a day before I knew I had to go. Simon had put together a group and so I asked to join his group."

"Well, you're here now. Let's get you settled," Wendell soothed, much to Conrad's annoyance as he made the introductions to the rest of the company.

"Looks like you've arrived just in time," Karl said, folding his arms as the burgomaster and aldermen came stumbling in. "We know," he said, rolling his eyes.

"This is getting ridiculous," Annabeth frowned.

"Look on the bright side," Raquel replied. "You get to improve your aim and we get to exercise a little bit."

"Exercise?" Conrad tittered. "Tiny doesn't even break a sweat."

"Tiny?" Tina asked.

"The biggest oaf in the city and our good friend," he said, jerking a thumb at Dieter. "You can come along and watch the fun."

The bread was still warm by the time they returned to the tavern. The banter continued but there was a distinct change. Though they had again defeated three orcs, the effort was minimal, like swatting a fly, and they dismissed the interruption with no more effort than having one's conversation interrupted.

Conrad and Wendell commandeered a table for the four dwarves and were regaling Tina with their escapades while Karl sat contemplating the repeated orc appearances when his stats screen appeared. His lips pursed at the intrusion. Just as he was about to exclaim how much he hated popups, he frowned, surprised to note that he had leveled up again.

Karl the Viking – Level 4

Strength: 20 points
Speech: 10 points
Magic: 4 points (locked)
Health: 20 points
Mana: 20 points
Combat: 24 points
Leadership: 16 points

Reputation: 16 points - You're a local hero

He turned to Raquel and Annabeth. "Something's not right."

"Like what?" Annabeth replied.

"Check your stats."

"Huh," Raquel muttered, reading her personal screen. "I'm a level 4 now. When did that happen?"

"Me too," Annabeth said, both surprised and pleased. "The last time I leveled up, I got this big flash across my screen telling me congratulations."

"I just wonder…" Karl began.

"Wonder what?" Annabeth inquired with a sweet smile.

"We've taken out three orcs for each of the past four nights. I wonder if that's why we leveled up."

"Just taking out a bunch of orcs?" Raquel shook her head in doubt. "That doesn't make sense."

"I agree. To test my theory, let's stay a couple of more days and see."

Three evenings later, having received the *Congratulations: You have completed the Quest - save the town from orcs, again, part VII* response, the company sat in the tavern, restless and distracted.

"When are we going to move on?" Carole muttered. "This is getting boring."

"I feel like we're in some sort of time warp," Ross complained.

"I understand," Karl said, listening to the grumbling. Standing, he addressed the group. "Before I say anything, I want each of you to check your stats."

"Why?" Bruno questioned, his tone more of a challenge than a curiosity.

"Just do what I asked," Karl tartly replied.

"My God," Carole burst. "I'm a level six."

"So am I," Sakura added, soon followed by the rest of the company, all except Tina who was a level five."

"How is that possible?" Brad frowned. "What have we done to warrant increasing our levels other than killing a bunch of orcs?"

"My point exactly," Karl answered. "My thought is to stay here until we are all level 10s and then move on."

"Why Level 10?" Ross asked.

Karl shrugged. "It was the first number that popped into my mind. I figure Level 10 ought to get us some traction as we cross the island."

"Sounds good to me," Conrad loudly announced.

The mood dramatically changed as the members calculated how long it would take to level up.

"Speaking of leveling up," Raquel grinned at Karl, flicking her eyebrows and ticking her head towards the upstairs door.

"You two are insatiable," he replied with a tired smile. "How am I supposed to get any sleep?"

Annabeth patted his hand in sympathetic understanding. "Now, now, stop complaining. We do our best to wear you out. If you'd stop waking up so early in the morning, everything would be fine." She winked at Raquel.

Chapter 4

Mister Landon's office occupied the top floor of the Landon building. The view from the north bank of windows looked out over the Tennessee River towards Signal Mountain.

Felix Hubach had looked out those windows once when he tagged along with the former acting Director of Gaming who had gone to brief Mister Landon on the newest project, a game called Bridge Quest. Now here Felix was, the new CEO of ITL, riding the elevator to the top floor to brief Mister Landon.

Instead of the usual nondescript colors, the elevator's walls were mirrors, causing Felix to wonder if they were some sort of strange quirk to cause folks to examine themselves, ensure they were presentable before they arrived to see Landon. Despite the urge to look elsewhere, Felix stared at his reflection, a man in his early 40's, short wavy auburn hair, brown eyes, trim and fit from daily exercise, neatly dressed in a three piece pin-striped black suit. He had been hired because of his reputation of ruthless organizational efficiency.

ITL had become lax, too lax and Mister Landon wanted it fixed... now. Felix's predecessor was fired, or to use the more politically correct term – 'downsized.' Although, Felix was surprised to discover that the man had immersed into a harem quest game... leaving behind a wife of thirty-five years and two grown children. Needless to say the wife was more than a 'little pissed.' She had threatened to sue the particular gaming company, a rapidly growing outfit out of Boulder, Colorado. Unfortunately, the man's wishes were perfectly legal and there was nothing she could do about it... other than to immerse into a reverse harem game, leaving the children to wonder if they ever really knew their parents.

Still, why they had chosen Felix, a man with no gaming experience to lead ITL, surprised him almost as much as his chutzpah for applying for the position. It had been a lark, a gamble to see if he could do it, for the increase in salary was substantial.

But he determined to prove himself and very quickly the atmosphere at ITL became efficient, professional when Felix fired several department heads in his first two weeks on the job. Word spread faster than a STD and folks' attitude rose to meet the challenge.

Mister Landon was so impressed that he raised Felix's salary another step level. Though thrilled with the recognition, Felix knew he had one area that needed immediate attention, now that the organization was running smoothly. He knew nothing about gaming development and initiated a crash course into the gaming world, quickly realizing talent in organization efficiency didn't necessarily translate into absorbing gaming and computer knowledge. So it was with a bit of trepidation that he stood staring at his reflection on his way to meet Mister Landon.

Mister Landon had a first name, but no one ever used it, not even those who considered themselves reasonably close to the man. Yet, 'reasonably close' was not quite right, for no one could claim they were close to the man.

An only child and son of the founder of Landon Limited, Mister Landon was a stark contrast to his father, Albert Landon who was as gregarious as his son was reticent and hermetical, rarely venturing out beyond the walls of the top floor, which contained his office and living quarters.

As the elevator approached the top floor, Felix mused that he knew no one who had ever been in Mister Landon's apartment. Well, that wasn't quite accurate. Mister Landon had a butler who took care of the day to day essentials. And there was a cleaning crew and a cook. But none would relate even the slightest detail of Mister Landon's living arrangements, as though they were sworn to secrecy, which sort of made sense as secrecy was the middle name of Landon Limited.

The elevator slowed imperceptibly and the doors opened. Felix stepped out into the silent world of busy executives, assistants, lawyers, and support staff. Conversations, if any, were muted or held behind sound proof glass in meticulously organized offices. All employees, regardless of position, were dressed in business professional; even the lowly copier repairman dressed in suit and vest.

Felix made his way down the aisle, past the numerous cubicles where accountants, admin assistants, payroll managers, and a multitude of other middle managers quietly worked, towards the massive double doors that reached floor to ceiling at the far end.

Opening the door, which swung smoothly and easily for its size, Felix stepped into the inner sanctum, the front office leading to Mister Landon's abode. The front office spread the width of the building and contained a single desk in the center, in front of which were arranged a sofa and several overstuffed chairs. Behind the desk was a tall curvaceous and stunningly beautiful woman with long black hair done up in a bun, who smiled at him with only her lips. An ornately carved canary wood nameplate, perched at the edge of her desk, announced that she was Alyson Whitmer.

"Mister Hubach?" she said, her voice almost sensual.

"Yes."

"He is expecting you. Please sit."

Momentarily overwhelmed by her dazzling beauty, Felix nodded politely, off-balance as she seemed to be studying him, though in a detached manner. In an attempt to break her scrutiny, he moved to a chair and sat, thankful that she had resumed her work. He did a quick perfunctory scan of the room. It was wide and narrow with windows at both ends. One or two tall plants sat next to the windows, doing little to block the view. The office walls were a rich oak with paneling and wainscoting. The smoothness of the walls was interrupted at regular intervals with neatly placed doors. Behind the secretary were the double doors leading to the stairs to Mister Landon's office. Curiously, every now and then he caught the secretary, or was it admin assistant, shifting a surreptitious glance at him

At precisely one o'clock, Miss Whitmer, or was it Ms or maybe it was Missus, Felix wasn't sure as he failed to see if she wore a wedding ring, announced, "He is ready to see you." She pressed a button on her desk, causing the doors to swing wide, revealing a broad set of stairs and another set of doors at the top. By the time he climbed the stairs, the doors at the top opened, and he stepped into Mister Landon's office, the sanctum sanctorum.

The office stretched wide like the secretary's office. In contrast to the stark emptiness of the secretary's front office, Landon's office was replete with sculptures, antiques, artifacts and antiquities, oil paintings, drawings, plants and book shelves crammed with tomes that lined an entire wall.

Mister Landon stood at the window behind his desk, gazing out over the city. Landon was in his early 50s, slim, average height, with short auburn hair and a pencil moustache, the one vanity he allowed himself. He had no tattoos and though he disliked the inking of one's body, he realized he would have no employees if he held fast to his aversion.

The doors closed behind Felix and he approached the desk. "You wished to receive the latest on the Bridge Quest project, Sir."

Mister Landon paused then turned, his coal black eyes piercing Felix as though he were penetrating into his soul. "Yes. I understand there is a glitch in the game." His voice was nonchalant, which Felix knew was dangerous.

"Yes, Sir," he nervously began. "We're working on correcting it."

"Working on it?" He folded his arms and his stare intensified. "This problem has been going on for a week, has it not?"

"Uh... I believe so, Sir."

"You believe so?" he repeated, his voice suddenly cold. "Why is it taking so long?"

"I didn't find out about it until yesterday," he explained.

"Yesterday?" Landon questioned, an eyebrow arched in feigned surprise. "How is it that I knew about this problem the day after it occurred?"

"I… uh, I don't know sir." Felix silently kicked himself for such a stupid answer.

"You don't know?" It wasn't a question. "I pay you good money to know. I expect you to know. You *will* know or I'll find someone who *can* know."

"Yes, Sir. I understand, Sir." Felix's armpits were gushing like fountains and he felt the drops of sweat running down his sides as he silently prayed that Landon would not notice, though how could he not when the beads of sweat were forming on his temples.

"So then, Mister Hubach, why don't you tell me what you *do* know."

"The glitch is in the town of Abeloft on the first island. For some reason, once the orcs are killed outside the front gate, the program assumes the quest is successful and that a new individual has arrived for the same quest. In other words, once the orcs are killed the program reactivates the quest and keeps reactivating it, despite the fact that it is the same team completing the quest."

"What else?"

"Well," he added with a nervous breath. "Those involved with completing the quest are leveling up beyond where they should be at this point in the game."

"They are already at level 6," Mister Landon sharply pointed out. "They should not be level 6 until they are on the second island. Is that not correct?"

"No, Sir."

"No?"

Despite the ominous sound of his reply, Felix relaxed slightly as he realized Mister Landon didn't know everything. "No Sir. They need to be at level 10 in order to cross to the next island."

"Ah, yes," he replied with a knowing smile. "You are right. However, they are still leveling up too quickly. What do you intend to do about it?"

"It's the interface between the leveling parameters and quest control. We've already identified the programming error and are in the process of correcting it. It should be finished by the end of the day."

"Should be?"

"I meant *will be*, Sir. They were running some tests while I was on my way here."

Landon relaxed slightly. "So what do you recommend we do about their levels?"

"Leave them, Sir."

"Leave them alone?" he said, frowning.

"Yes, Sir. I believe they realized why they were leveling up and were staying in Abeloft to continue the leveling. If we take away their levels, it might affect their morale. Right now, the leader –"

"Our Viking, Karl," Landon interjected.

"Yes, Sir, Karl. He's put together a tight team and they're operating rather well, just like we wanted. He's a natural leader."

"We knew that," Landon nodded. "That's why we chose him."

"Yes, Sir. As I was saying, reducing their levels will impact the team. I believe we should leave them like they are. It will get them across the bridge faster and they'll be where they should be. Also, once we cease the leveling in Abeloft, they'll take the hint and move on."

Landon mused a bit then gave Felix a rare smile. "Fine. I accept your recommendation. But no more glitches."

"No Sir," he answered with a relieved smile. He could see that Landon was about to dismiss him when he said, "There's one more thing, Sir. Minor really, but I think might help overall in the game."

"Yes?"

"Coffee."

"Coffee?" he furrowed his brows, puzzled.

"Yes, Sir. We've created a dazzling world for our experiment, but the one thing missing is coffee."

Landon's smile turned into a grin. "Of course. There's no coffee in the medieval universe we created. So intent on developing our creations into useful weapons of war, we've neglected the essential creature comforts." He smiled again at Felix. "By all means, we need to add coffee to the game."

"My thought, Sir, is to add it on the second island, sort of as a reward for leaving the first island."

"I'll leave that to you," he replied with a flip of his hand, his reserved demeanor returning.

Recognizing he had been dismissed, he dipped his head in a respectful bow. "Good day, Sir."

"Yes, yes. Good day to you, Felix." He turned back to gaze out the window.

Felix was halfway down the hallway to the elevator when he suddenly realized that Mister Landon had called him by his first name. Controlling his giddiness, he calmed himself, quickly remembering that he needed to discover how Mister Landon knew about the glitch before he did, which meant there either was a mole in his office or the supposedly shielded lines running the program weren't as shielded as he believed. All which meant that he had a security problem, one that he intended to eradicate.

There was a buzz of anticipation as Karl and company sat in the tavern, waiting for the burgomaster and alderman to come traipsing in. While some were thinking of the number of days it would take to level up to 10, others checked weapons or rehearsed spells.

'Why don't we just head on out to the gate," Conrad said aloud, "and surprise them before they even have a chance to know we're there?"

"Because we want the burgomaster and aldermen to come to us and beg us for help," Karl answered. "Showing up uninvited gets them off the hook. We want an overt quid pro quo."

"A what?"

"It's Latin, dummy," Wendell loftily replied.

"So what's it mean, Mister Latin scholar?" Conrad retorted, calling his bluff.

"Uh…" He cleared his throat as he tried to think of an answer that might be close to the truth or was so wildly silly that everyone would laugh and move on and forget that he hadn't a clue.

Tina came to his rescue when she answered for him. "It means a favor granted in return for something," Tina replied.

The two dwarves stared blankly at her before Wendell asked, "How'd you know that?"

"I studied Latin in High School," she demurely answered. "I had once thought to study languages when I went to college. Latin was a good foundation language."

"You speak other languages?" Conrad asked, impressed.

"Yes."

When she didn't elaborate, Kendra pressed, "How many?"

"I don't know," she shrugged, while blushing. "A couple, I guess."

"Which ones?" Wendell asked, interested.

"Oh, um... Spanish, Italian, German, French, Portuguese, Romanian, and I'm pretty good in English too."

Conrad's and Wendell's mouth slacked open as they blankly stared at her.

"You can actually carry on a conversation in all those languages?" Conrad said, dumbfounded.

"Yes."

"I have enough problems in English," Wendell offered.

"Languages were always easy for me," she replied. "The problem was that just because I could speak another language didn't mean I could find a job, other than being some interpreter for the United Nations or an international corporation or teaching, and those jobs are hard to come by because so many people already speak English, so they didn't need an interpreter or another teacher."

"So what did you do?" Kendra asked.

"Nothing much yet. I was still looking for a job when I was diagnosed with leukemia. I was surprised when they came to me about this game. When I asked them why me, they said because I have special abilities that could be used in the game."

"Special abilities?" Wendell repeated.

"Yeah," she shrugged again. "I once won a Rubix cube competition."

"Wow," Conrad chuckled. "They still have those?"

"Yeah, I know, right?" She rolled her eyes.

"What's so special about winning a Rubix cube competition?" Wendell asked then quickly added, "Not that that isn't impressive."

"I was one hundredth of a second off the world record," she replied. "I would have beat it except the cube got stuck when I was twisting it. What did you two do before you came here?"

"I was an accountant," Conrad sheepishly admitted. He hooked a thumb at Wendell. "He was a restaurant manager."

"At least you had careers," she sighed. "I'd spent my life doing what I was good at and discovered too late that there wasn't much use for what I was good at. Then I was diagnosed as almost ready to die and I thought what a waste my life has been. You spend all those years preparing for the future only to have it robbed from you. And now here I am... in a game. Talk about irony. After all is said and done, my life is nothing more than a game."

"Wow. That was deep," Wendell said, dreamingly staring at her.

When Conrad saw her give Wendell a warm smile, he knew he was the odd man out. Clearing his throat, he pushed away from the table, wondering where Kendra was.

Karl scooted his chair back and stood then meandered around the tables, stopping to chat and visit. Heading over to the dwarf table, he was intercepted by Ross who motioned him to the side for a private conversation.

"What's up?" Karl asked.

Ross grinned at him then ticked his head at Raquel and Annabeth. "What's it take to get in on the action with those two?"

"I wouldn't know," he stiffly replied.

"Yeah, right," Ross snickered, eyes half-lidded. "How about sharing a little?"

Karl's lips tightened. "You don't need my permission. They're big girls. They make their own decisions. Go ahead. Ask them yourself." He walked away, more than a little irritated, not that Ross wanted to share in the fun, but the man's approach bespoke crassness. But something more was going on and he walked to the front door and opened it. Night had fallen and the orcs hadn't come.

"That's it, folks" he announced, turning around. "Looks like someone discovered our little secret. The orcs aren't coming tonight."

"They're not?" a voice called out, disappointed.

"No. Looks like we'll be moving on day after tomorrow. Team leaders, let's meet in about five minutes." He glanced over to an obviously crestfallen Humphrey. Though the taverner had born the costs of their lodging ever since they started killing orcs, his business had boomed due to the increase of city folk who wanted to spend time with the orc-killers.

"Sorry Humphrey," Karl commiserated. "We've had a great time here and you've been an incredible host. We'll miss this place. But don't worry. There will be more like us coming."

"Really?" Humphrey brightened.

"I'm sure if it," Karl smiled, not sure what made him say that as he had no clue as to what ITL's plans were. His attention was diverted when he saw Conrad and Wendell approach. Conrad curled a finger at Karl while the two dwarves veered off to not be overhead.

"Yes?" Karl asked with a curious smile.

"Uh, y'see, it's like this," Conrad began. "We were thinking, that Wendell and me that is if it's OK with you, him and me could do sort of a switcheroo."

"Like what?"

"Well, there's him and me on one team and Kendra and Tina on the other. What we wanna do is switch Kendra for me so that him and Tina would be on one team and me and Kendra would be on the other team."

Karl studied Wendell. "You sure?"

"Yup," Wendell replied without hesitation.

"What do the ladies think?"

"Haven't asked them yet?" Conrad sheepishly admitted. "Wanted to clear it with you first."

132

Karl thought a bit about the four dwarves. Conrad and Wendell were rogues, the two lady dwarves were healers. Switching out one of the rogues would actually help balance the teams.

"I'm fine with it as long as the two ladies are OK with it, as well as the team leaders."

"Thanks," Conrad beamed as the two rogues hustled off to convince the ladies of their brilliant idea.

Bemused by their enthusiasm, Karl headed upstairs to retrieve the island map. By the time he returned, Conrad and Wendell were still adroitly pressing their argument. Spreading the map out on the table where Raquel and Annabeth sat, he folded his arms as he studied the details.

The Misted Isle was shaped like a lopsided and squashed 'U.' Marbeck, the town of their arrival was on the tip of the upper arm of the 'U.' A little farther down the arm was Abeloft. The rest of the map contained symbols for mountains, rivers and other towns. Mountains occupied the center of the island. All the towns, except one were along the coast. One town lay in the center of the mountains. The bridge to the next island was at the tip of the other arm. The obvious shorter route would be to travel along the coast along the inside of the 'U.'

Dieter and Sakura walked up as he concentrated on the map.

"I've been studying this map ever since we found it," Karl said. "Logically, the shortest route to the bridge would make the most sense. However, in order to cross the bridge we have to accomplish a number of quests, which, I assume, would get us to a level high enough to cross. In our present situation, I make the assumption that we have leveled high enough. However, that may not be the case, for, in truth, I have no idea what level we need to be to cross."

"So we're here," Dieter said pointing to the town symbol labelled 'Abeloft' on the left side of the map. "And we gotta get there." He pointed to a town labeled 'Hulgard,' with a bridge symbol extending out from the town and ending across an expanse of water at the tip of another island at the edge of the map.

"Yes."

"The only roads I see marked go into the mountains or along the west coast," Dieter said. "I don't see any going the shorter route."

"You're right," Karl agreed. "But that doesn't mean there aren't any as we don't know how old the map is. That aside, I'm looking for input."

"Why not take a vote?" Sakura proposed.

"Because this isn't a democracy," Raquel answered.

"She's right," Dieter quietly said. "Karl is in charge and he has the final decision."

"I just meant to get more input," Sakura defensively stated.

"I don't need everyone's input," Karl responded. "That's why you're the team leader. What are *your* thoughts?"

Sakura looked like she was about to argue when she backed down. "I say we take the longer route. It's not like we're in a rush to get to the next island. There's no deadline or timeline we have to follow. Take our time and get leveled up as high as we can on the way."

"I agree with Sakura," Dieter nodded. "We take our time, enjoy ourselves where and when we can, and move on when we need to, like we did here."

Karl turned to Raquel and Annabeth who both nodded, concurring with the plan.

"There it is then. It took us two days to get from Marbeck to Abeloft. If the map is to scale, I calculate the distance to Hulgard probably another week to ten days, without any diversions or interruptions, which means it'll take longer than that as we all know we can expect to be interrupted along the way. We move out day after tomorrow, as soon as the mist burns off. Oh, one more thing," he said, looking past Sakura to see Conrad and Wendell smiling. "Conrad and Wendell have a proposal concerning dwarf composition on your teams," he said, addressing Dieter and Sakura. "I have no objection to their proposal, but the choice is yours."

"What's the proposal?" Sakura asked.

"I'll let them explain," he replied with a smile.

As Sakura moved off to find out what Conrad and Wendell had in mind, Dieter lingered, giving Karl a hopeful stare.

"Have you made a decision yet, Boss?"

"I have. As long as everyone involved agrees, you may take Elena with you."

"Awesome," Dieter said, pumping his fist. "I'll go let her know."

By the size of the crowd, it looked like the entire city had turned out to see them off. A relieved burgomaster, glad to be freed of the cost of supporting and supplying Karl and company stood at the gate and shook hands with each one of the team as they passed by.

"Don't forget us," he said with a broad smile. "Come back anytime," he added, praying they never did.

They traveled in over-watch with rangers Raquel and Ross out front, traveling along the single road leading south out of Abeloft. Though cautious, nothing out of the ordinary occurred as the day was warm, pleasant and sunny. As evening approached the scouts found a large home set back away from the main road.

"It looks a lot like that one home with the spiders," Raquel said with a grimace, "but it's larger."

"We need to hunker down for the night," Karl said. "Let's clean the place up before we settle."

Walking down the path to the house, the first thing Karl noted was the well-worn track leading to the front door, causing him to wonder who or what lived there. Instead of entering, Karl decided to walk around the outside of the home to study the building and the surrounding area.

The house was constructed of stone with a bright red front door, flanked by shuttered windows. Half a dozen windows, likewise shuttered lined the sides of the house. Two red brick chimneys protruded from the thatched roof, one in the middle and one in the back. It looked like the quintessential rustic home art piece one would find for sale in so many cheap arts and craft stores.

On his way to the other side of the house, a small torn bit of colored cloth tangled on the brambles at the edge of the forest surrounding the house caught his attention. Walking over to inspect it, he noted the smallest threads of spider silk waving in the gentle breeze. He immediately gave orders to collect as much burnable wood as each member could carry.

Walking into the house, he took notice of the layout of the large room along with the cooking pot and clean fireplace, table with maps and the striking similarity to the spider house. Passing through to the next room, he saw the fire place at the back wall then counted six double beds, three against each side wall. Either someone had a very large family, or someone was expecting them.

"Get a fire roaring in both fireplaces then collect more wood. I have a feeling we'll want to keep a fire going the entire night"

"Spiders?" Annabeth shuddered.

"We'll find out," he replied. "Dieter and Sakura," he called out to the two team leaders. "Position your teams around the outside of the house and watch for what comes out of the chimneys. The rest of us will back you up."

Dieter turned to Elena, his berserker rage already beginning to build. "Stay inside. You'll be safe here."

"OK," she meekly replied, having never seen this side of her lover.

It didn't take long to find out as once the wood caught fire and the smoke curled up the chimney, spiders began pouring out the top, smaller ones at first, then when the flames roared down below, larger ones popped out.

It was a war of attrition as the spiders cascaded down the roof to be met by dwarven hammers, elf arrows, a Viking sword, and a berserker hammer. Annabeth and Lana cast spells and launched freeze and fire bolts as rapidly as they formed them.

Yet some spiders did not take kindly to being attacked and launched themselves in suicidal assaults from the rooftop. Several found their mark and Carole screamed and collapsed under the weight of the spiders.

Dieter's berserker rage grew and the swath of his hammer cut such a deadly path that the spiders fell back as he made his way to the fallen Carole who lay crumpled and limp on the ground. Under the continued onslaught of the teams and with their lair and treachery exposed, the spiders fled into the surrounding forest. With the threat removed, Dieter picked up the wounded elf and carried her inside the house.

Karl's screen popped up.

Congratulations: You have defeated the Spiders of Iria Forest.
You've received: Experience.
You've received: Leadership +6 points.

Ignoring the prompt, he gathered everyone inside the cottage and positioned the company around the interior, near windows and the door as well as ensuring the fires continued rippling then went to check on Kendra and Tina who attended Carole, casting Remove Paralysis and Cure Light Wounds Spells.

"She's been bitten several times," Kendra said. "We've managed to take away the paralysis, and you can see we've healed the puncture bites, but the poison still runs in her blood. Neither of us have high enough healing skills to cure her."

"We've given her healing potions," Tina added, "but we only have so much. They've restored some of her health points, but she's still in danger the longer the poison stays inside her."

Karl looked down at the high elf's body bathed in a sheen of sweat. "Do your best," he grimly replied.

He walked over to where Dieter sat exhausted, propped against the wall, his berserker rage spent. Elena sat next to him, feeding him bits of dried meat, helping him regain his strength.

"How you feeling?"

"I'm doing better. Give me about half an hour to rest and I should be back to normal, maybe sooner with the food Elena is feeding me." He smiled affectionately at her.

As Karl continued his rounds, his worry grew as he realized everyone needed rest in order to recoup their strength. If a more powerful enemy than the spiders attacked now, they would be in big trouble.

'If you haven't already done so," he said in a calm voice, "change your bind spot to Abeloft."

"Preferably your bedroom and not the main tavern," Wendell cracked, looking at Conrad.

"Aren't you the comedian," Conrad retorted, hoping Kendra and Tina were too engrossed healing Carole to pay attention.

"Suppose your room is already rented out," Brad observed with a chuckle. "Can you imagine showing up and the person is in room?"

"Or two lovers in the middle of getting frisky," Bruno laughed. "Can you imagine the look on their faces, especially when you show up nude? One of them is not going to be happy."

"Oh I don't know," Annabeth giggled. "Depends who it is."

"I changed mine to the kitchen," Wendell announced. "That way it'll be warm when I respawn and I'll be surrounded by food and ale."

"You and your food," Conrad groused. "I'm surprised Humphrey is still in business after feeding you."

"Look who's talking, Mister Piglet," Wendell huffed.

"Or how about some grizzled old man or woman who hasn't had any in years," Bruno interrupted, "and they get the idea that you were heaven sent for their pleasure."

"I'd be running down the hall," Ross said, "clothes or no clothes."

A heavy thud at the door snapped them to alert. Ross, standing by the door, checked the two crossbars that held the door closed then pressed his head against the thick wooden door, trying to listen when another thud bounced his head away from the door.

"Check the windows," Karl quietly commanded, racing to the back bedroom where half the company had been relaxing but were now on edge, double checking the bars across the windows holding the shutters tight.

"I can hear something," Ross said, his head not so close to the door this time. "It sounds like voices, but I can't make any sense of it."

"Ho inside house," a voice yelled from outside, the accent thick and rough. "Open door. We want talk."

"Who are you?" Karl called back, needing to stall for time.

"Ho, we friends. Nice. Want talk."

"Who are you? Karl repeated.

There was a pause as Ross heard voices back and forth.

"We dwarf."

"No you're not," Conrad barked.

Another pause and more voices in what sounded like arguing.

"We elfs."

"No you're not," Bruno called back.

"Ale seller."

"No," Karl answered.

"Priest."

"No."

"Bunny," another voice called out, immediately followed by angry retorts and another voice saying, "Him joking. No bunny here."

Brad whispered in Karl's ear.

"You sound like goblins," Karl called back.

There was a long awkward pause. Ross heard the low undertones of a discussion.

"Yes. We goblin. Nice goblin. Happy goblin. Want to talk. Share food?"

Deciding he needed to know more about goblins, Karl pulled up his data screen and pressed the character information link, pulling up goblins.

Description: Goblins are short, ugly creatures, humanoid in appearance and stand just over 3 feet tall. Though rare, taller goblins are not unknown. The tallest goblin reported was close to 5 feet tall. Their bodies tend to be gaunt and crowned with an oversized head that is usually hairless. Goblins with hair tend to be female. All goblins have the usual trait of massive ears and beady red eyes, though orange and yellow eyes have also been reported. Goblins' skin tone varies in accordance with the surrounding environment. For example, forest goblins tend to have green and dull brown skin tones. Other prevalent tones are gray and blue. More rare are black and even pale white. Goblins have a voracious appetite, which explains their large mouths filled with jagged teeth. Goblins are greedy, capricious, and destructive by nature.

Personality: Goblins are a race of creatures with a mix of childlike naiveté and destructive passions that make them almost universally loathed. They are weak and cowardly, and because of their diminutive stature, they are frequently enslaved by stronger creatures that use them as disposable foot soldiers whose appetite for destruction provides a base for expansion. Most races view goblins as destructive cockroaches – despite the best efforts, they are impossible to exterminate. Goblins eat nearly anything and view other beings as sources of food. Their appetites are voracious and are the compelling reason for their existence. They live to eat. The preferred diet is meat, especially the flesh of humans and other high races, which they consider a difficult-to-obtain delicacy.

Karl scanned through the rest of the information, taking note that goblins were fast, but weak and quite unpleasant to be around.

"How much food do you have?" he asked.

This caused a burst of conversation on the other side of the door.

"No. No food. You share with us."

"We don't have enough," Karl replied. "Why don't you go hunt for some food and bring it back for us to cook?" Looking over his shoulder, he lowered his voice. "Anyone know what time it is?"

"It was still daylight when we took on the spiders," Raquel answered.

"It's still daylight now," Ross said, "though it won't be for long. I can see through a tiny slit in the shutters."

"OK folks," Karl said in muted tones. "Rolling watches throughout the night. Everyone needs to regain full strength as well as some rest."

"OK," the voice outside called out. "We go find food. Bring back. You cook. OK?"

"OK," Karl answered.

Five minutes later the voice called out. "Ho inside house. We back. Catch nice big deer." He was interrupted by a several voices. "No," he started again. "We catch two –" overlapping voices interrupted him again. "We catch three –"

What ensued was an angry exchange followed by final burst of anger and clearing of his throat.

"We catch five big fat deer. You cook for us. Yes?"

"We'll need more wood to cook all that," Karl called back.

An impatient burst of goblin spewed forth then stopped as the goblin collected himself. "OK. We get wood. You cook then. OK?"

"OK."

Five minutes later the voice sang out. "Ho inside house. We have wood."

"What about spices?" Karl asked, smirking. "We can't cook it unless we have spices."

"Spices?" the voice angrily repeated. "You no need spices. You cook now."

"That's too many deer," Karl explained. "We only have two fireplaces and you have five deer. Why don't you cook them and we can eat with you."

With an exasperated sigh, the voice said, "OK. We cook."

Five minutes later, the voice called out. "OK. All done."

"What?" Karl replied. "That's too quick. The meat is not cooked enough. We like it cooked all the way through."

141

Another torrent of words that Karl figured had to be swear words erupted.

The back and forth continued with the voice announcing the meat done and Karl asking which portions were done, had they cut off the fat because he doesn't like fat and Annabeth liked her venison lean, and make sure it wasn't charred because Brad didn't like it charred and by the way did they say an animal prayer over the deer after they killed them.

As time went on, Karl solicited replies, much to the amusement of those in the house. During a lull in the exchanges, Kendra came up.

"She's not getting any worse, but she's not getting any better. As far as Tina and I can tell, it's a slow acting poison. We've done all we can. She needs help from someone with more skills."

"Thanks," he nodded in appreciation. Turning to Ross still at the door, he said, "Can you handle the chatter while I talk with the team leaders?"

"Be happy to," he grinned.

Karl motioned for Dieter, Sakura, Annabeth and Raquel to meet at the table near the fireplace.

"We need to get Carole to someone with healing power," he said. "That means we have to break out of here as soon as possible. We launch our attack in the morning just before the mist disappears and head south to Westhaven. Hopefully someone will be there who can help."

"Suppose there isn't?" Sakura asked.

"Then she dies," Dieter answered.

"Why not just let her die here and she can respawn back in Abeloft?" Sakura said without emotion.

"How charitable of you," Raquel coldly responded.

"I'm serious. Taking her with us endangers us all. How many have to carry her, watch out for her, while the rest of us fight goblins? I say we sacrifice the one for the good of the many."

"It doesn't work that way," Karl quietly replied. "Though your reasoning has merit, it is bad for morale if anytime someone is hurt they are abandoned. There are fifteen of us here, now. There will be fifteen of us when we reach the bridge. We leave no man behind unless we absolutely can't help it. In this instance, we can help it. Besides, are there residual effects of the poison should she respawn in Abeloft? We all know there is no one there who has the healing capabilities she needs. The answer is simple. She comes with us."

Sakura closed her mouth, signifying she had nothing more to say.

"Do a weapons and skills check of your team," Karl continued. "Make sure everyone gets rest." He then gazed pointedly at Sakura. "You're an assassin by trade. An hour before our attack, I want you to do a recon."

"How will I get out?" she scowled.

"Through the roof," he answered.

She looked up, realizing the roof was thatch, silently berating herself for not analyzing the whole thing through before making snap statements.

"OK."

"Questions?"

"Yeah, "Annabeth said. "Who takes care of Carole?"

"Kendra and Tina," Karl answered. "They're dwarves. They're strong and can carry her. Likewise, they're healers and so wouldn't be an active part of the battle."

"Providing we don't need any healing," Raquel pointed out.

"I know," Karl acknowledged. "It's a gamble we'll have to take."

He paused when he heard Ross call out through the door, "It's too late to eat now. Everyone is trying to get some sleep except for me and I can't eat that much. I tell you what. Let's have a big meal tomorrow after the mist goes away, in the middle of the day. That will give you a chance to find some ale. Surely you don't expect us to have a feast without ale."

The response was a tired mumble of inarticulate words.

Karl smiled at him. "Cleverly done."

Ross grinned. "That was fun. Thanks."

"I have a question," Raquel said. "Goblins see well in the dark, but what about the heavy mist? And don't gnolls come out at night?   What's the chance of gnolls and goblins bumping into each other?"

"That would be to our advantage," Karl said. "We can hope for the best."

Karl woke at the sound of a loud disturbance in the middle of the night, like two clashing forces. Shouts and the clang of metal on metal pierced the quiet of the house. But it died down as quickly as it started.

He listened for another ten minutes and when no further sounds emerged, he stretched out again. He no sooner lay back than pounding and prying on the doors and windows began. Bolting up, he quickly saw everyone else was awake.

"To the windows," he commanded. "Hit them before they have a chance to get in."

The banging and prying were now accompanied by overlapping growls and yells of urgency. A window in the bedroom began to yield and the shutters slowly pried apart.

When the gap was wide enough, Sharyn sent an arrow through it causing a screech and the shutters to momentarily close.

Other window shutters were splintering under the incessant rain of blows from goblin clubs. With the two dwarf healers guarding Carole, the rest of the company split into twos for each window, believing the door could hold out longer than the windows.

Annabeth and Raquel were at the first window that burst. Before the goblins had a chance to push in, Annabeth hurled a fire bolt that caught the first goblin full in the face, exploding on contact and propelling him backwards into his cohorts. No sooner had the goblin fallen back that Raquel launched a flurry of arrows causing screams of pain and terror.

Lana and Brad stood ready at the window next to them, both working feverously on spells. As their window buckled, Lana drew a star circumscribed with a pentagram in the air then dropped to a knee and pressed her palm on the floor, fingers pointed to the wall. A narrow yet violent tremor shot out from her hand like a fissure from an earthquake. At the same time, Brad stretched a hand out and uttered a Fear Curse. The result was an eruption of panic among the goblins, for when the Fear Curse fell upon the single goblin, his alarm of dread coupled with the ground shake caused the others to follow him in a stampede away from the window.

While others jabbed swords through the shutter slits, finding their marks, Dieter stalked like a caged animal, his berserker rage building.

"This is bullshit," he bellowed. Hefting his battle axe, he strode across the floor, pulled off the bars securing the front door and yanked it open.

"No," Karl yelled, racing after him.

Dieter bent over to clear the doorway then unfolded to full height. Despite the heavy mist, those goblins close enough to distinguish that someone had opened the door suddenly found themselves cut in half as Dieter let out a loud bloodcurdling growl and swung his giant ax in a wide swath.

"Lock the door behind us," Karl called out as he followed Dieter.

Together, they worked their way around the perimeter of the house, Dieter swinging the savage blade in a wide furious arc while Karl protected his back.

The mist aided their efforts as the goblins, unaware of the approaching doom, continued their attacks on the windows, only to discover too late, when the bodies and heads of their compatriots split apart beside them, that death and destruction had arrived.

Twice, Karl had to call out "Hold your fire," as they came to an open window.

By the time they arrived back at the front door, an eerie quiet had settled, broken by the occasional anguished cry of a wounded goblin. Karl pounded on the door with the pommel of his sword.

"Open up. We're back."

"How do we know it's you?" a voice mocked.

"Very funny, Ross," Karl answered, shaking his head.

The door opened and the two warriors entered. Dieter was spattered in goblin blood while Karl's rear defense earned him very little in the gore department. Elena was about to rush over to Dieter when she saw that the rage had not left him yet, so she bided her time, coming up to stand beside him.

Karl smiled at Ross' innocent face then went to check on the company, pleased that they had already jammed beds into the spaces of the broken shutters.

"Everyone OK?" he queried.   Receiving affirmative nods, he complimented, "Nice work everyone. Well done. That was a nice touch you two," he said to Lana and Brad. "Very effective."

"Tiny looks a mess," Conrad chuckled.

The rage gone, Dieter looked down at his splattered clothing then shrugged. "How'd we do?"

"You were amazing," Karl grinned. "But maybe you can give me a warning the next time."

"Sorry, Boss," he sheepishly replied.

"Dawn's coming," Ross said, gazing out through one of the windows. "Mist should burn off in a couple of hours."

Karl was about to ask him how he knew then remembered the man was a Ranger and knew the lore of the outside world.

Congratulations: You've defeated a goblin regiment.

Reward: Reputation.   You and your company have increased your reputation: +6 points.   You've gone from local hero to 'Your name sounds familiar.'

"Looks like things might finally settle down," Karl announced. "For those of you not on watch, check your weapons then try to get some sleep if you can. We'll head out as soon as the mist gives us enough visibility."

Despite being tired, no one could sleep and instead chose to clean weapons and talk quietly amongst themselves. Then true to Ross' prognosis, the outside mist began to brighten and slowly dissolve.

An hour later, the mist was thin enough to open the door. What greeted them was the gruesome visage of the aftermath of battle with bodies of goblins, dozens upon dozens of them, scattered around the house. The largest number lay close to the house where Dieter had wreaked his havoc. Many bodies were decapitated, others missing whole limbs, and still others with their overlarge heads smashed in.

Conrad decided to count the toll, but stopped when he reached thirty one and he realized he still had the other side of the house to count.

"Do we check for any potions or other things?" Lana asked.

Karl surveyed the carnage, at once repulsed by memories of other battlefields, but satisfied that he had kept his company whole. "No. I don't see a need to spend any more time here."

"I quite agree," Ross said. "The sooner we get away from here the better. How far is it to the next town?"

"We should get there this afternoon," Karl answered. "Raquel. Ross. You take point. Sakura's team next then Dieter's team. Kendra and Tina. You OK with Carole?"

"Yes," Tina replied. They had rigged a stretcher using the boards from one of the bed frames and the cotton mattress covering, leaving some of the batting in it for Carole's comfort. The two dwarves carried her with ease.

"OK, good. The rest fall in where needed. Let's move out."

The road through the forest was wide enough for a single merchant's wagon and the ruts in the road made it appear the road was well traveled, yet during their entire time traveling, they had yet to meet another individual in passing.

The forest edging the road was thick with interlacing branches creating a canopy overhead. Shafts of sunlight pierced the cover, briefly illuminating the travelers as they passed through the light. The warmth of the day and the vivid greens and browns of the leaves and trees, along with the bright whites, reds, and purples of wildflowers created a lazy ambiance of a summer day with nothing urgent to do or place to go.

The careless feel to the day caused Karl to be more on edge. When defenses were down was the time when things went wrong. He circulated back and forth among the company, briefly making small talk, twice calling a halt to check the map.

By midafternoon, he was beginning to doubt the accuracy of the map. There was only one road on the map that led all the way from Marbeck through Abeloft to Westhaven. At least that was what the map said, and there had been no other roads that they had seen.

He was calculating how they were going to set up a camp in the forest when Raquel came back.

"There's a break in the woods up ahead. There's a good sized city on a hill. Looks like probably another hour or two before we get there."

"We need to pick up the pace," Karl said, "if we're going to make it in time." He strode back to where Tina and Kendra stood watch over Carole, the litter on the ground. "You two doing OK?"

"We're fine," Tina smiled.

"She's not heavy," Kendra added.

Tina gave Kendra a knowing smile. "We're strong. We're dwarves."

"There's a town about an hour or two away. We're going to have to pick up the pace if we're going to make it before they lock the gates."

"We can do it," Tina announced, bending down to grab hold of the ends of the litter. Kendra grabbed the other end and together they lifted.

Karl stared briefly down at Carole, her body a pale death gray then spun around and flicked a finger at Raquel telling her to resume the march. "We gotta pick up the pace," he informed the rest of the company.

As they moved out, Karl was both surprised and impressed with their determination and effort for once the group crested the road and saw their goal in the distance, they picked up the pace and arrived at the main gate in a little more than an hour.

The city of Westhaven covered a high broad hill, surrounded by a concentric series of thick crenellated walls of dark stone. In the middle and at the highest point of the hill was a castle that looked like the quintessential medieval castle along the lines of Hohenzollern Castle in Germany. In between the city walls and the surrounding forest was a wide gap of vibrant farm fields billowing with grains, protected at the forest's edge by a wide and impressively tall solid wall of smooth stone.

The guards at the gate were in the process of closing one of the massive oak doors when they were startled by Raquel calling out, "Hold fast."

They were further surprised when the rest of the company jogged the road leading up to the gate.

"Is there a healer in the city?" Karl asked.

"Of course there is," one guard replied. He was a medium height young man wearing chainmail and a Spangenhelm helmet. He cast a snide eye upon the group, though still taken aback at Dieter's size

"Who are you?" the other guard snapped. "What are you doing here? Where do you come from?" He was a middle aged man, dressed like his compatriot.

"I am Karl the Viking and these are my friends. We've come from Marbeck."

"Marbeck?" the first guard repeated with surprise.

"Karl the Viking?" the other guard slowly said. "I think I may have heard of you."

Karl chuckled thinking that the reputation trait might prove useful. "We've a deathly ill elf who's in need of a healer. She was bitten by spiders."

The eyes on both the guards widened in apprehension and respect.

"Did you kill any of them?" the older guard asked.

"Lots," Karl impatiently replied, "along with a whole slew of goblins. But we really need a healer."

"Of course," the older guard sympathetically said. "I can take you to her once we finish here."

"How long will that take?" Raquel asked.

"You can't do that," the younger guard interrupted. "They have to go to the Administrator."

"They can do both," the older guard answered with an indulgent sigh. "The entire group doesn't have to go to the

149

Administrator. C'mon. Let get these doors closed so they can get her to the healer."

"But... but..." the younger guard began but found he was ignored by the older guard who pulled the one gate door closed.

With the doors shut and bolted, the group passed through the gate house and stood just outside as the portcullis was lowered.

"Follow me," the older guard said with a curl of his hand. "My name's Jethdar. The lad over there is called Meinke." He looked at Tina and Kendra holding Carole. "You've two healers with you."

"We don't have enough power to heal her," Kendra explained.

"I understand," he nodded. "A single spider's bite is deadly. I'm surprised the elf still lives."

As Jethdar led the way past the farm fields, some rippling with grain, others as pasture for livestock, Karl glanced back over his shoulder and noted the guards spaced at intervals, manning the walls. He turned back to look ahead and calculated the distance to the next wall to be at least 1000 meters. Glancing to his left and right, he traced the outer wall, through which they entered, until it disappeared in the distance and realized it probably encircled the entire city and farms.

They walked in silence as the road gently climbed towards another wall and another gate, protected by four guards who gave Jethdar a friendly wave while regarding the newcomers with more than curious attention, bordering on fascination when they saw the dwarves.

"The elf suffers a spider's bite," Jethdar explained, causing the guards to tense up. "Tell the captain they're here. We go to the Lady for healing."

As dusk began to settle, Jethdar led them through the gate, which was partially blocked, forcing them to make a sharp left. Karl immediately understood the design as forcing an invader to narrow his forces in an awkward position.

Following the cobbled street another short distance, they came to another wall forcing them to make two quick right turns before finally opening up to the city's main street, active with merchants, soldiers, mothers with gamboling children, and revelers heading to numerous taverns, who were strangely subdued as those out and about talked in hushed tones.

"Why is everyone so quiet?" Conrad asked.

"It's out of respect for the queen."

"Something happen?" Conrad boldly asked.

"She was murdered by Lord Cyril's henchmen last week. Her dismembered body was tossed over the city walls of Durness."

"My God," Annabeth uttered. "That's terrible."

"That's not the half of it," he said, rolling his eyes in frustration. "It's said that Cyril has joined forces with the Trolls of Stonefell. We expect an attack any day now."

"So who rules here," Raquel asked, "now that the queen is dead."

"Oh, it's still Lady Gwen. She's Lady Briet's younger sister. The queen, Lady Briet, lives... or rather lived in Durness, the capital of Montgrec." He stopped and studied them with an intense stare. "I should think you would know all this."

"We've been gone for a while," Karl lamely replied, "sort of out of touch with what's been happening lately."

Jethdar frowned, shook his head and resumed walking. "You remind me of several of your kind who came through here a couple of months ago."

"Our kind?" Karl said.

"Yes, an assassin much like the dark one you have with you came through here and was gone before the Administrator had a chance to complete his interview with him. Two elves came later and the Administrator detained them until Lady Gwen intervened and allowed them to move on, once she got the assurance they would not join Cyril's campaign against us. "Your dwarves are the first to appear here in Westhaven,"

"You don't seem all that surprised," Karl commented.

Jethdar shrugged. "Elves, trolls, orcs, gnolls, giant spiders... what's the big deal about dwarves?"

"Hey," Conrad said with indignation.

"No offense," Jethdar offered, "just pointing out in the overall scheme of things, dwarves are the least of our worries."

"How long have you and Cyril been fighting?" Raquel asked.

"For as long as I can remember," he replied. "That we are at the far edges of the kingdom means we haven't had to endure the same trials those to the south have."

"Are Marbeck and Abeloft part of Montgrec?" Karl asked.

"Until a couple of months ago, we didn't even know they existed."

"What?" Karl raised an eyebrow in doubt. "How is that possible?"

Jethdar sighed, again shaking his head. "You forget that our attention is focused to the south. The only thing to the north was a forest filled with goblins, gnolls, and orcs. Those who ventured into the forest never came back. That is why your tale will be of interest to the Administrator."

"Our tale?"

"Yes," he answered. "Until the elves came and likewise stated they had come from a town called Marbeck through Abeloft to here, we all believed the assassin was sent by Cyril."

"How large is Westhaven?" Raquel asked.

Jethdar fixed her with a sharp glance.

"We're not spies, if that's what you're thinking," she said. "I should think that would be obvious to a professional soldier like yourself."

"I'm not a professional soldier," he answered, "though thank you for the compliment. I'm just a simple farmer. My spread's on the other side of the city. As to your question, there are just under ten thousand who live here."

Noting the size of the farms, Karl said, "You produce everything you need so that no one need leave the city?"

"Exactly."

"Why was the gate open then?"

"Custom," he chuckled. "We open the gate for an hour twice a day, once mid-morning and the other at the end of the day. You arrived just in time."

Karl did a rough mental calculation of the length of the outer city wall. "Ten thousand citizens seem too few to man all the walls and still maintain a living."

"We manage," he evasively answered.

Passing through another second gate, this one unmanned, they were met with the bustle of life and tall three story houses that lined both sides of the street. The first building opposite the gate was of solid dull red brick and contained a tavern doing a brisk business.

"We need to come back here," Wendell happily observed.

"The Brickhouse is an excellent tavern, but there are better ones closer to the castle," Meinke said.

"And more expensive," Jethdar added with a wink.

Jethdar led them up the main road then through a series of back roads and alleyways so that after fifteen minutes, they were utterly lost.

"I understand what you're doing," Raquel wryly observed, "and point out again that we are not spies."

"No doubt," Jethdar nodded. "Still, I do have to answer for my actions."

They emerged from one side-street onto a wide road bordered on one side by large homes facing a large verdant commons where mothers watched children playing games, lovers strolled hand in hand, and old men and women sat on benches sharing the latest gossip and aches and pains. Just beyond the park, the castle rose in domination.

Jethdar led them across the park causing those who saw them to stop and stare. Seeing the dwarves, children cast aside their inhibitions and raced over to get a closer look, standing in fascinated awe as the four diminutive beings passed by. One little girl squealed with delight when Conrad smiled and winked at her.

Once across the park and away from the inquisitive stares, Jethdar led them through the open gate of the castle then up a wide paved path that curled in a circle to another gate above the first gate, through that gate then again in a wide circle to a third gate above the first two.

Karl nodded in admiration that any enemy attempting to attack the castle was forced into these narrow circular routes and far too many gates. He was further surprised by the presence of a fourth gate that led to the main castle itself, 'J' shaped and comprised of three stories of smooth stone, all topped with tall turrets.

Crossing the courtyard, they entered the foyer and were greeted by a wide set of double stairs, supported by thick ornate columns, that curled around and joined together on the second floor. Several guards took one look at Jethdar's guests and stood aside.

"I thought you said there was someone who could heal our comrade," Karl urgently reminded Jethdar.

"I did. She lives here, as does the Administrator."

The castle seemed strangely vacant, considering the size as Karl and company were led through long halls, richly decorated with tapestries, paintings, and sculptures. Wide chandeliers adorned with cream colored candles suspended from the ceiling, which was often painted with clouds and blue sky.

Up another set of stairs and down three more hallways, Karl noted that they passed few people, and those they did were all fixed on their jobs, whether maid, butler, or attendant. They passed one or two nobility to which Jethdar deferentially nodded, yet none seemed the slightest bit interested in the newcomers.

Finally, Jethdar stopped them before an artfully carved door of woodland scenes, flanked by two tall burly guards who nodded in recognition at Jethdar. Seeing the stretcher, one of the guards turned and knocked. Though no 'Come in' sounded, he opened the door and waved them inside.

Karl found himself in a large anteroom almost as long as one of the hallways. At the far end, a woman stood near the fireplace, reading a book on a bookstand. She looked up when they entered then calmly placed a bookmark in the book and closed it.

"Lady Gwen," Jethdar reverently said as they approached. "These are visitors who have just arrived. One of them, an elf woman, has sustained a mortal wound. This one," he indicated Karl with a tick of his head, "is called Karl the Viking."

Karl sucked in his breath as he approached for Lady Gwen was of exquisite beauty. Her strawberry blond hair fell off her shoulders to below her breasts, which were neither large nor small but firm and covered in a gown of flowing white silk. Her waist was narrow as were her hips. But it was her bright emerald green eyes on a porcelain smooth face that immediately caught his attention, for her eyes spoke even before her lips moved.

"Welcome," she said, her voice warm and mellifluous, staring intently at Karl, holding him captive with her gaze before breaking away to take in the rest of the company. "You are all welcome. Karl the Viking. I believe I have heard of you."

Though flattered, Karl wasn't sure what benefit it was that someone might have heard of him.

"Now let's see what we have here. Put her on the couch there." She pointed to a thick cushioned settee by the tall windows of the outer wall.

Kendra and Tina carried Carole over and gently laid her on the settee then stepped to the side as Lady Gwen glided gracefully over to stand beside her. Reaching down, she felt Carole's forehead then took hold of her hand.

"There is death here, though life lurks along the edges. Tell me what happened." Though it was a command, it was said like a request.

"We were on the way here from Abeloft –" Karl began.

"It's true then," Lady Gwen said with keen interest.

"Yes, m'Lady," Jethdar answered.

"Continue," she said to Karl, "but you will tell me about Abeloft when we are finished here."

"Yes, m'Lady," Karl answered, mimicking Jethdar's respect. "We were on our way here from Abeloft and stopped at a house midway between here and there. The house was infested with spiders."

"Spiders of Iria," she nodded in understanding, "very poisonous. They capture the unsuspecting by luring them to abandoned houses, wrapping them up in spider silk when they sleep and take them away to dine on their flesh. Yes, we know the stories, though none venture into the forest anymore to confirm them."

"We killed many of them and in the battle, Carole was bitten several times. We would have left had it not been late and the mist. During the night, we were attacked by goblins but managed to inflict a severe loss upon them."

Lady Gwen nodded as she listened then hiking up her silk dress, she dropped to her knees, twisted her head and placed an ear on Carole's chest, listening to her breathing and heart. After a few moments she held out her hand to Karl to assist her to standing.

"I will do what I can. The rest will be up to her." Twisting her head to narrow her gaze at Karl, she added, "But it will come at a price."

"I understand," Karl nodded thinking they had more than enough gold to pay whatever the cost.

"No you do not," she stated. "My price is that you, all of you, will owe me a favor. All of you or there is no healing. Do you accept?"

Karl stood to full height, initially irritated at the demand. How dare this woman hold them hostage in order to heal Carole. Perhaps there was another, more reasonable healer in the city. He was about to infer as much when Conrad spoke up.

"What kind of favor?"

"You will know when I decide to tell you," Lady Gwen answered. "But you must choose quickly. I fear she will not last the remainder of the day."

His lips pursed, Karl war-gamed the worst that could happen, realizing the worst that could happen was that they all would be killed. But then, they would all respawn and life would resume. It was the pain of death and respawning that concerned him. Hearing Conrad retell it, it was not something one took flippantly for it involved immeasurable pain. Still... He turned to the rest of the company. "I will not make your decision for you. She has stated her terms, all or nothing. Are you willing to abide by the terms?"

"What choice do we have?" Tina asked. "She dies and respawns back in Abeloft, and we have lost one of our company."

"At least she'd be alive," Conrad pointed out. "Knowing what she does, it wouldn't take long for her to get back here."

"On her own?" Ross countered. "She was out when we fought the goblins, remember?"

"Then all she has to do is wait for another group to come by and join them." He countered.

Raquel fixed him with an intent stare. "I'll remember your words when you are the one mortally wounded."

"What?" Conrad defensively retorted. "All I'm doing is pointing out the possibilities."

"It's not as simple as you think," Lady Gwen interrupted. "There is only one man living in the city who survived the spider's bite. It took all my power to heal him. However, he has never been the same and is subject to fits of spasms and drooling."

Inhaling a deep breath, Karl looked at each of them in turn. "It sounds like our decision is made for us. For me, I will agree to her terms."

"As do I," Raquel and Annabeth said at the same time, followed by the rest, the last being a begrudging Conrad.

Karl turned back to Gwen. "We agree to your terms."

"Good." She then turned her attention to Kendra and Tina, she said, "You are both healers?"

"Yes, m' Lady," they replied.

"It is because of you that she still lives."

"We do not possess the skills to save her," Tina explained.

Lady Gwen noted their healer levels. "It is because you have not been trained. If matters work out, I will teach you."

"Yes, m'Lady. Thank you," Tina said with breathless gratitude, imagining the level she would be by the time they left.

Turning to Jethdar, Lady Gwen said, "Take them to the Administrator. Leave the two healers here with me... and

Karl the Viking. I wish him to remain here." Glancing up at Dieter she added, "And him too. He stays."

"Yes, m'Lady." Turning to the others, he motioned with his hand, "If you will follow me please."

Raquel and Annabeth gave each other a look that said they suspected the fair Lady had more in mind with Karl than simple conversation. Annabeth wanted to say something but by the time the door closed behind them, it was too late.

"Can you believe that," Annabeth sourly whispered to Raquel. "He belongs to us."

"Don't worry," Raquel whispered back. "Remember, we're crossing a bridge. I doubt she'll be coming along." She glanced over a fretting Elena. "Don't worry. He only has eyes for you."

"I hope so," she worried. "She's so beautiful and rich and powerful."

"Like I told Annabeth, our mission is to cross a bridge. She won't be there. You will."

That seemed to placate her and she relaxed, just a bit.

Back in Lady Gwen's room, Karl had surreptitiously pulled up Lady Gwen's stats.

Lady Gwen, Level 20, ruler of Westhaven and the northern country of the kingdom of Montgrec. Sister to Queen Briet and of the royal house of Bale.
Strength: 20 points
Speech: 25 points
Magic: 50 points
Healing: 75 points
Health: 50 points
Mana: 50 points
Combat: 12 points
Leadership: 40 points
Reputation: 35 points

Ignoring all the listed stats, he blinked in surprise that the woman was a Level 20. Suddenly he felt inadequate, like some nerdy freshman asking the prom queen for a date.

With a no-nonsense look, Lady Gwen addressed them. "I will pull out as much of the death poison as I can, but it means that my own strength and life force will diminish. Depending on how much poison is in her determines how long it will be before I am restored to health. During that time, the two healers will attend to the elf's health while you two warriors will protect us all."

"From what, m'Lady?" Karl asked confused. "Surely you are safe here."

"I wish that were true," she said with a sad sigh. "No one is safe, even behind these walls. Even now Cyril's agents actively seek my death. We have killed four of them so far, one who got so far as to be inside the castle. They will not rest until the kingdom is without rulers and in chaos. Once that occurs, I dread what will happen when the Trolls of Stonefell descend upon this land. Will you defend me now while I heal your companion?"

"Of course, m'Lady," Karl ardently responded. "We all pledge our lives for your safety."

With a grateful smile, she stepped over to Karl and placed a gentle hand on his cheek then kissed the other cheek. "Then I can rest easy... for now."

Turning to Kendra and Tina, she said, "You could not heal her because your healing powers are too little. I do not say this as condemnation, but as fact. Further, physical healing is not enough as you already know, having exhausted your healing potions and spells."

She again hiked up her dress and dropped to her knees. Placing one hand over Carole's heart, she placed the other on Carole's forehead then bent her head, closing her eyes.

Karl watched in wonder as Lady Gwen began a soft melodious humming as her body gently bobbed. His fascination quickly changed to concern as Lady Gwen's smooth porcelain white skin began to change to an ash gray. At the same time, the red of Carole's health bar began to flutter and turned to a dull orange.

Karl suddenly remembered his responsibility and turned to Dieter. "Go ahead and block the door while I check the rest of the room."

"OK, Boss."

While Dieter positioned himself by the door, Karl circulated around the room, noting a door by the fireplace. Pulling it open, he found it led to her bedroom, which seemed almost as large as the anteroom. Pulling the door closed, he repositioned a tall high-back wing chair before the door. His preparations were interrupted he when heard Kendra call out.

"Karl."

Looking over his shoulder, he saw her worried frown as she stared down at Lady Gwen and walked over. He was startled as he approached for long thin black cracks now appeared on Lady Gwen's skin, some of them connected in what looked like spider webbing.

Carole's health was now a solid orange, but Lady Gwen's health and mana had fallen to blinking orange. As he reached down to grab her hands to break the spell, she let out an anguished groan and collapsed to the floor.

Karl immediately scooped her up, amazed at how light she was then strode across the floor, kicked the chair out of the way and entered the bedroom, gently placing her on the bed.

"You have any more potions?" he called through the open door.

"Yes," Tina replied, collected the last vials from Kendra and scooting across the room and into the bedroom.

"Give them to her," he ordered.

"This is the last of what we have," Tina reminded him.

"I know. Give them to her."

As Tina uncorked the first vial, Karl raised Lady Gwen's head. It wasn't until the third vial that the orange of her health and mana bars stopped blinking. Tina was about to uncork their last vial when Lady Gwen raised a weak hand.

"No more," she breathed, her voice frail. "Thank you. Let me sleep."

Karl pulled back the top cover and placed it over her, noting how fragile the woman looked. Her porcelain skin still retained the ash color, but the cracks were slowly disappearing. Yet even in this state of brokenness, the woman still retained the auras of grace and beauty. He found himself enchanted for she seemed a fairytale princess.

"Carole's opened her eyes," Tina announced, standing in the doorway. "She even asked where we were. She needs food."

"Tell Dieter to ask the guards." Karl remained standing beside Lady Gwen, searching the room for possible entrances. The door was obvious, but he guessed there had to be a secret entrance or two in the room.

In the ante room, Dieter reached for the door and was surprised by a knock. Opening the door, he saw a servant holding a tray of food.

Apprehension flashed across the man's face but he quickly regained his composure. "The Administrator thought you might be hungry."

"Come in," Dieter replied, stepping aside. There was something about the man that looked off, not quite right, but he couldn't place it until he saw the man's shoes. They were worn and dirty.

Before the man had a chance to cross the room, Dieter grabbed him by the neck and lifted him off the ground, causing the tray to crash to the floor, splattering the contents onto the carpet covering the veined marble, while simultaneously butting the door closed.

His instincts were on the mark for as the man struggled in the vice grip, he jerked his foot up and withdrew a stiletto from inside his boot. Yet to no avail as Dieter grabbed his hand and twisted his arm behind his back with such force that the man's shoulder popped and he dropped the knife. He then slammed the man onto the floor on his other shoulder, soliciting a pained grunt and effectively dislocating the man's elbow before placing a heavy foot on the man's back and holding in in place.

Hearing the commotion, Karl burst in then relaxed slightly when he saw Dieter had everything under control. Looking back over his shoulder, ensuring the Lady was safe, he strode over to study the man.

"How'd you know?" Kendra said with wonder.

"The shoes," Dieter answered. "They're dirty from travel. A servant here would have clean shoes."

"Good job," Karl grimly mused, looking around the room for something suitable to tie the man up. Walking over to a window, he grabbed a cord for a curtain and gave it a hard yank, which ended up pulling down the entire curtain. Dismissing the mess, he cut a long length of cord and walked back to tie the man's hands behind him.

Once finished, Karl searched the man's clothing finding a small vial that he held up. "My guess it's poison, either for him if captured or for her if successful." Placing the vial in his pocket, he finished frisking the man and found little else except for a few coins.

Dieter yanked the assassin up and thrust him into a chair then helped Karl wrap the rest of the cord around the man and the chair. With the assassin secured, Dieter returned to the door and opened it, surprised to see the two guards still there.

"Did you not hear all the noise inside?" he demanded.

"We did," the one guard answered.

"Then why the hell didn't you come in?"

"Our orders are to enter only with the permission of Lady Gwen," he said with a tone of condescension.

"Are you two that stupid?" Dieter sneered. "How'd you know it wasn't an assassin trying to kill the Lady?"

"We figured the clumsy servant just dropped the food tray," the other guard answered.

Dieter looked at them and shook his head in disbelief. "So I was right. You two really *are* that stupid. That servant you just happened to let in was an assassin, and you let him breeze right past you. Had we not been here, your Lady Gwen would be dead. One of you go get the Administrator. Now," he barked, jolting the other guard to race down the hallway.

Closing the door, he walked back to stand beside Karl who was studying the assassin. He was an average height lithe man, nondescript, with short brown hair. He looked to be the sort of man one would take no notice of, one who would blend into a crowd of common folk. If one were to

162

ask for a description, the single answer would be 'average.' The assassin did his best not to grimace, but the pain of the separated shoulder and dislocated elbow caused him to scowl.

"I'm not going to ask you why you are here," Karl smiled. "But what I am hoping is that they'll let me interrogate and torture you."

The bedroom door burst open and the Administrator stalked in, guards and the rest of Karl's company trailing him. The Administrator was a slender man, almost as tall as Raquel. He wore crimson robes with puffed shoulders over a silk embroidered shirt and calf-skin leggings tucked into knee-high boots. The heavy chain and medallion of office hung around his neck. He rubbed his bald head as he took in the scene with his penetrating brown eyes, looking into the bedroom where Lady Gwen lay sleeping. Karl guessed he looked to be in his early fifties.

The Administrator brusquely brushed past them and went into the bedroom to stand by the bed, reassuring himself that Lady Gwen was unharmed then spun around and strode back to confront Dieter and Karl, breathing a sigh of relief. "Thank the gods you were here. Is this the villain?" He pointed an accusing finger at the assassin.

"Yes," Karl replied, surprised at the man's voice for it was high-pitched like a boy who had not yet reached puberty.

"Tell me what happened."

"I was in with the Lady," Karl explained. "There was a knock on the door and this man brought in some food. Dieter here immediately saw that something was not right and waylaid him, rather roughly I might add," he grinned.

Karl reached into his pocket and withdrew the vial. "He had this with him."

Accepting the vial, the Administrator nodded. "Poison no doubt." He handed it to one of the guards. "Take this to the alchemist. I want to know what it is."

"Yes, Sir."

As the guard dashed off, the Administrator turned a kind eye back to Karl. "How is our Lady?"

"She is resting," Karl answered. "I don't know how long until she is back to normal, but we are obligated to stay here until she is whole."

The Administrator regarded him with both surprise and satisfaction, dipping his head in understanding. "I'm sure she will appreciate that. Until then, you are to be guests here at the castle, where you may roam at your pleasure. You have done a great service to the kingdom. I'm sure the Lady will reward you appropriately."

"She already has by the healing of our friend. We are indebted to her," Karl gallantly replied.

"Well spoken, my friend, if I may call you such," the Administrator said with a polite smile before turning to the assassin. "And what should we do you with you?"

Karl watched the assassin stare up at the Administrator and for a fleeting moment, he swore he saw a glimpse of a smile.

"If you will allow me," Karl proposed, "I'd like a chance to interrogate him."

"We have our own very capable interrogators," the Administrator rebuffed.

"No doubt you do, but if I might ask the favor of having the first shot. If I fail," he shrugged, "then your men can take up where I failed."

The Administrator folded his arms and gave Karl an indulgent smile. "I'm intrigued. Just how would you interrogate him?"

Karl focused his attention of the assassin, keenly studying the body language as he spoke. "First, I would ask for the finest butcher in the city, one skilled in removing the thinnest of fat and skin."

"A butcher?" the Administrator chuckled. "That's a new one. Then what?"

"I would have the butcher remove the man's eyelids."

"My God," the Administrator choked. "Why?"

"Because removing the eyelids wouldn't' kill him, but the inability to shut out light will eventually drive him insane."

The assassin's breathing grew labored and his eyes widened as he jerked his head to stare up at the Administrator who seemed interested in the Vikings' approach.

"Then what?" the Administrator inquired.

"Then I would shave a couple layers of skin off his feet and hands."

"You are downright diabolical," the Administrator grinned.

"And then I would toss him over the wall. He'd still be quite alive, but the pain would be intense and ever present. If he was lucky and the animals or monsters didn't get him, he might make it all the way back home. Of course, that implies he was very lucky for once word got out that he was an assassin and everyone told to leave him alone, it's just possible he might starve to death before he made his way out of the kingdom. But, if he did survive, he would be forever branded as an assassin, a failed assassin."

"I like your approach," the Administrator smiled. "But there's still the problem of getting information from him. All these marvelous tortures and no results."

"Do you really expect him to talk?" Karl replied. "He expects to be tortured to death. He accepts that. However, to be allowed to live, deformed and broken... that he has not accepted."

"Interesting... perhaps you're right." The Administrator leaned down placing a knuckle under the man's chin and forcibly lifting his head to face him. Though looking at the assassin, he spoke to Karl. "So be it. He's all yours. Do with him as you wish."

Hatred filled the assassin's eyes. "You bastard. You really think they're going to let you rule? You're a dead man as soon as he gets here. And then I'll be the one gloating."

"Gloating?" the Administrator mocked. "You'll never have anything to gloat about the rest of your short life." He straightened and turned to Karl. "If you need anything, simply tell one of the guards or servants and they will provide you. If you have any problems, come get me."

"You are most kind, Sir," Karl said with a polite, yet slight, bow, wondering what the assassin meant by 'You really think they're going to let you rule.'

"I leave it to you then," the Administrator smiled. "I'll send someone for your butcher. The interrogation rooms are in the lowest levels, for obvious reasons." He grinned and leaned in, lowering his voice but ensuring the assassin heard. "Very few like listening to screams, although I've known some Inquisitors who rather enjoy their work. In fact, I just might come down myself to watch." Turning on his heels, his robe swirling, he strode through the door and was gone, his guards in orderly file behind him.

An awkward silence filled the room as Ross frowned at Karl. "Are you really going to torture him?"

"Of course," he replied, the answer obvious. "Why wouldn't I? He came here specifically to kill Lady Gwen, and anyone else who got in his way. Are you OK with that?"

"Of course not," he bluntly stated. "But torture? Why not just kill him and be done with it?"

"What do you suggest?" he tersely replied. "Feed him dinner and give him a warm send off? If you haven't noticed, we seemed to have landed in the middle of a war."

"I noticed," Ross tartly answered. "But torture... it's so... medieval, so beneath us."

Karl stared at him. "So your solution is to kill him outright, a sword thrust through the heart, a nice clean kill, an antiseptic approach. No one has to feel bad about what you've done because it was quick and he didn't suffer. Is that it?"

"No, well yes," Ross mumbled. "That's not what I mean."

"Come here," Karl commanded and walked over to stand inside the doorway of Lady Gwen's bedroom. When Ross stood beside him, Karl quietly spoke, his voice cold and hard. "Don't ever question my authority again. Understood?"

Ross's nostrils flared and his jaw tightened. "I wasn't questioning your authority," he growled.

"You were questioning my decision, which is the same thing," Karl shot back. "Do it again and you're out, on your own. Am I clear?"

"Who the hell do you think you are?" Ross snarled.

"What I am is your boss, your commander. If you have a problem with that you're free to find another outfit. No one is forcing you to stay here. But if you do stay, remember your agreement when you first signed on. I am the unquestioned leader of this group. Now which is it? You staying or leaving?" He folded his arms and narrowed his stare at him.

Ross pursed his lips and twisted his head to look over his shoulder at the rest of the company who were watching the interaction. Realizing he had little choice, he said, "Guess I'll stay... for now."

"It doesn't work that way," Karl replied, standing to full height. He turned and walked to the center of the room, Ross slowly following behind. "OK everyone, listen up. Ross here is not sure he wants to belong to this group. As I said to him, I tell you all now. No one is forcing any of you to be part of this team. However, once you make a commitment to the team, you are forever a part of it. We have each other's backs no matter what the circumstances."

The assassin snickered, shifting a derisive glance at Karl. "Trouble in paradise?"

Karl slowly turned to glare at him. "One more word from you and I cut your tongue out. Not only will you never be able to close your eyes, you'll never be able to talk again, so choose your next words wisely."

The assassin swallowed hard and looked away.

Karl turned back to the group. "This isn't a democracy. While I look for input from time to time, I make the decisions that affect the group. If you are unhappy with that, then you need to find another group or set out on your own. Questions?"

Dieter curled a lip and stared at Ross. "If I can't trust you to have my back, you can just leave right now."

Ross bristled then looked at the rest of the team, rapidly realizing they were completely loyal to Karl. If he left now, he would truly be alone.

"Aw hell," he grumbled. "What kind of soldier would I be if I didn't complain every now and then?"

"I accept complaints," Karl said, "but that's about it. What's your decision?"

"I'm not going anywhere," he lightly replied. "You have my word."

Chapter 5

Felix Hubach sat at the head of the table in the conference room in the ITL headquarters in Chattanooga. Located in a nine story Art Moderne style structure looking much like the old Federal Office Building in Seattle, Washington, the ITL headquarters overlooked the South Chickamauga Creek to the front and the Tennessee River to the rear. The view from the wall of windows in the conference room that overlooked the Tennessee River reached all the way to Signal Mountain.

Seated at the other eight places at the table was the design team for the Misted Isle part of Bridge Quest. Felix rested his elbows on the cushioned arms of the plush chair and interlaced his fingers as he listened to Scott Carleson, the Design Manager, talk about the latest developments.

Scott, sitting to Felix's immediate left, brushed an errant strand of blond hair out of his face. "Viking Karl has some, um... rather unusual means of dealing with various situations. The first is disaffected team members." He looked at Felix and then at the others siting at the table. "You'll remember that we initially chose Karl based upon his credentials of leadership and military experience. So far he's been what we had hoped. Ross the ranger, whom we had chosen for his intellect and potential leadership skills, came into conflict with Karl in a sort of power struggle. Karl made it quite plain that he was in charge and if Ross didn't like it, he could leave."

"What happened?" Felix asked.

Scott looked across the table to an attractive red-headed woman in her mid-twenties who preferred glasses instead of contacts and was constantly pushing them back up the bridge of her nose. "Tell us Maggie."

169

"Ross backed down," she answered with a neutral smile. "I think he took one look at the support Karl had and realized he would be on his own."

"And then there was the ingenious torture method," Scott said with a sparkle in his eyes.

Felix noticed some of the others cringe. "Go on."

"He had the man's eyelids removed."

Felix frowned and inhaled sharply. "Was that really necessary? Wasn't the assassin programed to reveal some tidbit of information already?"

"Well yes," Scott said, "but in this instance the PC took it upon himself to accelerate the process. In fact, we had to spend some time working up an additional set of algorithms to make it happen."

"How does this impact the two warring kingdoms?"

"It doesn't really," Scott replied. "Yes, there will be some variations we'll have to watch for, but for the most part, everything is going as planned."

"We've taken into account the level of our PCs," Maggie said, "remembering our objective is to get them to the next island. While some of the NPCs are higher levels to prevent PCs from leveling up too high, the majority of NPCs are within the skill sets of the players. For example, the trolls on Misted Isle are level 10s, with the king troll a level 15."

"And what level do our PCs have to be to cross the bridge?" Felix asked, knowing the answer.

"10," Maggie answered, using her middle finger to push her glasses up.

"And right now all of them are level 6 when they should only be level 4 by now," Felix admonished.

"Yes, Sir," Scott said, acknowledging the flaw in the programming. "That's why we've spent time building in more complexity to the quest. This quest should be more difficult and place them where they should be when they cross the bridge."

Felix templed his fingers and turned to Scott. "Let me know when they get to the bridge."

Karl sat on the edge of Lady Gwen's bed, intimating a familiarity of which the Administrator did not approve, neither did Annabeth or Raquel. During the past week, Karl and Dieter had spent most of their waking hours guarding the Lady, handing off the responsibility to others when they needed sleep.

As the days progressed, Lady Gwen's skin lost its ash color and returned to the smooth porcelain whiteness, but it still required effort to move around and she made known her preference that Karl and Dieter were her preferred escorts as she healed.

True to Karl's threats, the assassin's eyelids were removed and several layers of skin were taken from him feet and hands. Word quickly spread throughout the city, especially when the assassin was paraded out of the city and dumped outside the far walls. Karl's reputation as a ruthless commander grew and the people were both impressed and afraid of him.

Carole had regained a large portion of her health and had taken to walking around the castle and grounds as she continued to heal. The rest of the team enjoyed the exceptional cuisine and ale, Conrad and Wendell being the most pleased.

However, their time was not spent in idleness. News that Cyril's armies were on the march reached the city by a fleet-footed messenger who begged Lady Gwen to send as many troops as possible to help her brother-in-law defeat the enemy.

Sitting at the edge of Lady Gwen's bed, Karl listened to the messenger relay his instructions.

The messenger was a young man and wore the livery of the royal house of Bale. He was tired, dusty, and hungry as he had ridden without pause since the day before.

"My Lady," he said, surprised at the Viking sitting so irreverently on bed. "The king, your brother-in-law, requests your immediate support by supplying 1,000 men and women at arms."

"One thousand?" she gasped. "That is my entire army. What do I use to defend my own domain?"

"I do not know my Lady," he awkwardly replied. "What am I to tell the king, your brother-in-law?"

"Leave us," she commanded. "Let me think on this a bit."

"Your pardon, my Lady," he said, bowing his head, "but there is not much time left."

"You will get your answer within the hour. Now go."

"Yes, m'Lady."

Waiting until he was outside the far door, she then turned to Karl. "It is now time to call in my favor."

"Yes, my Lady," he answered, standing.

"My favor is this; you and your friends will defend my domain until the enemy is slain or we are all dead."

Quest Alert: Save Lady Gwen's domain of Westhaven from Cyril's armies

Reward: Unlimited access to supplies, scrolls, potions, and weapons currently in the domain

Reward: Escort to the Bridge connecting Misted Isle to the next island

Reward: Reputation: increase from 'Your name sounds familiar' to 'I have heard of you and I am impressed.'

Do you accept this quest? Yes No

Karl barely read the alert. With the messenger's dire news, Karl knew what Gwen's demand would be. Pressing the 'Yes' icon, he said, "How much time do we have to prepare?"

"Fetch the messenger."

Karl crossed the room and to the main door to the apartment, opening the door. The messenger sat slumped against the opposite wall.

"She wants you."

Despite his exhaustion, he pushed himself up and followed Karl to stand before the Lady."

"I will send 500," she stated. "To do more leaves me defenseless."

"Yes, m'Lady," he said with some relief. "When can they march?"

"They will be on the road tomorrow. Tell me, how does the king fare?"

"It is bad, m'Lady," he answered. "Cyril's forces have already invaded the outer lands. Trolls have been reported in Lord Martin's domain and he has sent his wife and children to the king. His two oldest remain to do battle."

"Can they hold out?"

The messenger's shoulders dropped and he let out a soft sigh. "I do not see how, m'Lady. Cyril's army has grown with trolls and orcs and even gnolls. Who can defeat such creatures?"

"But how long can he hold out?"

"Who can tell, m'Lady? A few days, a week, perhaps two? What is stopping Cyril from bypassing Lord Martin and coming straight to Durness?"

Realizing she was going to get nothing more from him, she dismissed him. Throwing the covers off, she held her hand out.

Karl took her hand and helped her to a circular table set close to the hearth. Sliding a chair out for her, he helped her sit then pulled out a chair and sat next to her.

The top of the table consisted of smooth clear glass that reached almost to the edges. Beneath the glass was a terrain map in the shape of the Misted Isle skillfully crafted from various hardwoods. The kingdom of Montgrec was outlined in white oak. To the south, Cyril's kingdom was etched in mahogany. Mountainous terrain filled most of the island except for the two arms and the coast along the southeast. Towns, rivers and farms were shown in the kingdom, while Cyril's domains had just as many locations identified. At the tip of the lower arm, the bridge to the next island ended into the edge of the table.

"You can see that our knowledge of the world is not as great as it should be," she said.

"Who is Lord Cyril?" Karl asked. "I've asked the Administrator and can't seem to get a satisfactory answer."

Lady Gwen gazed at him with a sad yet kind look. "He is my brother-in-law."

"Pardon?" Karl blinked in surprise.

"He is the brother to the king."

Karl sat back and chuckled. "So this is a family war."

"You might say that," she sighed. "Cyril and Coirthan have never been close. Coirthan was the oldest and obviously the heir to the throne. Cyril was... *is* your typical jealous younger brother. But make no mistake. His jealousy to prove himself the more deserving caused him to seek the battlefield where he earned well-deserved honors. His father was so pleased that he gave him half the kingdom. So long as the father lived, the two brothers kept their distance. When the father died, Cyril made no effort to hide his desire to unite the kingdom."

"What happened?"

Lady Gwen offered a weak shrug. "We've been at war ever since. No, that's not quite right. There was a ten year lull where we had all hoped life would return to some normalcy. Trade increased between the two parts of kingdoms and things seemed to be getting better. Then abruptly, six months ago, Cyril shut his borders and cut off all trade. Many of our farmers and merchants were ruined because they had put all their efforts in business and trade with his part of the kingdom. Then the border incursions started, not much at first, but enough to cause concern. We sent the usual diplomatic letters. The first time the letters were ignored and the raids across our borders became land grabs. The second time we sent letters, our messengers' heads were returned to us, stuck on poles attached to a wagon. Their bodies were dumped in the wagon itself. That was enough and Coirthan declared war. Now we have learned that Cyril has formed an alliance with the mountain trolls, a tribe of nasty creatures we once kept at bay."

"How large do you think Cyril's army is?"

"Who can say?" She turned her head to gaze out the window. "We are being defeated piecemeal. I fear once they arrive here, we are doomed." She turned to face him, her eyes filled with a great sadness. "I realize now that it is unfair of me to ask you to stay. You have no stake in the war. I release you from your obligation."

"That's very noble of you, m'Lady," he replied, fixing her with a firm stare, "but we're staying here to see this through. As far as we're concerned, it's like King Leonidas of Sparta said, you want Westhaven, Μολών λαβέ."

"Mo-lone lah-beh?"

"Yes," his visage hardened. "Come and take it."

Her eyes misted and she blinked the wetness away. "I am neither a warrior nor a military strategist. I do best amidst the swirls of political intrigue."

"Who is your commander?"

"His name is Manas. He was a valiant fighter in his younger years. He is older now, but still very wise."

"Then I need to speak with him," he said, standing. "You need to rethink your decision to send warriors to your brother-in-law. If we assume Cyril's army will overrun Lord Martin's forces, then sending your forces to support the king is a total loss of manpower, forces we could better use here."

"I'm afraid it doesn't work like that," she replied with a half-smile. "I am under obligation to send forces when the king demands."

"Even if it means the destruction of the entire kingdom?" he countered. "If we can hold them here and whittle them down, perhaps those remnant forces of the king could sway the balance to our favor. Simply sending forces to battle without an overall plan is foolish."

"We are not the ones being overrun at present," she reminded him. "They have been suffering ever since this war began."

"We can't change that," he said then had an idea. "If you want to save this domain and the kingdom, you're going to have to break some rules."

"I'll think about it," she stubbornly replied.

Leaning on the table, he narrowed his stare at her. "When Westhaven is surrounded, you'll wish you had those 500 warriors."

Lady Gwen stiffened, not liking his tone and what seemed like a reprimand, yet she knew he was right. "Let me discuss this with Manas."

"In the meantime, my team and I need access to any and all shops and persons that specialize in potions, spells, weapons, scrolls and the like, the more then better."

"Many of those items are beyond your team's abilities, skills, and levels," she pointed out.

"I know that. I'm looking for anything we can use. Where do I find Manas?"

"I'll send for him," she said, holding her hand up. Taking his hand, she stood then hung onto his arm as he escorted her to the bed.

"Does it always take this long," he quietly intoned.

"She was almost dead, remember? And the poison of the spiders is worse than most. Another day or two and I should be back to normal."

"It would not do for the people to see you like this when the enemy comes, even if they do understand why," he counseled.

"I know," she replied, sitting on the edge of the bed.

"When Manas arrives, I'd like for the rest of my team to be here."

Lady Gwen looked around the bedroom then into the anteroom, seeing no guards or waiting ladies. "Of course. This decision affects them as well. Where is everyone?"

"I believe they're outside waiting for us to let them in," he said with a smile.

"Give me an hour," she said. "We'll meet with Manas then."

An hour later, Karl stood in Lady Gwen's anteroom, the rest of the company lounging on the divans and additional chairs. The door to the bedroom was closed, but he could hear the tittering of Lady Gwen's ladies- in-waiting.

"So what's the prognosis, Boss?" Dieter said, more to break the monotony of waiting than actual interest.

"Doesn't look good," he answered, folding his arms. "Cyril's armies are marching. The prognosis is that the king's forces will fold like a house of cards, which means we're the last bastion remaining. Cyril's got trolls and gnolls fighting with him. Pull up the troll info and you can see what we're up against."

He flicked on his stat screen and hit the INFO button then scrolled down to MONSTERS then to TROLLS.

Trolls are humanoid in appearance, though rather ugly and loathsome. They tend to be large, usually over ten feet tall. The Trolls of Stonefell are unusual in that they tend to be smaller than normal trolls – averaging 8 feet in height. Like all trolls, they appear shorter due to their hunched postures. While they can be a variety of colors, the most frequent are shades of brown and green. They are quite strong with thick heavy bones and muscles. Their strength allows them to rip apart flesh and bone and they have been known to crush stone with their bare hands. A troll's motivation is his stomach. Trolls live to eat. It is not unusual for a troll, or even a group of trolls, to be in the thick of battle only to discover an available meal close by and to lose complete interest in the battle. What a troll eats is rather varied, the most common being the latest combatant, whether human, goblin, elf, or even another troll. Trolls eat everything raw.

Trolls possess an incredibly strong grip and are capable of wielding two weapons with equal skill. The one fear they have is fire. Even the mountain trolls, though they have been known to use torches in caves, give fire a wide berth. Trolls are known for their cruelty in battle and will not negotiate a surrender, believing it is better to die in battle than to lose face and slink home in defeat.

Male trolls tend to be solitary creatures, though it is not uncommon for two to three to work together for a joint effort. Trolls will follow orders if they believe the troll issuing the order is stronger. Getting five or more trolls to work together takes effort and requires a strong leader. The stronger the leader, the more trolls can be assembled as a unit.

The preferred weapons for trolls are battle axes and falchions. Armor, if worn is usually leather, covering the shoulder of the non-weapon arm.

Trolls are not known for their intelligence and can be easily confused given instructions or directions beyond their understanding. Most trolls have lost the ability to speak Trollsprach when the common tongue became prevalent. Most now speak common tongue, though poorly.

Karl continued reading, occasionally thinking of ways to defeat the brutish beasts. Yet trolls were only one part of the equation. There was still the tyrannical ambition of Cyril.

The door to the anteroom opened and a fit older man walked in. His once black hair now heavily salted, was long, despite a receding hairline, and tied in a ponytail. His close cropped beard hid a leather tanned face. Black bushy eyebrows, a sharp contrast to the grey in his hair, perched over dark brown eyes that darted around the room. He wore a sleeveless leather jerkin, revealing taut and strong arms. Resting his hand on the pommel of the sword at his hip, he narrowed his gaze at Karl.

"You the leader of this motley crew?" he asked, his voice a gravel baritone.

"Guilty as charged," Karl answered. "You must be Manas."

"That I am," he said, striding in then looking at the closed bedroom door. "She coming?"

"She'll be here in a moment," he said, though he had no idea when she would come out.

"We got ourselves a real problem," Manas said, once again looking at each of the team members. He paused when he sized up Dieter. "I could use a hundred more like you."

"You'll have to be satisfied with just one of me for the time being," Dieter replied.

"I'll take it."

"Before she comes out," Karl said, "I want to get one thing settled between us. We operate independently. We are not part of your army for you to command or piecemeal as you see fit. We are a fighting team that fights together. We will do more than is asked and give back more than is expected."

Manas stroked his chin and cocked his head. "I see you take me for either a dotard or a new recruit. I figured as much when I heard about you and the spiders and orcs. But I'm neither a dotard nor a young novice. I've fought trolls and orcs and all sorts of beasts. Even fought against Cyril when I was younger."

"You did?" Karl said, caught off guard.

"That surprises you, does it? It might surprise you that I also defeated him."

"When?"

"Back in the days when the old King still ruled. We had contests back then. Life was simpler and noble then. I kicked his ass in hand-to-hand combat. Never forgave me for that. That's why I'm here. Decided to get as far away from him as possible. Looks like this time he finally caught up with me."

The bedroom door opened and Lady Gwen emerged, causing Karl to suck in his breath. She was dressed in a long flowing silk gown of emerald green. Her hair was done up in Josephine curls revealing bare perfect shoulders. He thought to himself that she had been beautiful even when she was recovering. Now she was stunning. She held her hand out to Karl who crossed the floor in quick strides.

"I see you two have met," she smiled to Manas as Karl escorted her to a chair.

Karl pretended not to notice a scowl flash across the old man's face as this newcomer took his place.

"Now that we're all here," she spoke. "Let's get down to business. I believe we all know why we are here?" Receiving a collective nodding of heads, she continued. "The king's messenger arrived today with the king's request for us to send one thousand warriors –"

"One thousand," Manas exclaimed. "That's insane, m'Lady. He knows that would leave us completely defenseless. There would be no one left to man the walls except for farmers and merchants."

"Pretty much what I said," Karl said, giving Gwen an 'I-told-you-so' look.

179

"You both made your point," Lady Gwen nodded. "I had initially thought to send five hundred –"

"Even that's too many," Manas interrupted.

Karl said nothing but merely smiled at her.

"Let me finish, Manas."

"I apologize, my Lady," he said, dipping his head in respect.

"After talking with my favorite Viking here," she reached up and gently touched Karl's arm, much to Annabeth's and Raquel's irritation, "he's convinced me that our soldiers are needed here, so I've decided to send no troops at this time."

"Good," Manas grumped.

"But that means we need a stout defense, one that will not just hold the enemy in place, but defeat them." She leaned forward, emerald eyes blazing. "We need to end this once and for all. What that means is that whatever time we have between now and their arrival, we need to be ready. In fact," she added looking at Manas, "incorporate that messenger into our forces. We can use another warrior."

"Yes, m'Lady," Manas grinned.

She looked at each of them in turn and solemnly intoned, "We do not have the option of defeat or surrender. Know this. My brother-in-law is ruthless. I will be the first one he tortures and kills. Then he will systematically eliminate anyone he views as a threat to his throne."

"We understand, my Lady," Dieter replied, answering for the group.

Redirecting her gaze at Manas and Karl, she said, "Then I leave you to it. Keep me informed."

"Of course, m'Lady," Manas crisply answered.

She again touched Karl on the arm. "I know you must be about the business of defending my domain, but I would like for you to return here as often as you are able."

"With pleasure, my Lady," he smiled in reply, placing a hand over hers. He then turned to address his team, purposely ignoring the sour looks on Annabeth's and Raquel's faces. "I don't know how many days we have, but you need to go into the city and find any and every one who can help you in any way: spells, potions, scrolls, better weapons, things like that. Lady Gwen has charged the people to provide us anything we want. That doesn't mean we take whatever we want. Take only what you can use and pay for it if you can. If you find a better weapon or stronger potion, return the lesser back to the original owner. While you're doing that, Manas and I will work out a strategy. If you think of an idea or come across something we can use, be sure to let us know, no matter how insignificant you might think it. Questions?"

When no one replied, he briskly nodded. "Let's do it."

At that moment the door burst open and the Administrator bustled in then jerked to a stop midway between the door and the group, his jaw set. "Did my Lady forget she has a city Administrator?"

"No, Regnan, I have not forgotten," she calmly answered, "but as you see, these are warriors strategizing the battle to save this domain. Are you telling me that you wish to don a sword and fight alongside them?"

The Administrator's lips tightened at the not so subtle taunt. "You know my abilities, my Lady," he countered. "I have been in charge of running this city since you were just a child. I believe you will agree that the city has flourished under my direction."

Lady Gwen held up a placating hand. "No one is questioning your talents, Regnan. But from this time forward, Manas and Karl will be my leaders. This city and this domain will yield to their commands, including you. Whatever they need or ask, you will ensure it is swiftly delivered. I expect you to place yourself at their disposal."

The Administrator's nostrils flared at his overt demotion. He was about to retort when Karl interrupted.

"My Lord Administrator," he soothed. "General Manas and I have no intention of pretending to know how to manage a city like this, something you have done so effectively all these years. It would greatly reduce our own distractions if you would assert your talents as you have always done. While we will be planning for battle, we will need and value your insight."

"Well spoken," Lady Gwen complimented before turning to the Administrator. "Perhaps my words were poorly chosen. My Viking friend has put it as I should have said it."

The Administrator clicked his heels and dipped his head. "My apologies, my Lady, for misunderstanding." Turning his attention to Karl only, he said, "I will be available whenever you wish, most likely in my offices here in the castle."

"Thank you," Karl answered with a warm smile, wondering why Manas and Gwen didn't seem to care much for the man.

With that, the Administrator bowed out of the room.

Once he was gone, Lady Gwen yet again touched Karl's arm, gazing affectionately into his eyes. "That was tactfully done."

When neither he nor Lady Gwen said anything more but continued to gaze at each other, Annabeth broke the silence with a curt, "Don't we have a war to plan or something?"

"Yes, we do," Karl answered, breaking away from Lady Gwen's captivating eyes, yet patting her hand with a quiet, "I'll be back."

"Please do," she answered. "I've gotten used to having you close by."

Karl gave her another intimate smile then turned to Manas. "I think we need to walk the far outer walls so I can get a layout of the land. I have a couple of ideas I'd like to share with you."

"I'll meet you at the gate. I need to issue a warning order first." Manas bowed to Lady Gwen and walked out.

It was as Karl and the rest of the team walked down the hallways of the castle that Annabeth and Raquel sidled up to Karl.

"She seems rather friendly," Annabeth acidly observed.

"Yes, she is," Karl cheerily responded.

"A little touchy-feely don't you think?"

"I hadn't noticed," he blandly said.

"Hadn't noticed? I've gotten used to having you close by," she mimicked with more than a hint of sarcasm. "I'm surprised she didn't jump your bones right there."

"Oh, I don't think she's into exhibitionism," he smirked.

"So what's going on between you two?" Raquel asked. "We haven't had time with you since we got here."

"If you remember," he said as they turned a corner, "not only did she heal Carole, there was an assassin sent to kill her. She's been a little busy lately. She felt safe with Dieter and I there."

"I don't think that's all she feels," Annabeth sourly stated.

"So what if there *was* more?" Karl said. "So what if she and I jump in the sack together? Why are you so concerned?"

"Because you belong to us," Annabeth flatly stated. "We're willing to share with each other but not with anyone else... at least not yet."

"She's going to want you to stay after this is all over," Raquel said. "If you play your cards right, you could co-rule with her."

"Huh," Karl mused. "I never thought about that. I suppose I could."

"What then?"

"What then nothing," he answered as they emerged into the courtyard. He stopped, causing the two women to stop with him. As the rest of the team wandered off, he folded his arms and said, "I know where you're going with this so let's clear things up. First, if she and I jump in the sack together, it'll be for what it is, an evening of pleasure. Second, I'm not Dieter. I know she's an NPC, which means that even if the sex is great, she's still not real in the sense that you two are. It's like having sex with an android. It may be awesome, but there will always be something missing, the human part of it. Third, why would I stay here? We've got a bridge to cross. Staying here would be the same thing as staying in Marbeck. Fourth, you two are pretty much more than I can handle, so why would I want to replace you two? Fifth," he paused for effect, "you two are far more important to me than you realize. Does that answer your concerns?"

Mollified, Raquel said, "She *is* beautiful."

"Yes, she is," Karl agreed. "Still doesn't change a thing."

Annabeth flashed him a relaxed smile. "If you do have sex with her, you'll have to share the details with us."

Laughing, Karl shook his head. "If that's what you want."

An hour later, Karl and Manas walked south along the top of the far outer wall. Forest encroached most of the terrain until the wall curved to the east and the land opened up in a broad vista of open fields and far mountains.

Pausing to absorb the grandeur of the view, Karl remarked, "What's going on between Lady Gwen and the Administrator?"

"What do you mean? Manas asked.

"There didn't seem to be any love lost between them."

"Oh," he chuckled. "There isn't. Regnan was the Administrator long before Gwen showed up, appointed by the old king. When Gwen's sister married the son, part of the agreement was that Gwen would rule this part of the kingdom when the son ascended the throne. That was less than two years ago. Before then, there was no designated ruler and Regnan ruled here by himself, assuming all the trappings of royalty, even living in what are now Gwen's quarters. When she showed up and told him to move, he wasn't happy."

"Why doesn't she just get rid of him?"

Manas smiled at him. "You and I think like military men. We see a weakness or a problem and we get rid of it. It's not as easy as one would think. Coirthan, though agreeing to let his sister-in-law rule the northern domain, wasn't about to give his queen that much power in the kingdom. So he declared that any appointments concerning administrators in each of his subordinate domains had to have his approval."

Karl nodded in understanding. "So how is it that the queen was killed?"

Manas paused long before answering, choosing to gaze out over the verdant land before finally saying, "When the trouble started with Cyril and the last batch of messengers were brutally killed, Coirthan decided to send Briet with an escort as a final arbiter to end the discord between them." He turned to face Karl. "There are some who believe he did so knowing full well Cyril would kill her."

"Why would he do that?" Karl asked, raising an eyebrow.

Manas shook his head and shrugged. "Who knows? Some say he was tired of her. Others say his affection had wandered to another. She was a strong-willed woman, beautiful like her sister, mind you, but strong-willed. Whatever the reason, it was a calculated one. Perhaps he did it to openly declare war on his brother. Who knows? The reasons why, while satisfying our curiosity, do little to help us now."

"Wisely spoken."

Manas studied him a moment. "We have walked this wall for the past hour and I have answered your questions, yet I still do not have an answer as to how you intend to fight."

"I was wondering," he replied, scanning the land before and behind him. "Is there a way to get out into the forest here without being discovered, a sort of secret entrance to get in and out of the city?"

Manas' stare narrowed to a hard focus. "What have you heard?"

"I haven't heard anything," he stated.

Manas studied him for a long awkward moment before looking rapidly around then leaning in and lowering his voice. "There is, but it is known to only three individuals. Not even Regnan knows about it."

"Why so secret?"

"Because its knowledge and use would not only compromise the domain, it would imperil Lady Gwen herself."

"So why tell me now, if it's so secret?"

Manas inhaled a deep breath. "Because the kingdom is in peril and we are all that remain to prevent Cyril from destroying it. I need someone I can trust to help save us. I have an idea of why you want to use it. Striking at the enemy's rear could do great damage and throw them off balance. To do so, you must strike hard and fast, with devastating results. You and your team have weapons at your disposal that add to your abilities to inflict damage and destroy."

"I assume it is a tunnel?" Karl said.

Manas again paused before answering. "Before I say one way or another, know this, under no circumstances should you or anyone on your team let Regnan or anyone else know of its existence. Warn them. I hold you responsible for their silence."

"It will be as you wish."

Manas inhaled a slow deep breath. "Yes, it is a tunnel. It begins in the castle, goes under the main gate and ends about a kilometer beyond in the forest."

Karl welcomed the good news then commented, "You said there were three people who knew about this."

"Yes. Lady Gwen, myself, and the sorceress who maintains the spell of hidden portal on the two entrances. You will meet her when we are finished here."

"I think we're finished here," Karl said with a grin.

Manas held up a hand in warning. "Remember the secrecy of the tunnel."

Karl nodded his understanding. "So why not the Administrator?"

Manas folded his arms. "I do not trust him. You saw how easy it was for an assassin to gain entrance into the castle. Now imagine what knowledge of a hidden tunnel would do. Do I have your word that you and your team will remain silent?"

"You have my word," he said then gave voice to his thoughts. "There are fifteen of us, well fourteen as Carole is still in-op, but how do fifteen warriors of various sizes with all sorts of weapons get out of the castle without being seen or someone noticing that we're all gone at the same time?"

"A good question, one I'm sure the sorceress will help us with. Come. Let's meet with her so you can test the tunnel before we need it."

The afternoon sun stretched long shadows by the time they walked back down the wall stairs by the gate and across the farm fields to the outer wall of the city. Manas led the way from there, weaving a path of many turns, which Karl swore led them to cross a path they had just travelled.

Finally, after the last torturous weaving, they came to a nondescript home wedged into part of an ancient wall on the east side of the city. Karl studied the door and shuttered windows on either side of the door and then the surroundings in what looked to be what was once a fortification wall and was now a back alley.

Seeing his puzzlement, Manas said, "This was once the outer wall of the early version of Westhaven. It was called Wes-to-hoven back then. The city fell when an earthquake destroyed it. What lies on the other side of the wall is a jumbled mess of buildings and wreckage."

"She lives there?"

"Yes," Manas smiled, "away from inquisitive eyes and curiosity." He turned the door handle and pushed the door open. It swung soundlessly, revealing a short tunnel that led to the other side of the wall and the tumbled debris of an ancient city.

Karl followed Manas as they once again weaved their way amidst the moss covered stones. Trees grew in the midst of home foundations and what were once living rooms and bedrooms. Karl noted that the city had been built on the side of the hill, facing east toward the mountains.

As they descended on a snaking path, Karl realized that they were following a trail, though not well worn. He was brought to a halt when Manas stopped in front of a set of Corinthian pillars that had been broken in half, the bottom halves still standing and the top halves stretched out in an orderly fashion pointing towards the path.

Manas walked in between the two top halves and paused by the right pillar, pressing his palm against the cold stone.

A moment later, a voice crooned, "Welcome friend. It has been a while. Please come in. Bring your friend with you."

Manas turned to Karl. "Follow me." He stepped in between the two upright pillars and vanished.

Startled, Karl froze and stared at the empty space between the pillars and the collapsed rubble surrounding the pillars. He was even more shocked when a hand and arm emerged in the air between the pillars and waved him forward by Manas' voice saying, "C'mon."

Striding into the space between the pillars, his amazement grew as he suddenly found himself standing on the pathway leading to a beautiful two story home of white granite. Manas stood close by, his grin almost a smirk.

"She's waiting for us inside."

As they walked the path down to the home, Karl took in the surroundings. There was no wreckage here, no sign of an earthquake. Instead, there was a beautiful home surrounded by gardens and fountains.

"How..." he began.

"Remember what I said before about the hidden portal spell?" Manas said.

"This is beautiful," Karl marveled.

"Wait until you see *her*," Manas confided.

The front door opened and the necromancer stood in the doorway. "Welcome Manas. I see you have finally brought him."

Karl was suddenly tongue-tied, for the woman was a stunning beauty with long raven hair that fell to her small flat stomach. She reminded him of Gwen in that she had that same porcelain skin, flawless like a doll. She wore a long flowing dress of black silk that seemed to billow and flow though he could discern no wind. The movement of the dress caressed, folded, and danced, revealing a voluptuous body of firm breasts almost as large as Annabeth's. His gaze followed the movement of the dress, down to her stomach and then the valley between her legs, and he felt his heart quickening and his mind suddenly consumed with things more than adoration.

Then just as quickly, his lust faded and he felt like himself once again.

She smiled mischievously at him, her coal black eyes penetrating into his soul. "Welcome Karl the Viking.

Knowing you would soon be here, I looked forward to our first meeting."

"This is Kamdyn the Hallowed," Manas said by way of introduction as they stood before her.

She was tall, though not as tall as Manas. "Come in. I've been expecting you." She stood to the side and waved them in, following behind them as the door closed by itself.

They stood in a foyer that led to a wide set of stairs that split on the second floor and wrapped around and ascended once again. Karl frowned thinking that the stairs seemed too large for what he had seen was the size of the house, especially as the stairs went up at least three levels and the house he saw was only two levels.

Kamdyn led the way through the foyer and into a large reception room. A thick Turkish rug covered the floor. Floor to ceiling windows covered the opposite wall, providing a clear view to the distant mountains now fading in the approaching night. To the right was a wide hearth adorned with a carved granite mantel. Though the days and nights were warm, a fire rippled in the fireplace.

A couch and two chairs facing the couch were positioned close to the windows. In between the couch and chairs was a low table with trays of food and wine.

"Please sit," Kamdyn said. Her voice was soft, though sensual.

For some reason, Karl felt exposed as though she had read his initial desire. Why it abruptly disappeared surprised him.

As Karl and Manas sat on the chairs, Kamdyn positioned herself on the couch, tucking her long legs beneath her. Reaching for a morsel of cheese, she smiled seductively at Karl. "Please help yourselves. I'm sure you must be hungry from your hike along the wall this afternoon."

Manas filled the wine glasses, handing one to Kamdyn and one to Karl. "You know why we are here."

"Yes, I do," she answered, "and I agree that it is necessary."

"I wanted to make sure before I revealed the doors to him," he explained.

"He knows the rules and consequences?"

Her dark eyes settled on Karl and once again he felt an overwhelming arousal, so much so that he found it difficult to concentrate on anything else, no matter how hard he tried or reminded himself why they were there.

"I see you are a man of strong passions," she said with a sly smile.

Then just as before, his cravings vanished and he felt himself again. Confused, he mumbled, "I... I suppose." Reaching for the wine glass, he took a deep draught, surprised by the sweetness.

Kamdyn turned to Manas. "You do not have much time. Cyril's armies are on the march. Even now they approach Durness. Coirthan will last perhaps two or three days then Cyril will turn his attention here."

"If he doesn't send out scouts before then," Karl said.

"Wisely spoken," Kamdyn smiled. "I see you are more than a simple warrior."

Karl stared into her eyes and this time the desire to possess her body raged inside him and he struggled to control himself. In an act of his inner battle, he broke eye contact and the consuming desire abruptly vanished. An epiphany awoke his realization that she was responsible for his raging lust. When he shot an angry and suspicious look at her, he found her smiling impishly at him.

"I see you have discovered my little secret."

Manas looked at her then at Karl and burst out laughing. "You are so bad, Kamdyn." He turned to Karl with bemused sympathy. "Don't feel bad. She did that to me the first time too. In fact, she tries that just about every time I come here."

"I'll give him credit though," she said, grinning at Manas. "He figured out what was happening a lot sooner than you did." She leaned forward as though confiding and said, "It took him almost an hour before it finally dawned on him what I was doing."

"Can we get back to the reason why we're here?" Manas grumbled though smiling.

"The tunnel," Kamdyn said.

"Yes."

She focused her gaze on Karl with an intensity that made him uncomfortable. "What are your intentions after the battle?"

"My intentions?" he frowned, wondering what that had to do with the defense of the city.

"Yes. I sense an attraction between you and Gwen. Do you intend to stay and rule with her?"

"No," he asserted.

"Why not?" she said, her tone direct.

"Because I have a bridge to cross."

Her gaze narrowed. "And what bridge would that be?"

"The bridge at Hulgard."

Her gaze grew suddenly cold and she stood, folding her arms then turned her attention to Manas. "He is no different from the other one who passed through here. You would jeopardize the city for him?"

"He is not the same as the other one," Manas countered. "You'll notice that Karl the Viking is sitting here, unlike the other one who left as soon as he could. Even Gwen couldn't dissuade him from leaving."

Unconvinced, she twisted her head to stare at Karl. "Why *are* you here?"

"I am here to repay a debt," he answered. "Lady Gwen healed one of my friends."

"You have healers with you," she challenged. "Could they not heal your friend?"

"She was dead, or near dead."

Kamdyn silently stared at him then said, "I know all about your friend and the venomous bites she endured from the spiders. Tell me, had she not been wounded or near death, would you have agreed to stay?"

"Who knows?" he shrugged in reply. "Is it not enough that I am here, now?"

"No, it is not enough," she replied, crossing the floor to peer out into the gathering darkness. "This fight is not yours. You are free at any time to leave, or change sides if that suited you."

"You're right," he agreed, beginning to get irritated. "This fight is not mine. But, do you think me so

191

dishonorable that I would betray a trust or go back on my word? You meet me for the first time and use your powers to play with my emotions like it was a game. If you're so concerned with defending this city, why aren't you out front leading?"

Turning around, she locked her eyes on him and he returned her stare. He felt the stirrings of arousal again and through sheer will squashed them.

A smile curled the corners of her lips. "I see you have greater strength than I realized." Walking back to the couch, she sat down, again tucking her legs beneath her then turned to Manas. "Do you trust him?"

Manas looked at Karl then back to her. "Yes."

"So be it," she acknowledged.

"You still haven't told me why you're not out front mobilizing the city," Karl snipped.

She smiled kindly at him. "I'm a sorceress. If the battle should go against us, I will be fighting for my life from both sides. If the battle is for us, I am still held at arms' length, always suspected and never trusted. But do not mistake my visible absence for apathy. You will see me if and when you need me."

It was then that Karl saw her stats bar and wondered why he hadn't noticed it before. Had he been so preoccupied with her beauty that he was totally oblivious? It then dawned on him that he never saw a stats bar unless he thought about it. Otherwise, the bar vanished, unless there was a change to the stats as a result of some action, like after a battle.

Kamdyn the Hallowed: Sorceress, Level 20
Strength: 50 points
Speech: 50 points
Magic: 50 points
Health: 50 points
Mana: 50 points
Combat: 50 points
Leadership: 25 points

Karl was surprised to see the strength and combat points, wondering aloud, "You are a strong sorceress. I'm sure the city could use you in its defense."

Her smile vanished. "I have already answered your question, Viking." She twisted her head to give Manas a stern stare. "You may use the portals as you wish. I hold you responsible for their continued safety."

Night had fallen as Manas and Karl emerged from between the two pillars. Manas led the way and the two were silent for a while until they approached the door in the wall. Karl spoke as Manas opened the door.

"I understand your position."

"Do you?" Manas challenged. "I've kept the secret of the portals for over thirty years and now I'm supposed to entrust this secret to a group of strangers who show up and claim they're going to help defend us against a dreaded enemy, in a war they have no part of. For all I know, you all could be spies and Westhaven is dead already, as is Lady Gwen."

"I will never let anything happen to the Lady," Karl fiercely answered.

"Never is a pretty long time," Manas tartly pointed out. "Do you intend to stay?"

"I... I haven't decided yet," Karl waffled.

"Apparently 'never' lasts only as long as you are here," Manas stated.

"Who knows how long any of us are here?" Karl countered. "There is still a battle to not only win, but survive. As for me and my team, we have given our word to defend Westhaven and the Lady, even if it means our death. How many strangers offer such a bargain?" He abruptly remembered that he and his team could respawn, and just as suddenly his words rang hollow. But then, if the orcs at Abeloft could regenerate, did all the NPCs have the same capability? Was the approaching war a never ending affair?

"Point taken," Manas said with a begrudging smile. Stepping through the door, he said, "What do you think of her?"

193

"Lady Gwen?" he replied, his thoughts still somewhat distracted with the implications of respawning and regenerating. What was the difference?

"No," he chuckled, "Kamdyn."

"She's a strange one," Karl replied, remembering the rising lust he felt even as they took their leave.

Manas chuckled, stepping out onto the quiet alleyway. Above them in the near distance, dim streetlamps provided flickering beacons.

"That's because she's part succubus."

"Succubus?" Karl repeated, walking beside him. "What's a succubus?"

"You don't know what a succubus is?" Manas shot him a condescending glance.

"Obviously not," Karl retorted, hearing the man's patronizing tone.

"Odd. Don't they have succubi where you come from?"

"If I knew what it was, perhaps I could answer your question," Karl tartly replied.

"A succubus," Manas said as though repeating the word would somehow explain it. "You know. A demon woman who uses her seductive powers to steal a man's soul."

Karl startled. "Kamdyn's a demon?"

"No," Manas huffed, "she's not a demon. If she was, she wouldn't be allowed to live... at least not here. But she's enough of one to be forced to live where she does."

Karl pondered the woman for a moment before asking, "So what does a succubus actually do?"

"You felt it," Manas pointed out. "It's an incredible urge to yield to her sexuality. She does it as a game. If she had wanted, both of us would have crawled on our knees to pleasure her."

"Then what?"

"Then there would have been nothing left of us. We'd be mere shells of what we are now, our life sucked right out of us."

Karl pulled up his screen and punched in 'succubus' and began reading. It was when he got to the powers and abilities that he uttered a low whistle. "No wonder she had such impressive stats. She's immortal too."

"No she's not," Manas said as they passed through an alleyway and out onto a wide street crowded with folks headed home or to the nearest tavern. "She's only part succubus," then changed the subject when he saw a passing reveler's ears perk up at the word. "Let's get back so you can brief your team."

"I'd rather check out the..." he hesitated, realizing there were too many ears to hear. "I'd rather check out the place myself first."

Manas nodded and they kept their silence until they were back in the safety of the castle walls.

"Where do we begin?" Karl asked, still aware that anyone could eavesdrop.

"Follow me." Manas led the way back to Lady Gwen's chambers.

"Here?" Karl sputtered.

"Yes," Manas answered with a sly grin, giving a curt nod to the two door guards. One of the guards knocked loudly, waited a moment then opened the door for them.

Lady Gwen sat by the hearth, looking up and smiling when they entered. "I was wondering where you both ran off to. Last I heard you were traipsing the outer wall."

"We went to visit Kamdyn," Manas said.

"And how is she?"

"Well."

Gwen's smile turned impish as she focused her gaze on Karl. "And did she tease you too?"

Karl reddened under her stare and suddenly he felt the same primordial sexual urge that he felt when Kamdyn locked her eyes on him. It rose within and the desire to rush over there and tear her clothing off and force himself upon her shocked him. He struggled to break eye contact, finally succeeding and caught his breath as the urge dissipated. His lips tightened and his eyes hardened as he turned once again to look at her.

"Yes," she admitted with a calm smile. "I too have the blood of the succubus."

"Is that why I agreed to stay and fight for you?" He stood erect, staring down his nose at her.

"Do not be angry with me," she sighed. "And no, that is not why you agreed to stay and fight for me. You agreed because you are an honorable man. The fact that I can use my power doesn't mean that I do."

"What's the difference between you and Kamdyn?"

"I am not a sorceress," she answered with a shrug.

"But she is forced to live where she does while you sit here and rule a domain," Karl tersely stated.

"She was forced there long before I came here. She does so now out of respect for my position."

"So she doesn't have to live there?"

"Well... yes and no," she said, patting the seat next to her. "Come sit and I'll explain." When he hesitated, she tilted her head and gave him a seductive smile. "I won't bite. I promise."

"How do I know you won't be toying with my emotions?" Karl demanded.

"If I promise never to do that to you, would that suffice?"

"By the gods, man," Manas interrupted, rolling his eyes. "Either you trust her or you don't. If you don't, just go ahead and leave. No one's forcing you to stay. Otherwise, sit your ass down. My apologies, m'Lady for the inappropriate language."

"No apologies necessary, Manas," she laughed. "Your candor is one of the many qualities about you that I like and trust."

Karl's visage softened as he felt somewhat abashed. So what if she did use her powers to compel him to make love to her. What could be the downside? She was beautiful. And then he remembered the little part about having one's soul sucked out and his flight of fancy quickly sobered. Yet she had given her word, just as he had done.

He walked over to stand before her. "Might I delay the lesson so that I can see the tunnel first?"

"Of course," she sweetly replied, holding her hand out.

Karl took her hand and helped her up. She stood so close to him that their faces almost touched and for an instant he felt his heart quicken.

Peering into his eyes, she spoke, her voice warm and sensual. "See? I don't need magic to make you feel what you feel. But I ask you, what magic is yours that makes me feel the same?"

Karl sucked in a breath, staring into her eyes, searching for the right response when Manas cleared his throat.

"Beg pardon, m'Lady, but time is of the essence. We need to be prepared."

"Of course, Manas," she answered, her gaze firmly locked on Karl. Turning, she slipped a hand in Karl's hand, placing the other hand on top. "Follow me." She gently tugged his hand and he yielded to her touch as she guided them into her bedroom.

Pausing in front of the hearth opposite the large canopied four-poster bed, she pointed to the mirror on the side. "That's the door."

Karl stood staring at the reflection of Lady Gwen standing close beside him, one hand in his and the other tenderly grasping his arm. Again his heart skipped and he felt the urge to sweep her up in his arms and devour her. Behind them and to the side, grim-faced Manas waited.

"How does it work?" Karl asked, forcing himself to focus.

"You simply walk through the mirror," she explained, using the mirror's reflection to stare into his eyes.

"Like this," Manas gruffly said, moving around them and stepping halfway through the mirror so that only the back half of him was visible before completely disappearing.

"You'd better go," she said, reaching up and gently turning his face to hers.

When she kissed him, he felt his knees buckle as she poured out an intense passion that overwhelmed him and he wrapped his arms around her, crushing her to him. They lingered entwined in each other, lips locked together, tongues probing each other's mouth.

It wasn't until they heard the not so polite cough of a returned Manas that they separated.

"You'd better go," she said with disappointment then whispered. "I'll be here when you get back."

Reluctantly nodding, Karl followed Manas into the mirror, turning around when through. He could see Gwen's hazy form standing on the other side.

"C'mon lover boy," Manas said. "We got things to do and a city to defend."

Smiling despite himself, Karl turned around to find himself on a small platform enclosed within the stone of the castle. To the side, a set of spiral stairs descended into darkness, the light coming through the mirror the only light in the room. Following Manas, he descended into the darkness that was pushed away by a soft glow emanating from the stone wall by the steps creating a dizzying corkscrew.

"How far down does this go?" Karl quietly asked.

"It goes down until we are below the castle's foundation."

They hit another platform with a thick iron door to the side. It was barred and locked on this side.

"That leads to another escape route," Manas said. "Never been used as far as I know."

"Where does it lead?"

"Kamdyn's place," Manas answered, continuing down the steps.

Fifteen minutes later, the stairs ended in the middle of a large circular room, lit by the same low glowing stone lights at the edges where the ceiling and walls met. Karl glanced around, noting there were at least a dozen doors recessed in the wall surrounding the stairs.

"All except one is a false door. Take the wrong door at your peril."

"Why?"

"They all lead to traps and a lingering death."

"Which door is the right one?"

Manas stood at the bottom step and faced the door directly opposite them. He then executed a left face and faced the door to the left of the stairs. Marching towards it, he stopped two paces away and pointed to the next door to the left. "This is the door. You make a left and a left."

Karl stood at the bottom of the stairs and repeated the steps.

Manas motioned him closer and had him feel along the door jamb towards the top. "Feel this?"

Karl raised a hand and felt the spot where Manas directed. It was a small smooth spot on the stone, warm, almost hot, but only in the spot where he touched. Move a centimeter away and the stone was cold.

"You know this is the right door by the hot stone." Manas slid the bars back and opened the door to a tunnel paved and lined in the same stone as the castle. He was surprised that the air was dry and cool. As soon as they stepped inside, a series of lights set in the stone walls rippled down the tunnel.

"It's pretty much a straight shot to the other end. There's only two instances where you have to pay attention."

They walked in silence for a bit before Manas warned, "You need to be careful."

Karl glanced around yet saw nothing unusual. "Is there some sort of trap ahead?"

"That's not what I mean," he said, stopping abruptly, causing Karl to stutter to a halt. "I'm talking about Lady Gwen."

"How so?" Karl cocked an eyebrow, thinking whatever passed between Gwen and himself was nobody's business.

"She's not one to be trifled with."

Karl folded his arms and stared down at the man. "Why don't you just make your point?"

Manas returned the stare with equal strength. "It's obvious you two are taken with each other. The fact is, you intend on leaving when the battle is over. What happens to her when you go?"

"Why does anything have to *happen* to her?" he replied.

"Don't be daft, man," Manas retorted. "The woman's in love with you. A blind man can see that."

"I'm sure it's not the first time she's been in love," Karl defended himself. Before he had a chance to say, 'She'll get over it,' Manas jabbed a finger in his chest.

"Yes it *is* the first time. I've known the woman a long time and I've never seen her like this, distracted and almost reckless, seeming not to care who sees how she acts. She's acting like some fool of a young girl, starry eyed in love."

"It's not my fault how she acts," Karl stiffly replied. "She's a big girl and responsible for her own actions."

Manas bowed up and his face hardened then just as quickly, he sighed and relaxed his shoulders. "Yes, she is a big girl. I'm just saying you need to be careful. You truly don't know what you're getting into."

"I'll be careful," Karl nonchalantly answered, beginning to think that the man standing before him might be carrying his own torch for the lady in question. "How much farther 'til we get to the end?"

"Not much further," Manas said, stepping forward.

A short while later, they came to an intersection leading left and right.

"We go left," Manas instructed. "Remember – left out, right in. You always go left when you go out and right when you come back in."

"Where does that go?" Karl asked, ticking his head at the other direction.

"More traps," Manas answered. "C'mon."

Past another intersection later, they came to a door leading to a dimly lit circular room with a dozen doors, an imitation of the room at the other end. A set of winding stairs ascended in the middle of the room, disappearing into the darkness above.

"Just like the other room," Manas explained, reaching up. "You can feel the smooth warm stone and know it's the right door. When you come back down the stairs, you turn to your right and then pick the door to the right. Got it?"

"I think so." Karl looked at the door and reached up to touch the warm stone.

"Not much further," Manas said, leading the way up the stairs.

The climb was much shorter than the descent at the castle and Karl found himself following Manas thorough a heavy door held together with iron straps then into an empty room with a single door at the opposite end. The room was lit by moonlight that illuminated the ethereal walls and roof of what was a small cottage.

"We're about half a kilometer beyond the outer walls," Manas said.

Mystified, Karl did a slow circle around the room, peering through the shimmering walls at the hazy forms of trees and shrubs that occasionally pierced through the translucent roof and walls.

"How is this possible?" he asked, filled with wonder.

"One of Kamdyn's spells," Manas answered. "I think she calls it the 'invisible portal' or something like that. You can see out, but no one can see in."

"Can someone walk though it?"

"Not unless you know the spell is here," he said. "Whenever anyone comes close, they think there's an impenetrable mass of thorny shrubs and go around it."

Karl went over to the door through which they had entered the cottage, and tested the wood. "This seems real enough."

"It is," Manas chuckled. "It's the only real thing here."

Karl opened the door and saw the small platform and the descending stairs. Closing the door, he looked around and behind it and saw nothing but trees and underbrush.

"Fascinating," he marveled, shaking his head. "How do we know where to come back to?"

"I'll show you in the morning," Manas said. "It's easier to see in the daylight."

"And no one can see us, even in the daytime?"

"No."

"Why is there no mist here?"

"There is," Manas smiled. "That's the beauty of it. In the daytime, it looks like thick brambles. In the deep mist of the night, no one would dare venture here, thinking it full of thorns. Yet to those who come through the portal, all is made visible. You can see through the mist almost as if it was daytime."

"So if I step outside this portal, I can still see like I can now?"

"Try it," Manas challenged.

Karl strode to the edge of the cottage wall then passed through it and was shocked to see trees, bushes, and undergrowth as more than distinct. Not only was the mist gone, but there was a brightness to the landscape, not quite the light of day, but the kind of light one would have on an open road in the light of a brilliant full moon.

Passing back through the wall, he was energized. "This will allow us to wreak havoc on the enemy. They won't know what hit them."

Manas smiled, thankful the response was as he had hoped. While he and the soldiers of Westhaven held the line, Karl and his team of killers would destroy the enemy from behind. With a little luck, they would defeat Cyril and Gwen would become queen. And then, perhaps, he would become general of the armies.

Karl glanced around a bit more then said, "I'll need the entire team with me. We need to learn the area around here so we can find this place with our eyes closed."

"Agreed. You ready?"

"Yes."

Manas followed behind Karl for the return trip, impressed that Karl had no problems finding his way back. When they emerged through the mirror into Gwen's bedroom, Karl was surprised to hear Annabeth's voice in the other room.

"So where have you been hiding?" Annabeth blurted when Karl entered the room. Her frown of disapproval turned to confusion as Manas followed him into the room.

"You'll find out tomorrow," Karl answered, taking in the scene. Gwen demurely sat on the divan, with Annabeth and Raquel sitting on overstuffed high-back chairs opposite her. Raquel's face was one of forced politeness.

"Why tomorrow? Why not now?" Annabeth demanded.

"Because it's too dark to make sense of anything now," Karl patiently explained then furrowed his brow. "What are you doing here?"

"We noticed that you seem to be spending an inordinate amount of time here," Annabeth said with a hint of self-righteousness as she ticked her head towards Gwen, "and we thought that we ought to explain the rules in place. We were explaining to Lady Gwen here that we were willing to share, even if it means waiting three days to have you to oneself. But that meant sharing and not keeping you to herself."

Gwen fixed her emerald green on him and he felt his passions rising.

"They were most polite and informative," she said. "I quickly realized that I have intruded on an established precedent and conveyed my deepest apologies. As to their proposal, while I find it very generous and interesting, I have yet to determine whether it is something that suits me."

Karl felt his heart quicken at the thought that she was no longer interested in him, at once cursing women for being so fickle while at the same time remembering the lingering kiss before he went into the tunnel.

"But that must wait for the moment," Gwen regally stated then turned to the two women. "For now, I must discuss the future of my domain with these two. I find your proposal most interesting, yet need to think about it. Perhaps we can resume our discussion tomorrow."

"Of course," Annabeth cheerily replied standing, a reluctant Raquel also standing. She looked over at Karl. "We'll wait for you outside."

"Perhaps it would be better if you waited in your rooms," Gwen stated. "I do not know how long it will be before your commander is available to you."

"That's alright," Annabeth answered, tugging Raquel to follow. "We don't mind, do we?" They were out the door before Gwen had a chance to respond.

She gazed up at Karl with a bemused smile. "Such delightful and entertaining ladies. You're very fortunate to have them as friends."

"Yes I am," he replied, unsure of both his answer and her comment.

"Well?" she inquired. "What do you think of our little secret?"

Karl paused before answering, wondering whether she was asking about the secret that they were infatuated with each other or about the tunnel. Fortunately, Manas came to his rescue.

"We'll need to go back during the day so they can get a feel for the land and the entrance spot."

"We'll go back out tomorrow," Karl said, giving Manas a 'thank you' nod. "I'll need to brief my team."

"I'd like that to happen here," she said, "for obvious reasons. I don't need to remind you of the necessity of secrecy."

"I understand."

Standing, she moved towards the door to the outer hall. "Until tomorrow then."

Once Manas passed through the open door, it closed behind him.

"That was quick," Annabeth said, her frown deepening. "What's going on?"

Pursing his lips, Manas stared at the closed door. "She had something she wished to discuss in private." He turned and headed down the hallway.

"Like what?" Annabeth called after him.

"I don't know," he said over his shoulder. "That's why it's called 'private'."

Crossing her arms, she spun around to face Raquel. "Well we're just gonna stay here until he comes out."

With a sigh, Raquel shook her head. "Right now, she has the advantage. Once the battle is over and we're on our way, it'll be back to normal."

"What?" Annabeth fussed. "You're gonna let that woman interfere with our fun?"

"Doesn't look like we have a choice. It's not like he's fighting to get away from her."

"What are we gonna do?" Annabeth pouted then scowled at the door.

"I'm going to bed," Raquel answered then turned to amble down the hallway.

"It's not fair," Annabeth grumbled, standing in indecision before chasing after Raquel. "He was supposed to be with me tonight."

On the other side of the door, Karl and Gwen were wrapped in each other's arms, their mouths locked in a long deep kiss. When they broke to catch their breaths, Gwen grabbed his hand and led him to the bedroom, closing the door behind him. Positioning him by the bed, she gently pressed her hand on his chest, forcing him to sit on the edge of the bed then took a step back.

"Stay there and watch, my gorgeous Viking."

Karl's heart thudded in his chest as lust and desire rose to maddening heights, watching as she reached up and unclasped the broach at her shoulder. The gossamer fabric of her dress gently billowed as it slipped off her shoulders, cresting over her breasts then dropped to the floor, leaving her quite naked, stunningly naked.

Karl sucked in a breath and reached for her, but she pushed him onto his back and straddled him.

"Take me now," she begged.

Chapter 6

Felix twisted his head to gaze longingly out the window. It was one of those days where the siren call of the golf course taunted him as he half listened to Scott ramble on about the latest additions and variants to Bridge Quest. Though he knew he ought to be interested, why he should care now about developments on islands six to eight when none of the players had crossed the first bridge yet was stretching his patience. With a disappointed sigh that he'd be lucky to get in nine holes this afternoon, he held up his hand for Scott to stop.

"Talk to me about the NPC that's with the group in Westhaven."

"Elena?"

"I believe that is her name," he said, turning his head away from the window and twisting around to face Scott who sat in an overstuffed chair in front of Felix's desk. "What is she doing there?"

Scott stared at him, wondering if he was testing him or if he really didn't know. Deciding to show off his intimate knowledge of the latest developments within the game, he said, "She and Dieter have formed an affection for each other. It's really quite interesting. Using the Vienna studies of human behavior and electronic impulse, we've managed to give the feeling of being in love to a number of NPCs. It's been a recent development in the game, but it's added a fascinating parameter and exponential."

His excitement grew as he explained, "If we choose, we can infuse an NPC with a number of very human emotions. Take jealousy for example. We can input jealousy into NPCs and create all sorts of deviations for game play. Right now, we're in the process of adding human emotion layers to as many NPCs as possible... well, human NPCs. We're still working on the non-human side."

"I thought all our human NPCs were already constructed to act like humans," Felix said with a frown.

"They were," Scott replied, "to a point. With the addition of the Vienna parameters, we've made them even more human."

"How far along are we?"

"We've made the additions to all NPCs on the first three islands. We should have the rest of the changes completed by the end of the month."

Felix swiveled around in his chair to once again gaze out the window. The siren call was growing louder, especially as his eyes fell onto the golf course directly across the Tennessee River. There was a foursome on the 5th hole fairway with another foursome waiting to Tee off.

"So you're telling me," he said, though still looking out the window, "that Dieter and Elena are in love?"

"Yes."

"What was her place before she left Abeloft?"

The question surprised Scott for it intimated that Felix knew all about the relationship. "She was a serving girl."

"What happens when they get to the bridge?"

"Ah, yes," Scott acknowledged. "We've been debating that. My thoughts are that non-essential NPCs be allowed to cross bridges, NPCs that aren't critical to the execution of the game."

"And how can you determine which ones are non-critical?" He watched a golfer hit a shot then pump his fist, pleased with the result.

"There are plenty of nonessential NPCs," Scott replied.

"I understand that," Felix said, cutting him off. "If Dieter is consumed with Elena, haven't you made her an essential NPC? If, in fact, they 'love' each other," he used both hands to make quotation marks, "that means that Dieter will do his best to protect her. If she can't cross the bridge, wouldn't that imply that there's more than a fair chance that Dieter will remain with her?"

"That's why I recommend she be allowed to cross over to the next island."

Felix slowly nodded. "Suppose something happens to her?"

Scott shrugged. "Just like it does in real life. If she is killed, she's gone forever... at least to Dieter. We'll just reintroduce her back into the tavern in Abeloft if that happens."

"Will she have the memory of Dieter?"

Scott paused. "That's a good question. Memory is still one of those areas we're exploring and testing. All NPCs have short term memory and game required memory. The worst that can happen, from my perspective is that she has memory of Dieter. If it proves problematic, we simply eliminate her as an NPC, though I can see advantages to the memory aspect."

"And complications," Felix pointed out, turning back around. "If she has memory, then she has memory of everything between leaving Abeloft and her death, which means if you put her back in Abeloft, she can tell anyone what to expect... as well as what happened when she died."

"Yes," Scott admitted, "there is that. We're working on it."

"Then you need to work faster," he said.

"Yes, Sir," Scott answered.

"I have another question," Felix said, narrowing his gaze at him. "Our monsters and certain NPCs respawn so that subsequent PCs have the benefit of interacting with them after other PCs have moved on, like orcs at Abeloft for example."

"We fixed that," Scotts interjected.

"That's not the point," Felix replied, waving away the response. "Essential NPCs respawn so that other PCs can interact with them. You've made Elena an essential NPC –"

"With no memory," Scott interrupted, eyes bright. "That's perfect. That way, any PC could take an NPC with them and should something happen to it, it merely respawns back at the original spot with no memory of what happened before then."

"You're still removing an NPC from the game though," Felix objected.

"Not really," Scott countered. "The NPC is still in the game and assumes an ever greater role in either aiding or hindering the quest. This is brilliant."

"How so?" Felix smiled at the man's excitement.

"Just think of the variations. Further, not every player interacts with NPCs that other players do, so it doesn't really matter if one or more NPCs are unavailable to them."

"So if all the members of Karl's team decided to take an NPC as a lover?" Felix cocked an eyebrow.

"It doesn't matter. Worse casing it, we can always add a character if necessary."

"Suppose a player falls in love and decides to remain where he is, what then?"

Scott gave him a wicked smile. "We make him an offer he can't refuse."

Felix chuckled. "Anything else?"

"What about the bridge? My recommendation is to let her cross."

"I'm leaning towards your favor. Let me think on it," Felix loftily replied. "Once this present quest is near completion, come back to me and let's finalize our approach." His attention again wandered to the golf course across the river as he swiveled around and leaned back in his chair.

"Yes, Sir," Scott said with a hint of frustration then decided he would proceed as he had planned. As the saying went, 'It's easier to ask for forgiveness than it is for permission.' "There is one more thing."

"Yes?" Felix's focus remained on the fairway across the river.

"It's about personnel shortages," Scott said. "I'm down a third from a little more than a month ago. I can't continue like this. I'm losing too many employees to immersion."

Frowning, Felix swiveled back around. "Anyone critical?"

"Two," Scott replied, "but that's beside the point. I'm asked to develop gaming parameters, variations, and solutions within time constraints without the manpower to make it happen... even with AI assistance."

"You can put a stop to that," Felix stated.

"Only if it's internal," Scott reminded him. "We have no control over external immersion. If an employee wants to immerse in another company's game, we can't stop them, especially when we find out after the fact."

Felix pursed his lips. Scott's division was not the only one losing employees to immersion, and ITL was not the only company who found itself at the mercy of gaming success.

"You'll have to ramp up the AI," Felix said, though not liking the solution.

"I'm already doing that," Scott sighed. "I lost Jackson Clark from Designers section yesterday."

"Where'd he go?" Felix asked, both disappointed and surprised.

"Harem Quest," Scott replied, rolling his eyes.

Felix stifled a smile. "AI backup?"

"Well sure," Scott answered, "but AI can only do so much. It doesn't have the creativity that an out of the box thinker like Jackson does."

While Scott was technically correct, Felix knew it was merely a matter of time before AI caught up and surpassed the Jacksons of ITL.

Turning back around to stare out the window, Felix quietly said, "Do your best."

Scott pushed himself up, hesitating only a moment to see if Felix would acknowledge his departure. When none came, he turned and walked out, leaving Felix to watch the next foursome tee off.

Sensing he was alone, Felix looked back over his shoulder to make sure. He knew Scott was right. ITL was bleeding employees... as was every other business. It was even getting harder to find a good restaurant that had enough staff to stay open. Immersion was all the rage. Looking back across the river, he wondered how soon it would be before he was the only one left.

A thumping on the door woke them and Karl blinked as the morning's sunlight filtered in through the windows. Propping up on his elbow, he turned to gaze down at the beautiful woman beside him. She looked up at him and he felt his passions again stirring. What was it about this woman that so consumed him? Not only was she beautiful, she was an amazing and voracious lover. In fact, her appetite and techniques caused him to wonder whether Manas had told him the truth that she had never been in love before.

"Unless they're bringing breakfast, they need to leave us alone," she said with an impish smile, pressing herself against him.

On the other side of the door came a muffled but urgent, "M'Lady," followed by a louder knock.

"You better see what they want," Karl urged.

Giving him a quick kiss, she scooted out of the bed and wrapped a silk robe around her, which did little to hide her voluptuous body.

Prying open the door enough to see who had interrupted their sleep, she listened as the messenger related that Cyril's armies were attacking Durness and that many fleeing the battle were now at the outer gates of Westhaven.

"Notify General Manas. And have someone send up breakfast enough for three."

"Yes, m'Lady."

Locking the door, she turned and crossed the floor, losing the robe in the process. Once on the bed, she straddled Karl and leaned down to kiss him then whispered in his ear, "We have time for one more." She kissed down his chest as she pulled the blanket off him.

They were both dressed when she finally answered the door and allowed the servants to bring breakfast in. The once fresh hot bread had cooled and the steaming eggs were lukewarm. It mattered little to Karl, for his heart was filled with Gwen. And suddenly he understood why Dieter was so captivated by Elena. Yet, he was faced with a dilemma. Should he stay here with Gwen? By all likelihood, she would become queen. If he stayed, would that make him king? But he had to move on, cross that bridge... didn't he? But what was wrong with staying here? It wasn't like he *had* to cross the bridge.

He gave voice to his thoughts. Slicing a slender bit of cheese, he said, "What happens after the battle is won?"

Her emerald green eyes brightened as she gazed upon him. "You are the most amazing and incredible lover a woman could ever want. No wonder those two are so possessive of you. You are beyond handsome and gracious. You are the perfect man."

Karl laughed. "Let's not get carried away. Seriously. What happens after we win?"

"Who knows?" she evasively shrugged.

"Isn't it possible that you would become queen?"

"Only if Coirthan is dead."

"And if he is?"

"Then it's possible, I suppose." She daintily nibbled on a piece of bread.

Karl felt his concentration fade and all he could see was her. "My God, you are so beautiful."

"I'm glad you think so," she blushed.

A knock interrupted their reverie and the door to the suite burst open, Manas charging in. "M'Lady." Grim faced, he dipped his head, his lips tightening at the intimacy of the Viking with his Lady. Propriety demanded he recognize the man and he nodded at Karl yet said nothing, instead choosing to address the more pressing matter.

"There is a steady stream of people fleeing Durness. They line up outside the gates, demanding sanctuary."

"Let them in," she replied as though the answer was obvious.

"M'Lady," Manas sighed in frustration. "Any number of them could be someone sent here to harm you."

"He's right," Karl asserted. "They need to be vetted."

"How do we do that?" she asked.

Manas hesitated, for his first inclination was to keep those able to bear arms while sending the rest away.

"Have someone vouch for them," Karl suggested. "That way they are also responsible for their guest. Anyone without a sponsor will have to wait outside the gates."

"What happens when Cyril's army approaches?" she worried.

"By that time they will either have sought refuge farther away or found a place to climb the walls. Either way, your safety and the safety of our citizens take precedence over their needs."

"He's right, m'Lady," Manas readily agreed, though noting Karl said *our* citizens, which caused him to wonder if the man's intentions had changed. A passing thought slipped by as he pondered whether it was the succubus part of Lady Gwen doing its magic.

'Then I leave it to you to make it happen. No," she said stopping him. "Get the Administrator. It's his job to ensure things like this are properly handled. You need to focus on defending the domain."

"Yes, m'Lady." He turned to Karl. "When will you brief your group?"

"As soon as I finish breakfast," he said, lacking the sense of urgency that Manas felt.

"I want to be here when you do."

"Of course. I was hoping you would come with us."

Pleased, Manas bowed to Lady Gwen. "I'll be back shortly."

The words scarcely left his lips when the Administrator bustled in. He wore the same crimson robes with puffed shoulders over a beige silk embroidered shirt and calf-skin leggings tucked into knee-high boots that Karl had seen the first time they had met. The heavy chain and medallion of office hung around his neck and Karl wondered if he slept with it on.

His lips pursed as his penetrating brown eyes focused on Westhaven's commanding general, standing like some supplicant while this trespassing Viking was sitting and dining with the Lady. Yet he already knew the two had spent the night together. Not only was that entirely inappropriate, it was also another obstacle to his ambition. He would have to put a stop to it.

"Our city is under a virtual siege and my Lady has time for a leisurely breakfast?" He turned a cold eye on Karl. "Shouldn't you be out reconnoitering or something useful like that, instead of distracting our lady from her responsibilities?"

Ignoring him, Karl smiled at Gwen. "Sounds like someone got up on the wrong side of the bed."

Gwen suppressed a snicker, which only increased the man's irritation. "My Lady," he said with indignation. "This is unseemly. This... this common warrior has bewitched you. The walls are fairly crumbling due to the turbulence of the frightened mobs escaping the armies of your brother-in-law. Yet you sit here as though life is grand and nothing to fret about."

Gwen patiently listened, all the while gazing lovingly at Karl. Reaching for his hands, she said, "Yes, you are right Regnan. He has bewitched me, just as I have bewitched him. We have bewitched each other." Her melodious and childlike laugh caused Karl to squeeze her hand with adoration.

Abruptly, her voice and tone changed as she twisted her head to glare at him, her emerald green eyes blazing in determination. "Yet you cross the line when you think it is your place to tell me what is unseemly or not."

"But... but, my Lady –"

"Be quiet," she commanded. "We are faced with a dangerous situation here. As you correctly point out, the crowds even now press against the gates. Yet it is my general who comes to tell me instead of my Administrator. Why is that?"

Regnan's jaw tightened. "If you remember, my Lady," he slowly enunciated, "you gave responsibility of defending this city and the domain to General Manas and the Viking here."

"The Viking has a name," she tersely reminded him. "And if *you* remember, this Viking here, whose name is Karl, informed you that he had no wish to interfere with how you ran this city. Does that strike a bell or have your wits left you too?"

His nostrils flaring at the insult, he caught himself and swallowed his pride, smiling apologetically at Karl and reminding himself that revenge is sweet. "You are right, my Lady. I am in the wrong."

"What are your plans for these newcomers?" she asked, giving him no respite.

"I… had not yet finalized a plan."

"While you were running around here feeling sorry for yourself, these two were doing your work for you. Wait outside. General Manas will explain it to you."

Stiffening at the curt dismissal like he was some recalcitrant school boy, Regnan dipped his head in respect and marched through the door and into the hallway, his anger boiling then settling as he reworked through his plans.

"Was that wise, m'Lady?" Manas softly asked.

"It was about time the man was put in his place," she answered.

"That is true, m'Lady, but I fear it will do more harm than good."

Gwen stared at him, her gaze penetrating. "If he gets in the way, eliminate him."

Startled, Manas said, "Who will run the city?"

"Do you think me so innocent and naïve to be unable to do it myself?"

"Not at all," he quickly replied.

"Go tell him what he needs to do then return. Our dearest Viking friend here needs to collect his team and I can tell he is itching to go."

"Yes, m'Lady." Bowing he went out to find the Administrator.

"Impressive," Karl teased then added, "but needed to be done." Standing, he went to her side and bent down and kissed her, his passions rising as he felt the touch of her lips and the sensual smoothness of her face. "My God you are stunning."

"Hurry back," she whispered then shifted a glance to the bedroom.

Following her glance, he grinned, fervently wishing Cyril was on another island.

Karl found the rest of the group lounging in a large reception room on the floor below. "Is everyone here?"

"Yes," Raquel answered, her face a mask of indifference.

Doing a quick count to verify, he walked to the center of the group. "Listen up. Cyril's army is on the move. It's anyone's guess how long it will be before they get here. Our job –"

"We know our job," Ross snidely interrupted.

"Let him finish," Conrad scowled.

Karl looked about the group and noted more than several sour faces. "What's the problem?"

"We're bored," Bruno replied. "I'm a thief but haven't been able to practice or improve my skills because we're got to be good here."

"Yeah," Ross added. "While you're upstairs playing kissy-face with Gwen, we're left on our own to hang around with nothing to do. What's goin' on with you and that lady?"

"None of your business," he shot back then addressed the rest of the group. "Instead of moping around, you all should have been working on your skills or spells, double checking potions. Take the initiative and figure out what needs to be done. So if you all are through with your pity party, we've got some scouting to do today. We meet in Lady Gwen's suite in five minutes. Questions?" He gave Ross a piercing stare.

When no one responded, he turned to Dieter. "We need to talk."

"OK, Boss." He gave Elena a wink of reassurance and walked over to match strides with Karl as they moved away from the group.

"We'll be operating behind enemy lines," Karl said as they walked to the far edge of the room. "Obviously we can't take Elena with us. We need to place her somewhere safe. I can think of two places, neither of them completely safe, but better than most."

"Thanks, Boss." Dieter placed a massive hand on Karl's shoulder.

"You can thank me when this is over and we're all safe," he said with a paternal smile.

"Where do you want her?"

"Either with Gwen or with a sorceress named Kamdyn."

"Sorceress?" Dieter cocked an eyebrow.

"She's a good sorceress," Karl replied then wondered if Kamdyn's succubus skills likewise worked on women and thinking perhaps it might not be such a good idea for Elena to be with her. "But, I think it would be best if Elena stayed with Gwen. I know Gwen will protect her."

Dieter relaxed. "I think that's a better idea."

"One more thing," he said. "What we're about to do is of utmost secrecy. Elena is part of this team, but you need to impress upon her that she can never tell a soul what she is about to witness. Lives depend on it."

"She's as trustworthy as Ross," Dieter emphasized.

Karl sniffed in disdain. "I trust her more than I do him."

They assembled in Gwen's outer room, waiting for Manas. Gwen was a gracious hostess, moving among the team members, offering encouragement and listening patiently. Even Annabeth and Raquel sloughed off their sour dispositions and chatted amiably with her. Karl noted that Gwen seemed to spend more time with those two than the others.

Manas bolted the door closed behind him and turned to nod at Karl, letting him know all was ready.

"OK, folks. Here's the plan. When Cyril's army encamps around the city, we will be conducting harassment attacks in the rear areas."

"What the hell?" Ross exclaimed. "We'll be mowed down before we get out the gates."

"Perhaps you should wait until everything's explained," Dieter growled, "before spouting off in ignorance."

"Yeah," Conrad agreed. "Shut up and let him finish. Jeez."

Karl paused and stared at Ross, pondering whether he was necessary to the team anymore. The man was a royal pain in the ass. The problem was whether he was trustworthy enough to endure that pain. At that moment, he made a decision.

"While most of us will be operating behind enemy lines, others will be conducting operations with Manas' forces. In this instance, I need a take-charge kind of person, one who can lead and get things done. Further this individual will act as a liaison between the two forces, which means I need someone who can move fast and silent. That person is you, Ross."

Ross' previous chagrin immediately vanished, replaced by smug confidence and arrogance at the obvious recognition. He gave Karl a brisk nod of acknowledgement, effectively telling him he had chosen the right person.

"General Manas," Karl spoke, emphasizing Manas' positon as commander of Gwen's army, "would you please designate a suitable counterpart so that Ross can begin coordinating."

Watching the exchange between Karl and Ross, Manas had immediately understood what Karl was doing.

"Of course." Addressing Ross, he said, "Captain Vergun is the commander of the Imperial Guard. His office is at the barracks."

"I know where it is," Ross replied with self-satisfied assurance.

"Good. When you report there, tell him your mission and that I have directed he accommodate you in any way he can." He unbolted and opened the door.

Ross hesitated. "Shouldn't I stay for the rest of the briefing?"

"You don't need to," Karl answered. "Besides, time is of the essence. Already refugees are fleeing the capital and scrambling here. I need you to act quickly and get things done before Cyril gets here. We need to have so smooth a cooperation and operation that no one knows we're two separate forces."

"Got it," he grinned proudly and hustled out.

Bolting the door again, Manas nodded at Karl to proceed.

"Thank God," Conrad mumbled. "The man was driving us crazy."

"Let's get to the point," Karl said. "We here in this room are now vowed to keep a secret that not even Ross is to know about. As the saying goes, sharing this knowledge is on a need-to-know basis and I will determine the need-to-know. Is that clear?"

Seeing he had their rapt attention, Karl explained, "We will be hitting the enemy from a point of advantage. There is a tunnel that runs under the castle and beyond the far outer walls. Manas showed it to me yesterday. Until this moment, only three people knew about the tunnel. Now there are fourteen more. I warn each of you, if anyone finds out about this tunnel, the castle and the domain are doomed. Do you solemnly swear to keep this secret?"

The response was automatic and heartfelt, for they knew their own success depended on defeating Cyril.

"The entrance is in Gwen's bedroom and the other entrance is, like I said, beyond the far walls. They are both protected by a spell, so you spell casters, you're going to need to be sure you're not casting spells that might interfere with the spell."

"How do we know what or what not to cast?" Annabeth asked.

"I'm going to introduce both you and Lana to the sorceress responsible for the spell's power. She will know what to do."

Annabeth's smile widened at the thought of meeting a higher level sorceress and learning more powerful spells.

"I'll explain more when we get to the other portal," Karl said. "For now, we're going to the other side and scout the terrain. I want each of you to become intimate with the terrain and the portal's location. With this advantage, I expect us to do quite a bit of damage. Remember, when the battle starts, we take no prisoners. We destroy anyone and everything we can, including their supply trains. We want to make them regret they ever came this far."

"What happens after the battle?" Wendell asked, pointedly thinking about the bridge.

"We'll worry about that when the time comes," Karl said. "Right now, we have a war to win. While I think about it, has everyone changed their bind spot to your room here? If not, do so now." He waited while several team members called up their screens and made the change. "Manas will take point as we go through the tunnel. I'll bring up the rear."

Manas led the way into Gwen's bedroom and paused before the mirror, while Annabeth and Raquel took special note of the Lady's bed.

"The mirror is the portal," he said then demonstrated by disappearing through it amidst the surprised gasps of the team. Partially reappearing with half his body invisible, he said, "Watch your step."

One by one, the rest of the team followed until only Karl and Gwen remained. She held on to his hand, reluctant to let go. "I miss you already."

"I won't be long," he reassured her with an affectionate smile.

She reached a hand up to pull his head down and kissed him then whispered in his ear, "Hurry back. We have some unfinished business." She winked at him then frowned. "What's a bind spot?"

"I'll explain when I get back," he replied with an indulgent chuckle.

By the time he descended the stairs, Conrad, the last in line, was disappearing through the tunnel door. Catching up, he listened to the animated, though muted, conversations and his thoughts wandered to Gwen. The woman was all and more than he had ever wanted or hoped to have. Her sexual appetite had surprised him and he found himself once again wondering how many lovers the woman had before he came along. But then, he knew there were only a few players ahead of him. Did NPCs have sex? If not, was she programed to be like that?

The more he thought about it, the more frustrated he became and he reminded himself that she was just an NPC, a very lifelike one, mind you, a very sexually experienced one. He smiled at the reverie of their frolicking and he was suddenly reminded of Annabeth and Raquel. What was the difference between them and Gwen other than they were players and she was an NPC? They all had computer generated bodies. Would he be interested in any of them if they met in real life?

Real life? Who was he kidding? This was his 'real life' now. Who knew how long he would be here, immersed in a game? It could be scores of years before a cure was found, maybe even longer. Or… it could be days. The not-knowing was the hardest thing to accept. And the fact that he was nothing more than a series of electronic impulses gnawed at him, for he knew he was more than that. At least he hoped he was. Reducing man to a programmable matrix took away all of man's uniqueness. Was he nothing more than a series of on and off switches? He was convinced those in real life believed they were more than that.

They came to an intersection and he listened as Manas warned them about taking the wrong path.

Once they started off again, he resumed his musings then abruptly shook his head. Since when had he become a philosopher? The reality is what is here and now, regardless of what was behind the proverbial curtain or mirror. The truth was that he was having more fun now than he had in real life and more and more of him didn't want that to change, and it dawned on him that were he to stay in the game, he could live forever.

That thought excited him and he prayed that either his cure would never be found or that the developers would forget all about him.

In the dim lights ahead, he saw Annabeth and Raquel and their fluid and graceful strut gave them a sensual attractiveness. His mind drifted to the bedroom experiences with them and he had to admit that they were just as exciting as the times with Gwen, and he frowned when he realized his uncontrollable lust for Gwen had somehow diminished and it puzzled him.

Reminding himself that he was the leader of his group, he pushed his distractions to the side and focused on the present mission. They had a battle to fight and win if they were going to get to the bridge.

It was mid-morning when they emerged into the invisible cottage, and sunlight streamed through the gossamer roof and walls.

"No one can see or hear you," Manas lectured, "once you are inside the protective walls of the spell. That changes once you pass through. You become susceptible like anyone else."

"Dieter and Sakura," Karl ordered. "Take your teams and recon the surrounding area. Take your time."

"Take the time to remember where we are," Manas cautioned them. "You need to be able to find this place regardless of where you might be."

"The rest of you will be with Manas and me," Karl said. "We'll meet again back here at high noon. While you're out reconning, look for sites and places where your skills will be of special use, thieves and rogues especially. There may come a time where your skills will be put to use to learn about the enemy's plans."

Conrad rubbed his hands together. "Hot damn. Finally a chance to do some mischief."

"They're orcs," Wendell cautioned. "Remember?"

"That's why we get paid the big bucks."

"Big bucks?" Wendell's eyebrows scrunched. "We're not getting paid, are we?"

"Forget it," Conrad said rolling his eyes. "Subtle humor is lost on you."

"If there are no other questions," Karl said with a smile, "let's move out."

By the time they returned after the afternoon's recon, they'd had enough and were ready to settle down for a good meal and some ale.

"We go out again when it's dark," Karl said.

"Again?" Sharyn whined. "We've been over that ground for hours. Nothing's changed. It's all still the same."

"But it won't look the same when it's dark," Karl explained. He looked at Carole who was dragging a bit. "How you holding up?"

"I'm OK," she replied with false confidence.

"Why don't you stay back tonight," Karl offered. "You need the rest more than you do the recon."

"What about the rest of us," Sharyn asked.

"The rest of us are back out when it's dark. Now go get something to eat. Be back here at nine."

"It'll be past midnight before we're back," Sharyn complained.

"Most likely," Karl agreed. "But on the flip side, you get to sleep in because we won't go out again until the afternoon."

"Thank God," she said with a sigh of relief.

Gwen appeared in the doorway, and Karl felt his arousal stir and he wished everyone was gone because Gwen had intimated a shared bath was on the agenda.

"You coming?" Annabeth asked, breaking into his reverie.

"I've got some things to discuss with Lady Gwen and General Manas," he lamely answered.

"Sure," Annabeth nodded, giving him a 'you-know-I-don't believe-you' look. Turning to Raquel, she ticked her head towards the door. "C'mon girlfriend. Let's get something to eat and see what mischief we can get into together afterwards."

Karl watched them saunter away, their swaying hips subtly seductive, and he wondered what she meant by 'mischief together' and suddenly he wondered if they were intimate while he was up here with Gwen. The thought of them together diverted his attention and focus to the two luscious women and he took a hesitant step only to be brought to a standstill when Gwen stepped in his line of sight, giving him a demure yet alluring smile.

"Are you hungry?" she inquired.

Karl's lust for a shared experience with Annabeth and Raquel vanished, replaced by surging passion to rip Gwen's clothes off.

Gwen butted the door closed and bolted it then unhooked the broach at her shoulder and let the gown fall to floor. "I was hoping you'd be hungry for this instead."

It was well past midnight when the team dragged themselves through the portal. Though tired, they were excited about the spell's night vision effects.

"Wish we would have had this before," Conrad opined. "We'd be level 30's by now."

Raquel paused by Manas. "So once the mist descends, everything pretty much is at a standstill, because no one can see the nose on their face, which gives us an amazing advantage. It's like we're fighting a blind man."

"That's right."

Tilting her head in thought, she asked, "If we have a sorceress who can cast a spell like that, is it possible they have one too?"

Manas grew solemn. "Yes, it is possible, though I have heard of no one with that capability."

"So Cyril has sorceresses?"

"Most likely," he admitted.

"So it is possible."

"Yes."

"Is there a way we could find out?"

"It may be too late," he said, shaking his head. "I'll ask."

She turned to Karl. "We might have an advantage in the beginning, but once they figure out what's happening, we're screwed."

"Which means," he slowly nodded, "that we have to strike fast and hard, hit and run, disappear before they know what happened."

Gwen came up and slipped a hand around Karl's arm. "You all must be tired," she commiserated. Peering intently at Raquel, she offered a tender, "Thank you."

Raquel blinked as she felt the sudden urge to kiss her then blinked again when the feeling abruptly vanished when Gwen turned her attention to Karl. "No problem," she distractedly replied before joining up with Annabeth as she walked through the door and into the hallway.

"That was weird," Raquel said.

"What?"

"I'm standing there talking to Manas when Gwen comes up, looks at me and all she says is 'Thank you,' and I get this overwhelming urge to kiss her."

"Well she is pretty," Annabeth remarked.

"That's not what I mean," she said, shaking her head.

"Oh?"

"It was more sexual than a mere peck on the cheek."

"I know."

"You do?" Raquel quizzically regarded her friend.

"There've been a couple of times I've felt the same thing. It's like she's talking to someone then turns her attention on you and suddenly you want to make love to her. If it was just once, I would have passed it off as my imagination. But I noticed that anytime she focused her attention on me, I felt my body respond. And each time I think about doing something, as soon as she turns to someone else, the feeling goes away. I think I may have found an answer." She slowed down to give them distance from the others.

Annabeth leaned in and lowered her voice. "I've been looking at characters and their traits and personalities. There's one called a succubus."

"Succubus?"

"Yes. A succubus is a woman, actually a demoness in the appearance of a beautiful woman who seduces men and steals their energy and souls during sex. There's a man equivalent called an 'incubus.'"

"So you think she's a succubus?"

"What other logical explanation is there?"

"But Karl's energy isn't any different. Look at the way he ran all over the place when we were out on recon. I could barely keep up."

"Yeah, well, maybe that part's a little off, but look at the way he is around her, like he's some junior high nerd all starry-eyed because the cheerleader noticed him."

Raquel silently considered Annabeth's conclusion. "So what do we do?"

"I don't know," she said with a defeated shrug. "It's not like we can confront her. We show up to reveal her secret and we'd probably end up in a foursome. While it might be fun, it accomplishes nothing and we're back to square one."

"Then we have to get him away from her," Raquel asserted.

"How? You see the way they are together."

Raquel bristled at the image. Ever since they arrived in Westhaven, Karl had spent all his time with Gwen. It wasn't so much that she resented his interest in another woman... well, maybe a little, but it was the overt dismissal of her and Annabeth as though they were just mere team members and nothing more.

"I don't know yet," she said. "Think we ought to tell anyone else?"

"I think we ought to tell Dieter and probably Brad and Lana. I get the feeling that once this battle is over, our boy's gonna have second thoughts about moving on to the bridge."

Raquel's eyes widened. "I hadn't thought of that."

"We may have to end up kidnapping him to break the spell."

"You and Lana have spells that could do that?"

"You kidding me?" Annabeth scoffed. "You see her level? She's a 20 with 50 in magic. We try to match wits with her and she'd have us dancing like silly puppets. We gotta think of a better way."

In the early afternoon, the door to Lady Gwen's suite opened and a messenger strode in, his face awash in controlled fear. "My Lady. Cyril's army approaches. General Manas sends word that the battle will likely begin tomorrow as by the time they arrive and get into position, it will be too late to mount an attack." He turned his attention to Karl. "M'Lord, he said that you should be prepared to conduct your operations tonight."

"Do we have any idea of the size of his forces?"

The messenger shook his head. "Only that there are orcs along with the Trolls of Stonefell in his army."

Karl activated his screen and scrolled through the monster listings, settling on the 'Troll' link. While he remembered the basics, there was something about weaknesses that caused him to scroll through the Troll info until he slowed down at the last paragraphs.

Trolls have three weaknesses. The first relates to their voracious appetite. Trolls are forced to spend most of their time hunting for food, as they must consume vast amounts each day or face starvation. This quest, or need, to maintain sustenance causes trolls to lay claim to wide areas and fights between rivals or adjoining territories are common, though usually nonlethal. However, trolls know their lives depend on sufficient food supplies and have no qualms killing their own kind should food become scarce.

The second weakness is fire. As trolls have amazing regenerative powers, fire is the one substance that prevents regeneration. Thus, those who battle trolls know to burn all parts after a fight, for even the smallest bit of flesh can regrow to a full-size troll – given enough time. A word of caution – a troll's fear of fire does not mean he will back down from a fight. Trolls are head strong, fearless, and vicious. They are incredibly strong and are ever ready to charge headlong at its opponent and attack it with all its fury.

The third weakness is sunlight, though some troll variants have adapted to moderate sunlight. Those variants most affected by sunlight are stone trolls and rock trolls. Rock trolls live far beneath the earth in underground caverns and venture forth when the sun has set. Thus, their habits are the reverse of topside dwellers, sleeping during the day and active at night. Rock trolls caught in the sunlight will turn to solid stone.

Stone trolls, cousins to rock trolls, live nearer the surface and are able to function topside during the dawn hours and sunset hours – even when the sun has risen, using shadows to shield themselves against the sun's rays. Exposure to sunlight of any part of their body turns that specific part to stone as a permanent condition.

Karl scanned the rest of the parts about families and variants, instead choosing to focus on stats and skills, wondering aloud, "How is he employing the trolls if they are subject to sunlight? I assume the mist affects them just like everyone else." Then he read their dark vision stats.

Senses:
Dark vision: 60 feet (18.3m)
Lowlight: + 6
Sense: +6
Perception: +4

Thinking about their upcoming raid, he uttered a soft, "Damn."

Gwen's lips tightened at his response then relaxed as she quickly remembered the messenger waiting for her reply. "Thank you. Please relay to the General that we will do as he instructs."

"Yes, m'Lady," he answered with a crisp bow and hustled out.

Once left alone, Karl watched as Gwen, lost in thought, paced the room, her arms folded. "Don't worry," he reassured her. "I won't let you down." His smile was one of confidence.

She paused and twisted her head to stare at him, and for a fleeting instant the eyes were cold and piercing, instantly replaced by warmth and devotion.

"I know you won't," she answered with a forced smile. Suddenly she brightened. "Well. There's nothing I can do about it this moment. I think a certain lady needs some attention by a certain Viking."

"Now?" Karl replied, surprised. Yet what surprised him even more was the sudden arousal he felt, clouding his mind from his responsibilities. This time it was distinct, like the desire he felt in Kamdyn's home. "What are you doing to me?" he slurred, drunk with uncontrollable desire.

"What do you mean?" she teased with a coy smile as he crossed over to her and swept her up in his arms.

"I don't know what I mean," he answered, his mind consumed with only one desire.

Standing on the high crenellated walls surrounding Westhaven, Manas watched as Cyril's army spread out around the walls, cutting down trees and maneuvering catapults and trebuchets into the opening spaces. Initially mystified to see orcs and humans working together, he was somewhat mollified when he saw the not so subtle mutual distrust. His standing order of not to engage the enemy unless the target had the likelihood of being killed made the attackers less cautious until one bowman let fly a barbed arrow at a man pushing one of the catapults, piercing him through the throat and pinning him to the side of the machine.

The response was a flurry of arrows that fell harmlessly on the Westhaven side of the wall, where, to his delight, the fletchers and lesser skilled warriors collected over fifty perfectly good arrows.

Deciding he could always use more arrows, he selected four more master archers and told them to pick a target. Four more humans went down. By the time one of Cyril's captains saw what was going on and yelled out for the damned fools to stop wasting arrows, Manas' forces had collected three hundred and twenty seven arrows.

His mirth changed to anger once the machines were put to use. Instead of rocks and boulders, the first missiles fired were heads, human heads that bounced and rolled. The shock and horror soon turned to wails of grief as many recognized decapitated friends and relatives.

One head in particular caught Manas' attention when it was brought to him, its tormented grimace still defiant to the end. The twisted visage on King Coirthan's face reminded him that this same fate awaited him and Gwen and many others should they lose this war. He silently prayed that Karl and his team would prove successful.

Calling over one of his captains, a trim middle-aged man named Cuix, he commanded, "Send a messenger to Lady Gwen and inform her that the king is dead. I want you personally to inform the Lady of the circumstances. Take the head with you as a reminder to her and everyone else what we can expect from Cyril."

"Yes, General." He saluted then curled a finger at the man holding the king's head by the thick hair.

Cuix and the warrior holding the king's head, now stuffed in a bag, stood outside the door to Gwen's suite and waited while the guard knocked and opened the door, immediately noting the door to Gwen's bedroom door was closed.

"It'll be a while," the guard informed them, rolling his eyes and smiling.

"We don't have a while, you fool," Cuix snarled. "Get her out here."

Chastised, the guard scurried over to the bedroom door and hesitantly knocked. When he received no response, he knocked again with a bit more insistence. He knocked the third time, adding, "My Lady. Captain Cuix is here."

"Go away," came the muffled reply.

Cuix strode across the room and wacked the door. "My Lady," he loudly announced. "The king is dead."

Silence followed for but a moment when the door cracked open enough for Gwen's head to appear. Looking behind her, Cuix saw the Viking hastily dressing.

"Is it true?" she asked, her voice edged with disbelief.

Cuix motioned to the warrior holding the severed head in the bag. "His head was delivered to us just a little while ago." He stared firmly into her eyes as he added, "You are now the queen and sole ruler of Montgrec. What are your commands?"

"Give me a minute," she said, closing the door.

By the time Cuix and the warrior repositioned themselves in the middle of the outer room, the door to the bedroom opened and Gwen walked out, dressed in a flowered silk gown, followed by Karl who had managed to get dressed in the interval.

Gazing directly at Cuix then the warrior, her eyes dropped to the bag in his hand. "Show me."

The warrior gingerly removed a small statue from a narrow pedestal table and placed the bag on top, untying the top then slipping the fabric over the side of the head.

Gwen stepped closer sand studied the grotesque visage. Karl was impressed that she displayed no tearful emotion.

"Keep this safe," she admonished. "When this is all over, if we can find the body, he will be buried properly."

"Yes, your Majesty," the warrior reverently spoke.

She then turned her attention to the guard by the door. "Fetch the Administrator."

"Yes, m'Lady... er, uh, I mean, your Majesty."

"Anyone hurt?" she said, addressing Cuix.

"No. He," he said, waving a hand at the king's head, "and about fifty others were launched over the walls, hoping to affect our morale. It merely angered us."

"Has Cyril shown himself?"

"Not yet."

The Administrator burst through the door with an "O my God" as soon as he saw the king's head.

Karl watched the man, with a detached fascination. The Administrator's look of anguish was appropriately genuine, yet lacked the skill of a true actor. Karl stood to the side as the man fawned over the dead king as though he had been a martyred saint.

Finally enduring enough, Gwen held up a hand. "Your condolences are duly noted. With his demise, I am now the ruler of Montgrec. I expect you to inform the people, impressing upon them that their fate is tied to mine and that they are expected to defend this domain to the best of their abilities."

"Of course, my Lady," he acknowledged with curt bow.

Karl noticed a smug smile flicker and vanish.

"Attend to it then."

"Yes, my Lady."

"Your Majesty," Cuix intoned, correcting him.

"Ah yes," the Administrator smiled in feigned embarrassment at his faux pas, "your Majesty."

When the Administrator departed, Gwen focused her attention on Cuix. Karl watched and listened to the calm and efficient way Gwen issued commands. It was then he abruptly realized that his constant infatuation was absent. Also absent was his indecisiveness concerning the completion of this quest and moving on to the bridge. He frowned that he had actually contemplated remaining here.

Once Cuix and the warrior departed and the door firmly closed, Gwen turned to Karl and smiled. "Now where were we?"

Karl cocked an eyebrow, wondering how she could think of frolicking in the bedroom when her domain was in imminent peril. "I probably should check on my team. There's a battle about to start."

"They can wait," she purred, moving closer to him.

"Are you sure, your Majesty?" he said, returning the smile.

Gwen stepped up to him, gently placing a hand on his chest. "We are far too intimate, my dearest Viking, to be captive to such titles."

Karl felt his passions stir. "You promised you would never use your powers over me," he huskily said.

"And I won't," she assured him, "just like I promised. Now, let's see if we can pick up where we left off." Grabbing his hand, she led him to the bedroom.

It was early evening, that time of day when the sun dipped below the horizon yet daylight remained for a while longer, when Manas saw the man on the dappled stallion approaching the gate. He was surrounded by a coterie of vassals flying pennants of their respective cities. Behind them, several orcs and two large trolls haughtily stalked. The group stopped at the gates and Cyril looked up to see Manas high above him.

"And how is my sister-in-law's general doing these days?" He smiled as though sincerely interested. He was a trim man on the verge of going plump from too much pleasure, both in food and women. His ruddy face was offset with a trim Van Dyke beard of auburn hair streaked with grey. Instead of the long flowing head of hair favored by his brother, Cyril kept his cut short and well-trimmed. He was dressed for combat in a common warrior's tunic and leggings, though the material was of much finer quality. The one distinguishing trait was the coat of arms burnt into the leather of his vest.

"I'm fine, m'Lord," Manas smiled in return. He gazed out over the assembled force then back at Cyril. "Does my Lord intend to spend the evening hunting in the forest before he returns home?"

Cyril chuckled. "Come, my good general. We both know why I am here. Give me Lady Gwen and this city will be safe from further harm."

"You know I can't do that, m'Lord."

"Are you really willing to let Westhaven suffer for the life of one avaricious woman?"

"If it is one simple woman, as you claim, why did you come all the way here with this army? Were your assassins not able to accomplish what you wanted?"

Cyril's face tightened. "One last chance general. Surrender the woman or suffer the same fate as Durness."

Manas slowly shook his head, his contempt overt. "My Lord. Do you really expect us to believe that you would ensure the safety of this city when your army is filled with orcs and trolls?" He swiftly turned his attention to the orc and troll leaders. "What did he promise you? That you could feast to your hearts content on the flesh of the good citizens of Westhaven? What happens after that? Has he not revealed that he intends to kill you all once he has what he wants?"

Cyril heard the low grunts and grumbling behind him, irritated that he had allowed Manas to infuse doubt into his allies, let alone reveal his true intentions.

"Cleverly spoken," he retorted. "By the way, I'd like to meet the one responsible for this." He motioned with his hand and two men brought forward the assassin that Karl had tortured. He was dressed in torn clothing and bound with ropes and a chain at his neck. Drool slid from the corners of his mouth and his lidless eyes twitched and wandered incessantly. His hands and feet were bandaged in filthy rags. It was obvious the man had lost his mind.

"Ah yes," Manas said in recognition. "The handiwork of our confessor."

Cyril gave Manas a begrudging smile. "When we sweep through the city, be sure to point him out. I can use someone with his talents."

"I take it you intend to stay?"

Cyril locked his gaze on Manas and growled, "I always finish what I start. I give you one last chance, General. Surrender the woman and I guarantee the safety of you and everyone else in the city."

"Does that include the Administrator?" Manas frowned when the words came forth because he wasn't sure why he said them.

A sly smile split Cyril's mouth. "Is he safe?"

"For the moment," Manas replied, suddenly realizing why the assassins had such an easy time getting into the city.

"I hold you responsible for his safety."

"Why?" Manas mocked. "You're going to kill him anyway, just like you are all these orcs and trolls."

"Enough," Cyril commanded. "Do not try my patience. You have until the morrow's morning to deliver the woman. Otherwise, the fate of Westhaven is on your head."

"No. The fate of Westhaven is on *your* head. You will have our answer in the morning," Manas calmly answered then turned away, an overt slight to the Lord below.

Once down the steps, Manas collared one of his fastest messengers, a young man in his early teens. "Tell Lady Gwen to lock up the Administrator. If she asks you why, you tell her Manas said so. Now go."

Unwilling to leave such a mission to chance, Manas gave orders to the several captains and headed to the castle. By the time he swept up the set of stairs to Gwen's suite, he heard the commotion and indignation erupting from the

Administrator's quarters as two large guards frog-marched the man out into the hallway.

"This is outrageous," Regnan yelped. "Get your hands off of me." Seeing Manas, he shouted, "Is this your doing?"

Ignoring him, he nodded to the guards. "Make sure he is secure. Gag him if you need to. No one sees him unless I give the order."

"Yes, General," they replied in unison.

As they forcibly marched him down the hallway, Regnan called out over his shoulder, "You'll pay for this."

Karl and the rest of the team were in Gwen's quarters when he entered. Gwen's pursed lips revealed her suppressed anger as her suspicions about the Administrator seemed to be confirmed.

"Is it true?" she asked when their eyes met.

"Yes," he replied. "Your brother-in-law said as much."

"I'll have his head when this is over," she seethed.

"Hopefully it will be his and not yours. Cyril demands we turn you over to him."

"In exchange for what? The safety of the city?" she scoffed.

"Those were his words," he answered.

Gwen stared at him a moment before blurting, "And you believe him?"

"My Lady," Manas slowly replied, ignoring the momentary lack of trust. "Please do not think me a fool as to believe Cyril. Westhaven's safety is no more assured than your own."

Gwen's shoulders slumped. "Forgive me, Manas. That was unkind."

"There is nothing to forgive, m'Lady," he replied with a sympathetic smile. Turning to Karl, he asked, "You ready?"

"We've been ready since we got word they were here," Karl confidently replied.

"You know about trolls and their night vision," he warned, "though Kamdyn's spell should protect you."

Karl flashed a wicked smile. "I have an idea we're going to try. I'll tell you about it when we return."

Manas nodded and gave him the knowing smile of one warrior to another. "Good luck."

As the evening skies darkened, Manas took his time as he methodically walked along the outer wall walk, reassuring the sentries posted at intervals behind the crenellations. Though thankful the walls were high, he wished they were higher. It was only a matter of time before someone in Cyril's army discovered a weakness and the undermining process would begin.

"How will the attack go?" a young guard asked, doing his best to hide his nervousness.

"They'll work the gates first," Manas replied. "That's the weakest part of a wall." Seeing the man's eyes widen, he placed a comforting hand on his shoulder. "It's also contained inside the barbican that has two portcullis and solid oak gate that's a span thick, double barred on the inside. They'd be wiser to search along the wall to find a place to undermine it." He was about to say that they'd probably do both at the same time, but decided against further terrifying the young man.

"Are there really trolls in his army?" he asked, his fear growing.

"Yes," Manas matter-of-factly replied, "so you need to be alert."

"Can they get up here?" He cast a worried glance around the wall walk.

"Not unless they've sprouted wings and can fly," Manas retorted.

"But I heard they can climb better than people." He spoke as one with assured knowledge.

"Bah," Manas disdainfully answered. "Tell me lad, have you ever tried climbing this outer wall?"

"Tried when I was younger."

"How far did you get?"

"Didn't get far at all," he answered with understanding. "Wasn't nothing I could grab ahold of."

"Trolls have the same problem."

"But they're used to fighting in the dark," he countered.

"Son," he said, already tired at having to dispel a young man's fearful imagination, "if and when we send folks out to fight at night, you can worry about it then." He looked up at the night sky and then back down to follow the line of flickering torches that snaked along the top of the wall into the far distance. "Mist is coming soon. Make sure you keep the firelight going."

"Yes, Sir."

"You have enough arrows for that bow of yours?"

"Yes, Sir," he proudly replied. "Collected a bunch more earlier."

"Good. When the battle begins tomorrow, pick your targets with care. A wasted arrow is one more enemy we have to kill later."

Giving the man a confident nod, Manas continued his rounds, knowing he needed to get some sleep, but wanting to wait until Karl and his team returned.

Down below, beyond the outer wall, Karl and company had assembled in the room below the cottage. There was a palpable nervous excitement, the delay in conducting the hit and run attack adding to the anticipation.

"One more time," Karl quietly spoke. "We all know our assignments. Once the mist descends, the two combat teams take out as many orcs and humans as you can. Watch out for trolls as they can see well in the dark, though the mist should be a problem for them too. Stealth is the watch word. No flashy or bright spells unless it's an emergency. Remember, we don't want them to know we're here. My team and I will conduct a deeper recon to find where the trolls are. We have one hour to do our job and head back. Assembly point is right here. Any questions?"

"Yeah," Conrad grinned and pointed to the lengths of coiled rope around the shoulders of the five members of Karl's team. "What're you gonna do while we're out having fun?"

"Trying to find a way to neutralize part of Cyril's army. The more we can take out tonight, the better. Rest assured, they will expect us tomorrow night." He glanced around once more before focusing on Carole. "You sure you're OK?"

"I'm fine," she replied. "My mana and health are back to normal."

With a distracted nod, he said, "I think it's time."

Silently emerging into the cottage, Karl was startled to see the number of camp fires close to them. Though expecting the enemy to be encamped around them, he was still surprised at how close they were. Still, Kamdyn's spells were in full force and the presence of his force was unnoticed. The one thing he noted with satisfaction was that the enemy encamped around them was human.

They hunkered down and waited for the mist to descend.

Karl watched and studied the warriors as they bantered and drank and settled down for the night. They were far too relaxed and he noted that a guard had not been posted. If Cyril wasn't overconfident, these people were. Then he remembered why they had no guards posted for orcs prefer operating at night, preferably in overcast conditions, or in the predawn hours. Like trolls, sunlight affected their ability to wage combat. It was far worse for trolls and he worried they wouldn't find the troll encampment in time. Then it dawned on him that his plan would work for orcs as well, provided the next few days were bright with sunshine. Still, he preferred his target be trolls.

While he was musing his plan, the mist started enveloping the forest and soon activity around slowed until all movement stopped. Waiting another half-hour more, Karl stood and motioned for the attack to begin.

While Dieter and Sakura led their teams, entering tents and slicing throats, Karl led his small group away from the carnage and carefully snaked their way around the various tents and campfires, working their way to the catapults and trebuchets. They found six of them near the edge of the forest not far from the main gate. Once the weapons were located, they worked their way back into the forest, searching for the orc and troll bivouac sites.

They came up to the troll camp set apart and Karl was frustrated that despite the mist, the trolls were still very much awake and alert, jabbering and sharpening weapons for what was probably a pre-dawn attack. That meant the orcs were likewise preparing and he was running out of time.

Cyril had wisely brought along large tents, enough to accommodate those forces vulnerable to sunlight, which was why Karl and friends had lengths of rope. Karl quickly calculated the distance between the tents and the catapults and determined the distance required two full lengths of rope, or about 50 meters total. Sending an end each with Raquel and Annabeth towards the war machines, he and Lana square knotted the other ends with two other lengths of rope while Brad stood guard.

As Karl and Lana secured the two ends of the ropes, Raquel and Annabeth raced towards the war machines. Pleased that the catapult buckets were winched down, ready to launch the large stone resting in the bucket, the two players wrestled the ropes around the stones and feeding the line down along the end of the bucket, making it look like it was part of the release rope. Retracing their steps, they did their best to cover up the rope.

They repeated the process with the remaining ropes, attaching them to two more catapults and a mangonel. They then fed the other ends near wide tree trunks, finally attaching them to the corner tent poles of five tents, likewise covering up their handiwork.

By the time they returned to the cottage, the other two teams were silently waiting for them. Karl motioned them down and waited until the last one passed before closing the door behind them. Holding a finger up to his lips, he then led the way back to the castle.

It wasn't until they were safely in Gwen's suite that he relaxed and asked for a debrief. "You first, Dieter."

"We worked to the north and west of the cottage," he replied. "The humans were in small tents, no more than six warriors to a tent, which made it easier to slice their throats. My count may not be exact, but by the time we returned to base, we had taken out over sixty tents."

"So, about three hundred fifty or so," Karl calculated, pleased. "Sakura?"

"About the same," she replied.

The door to the suite opened and Manas strode in. "Well?"

"Possibly around seven hundred," Karl answered.

Manas's eyes bolted wide. "My God. You took out seven hundred of them?"

"That's what it adds up to. Hopefully once the sun comes up, it'll be more." He stretched and covered a yawn. "Get some rest folks. We still have a battle come daylight and once Cyril sees what happened, he's gonna be pissed."

Annabeth and Raquel lingered, hoping to encourage Karl to come along, but their not so subtle efforts were thwarted when Gwen interspersed herself between them and Karl. With a defeated sigh, the two women meandered out and back to their rooms.

"You are so brave," Gwen gushed, placing a hand on his chest.

Karl felt his heart skip as devotion and desire suddenly consumed him.

Manas saw the reaction to her touch. "My Lady," he gently reproached. "He needs to be focused on what lies ahead."

Karl gave him a puzzling glance. "What're you talking about?"

"I'm talking about tomorrow's battle," he answered. "I plan on getting what sleep I can up on the wall walk. Perhaps you should join me."

"He can get better rest here," Gwen said, coming to his defense. "You can get better rest in your own bed. Nothing will happen until the mist burns off."

"I accept no guarantees," Manas replied, defeated. "Tomorrow, as soon as it is clear enough to maneuver, Cyril will attack."

"I think he may be right," Karl quietly offered. "I need to be there when Cyril discovers what happened tonight. We need to see what changes he's likely to make." He grinned at the thought of Cyril's anger and frustration at losing so many warriors.

Gwen gave him a pout then nodded. "You're right of course. We need to win this war. The sooner, the better."

"Your command regarding Cyril?" Manas asked. "Dead or alive?"

Gwen's face tightened. "Dead."

Chapter 7

Karl spent an uncomfortable night on the wall walk, despite the thick blankets and mattress, courtesy of the garrison supply sergeant. His mind was too preoccupied to let him sleep, though he did doze some. Despite the warmth of the night, the dampness of the mist seemed to soak through his clothing. He was up and eating breakfast just as the dawn's brightness began illuminating the mist.

He was startled when he heard Manas standing next to him, say, "They'll wait for the sun to come out to harass us. While our attention is on them, they'll be probing where the walls are most vulnerable. He'll probably wait until it's dark and use sappers to undermine the wall. Once the wall is breached, he'll send the orcs and trolls to break through the gap and head up towards the city."

"So where's the weakest part of the walls?" Karl asked, wishing he had coffee instead of ale for breakfast.

"Probably the front gate," Manas chuckled. "The foundation rock for the rest of the wall goes down at least twenty feet. If he breaks through the gate doors, we can't stop them." He gazed down at Karl. "Let's hope your plan works."

"We've made a good start last night," he said. "Don't know how many humans he has in his army, but we whittled that faction down a good bit. Once the trolls are dealt with, I think he'll be having second thoughts about his success."

"Let's hope." Manas said, walking away to give last minute instructions and encouragement to his warriors.

As the sun burned away the mist, Manas' army waited by the gates while Karl's team readied their attack in the cottage in the forest.

The mist had thinned when a cry of alarm went up in the forest and Karl could hear the panicked voices of those in fear. Karl wished he was with the team in the cottage so he could see for himself, but he knew his presence was needed here.

Those in the cottage hunkered down, once the shrill cries of terror penetrated the surrounding forest. They watched as men and women raced among the tents of those slain, their faces stunned and scrunched in panic as they vainly tried to understand what had happened.

Into the midst of the scurrying warriors and leaders, Cyril strode purposely, an angry scowl permanently affixed to his face.

"How the hell did this happen?" he barked. When no one replied, he turned to one of his captains, a stern man with little patience for excuses. "How many are dead?"

"We've counted over 700, m'Lord."

"The gods damn it all," Cyril bellowed. "That's almost a third of my army."

"Yes, m'Lord."

"Well?" Cyril demanded staring at the captain.

"It's not magic," the captain replied. "I've had the trackers looking at the prints. Though the prints are mixed and heavily over-trodden, we know they were human."

One of the trackers approached, a middle aged man dressed in deerskin and calf-high boots. His hair was long and wild, and mostly white.

"Beg pardon, m'Lord."

"Yes, Sawluch?" the captain said.

"Far as me and them other trackers can tell, all them prints seem to lead back to there." He pointed to where Raquel and the others lay in wait. "Don't make no sense though. Them brambles is thick with thorns and snags."

Raquel put her finger to her lips, warning everyone as they watched Cyril walk up to the edge of the cottage and reach his hand out to gingerly touch a branch and thorn. From inside the cottage, it looked like Cyril was rubbing a thumb and fingers in the air, just above Wendell's head.

"Cut it down," Cyril commanded.

"Tried that already, we did," the tracker answered. "Every time we cuts it, it grows back thicker.

Cyril's scowl deepened. "This smells of sorcery. Where's Mavie?"

"She's still at Tal Olca," the captain answered.

"What?" Cyril roared. "Damn that woman. I gave orders for her to be here. Why is she still there?"

"If you remember, m'Lord, you had her stay behind to maintain control over your domain while you were on the march," the captain answered, "so that when you return, you are not hindered in your rule."

Somewhat mollified, Cyril stared again at the thick growth. "I still want this cut down. Burn it if you have to."

"Yes, m'Lord." The captain dipped his head.

"Ready the catapults. We launch in ten minutes. I want those projectiles battering the far walls. Focus on one spot. Are the other catapults ready?"

"Yes, m'Lord. We'll set them up and range them first thing as soon as the mist clears."

"Good. I'll be near the gates. Send someone to fetch the orc captain. I don't want them screwing this up."

"Yes, m'Lord."

Raquel and the others exhaled a slow breath as Cyril and the two men walked away.

"We wait until the signal," she whispered, warning them to be patient.

That lasted until a few moments later, when three men walked up, one holding a torch, the other two with falchions.

"Try cuttin' it down," the man with the torch said.

Those inside the cottage closest to the three men scooted away as the falchion swings encroached into the space above their heads.

"It ain't workin'," one of the men complained. "Every time we cut a branch, two grow in its place.

"Hell," the torchbearer snarled. "Lemme see if this works." He stepped forward to thrust the torch into imaginary brambles when Bruno grabbed his hand, jerked him forward and at the same time thrusting a stiletto blade deep into his chest then pushed the man backwards.

The man staggered back, dropped the torch and grabbed his chest before dropping to his knees and rolling over onto his side, dead.

"Gol damn," one warrior blurted as he stutter stepped backwards.

The other warrior kneeled beside the dead man. "He's done killed hisself. Looky that." He pointed to the slender stab wound in the chest, blood flowing out. "Them thorns are killers."

"What we gonna do?" the other man asked, casting fearful glances around at the few warriors still working through the encampment of dead bodies.

"I ain't gonna get myself killed," the other replied. He picked up the sputtering torch and just as he reared back to toss it into the brambles, an elf arrow burst through the branches, piercing his heart.

The other man gasped just before the second arrow found its mark in his own chest.

Had any of their compatriots paid attention, they would have seen three bodies tugged by their feet into the brambles then disappear.

Up on the wall, Karl waited with anticipation. The mist was almost gone and he could see the enemy positioning beyond the walls.

Then he heard it, the command to launch the catapult stones. His anticipation was rewarded when among the first volley were five large stones high in the air, troll tents streaming behind them.

There was a sudden lull in the assault as shouts of anger and fear spilled out through the forest.

Karl leaped down the stairs and strode to where Manas now stood in the front of his warriors, poised to attack. "Let's do it."

Two guards lifted the gate bar and pushed the gates ever wider as the army of Westhaven poured out.

Back at the cottage, Raquel heard the commotion and notched an arrow. "It's time."

The team abruptly materialized out of the brambles and launched their attack. Making quick work of the humans, they forged on to seek out the orcs. Along the way, they smirked and pointed at tent sites where trolls remained forever frozen in stone, some of them still prone on field cots, others looking up when the tents were snatched away. They stopped to destroy more tents, unhooking tent ropes, knocking down tent poles and yanking away the canvas.

While some trolls cowered in fear, others, more aware of what was happening, fought to keep the tents in place, struggling to hold onto the shade and darkness provided. Yet one by one, tents collapsed and the cover removed, and one by one, trolls exposed to the sunlight morphed to stone.

But the team's main objective lay beyond the troll encampment to where the orcs assembled.

The mist had vanished and the sun radiated brightness, causing confusion among the orcs as they fought and argued to find shelter from the sun. Expecting their human allies to fight during the day, they were ill prepared for Raquel's attack. Their attention focused on the army swarming out Westhaven's gates, on the catapults and the protection of their own tents, they were unaware when Raquel and the rest burst into the rear of their camp.

Raquel and Sharyn launched arrow after arrow as the berserker rage filled Dieter, his battle axe swinging in wide swaths, decapitating or dismembering all in his path. Sakura darted in and out of the enemy, materializing as if from the air, her daggers slicing throats or stabbing in the back of necks. Behind them, Lana sent out flare bursts to add to the orcs' disorientation. Annabeth cast a flurry of ice daggers, acid splashes, fire bolts and any other spells she could conjure with indiscriminate abandon. Trailing behind them, Tina and Kendra waited to send healing mana when needed, the remaining members protecting the healers.

They moved in one body, the orcs falling before them. It wasn't until some fifty orcs lay dead that the alarm went up that their rear was being attacked. Despite the effects of the sun, many orcs turned to fight, but were hard pressed as Manas' army was already at their front. Hemmed in on both sides, the orcs fought bravely, but were sorely outnumbered.

The orc battle captain, a hulking monster almost as tall as Dieter, decided that it was time to escape and fight another day. Besides, had he thought it through, he should have let the humans fight it out and then clean up after they destroyed each other. Placing a holding force to delay Manas' warriors, he gathered the rest of the orc army and plunged into the forest only to be confronted by Raquel and the team.

Immediately recognizing the orc as the battle captain, Raquel called out, "The one with the spider tattoo on his neck," and launched a flurry of arrows at him while Sharyn fired at those close by him.

Yet still the captain came on, arrows protruding from his arm and chest. Cursing a loud oath, he raised his battle axe just as Annabeth and Lana joined in a freeze spell, causing him to lock in place, his face an angry scowl as he vainly struggled against the spell. Yet his eyes revealed his fear and anger as Dieter, the blood lust still flowing, leaped forward and swung his axe, neatly severing the orc's head, which remained in place until Annabeth and Lana released the spell and the head fell to the ground followed by the body tumbling over.

Seeing their leader so easily destroyed, the remaining orcs fled for their lives. Raquel and the rest of the team continued chase until Manas' forces caught up with them. By the time they returned to the main assembly area, the battle was over, Cyril's army destroyed.

"This was almost too easy," Sharyn said, walking next to Raquel.

"I know," she agreed. "With the sorceress and druid here," she ticked her head at Annabeth and Lana walking beside them, "we have a distinct advantage. And then there's the benefit of the big guy."

"We're lucky to have him," Sharyn nodded, giving Dieter a pleasant smile.

Hearing the compliment, Dieter said nothing, but smiled. He was thankful to be a part of this team.

"So how'd we do?" Karl asked as the team approached. He stood outside a hastily erected tent. He was spattered with blood, but seemed unharmed.

"No one hurt, killed more than we could count," Raquel answered. She hooked a thumb at the closed tent flaps. "What's up?"

"A certain brother-in-law is suing for peace," he replied, shaking his head. "I pray she has the sense to eliminate him. It would not do us any good if he remains alive."

Raquel noted the 'us' in his statement, but decided to bide her time. Now was not the time to confront him.

The tent flap opened and Manas stepped out. Ignoring Karl and company for the moment, he beckoned one of his captains, a humorless man of efficiency. "Take Lord Cyril to the castle. He is to remain shackled, no matter how much he complains. Let no one talk to him or provide for him. If he needs to take a piss, there will be four guards watching him."

"I understand, General. He is under my watch. I will ensure he is dealt with as necessary and appropriate."

Manas' gaze lingered for a moment. "I want him alive."

"Yes, General, of course."

The man's stoic response caused Manas to smile. It wasn't far to the castle, but in the time it took to get there, Cyril would meet with several unfortunate accidents so that by the time he arrived, he would pray someone would kill him to relieve the pain.

"Good. He's all yours." As the captain entered the tent, Manas turned to Karl. "You and your team were the key to our success. Without you, Westhaven would have fallen. We owe you more than can ever be repaid."

A screen opened up for Karl.

Congratulations: You have completed the Quest - save Lady Gwen's domain of Westhaven from Cyril's armies.

Reward: Unlimited access to supplies, scrolls, potions, and weapons currently in the domain.

Reward: Escort to the Bridge connecting Misted Isle to the next island.

Reward: Reputation: increase from 'Your name sounds familiar' to 'I have heard of you and I am impressed.'

"As agreed," Manas continued, "we will provide you an escort all the way to the bridge to the next island, though in truth, no one in Westhaven has been much farther south than Durness in a long time. Likewise, Cyril's domain ends before one gets to the bridge. Still, we will honor our agreement."

"Thank you," Karl replied. "Let me talk with the team and we'll let you know if we need an escort. "

The tent flap opened and the captain exited followed by two guards then Lord Cyril with his hands shackled behind him then two more guards. Though defeated, Cyril maintained the aura of nobility, fully expecting people to respect his position and title even if they hated him.

"Where is the coach to take me to Lady Gwen?" he caustically demanded.

"We're walking," the captain replied.

"What? You don't expect me to walk all the way there. Fetch my horse." He stiffened as though rooted to the ground until the butt end of a spear jabbed in his back pushed him forward.

"You have a choice, my lord," the captain coldly responded. "You can either walk or we drag you by your ankles behind an ox cart."

"You wouldn't dare," Cyril shot back.

"I would, and I will if you don't start walking." The captain folded his arms and gave Cyril a hard stare.

Cyril stared back at the man, quickly realizing the man fully intended to do as he threatened. Bristling at the insult, Cyril started marching towards the gate, surrounded by the Captain and the four guards.

"I'll meet you back at the castle," Manas said, smiling as he watched Cyril walk away.

Karl and the team started walking back to the cottage, Karl wanting to hear a retelling of their attack. They were standing outside one of the troll tents when a runner came up.

"Your pardon, Lord Karl, but Lady Gwen asks that you attend her."

"Of course," he politely replied. Turning to the team, he said, "I'll catch up with you later."

When he was out of earshot, Ross said, "She has him on a string."

"That she does," Annabeth mumbled, watching Karl in the distance, walking as one without a care, chatting amiably with the runner.

"Don't we need to do something?" Ross asked.

"Like what?" Conrad retorted. "She's some sort of sorceress herself. None of us here is strong enough to break the spell."

"So why not do what I suggested in the first place?"

"Leave him?" Conrad demanded.

"Why not? Like you said, it's not like we can do anything about it."

"He just needs to be away from her for a bit then he'll see what's going on," Raquel reassured them. "C'mon, let's get back to the castle."

"Speaking of that," Ross interrupted. "How'd you guys get behind the enemy here? There's only one gate and I was there when it opened."

"There's a secret passage," Wendell said followed by an "Ouch," when Conrad kicked him. "What was that for?"

"It's not a secret if everyone knows about it," Conrad snapped.

"Secret passage?" Ross inquired with bright eyes followed by an immediate frown. "Why wasn't I told about it?"

"It's called 'need-to-know,'" Raquel answered. "You had your mission with Manas' army. Had you been captured, you honestly knew nothing about it and thus could not reveal its location."

"Well the battle is over and the war is won, so where is it?" he asked, his irritation at being left out obvious.

"It's complicated," Annabeth explained. "There's another gate in another part of the wall," she said, reasoning that she wasn't lying because she didn't say where the gate was and which wall.

"Where?"

"Slow down, Ross," Raquel chided, "and let her finish."

"The gate has a spell on it that allowed us to go through without being seen," Annabeth said. "That's how we got behind them."

"Where is it?" Ross again asked.

Annabeth pointed to the north. "Far enough away to be unnoticed by Cyril's army. If we're here long enough, I'll show you."

"Thanks."

"C'mon then," Raquel urged. "Let's go."

Their walk back was relaxed, almost lazy. Passing through the gate, they accepted the praise and appreciation of Westhaven's warriors. Halfway to the second gate leading to the city proper, they saw a beehive of activity inside it and then something being hoisted up on a pole to the side of the gate.

As they approached, they discovered the grizzly display of Cyril's head jammed on a pole, the visage one of complete shock, the flies already swarming.

"She doesn't waste any time," Conrad intoned, staring up at the gruesome spectacle.

"If someone butchered your sister and flung her over the city walls," Sakura said, "what would you do?"

"Pretty much the same thing," he coldly replied, "except I'd make him suffer to the point that he begged for death. I'd drag out his execution to the point that he'd go insane."

"And how would you do that?" Brad asked, interested.

"I'd mess with his mind. Tell him he's going to be hanged, drag him to the scaffold, put the noose around his neck then pull the lever but have the gallows built in such a way that he only drops something like a foot or two so that he doesn't hang."

"My God, that's evil," Kendra said, concerned about this undiscovered side of Conrad.

"There's more," he said as they walked on. "Then I'd tie him to a stake and have an archer ready to shoot him in the heart. I'd make sure Cyril knew this was the end for him and that the archer had but one shot to do the job. Of course the archer would miss the heart, but hit him in a non-vital part of his body. I'd take him down from the stake, bandage him up and tell him we're going to do it again the next day. But," he said with a wicked smile, "nothing would happen the next day and the day after. On the third day, he'd be dragged out for another shot and the same thing would happen. This time he might be shot in the thigh."

"That's torture and cruel," Kendra chided.

"Damn right it is," he countered. "The question was, what would I do to someone who hurt my family, or someone I love?" He narrowed his gaze at her, "and that includes you."

Kendra blinked as she absorbed the revelation. Part of her was repulsed by the acts of torture while another wondered if she would act the same way. Yet another larger part reveled in this declaration of his love. Her response was thwarted when Raquel interrupted.

"Now that we've satisfied the quest, it's time to move on. Everyone get your gear ready to move out."

Once inside the castle, while the others headed to their quarters, Raquel grabbed Annabeth by the elbow and guided her up the stairs.

"We need to check on a certain Viking."

When they entered Gwen's apartment, Manas was still there, his sour demeanor telling them he was not happy about something.

"I'm so glad you're here," Gwen sweetly said as the two women entered. "I think that it's important you hear it directly from him."

"Hear what?" Raquel asked, masking her alarm.

There was a pause before Karl quietly said, "I've decided to stay."

"You're what?" Annabeth exclaimed, her jaw dropping.

"I'm staying," Karl replied with a nonchalant shrug.

Nonplused, Annabeth wordlessly stared at him, until Raquel reached over and gently pushed her jaw up to close her mouth.

"What are you going to do?" Raquel asked.

"He's going to rule with me," Gwen answered for him.

"What about the bridge and the next island?" Annabeth demanded. "What about the team, our team?"

"You'll just have to move on without him," Gwen said.

"How about letting him answer the questions," Annabeth sourly complained.

"Like she said," he again shrugged. "You'll just have to get along without me."

"This is crazy," Annabeth blurted. "You just can't –"

"We're happy for you," Raquel interrupted.

"What?" Annabeth jerked her head around to glare at her friend.

"We're happy for them, aren't we," Raquel repeated, giving Annabeth a 'just-play-along-with-me' look.

"Uh, sure, I suppose," Annabeth unconvincingly replied.

"C'mon then," Raquel said. "We better start packing. We're leaving in a day or two." She turned to Gwen. "Do you mind if we come back later tonight or tomorrow morning to say our goodbyes?"

"Of course not," Gwen sweetly smiled in triumph.

"You bring the wine?" Raquel returned the smile.

"I have a special bottle I've been saving," Gwen answered.

Once outside the suite and out of earshot, Annabeth leaned in and whispered, "What's your plan?"

"We need to see a certain sorceress," Raquel said.

"Kamdyn? We don't have time and besides, how are we going to ever find her? I haven't a clue where she lives."

"I'm a ranger, remember?" Raquel grinned. "I paid attention the time Manas took us to see her."

"We never got past the columns," Annabeth replied, vaguely remembering the location, "when Manas changed his mind or something like that and we returned back to the castle. I was rather disappointed because I had wanted her to teach me how to use my magic."

"Maybe she'll give you some pointers now," Raquel replied, leading them along the same path that Manas had followed. In short order they stood before the door in the wall. Opening the door, they slipped past and descended the snaking path to the set of broken Corinthian columns.

Imitating Manas, Raquel walked in between the two top halves and paused by the right pillar, pressing her palm against the cold stone.

A moment later, a voice crooned, "Welcome Lady Ranger and Sorceress Annabeth. I've been expecting you. Please come in."

Stepping through the empty space between the pillars, the two women disappeared, emerging on the pathway leading to a Kamdyn's beautiful two story home of white granite. Ignoring the surrounding gardens and fountains, Raquel led the way to the front door where the necromancer stood in the doorway.

"Welcome, my friends." Kamdyn wore the same flowing dress of black silk, undulating in sensual billows, emphasizing her voluptuous body.

Annabeth felt a sudden surge of lust and she startled at the emotion, shaking her head in a vain attempt to clear her thoughts. Then just as quickly, the growing lust faded and she felt like herself once again.

Kamdyn smiled mischievously at Annabeth. "Sorry. It's become a habit, though you look like you could be fun, as do you," she added, staring intently at Raquel.

Raquel felt suddenly exposed and cleared her throat. "We need your help."

"Yes, I know," she chuckled. She stood to the side and waved them in, following behind them as the door closed by itself.

Kamdyn led the way through the foyer and into a large reception room. A couch and two chairs facing the couch were positioned close to the windows. In between the couch and chairs facing the windows was a low table with trays of food and wine.

"Please sit," Kamdyn said. Her voice was soft, though sensual.

As Raquel and Annabeth sat on the chairs, Kamdyn positioned herself on the couch, tucking her long legs beneath her. Reaching for a sweet roll, she smiled seductively at them. "Please help yourselves. I'd hate to see all this food go to waste."

Annabeth reached for the carafe of wine and filled the three crystal glasses. "Like Raquel said, we need your help." She stood up and handed a glass of wine to Kamdyn.

"Your Viking is too enchanted with the lady of the castle?" Kamdyn casually declared.

"Yes. How did you know?" Annabeth sat down and picked up a sweet roll.

"I know everything that goes on in the castle," she replied. "For instance, I know your precious Viking has decided to remain here in Westhaven, at least for the time being until Gwen decides to relocate to Durness where she will rule as queen."

Raquel noted a hint of envy in Kamdyn's reply. "Will you continue to live here?"

"I have no choice," she answered. Her mask of amiability momentarily vanished.

"Why not?" Annabeth asked.

"It's complicated," Kamdyn replied. When the two women simply stared at her, waiting, she explained, "I'm a known necromancer. You can imagine how people react when they learn who I am."

As Raquel nodded in empathy, Annabeth blurted, "What's the real reason?"

Kamdyn flashed a hard stare at her then relaxed. "I've been banished here."

"By whom?"

"By the former king."

"Why?" Raquel asked, her interest rising.

Kamdyn paused. "Because I'm a succubus."

"Just like Gwen?" Annabeth intoned.

Kamdyn smiled. "Yes, just like Gwen."

Silence settled as Raquel studied the sorceress. Leaning back, she sipped her wine, staring at Kamdyn over the rim of the glass. "You all are related, aren't you, Gwen, you, and the woman who was queen. Sisters or cousins, right?"

"Very good," Kamdyn nodded in recognition. "We are sisters."

"Then why are you stuck here?" Annabeth asked.

"A long story," Kamdyn sighed, "but I'll give you the short version. Yes, we are three sisters. Briet was the oldest then Gwen then me. We were all born succubi with powers to induce desire at will. Mine are the strongest. However, father kept our powers secret, especially when time came to find a bride for the king's son. As Briet was the oldest, she was the designee to woo Coirthan. Obviously she was successful and became queen. Father and Briet then managed to get Coirthan to name Gwen as viceroy for Westhaven."

"I can imagine how that happened," Annabeth chuckled.

Kamdyn smiled in return. "Men are so easy."

"Then what happened?" Raquel interrupted.

"Once Gwen was appointed as viceroy, father set about finding a position for me, not only to add family influence, but to counterbalance Cyril. Unfortunately, Coirthan discovered our secret."

"How?" Annabeth asked, intrigued.

Kamdyn waved away the question. "That's another story for another time. The result was that when he learned that I had the strongest powers, he threatened to ruin us. Father then threatened to expose certain, um, royal secrets that Briet had coaxed out of Coirthan. The bottom line was that in exchange for exiling me to this place," she waved her hand at the surroundings, "Briet would stay as queen and Gwen would remain as viceroy."

"Leaving you stuck here while they enjoyed life," Raquel observed, noting the subtle resentment.

"Yes."

"But if Gwen is now queen, shouldn't that release you from here?" Annabeth said.

"Yes, it should…"

"But?"

"There is more to this story than I am willing to reveal," Kamdyn stated. "For now, suffice it to say that I am waiting for Gwen to move to Durness before I make my move. However, if I am to be successful, I can't afford for her to have your Viking by her side. So, you see, we all benefit from his departure."

"So what do we do?" Annabeth asked.

Kamdyn turned a discerning eye towards her. "You already have part of that capability as a sorceress."

"I do?" she blinked in surprise.

"How many spells do you have?"

Annabeth rolled her eyes. "Something like over 150 of them."

"Have you experimented with each one?"

"Uh... not really. I'm still trying to figure out how to remember them all. Some of them make no sense, like an air bubble or mud ball. What's the purpose of those?"

"They have their place," Kamdyn smiled. "For now though, you really ought to concentrate and practice those spells you think you will use. I can think of two in this instance that will help us. The first is Implant Idea."

Raquel leaned forward, her eyes bright. "What does that do?"

"It places an idea into another character," Annabeth answered, looking at Kamdyn. "But she's a level 20, and what idea am I supposed to implant?"

"It doesn't matter if she is a level 20 or 50," Kamdyn replied, "though the higher the level, the greater likelihood of resistance to the spell. And then if she has a resistance to suggestion spell, it would counter-balance the Implant spell."

"This gets us nowhere," Annabeth complained. "Does she have a resistance to suggestion counter spell?"

"Not that I know of," Kamdyn slyly answered.

"Oh," Annabeth said. "So what idea do I implant?"

"That she's very very tired," Kamdyn said, "followed by the second spell, Sleep. The two spells together will cause her to fall asleep right where she is. As an added precaution," she held up a small vial containing an orange liquid, "add this to the wine. With the two spells and the sleep potion, she should remain asleep for at least six hours, enough time for you to put some distance between you."

"What about Karl?"

"I suggest you put the potion into his drink also. Her sway over him is clouding his judgment and he will be reluctant to leave. Use that big barbarian named Dieter to help you carry Karl away. He'll wake up far enough away to wonder why he was drugged in the first place and with a clearer mind."

"Perfect," Annabeth chortled, standing. "C'mon," she said to Raquel then abruptly frowned for Raquel had likewise stood, but was in the process of slowly unbuttoning her shirt, her eyes in a sensual gaze at Kamdyn. Annabeth looked at Kamdyn who was smiling at her.

Raquel was midway spreading her shirt wide and exposing her breasts when Annabeth angrily exclaimed, "We don't have time for this."

The spell broken, Raquel blinked then jerked her head down to see her exposed chest, quickly covering up. Her lips pursed, she seethed, "I can see now why you were exiled here."

"Oh don't be angry with me," Kamdyn teased. "I was just playing. Besides, you have a gorgeous body. Pity you're leaving."

"We're not leaving soon enough," Raquel mumbled, buttoning up her shirt.

Once outside on the path away from the house, Raquel complained, "Why didn't you stop her when you saw what was happening?"

"I didn't even know it *was* happening," Annabeth explained. "She was looking directly at me and the next thing I see is you unbuttoning your shirt. I wish I had that kind of power."

"What? Make people take their clothes off?" she sourly admonished.

"Yes, I mean no, well, yes, in part," Annabeth awkwardly replied. "I mean, to have the ability to focus on more than one person at the same time. Think about it. She was talking to me while she was manipulating you."

"Well maybe the next time you can be the one undressing," Raquel said as they emerged between the columns.

Annabeth thought for a moment then grinned. "That might be fun."

Raquel shot her a stern glare then abruptly laughed. "You are so bad. C'mon. We got a Viking to rescue."

Annabeth, Raquel, Karl and Gwen stood in the outer room of Gwen's suite. Gwen held Karl's hand with both of hers. A tray with a carafe of wine and four glasses sat on the low table by the hearth.

"We can't stay long," Raquel said. "Just wanted to say our goodbyes."

"Glad you're not too upset," Karl said.

"We understand," Raquel smiled. "You have a lot of potential right here. Might as well take advantage of it."

"Glad you see it that way." Karl smiled.

"We'll miss you," Gwen said with a sincere smile.

"Is the wine poured?" Raquel asked.

"Not yet," Gwen replied.

"I'll do it," Annabeth volunteered, walking over to the table and carefully pouring the wine into the four glasses.

As Annabeth poured the wine into the fourth glass, Raquel turned her head away from Annabeth to stare at the tapestry on the opposite wall. "I don't remember the colors in that tapestry being so vivid."

Gwen and Karl both turned their heads to gaze at the tapestry while Annabeth quickly poured the contents of the sleep potion into two wine glasses.

"That was here before I arrived," Gwen said, staring at the hunting scene of several ladies on horses giving chase to a fox. "It really doesn't do much for me so I'll be leaving it here when I, I mean when 'we,'" she squeezed Karl's hand, "move to Durness."

"Would you give me a hand here, Raquel," Annabeth called out.

Karl was about to walk over to help only to be restrained by Gwen, and Raquel cutting him off. As Annabeth handed two glasses to Raquel, she tapped the side of one with her forefinger and ticked her head at Karl and Gwen. At the same time, she cast the Implant Idea spell, noting with satisfaction Gwen's yawn and the blinking of suddenly tired eyes.

Raquel handed a glass to Gwen as Annabeth came up and gave a glass to Karl.

"Here's to the future," Raquel said, holding up her glass in a toast.

The four raised and clinked their glasses.

"May you achieve what you desire," Raquel again toasted, followed by another toast, and yet another.

When the final toast was proposed, Annabeth cast the sleep spell just as Gwen took a deep swallow of wine.

"Suddenly I'm really sleepy," Gwen slurred.

"Probably from all the excitement of these past days," Raquel offered.

"Most likely from all the activity in the bedroom," Annabeth teased.

Gwen replied with a weak grin, handed her wine glass to Raquel, and made a drunken bee line towards her bedroom door, completely ignoring everyone else in the room. Flinging the door open, she stumbled the last few meters to the bed, climbed up and promptly flopped face first onto the pillows.

Karl stood in place, mutely watching Gwen teeter away. Staring down at the remnants of wine at the bottom of his glass, he said, "Man, what's in this stuff." He started for the bedroom, glass in hand, then stopped and stared through the open door at the Queen of Montgrec sprawled on the bed. A sudden yawn overtook him and he resumed his march, ending up draped on the bed next to Gwen.

Annabeth was already across the room to the suite's door by the time Karl was asleep. Yanking the door open, she poked her head out to see Manas and Dieter amiably chatting with the rest of the team.

"C'mon," she urged.

Manas closed and bolted the door behind them when the last one entered then joined Annabeth and Raquel in the bedroom next to the bed.

"She's going to be mad at you when she wakes up," Raquel warned.

"It had to be done," he said.

"What are you going to tell her?" Annabeth asked.

"I'll tell her the truth," he firmly stated then slyly smiled, "that I was standing outside talking to the group when she fell asleep."

"And after that?"

"I'll have to think of something else," he shrugged then handed her a folded parchment. "You better get going before she wakes up. Here's a map of the rest of the kingdom. I don't know what's at the other end of Cyril's domain, so you're on your own after that. Stick to the main road and move quickly. I figure you should have a good half-day head start before she sends someone to drag him back. With luck, you should be beyond her reach by the time you leave the far borders."

"Thank you," Annabeth said. "We need one last bit of help. Though we've been through the tunnel a bunch of times, I didn't really pay attention to the doors and turns in the tunnel."

"I did," Raquel interrupted.

"I'm coming anyway," Manas replied, "just to make sure. Let's go."

They stepped back as Dieter moved in, grabbed Karl's arm and lifted him up onto his shoulder.

"I'm ready," Dieter said, shifting the Viking's weight for comfort.

Manas led the way, marveling that Dieter kept the pace, despite the added weight. Half an hour later they stepped through the door in the cottage.

"I'd forgotten about the mess we made," Annabeth said, gazing at the surrounding tents and dead bodies of what had been part of Cyril's army.

"We'll burn the bodies once we collect any useful weapons and valuables," Manas said by way of explanation. "And the catapults are a nice addition to the army." He walked with them to the edge of the cottage. "Your group is about half a kilometer beyond the outer walls, on the main road heading towards Durness. I recommend you halt only while the mist is active. Good luck... and thank you. We would not have been successful without your help."

He stood to the side and waited until they had all passed by then waved as they zigzagged their way around the campsites and finally disappeared. With a slow deep breath, he retreated back through the tunnel, rehearsing what he was going to tell Gwen.

Raquel led the group through the forest with practiced ease, passing the numerous trolls all turned into stone statues, emerging farther south from the main gate where it seemed not all that long ago they had entered. They maintained a steady pace and soon enough saw Ross impatiently standing next to a wagon, a large draft horse harnessed in front. The rest of the teams stood in the forest edge close by.

"About time you got here," he fussed. "I've had a hard time explaining why I was just waiting here." He frowned at Karl as Dieter hefted him into the wagon. "What's his problem?"

"A certain somebody wanted him to stay here," Annabeth sweetly replied, "and we're making sure he comes along."

Ross shook his head with disdain. "Whatever. Why not just leave him here. He was happy enough."

Raquel glared at him. "That's not the way we operate. He was under a spell and couldn't do anything to stop it."

"Like I said," he shrugged. "He was happy enough. What he don't know won't hurt him."

"Remind me to apply the same principle to you when you're in trouble," Raquel said. She turned to the group. "We ready?"

"Who made you boss?" Ross challenged.

"We all did," Dieter growled. "She's second in command. If you don't like it, you're free to stay here."

Ross held up his hands in defeat. "Down big guy. I was just asking."

"We're wasting time," Annabeth pointed out. "We need to get moving."

"Why all the secrecy and rush?" Ross asked.

"Because when the queen finds out he's gone, she's not gonna be happy," Conrad intoned. "Now can we get going?"

He climbed up onto the wagon and reached down to help Kendra up. Wendell followed suit with Tina.

When Conrad saw Ross' cocked eyebrow, he curtly explained, "We're dwarves, remember? Our feet don't cover as much ground as fast as you do. While we can march just as far as any of you, if you want to make time, you best let us ride." He then climbed into the driver's seat and took hold of the reins then patted the place next to him for Kendra to sit.

"Let's move out," Raquel commanded.

The road to Durness was well travelled and by the time the sun was at midday, they had put almost four hours of distance between them and Westhaven. Had they known that the sleeping potion Kamdyn gave to Annabeth was more placebo than spell, their confidence might have faltered. Coupled with that fact was Gwen's own strength and protection against spells reduced the effect of Annabeth's spells and what should have been a six hour sleep lasted but three hours. When Gwen awakened and discovered the plot, her wrath unfurled.

Knowing that he would be the first target, Manas had put his affairs in order, designated his successor and calmly waited for the guards to arrest him. A knock on the door to his apartment in the castle alerted him that his time as commander of Westhaven's army was about to end. He opened the door to four apologetic guards.

"I'm sorry, General," the sergeant, a middle aged wiry man, said, "but the Queen has sent us to escort you to her quarters."

Manas held out his wrists to be shackled.

The sergeant hesitated. "I can't do that to you, General. Your word that you will cooperate is enough."

Manas gave the man a respectful nod and smile. "Thank you, Sergeant Tyril. You have my word."

Manas led the way through the hallways to Gwen's suite, the guards sent to arrest him falling in behind. He was startled to see Kamdyn approaching from the other end of the hallway, the four guards sent to arrest her surrounding her like devoted puppies.

"Good to see you, my friend," she said with a smile.

"Good to see you too," he answered, "or should I say, surprised to see you. How long has it been since you roamed these halls?"

"Three years," she replied with a sigh. Pausing before the door, she leaned closer to him and while the door guard knocked, she said, "My sister is rather angry that we helped her lover escape. I fear I may be spending a lot more time in my prison."

The door opened and the two were ushered in, the two sets of guards tumbling in behind them.

Two hours past midday, Karl began to stir then finally sat up and yawned, scratched his head and frowned as he looked around.

"Well good morning sleepy beauty," Conrad teased. "Nice of you to join us."

"Where are we? Why am I riding in this wagon? How long have I been asleep?" He cracked his neck as he took in the surroundings. The vista had opened up to rolling hills covered in neatly ordered farm fields surrounded by low stone walls and small groves of fruit trees.

"We're about six hours out of Westhaven," Conrad answered. "You're riding in this wagon because that was the only way we could get you away from her. And third, you've been asleep for about six hours."

Karl licked his lips and shook his head. "The last thing I remember is drinking wine in Gwen's suite."

"She had your number, lover boy," Conrad chuckled.

"What do you mean?"

"He means that you were under her spell," Annabeth said dropping back when she saw that he was awake. "You know she's a succubus, right?"

"Yeah, sure," he replied, "but she promised she wouldn't do that to me."

Annabeth gave him a stare that said he was dumber than a box of rocks. "Puh-lease. I can't believe you fell for that line. Actually I can, because not only did you swallow the hook, you ate the entire fishing pole."

"What are you talking about?" Karl's frown deepened.

"Dude," Conrad chimed in. "You told us that you were going to stay with Gwen and rule with her."

"What?" Karl blurted. "That's crazy. Why would I do that?"

"Because, lover boy," Annabeth cooed, "she used her succubus powers to persuade you that you wanted to stay. Do you remember Raquel and me having a glass of wine with you and Gwen in her apartment in the castle?"

"That's pretty much the last thing I remember."

"Do you remember what you told us the day before?"

Karl thought for a moment then shook his head. "I don't remember anything of what was said."

"Do you remember the battle?" Conrad joked.

"Yes, I remember that," he huffed.

"Here's the short and sweet of what's been happening since we arrived in Westhaven," Annabeth said as Raquel slowed down to walk alongside the wagon. "Gwen healed Carole. We traded her healing for the quest to save Westhaven from Cyril's armies. During our stay here, you and the little tart, also vixen and succubus, by the name of Gwen, became rather intimate, so much so that you had us worried, rightfully so, that she was using her succubus powers on you. You, Mister Clueless, went right along with her. Thankfully, with the help of Manas and a certain sorceress named Kamdyn, we were able to drug you and kidnap you to bring you back to your senses. And here we are, or rather you are, riding in a wagon, escaping the evil clutches of a woman who wanted you all to herself, preventing you from not only leading the elite team of players, but of crossing the first bridge."

Karl sheepishly looked at Annabeth then Raquel. "That bad, eh?"

"That's just the good parts," Raquel smiled.

"What's the plan?" he asked, climbing out of the wagon to walk alongside the two women. He did another glance around the wagon, noting who was where. Sakura and Ross were at point with the remainder arrayed around the wagon.

"We're headed towards Durness," Raquel answered. "We turned down the offer of an escort due to the fact no one in Westhaven had even been farther south than Durness, and more importantly, we didn't want to be slowed down by having to deal with an escort."

"Map?"

"Here." Anticipating his request, Raquel handed him a folded map from one of the merchants in Westhaven. "This one's better than the others we have."

Karl opened the map while he called up his screen, tapping the map button to compare. After a moment of examining the two maps, he complained, "Why is our computer map so inferior to this one? All it shows is the towns we've been through, where we're headed and the old 'you-are-here' arrow."

"Yeah, I know," she nodded. "I think it's done on purpose so that we have to use the NPCs to help us achieve our quests. At least that's what I came up with."

"I suppose," he said, turning his attention to the map in his hand. "According to this, we're about two-thirds of the way to the bridge."

Annabeth chuckled at him. "You missed something important when you checked for the map."

"What?" He pulled the screen back up, scrutinizing the map. "I don't see anything unusual."

"That's because it's not on the map."

"So where is it?" he said, shaking his head, already tired of the game.

"What level were you when we came to Westhaven?"

"Level 6," he replied then blurted, "I'm a level 9 now."

"So are the rest of us."

Karl looked at the rest of his stats, noting the marked rise in leadership and strategy skills. His mana and XP were both over 100. Scrunching his face, he wondered again what it all meant. He thought he understood what mana was, but it still seemed confusing. Why was it important? Health he could understand. Mana? As far as he understood it, it had to do with magic, but his magic skill was still frozen so what did it matter how much mana he had?

Gazing at his other stats, he struggled to make sense of it all. From what they told him, he would lose health and mana if he was wounded in battle, and if he lost all health and mana he would die then respawn and regain his health and mana. It was all too confusing, especially as he hadn't so much as received a scratch in all the skirmishes he'd had. What was the purpose of having health and mana if he could keep regaining them once he respawned?

He looked at the two women and thought about asking their input, but quickly realized they were as ignorant as he was. In fact, no one on his team had ever gamed before, which was either good in that it gave them all equal footing, or it was crazy because they were all equally ignorant.

Finally, he gave thoughts to his questions. "Can anyone tell me what all the stats mean? Like, what does it matter how many points I have in a certain skill?"

"I think I have an answer," Annabeth replied. "It has to do with what you can accomplish. Take me for instance. I'm a Level 1 sorceress. I've got something like 165 spells, which I'm still trying to figure out what to do with. But some spells have no points in them because I haven't used them. Others, like my fireball spell, have more points in them because I've used them and my skill with them has improved, so the more I use it, the better I get and the more points I get so that when I use it again, it's a more effective spell. At least that's what I can figure out so far."

Ross meandered back, a look of puzzlement creasing his face. "I feel a disturbance in the force," he said.

"Like what?" Karl said with a grin at the reference.

"Something's just not right," he glanced up at the afternoon sky and pointed. "A few minutes ago, several birds flew by here, rather quickly."

"So?" Karl replied while Raquel's ears perked up.

"I tried using my 'Call Animal' spell, but they ignored me. I know I may only have level one spell skills at the moment, but I've been able to call down birds and hawks before."

"Which way were they heading?" Raquel asked.

"That way," he said pointing south, "towards Durness."

"Maybe they were out of range," Karl opined.

"No," Raquel said, her eyes fierce. "It's her. She's sending messages to Durness."

"Gimme a break," Karl moaned. "Why the sinister plot. Maybe it's just a couple of birds flying too high and they just happen to be heading south. Talk about conspiracy theory."

"You don't know her, like we do," Raquel solemnly said. "She'll stop at nothing to get what she wants."

"You're making something out of nothing," Karl objected.

"Even if I am," she answered, "it wouldn't hurt to be on our guard when we get there."

"At this pace, we're not getting there until tomorrow," he said. "We need to find a place to spend the night."

"We passed through three small villages and a larger town already, so we're about right here," Raquel said, pointing on the map in Karl's hands. "The next town is Brynford. I figured we'd spend the night there."

"Works for me." They walked in silence for a while. Ross wandered back to his place at point.

Once Ross was out of hearing, Karl turned to Raquel then Annabeth and back to Raquel. "Thank you for saving me," he whispered with heartfelt gratitude.

"Any time, lover boy," Annabeth said, affectionately patting his cheek. "Gotta take care of our own. No man left behind and all that."

"Besides," Raquel smiled impishly, pinching his butt and winking at Annabeth, "she was intruding on our claims."

Brynford wasn't much of a town, perhaps a dozen buildings arranged around a crossroads in the middle of broad farm fields. The road leading to town had a bridge just wide enough for a single farmer's wagon and crossed a creek one could almost jump across, providing one had a good running start.

Initially, the town seemed deserted, until a back door opened and a middle aged woman tossed out a pan full of table scraps into the small garden. She paused when she saw them, giving a friendly wave before disappearing back into the house.

Ross stopped at the edge of the bridge and gazed down at the creek only to realize it was far deeper than first impression and that the water moved rather quickly. Turning to the others, he grinned. "How about we play toss-a-dwarf? You all toss them and I'll get on the other side and catch them."

Conrad reined in the wagon and leveled a long suffering glare at him. "How about we play hunter-sailboat? We'll tie your hands and feet and see how long you can float?"

"I was just kidding. Jeez. Get over yourself," Ross smirked.

"How about you go scout the town while we wait here?" Karl said.

"What's to scout?" he sniffed in disdain glancing around at the few buildings. "I just hope this dump has a tavern."

"We're waiting," Karl said.

"Damn," Ross retorted. "Feeling our oats today? You sleep half the trip here and now it's suddenly 'do this' and 'do that.' You oughta be thankful you're even here. I was all for leaving your sorry ass back in Westhaven."

With a cold smile, Karl narrowed his gaze at him. "I'll ask you one last time. Go scout the town."

Ross returned the stare then shifted his gaze to the others who seemed to be either unaffected by his challenge to Karl's authority or smiling, waiting to see the outcome. Deciding now was the time, he retorted, "Go scout it yourself."

With a sigh and shaking his head, Karl stepped to the side as Raquel notched an arrow in her short bow and drew back the string, aiming at Ross.

"You're going to shoot me?" he mocked. "This is the way you lead? By threatening to kill someone if they don't obey your whims? I don't need this or you. I'm outta here." He was about to turn away when he heard Karl say, "Too late."

The arrow found its mark in Ross' chest, penetrating his heart. His shocked face twisted as the pain shot throughout his body and he dropped to his knees

"You... bastard. You're... gonna... pay..."

Sakura came up from behind him, jerked his head back and slit his throat.

As life sloughed from his body, he turned glazed eyes to give Karl one last hateful glare.

"Never did like the jerk," Conrad mumbled.

"See what he has that you can use," Karl said addressing the group, "before he disappears to respawn."

"He'll go back to Westhaven," Dieter said, "which means he's mad and he knows where we are."

"That's if he changed his respawn spot there," Annabeth said, hoping he forgot and was stuck back in Abeloft or Marbeck.

"We can't count on that," Dieter replied. "We're eight hours out of Westhaven."

"We can make the assumption that she's awake. That's why we saw the birds headed south. She's telling someone somewhere about us," Raquel observed. "Still, she can't send anyone out once it gets dark, and that will be soon enough."

"What about Ross?" Lana asked, looking down at the Ranger. "He's going to want revenge."

"That he is," Karl answered. "I doubt he'll travel alone. My guess is that he'll wait for another player to come along and team up."

A moment later, Ross' body softly fizzled and was gone.

"Let's find a place for the night," Karl said, crossing the bridge.

The largest building in the town turned out to be the tavern with two large bedrooms with ten beds per room. Despite the summer camp type sleeping arrangements, the ale was reasonably good and the food even better.

"They came through here not even a week ago," the proprietor recounted. He was a trim industrious man who owned a farm in addition to the tavern.

"The orcs was with 'em," the serving girl said with a shudder as she placed mugs of ale on the tables. A pretty blond, she looked to be in her late teens. "Never been so scared in my entire life."

"Haven't heard a peep as to what happened since they left," the proprietor said. "You're the first that's come that way since Cyril marched north."

"Cyril's dead and his army defeated," Karl said.

"Thank the gods," the man said with a relieved sigh. "What happened?

"Cyril depended too much on those who need the night to fight," Karl replied.

"And he didn't know that we were there," Annabeth grinned, "especially him." She hooked a thumb at Dieter who was absorbed with Elena and not paying attention.

"Yes, I can well imagine," the man nodded with approval. "Who is he?"

"His name's Dieter," she answered, "Dieter the Berserker."

At the sound of his name, Dieter looked up.

"I have heard of him," the man said, impressed.

"You have?" Dieter said, cocking an eyebrow.

The man turned his gaze to Karl. "You must be Karl the Viking. I am honored that you and your band have chosen my humble tavern to spend the night."

Giving him a friendly smile, Karl asked, "How far is it to Legurn?"

"Another day's journey. You should arrive this same time tomorrow."

Turning his attention to the group, Karl said, "We leave early tomorrow, as soon as we can see the road. We need to make time. So get your rest or whatever, but be ready first thing." Turning to the proprietor, he asked, "What time can we be served breakfast?"

"Whenever you want, m'Lord."

Karl was about to say, 'I'm not a lord,' but decided the title resulted in faster responses and better service. "I want to be finished eating by the time you can see the house next door.

"As you wish, m'Lord."

"Tell me what happened," Felix said, hoping Mister Landon hadn't found out yet.

"Raquel shot and killed Ross," Scott replied with amusement. "Then Sakura finished the job." He slid a thumb across his throat. "It was awesome. Ross had been a pain in the ass from the get go. Karl finally had had enough. He and Raquel and probably the others had to have arranged this beforehand, because no one seemed all that put out. It was like everyone was glad he's gone."

"Respawn spot?"

"Westhaven."

Standing at the window, his arms folded across his chest, Felix gazed out at the golf course on the other side of the Chattanooga River. He watched a golf cart slow down to a stop in the fairway. A man got out, selected a club and lined up for a shot. Felix waited until the swing and hit then followed the ball as it arced in a low trajectory on the other side of the green. With a wistful sigh, he turned around.

"This is indeed interesting news. Raquel unquestioningly takes out one of her own. She's coming along quite well."

"I have to admit," Scott said with respect. "You were right about her, though there is the little fact that she knew Ross would respawn. Would she be as accommodating if she knew he'd never come back?"

"Excellent question. Can we arrange it in the game? Should we arrange it?"

"Not with a player. Well... actually, I suppose we could with a player, the problem would be making sure the other players knew it was final. Unfortunately, that would impact their own trust and morale. I think it would be to our disadvantage to allow that, at least for now. I think what we're doing with molding a team together that obeys orders without qualms is the greater objective."

"I think you're probably right," Felix agreed. "What about Ross?"

"For one, the man is gonna be royally pissed. I figure he's gonna make it his life's mission to get back at Raquel, and especially Karl who ordered the hit."

"Good. See what you can do to help him out. We need to see how Karl deals with players coming after him."

"What's to see?" Scott chuckled. "Karl knows Ross is pissed and he's gonna be on his guard."

"That's why I want you to team Ross up with another group or another player who might have a vendetta against Karl. Karl might know that Ross is out to get him, but he won't know about the others. This will be a good test of his analytical skills.

Scott immediately understood. "I think we might be in a position to make that happen very soon."

"Excellent. What's the update on the bodies?"

"Bodies?"

"The players' bodies," Felix replied.

Scott stared blankly at him a moment before it dawned on him. "Oh, you mean the ones cryogenically frozen?"

"Yes," Felix said, "and the clones. What's the status?"

"Like I told Maggie, there are some that we need to leave alone. Karl for example. He's already a martial arts master, so why change that? Raquel is a marketeer, so we're gonna have to do something about that. It's that way with the rest of them. Some we'll leave as is, others we'll have to use new bodies. What's important, from my perspective at least, is that we give them bodies that closely match what they have now."

"Why?"

"Morale and desire," Scott replied. "Think of the confidence and attitude when you come back and you not only look awesome, but your new body is already trained to perform. You're an assassin in the game and now an assassin in real life."

Felix pondered the idea and raised an eyebrow, yet with an added smile. "So the dwarves become dwarves in real life?"

"Of course not," Scott grinned, "but their rogue skills become valuable."

"So it comes back to my original question: Why not just train the clone from the start? Seems to me to be more effective. That way you get what you want from the beginning."

"I've wondered the same thing," Scott said shaking his head. "But after doing a little deeper research, it's actually more cost effective to do what we're doing, training a killing team within a game. There is nothing like it in real life, so we gain a significant amount of training in a short period of time. Second, using reproductive donor clones, though incurring some initial long term cost allows us to physically train an individual to standards while waiting for the occupant to finalize."

"I still don't see why you couldn't train a clone to act as an assassin or an accountant for that matter."

"That's the point," Scott agreed. "What we need are assassins who obey orders and are good at what they do."

"You can find people like that already, without having to put people into games," Felix countered.

"With respect, Felix, I think you're missing the point," Scott said. "The gaming world is the future. But that aside, look at it like this. Take Karl as an example. IRL –"

"IRL?"

"In real life," Scott smiled though inwardly rolling his eyes, wondering how long Felix would last. "IRL, Karl is a martial arts master. It's taken him years and years to get there. Likewise, he's combat trained and has no problem killing people. He's also a leader. People like him are hard to find."

"So why the charade that he's dying of some incurable disease?"

"Because that's the only way a rational person would allow himself to be placed into a game."

"Why the game in the first place?"

Scott inwardly sighed, concealing a hint of frustration. How could Felix be so obtuse? "Like I said, a game provides us far more parameters and options than real life ever could. Further, it puts together a tight team that can respawn whenever someone gets killed. You can't do that IRL. So what we have here is a failsafe method of training a team to peak efficiency without the trouble of losing members."

"Then what?"

"Once we decide they're ready, we bring them out, they conduct the hit, and we put them back into the game. It's perfect. The target is dead and no one knows where the killers are, because they leave no prints behind and they're safely back in the game where no one can find them."

"Except us," Felix said. "What happens when other players see an entire team disappear and then suddenly reappear?"

"We take them out at the right time."

Felix quietly mused a bit. "What's the status on your personnel strength?"

"Pardon?" Scott frowned, momentarily confused.

"You personnel strength," Felix said. "You've lost another seven this past week to immersion. You've done well counterbalancing the loss with the increase in AI. And I noted that you're already working on redundancy in anticipation of losing more."

"I have to," Scott moaned, "if you want Designers Branch to still be viable."

Felix leaned forward. "You do realize that you are eventually putting yourself out of a job."

"I know." Scott let out a slow sigh. "The AI is advancing so quickly that there is little left for us to do these days other than to see if there are any hiccups in the process."

"Which brings me back to the point of our team, Karl's team," Felix said. "If the rate of immersion continues like it is –"

"We're not the only ones," Scott objected.

"True and you make my point," Felix replied. "If the world as we know it is disappearing, why the need for an assassination team? Why bother?"

Scott shrugged. "I've asked the same question. Despite the 'we need someone behind just in case' response, my take is that not everyone is going to escape into a game. There will be holdouts, those who still fear technology. While AI can protect itself for the most part, there is sure to be some evil genius left behind who will want to manipulate the system and rule the world."

Felix chuckled. "I suppose so." He turned to gaze out across the river again. "Have you thought about your future?"

"You mean, what game am I looking to immerse in?"

"Yes."

"I'm still undecided," Scott wistfully replied. "Choosing only one game for the rest of eternity isn't a choice lightly made."

"I understand," Felix sympathized then turned around. "Thanks for the update. Keep me posted on the status of your department. We'll need to make some tough decisions very soon."

Chapter 8

Legurn was a small town though larger than some of the towns they had wandered through since leaving Marbeck. Often, a town was no more than four or five houses close to each other at a crossroad. Legurn was a veritable city in comparison as it contained almost forty houses grouped around a crossroad.

The town was silent when they passed by the first home and continued up the main road. The only evidence of life was the bouquet of smoke curling out of the chimneys and the occasional rim of light around a window that hadn't shut properly.

In the middle of the town was a larger building with a road sign that creaked in the wind. As the evening was too dark to read it, Karl approached and ran his hand over the engraved letters, trying to feel the name. In the process of fingering a letter, the door opened and light spilled out along with the clamor of tavern revelers as a man in his cups came staggering out, singing a bawdy ditty and laughing. His song abruptly halted when he saw them.

"Is the ale good here, friend," Karl asked with smile.

"Good enough for the likes of me," he replied, still warily regarding them, especially Dieter before his eyes happily settled on the women. "Yer kinda late. Tavern's gonna close in a hour or so."

"Just looking for a place to get something to eat and drink and spend the night."

"He's got 'em enough alright. Why you out so late? You ain't from 'round here."

"No we're not," Karl answered with a quiet chuckle. Though tipsy, the man wasn't drunk enough to be unaware. "Just passing through."

"Where ya headed?"

"South."

"Ain't nuthin much south of here 'cept you be getting' to Cyril's lands."

"Close the damn door," a voice called out from inside the tavern.

Using that as a que, Karl motioned the team forward when the man peered up at him.

"Say, did you see an army of trolls and orcs when you was headed this way?"

"The troll and orcs were sent up to Westhaven," Karl replied, stepping past him. "They won't be coming back."

The hubbub ceased as soon as they entered the tavern as heads turned in unison to stare at them. Karl strode boldly forward to the center of the room.

"My name is Karl the Viking." He watched with satisfaction as heads nodded in recognition. "We've come from Westhaven where Cyril's army is defeated."

A boisterous cheer erupted and the taverner, a short roly-poly man, flapped his arms for quiet. "And Cyril?"

"Dead, his head on a stake at the gates of Westhaven." Cheers again erupted. Calling out above the din, Karl added, "Gwen now rules Montgrec." Though the cheers were not as raucous as before, there were the plenty of grinning faces.

"How do we know what you say is true, Colonel," a voice called out.

There was something in the way the question was asked that caused Karl to cock an eyebrow. It was a man's voice and the tone was that of a sneer. He scanned the room looking for the doubter. He found him leaning back in a chair on the other side of the room, dressed in the black of an assassin. He was well proportioned with coal black hair and a handsome face with a pencil moustache. An elf Ranger and a human sorcerer sat at the table with him. The way the man stared at Karl aroused an immediate dislike.

The room grew quiet as Karl narrowed his gaze on the man. "You know what I say is true because my friends and I were there. We were there when Cyril's army attacked. We were there when Cyril was captured and sent to the castle. We were there when we walked by to stare at his head jammed on a stake, the flies already circling. We joined with the armies of Westhaven and Montgrec to defeat their enemies. We killed trolls and orcs. So where were you?"

Patrons grunted and nodded respect and admiration, waiting for the answer.

"I was here. I had no dog in that fight... Colonel."

The response was a mixture of disapproval and apathy, many thinking he was smart to not get tangled in the affairs of state.

"You keep calling me that. Why?"

"Because you are, or at least once were a Colonel... a Lieutenant Colonel." The man turned to those in the tavern. "Let me tell you about the Lieutenant Colonel here, or as he is known in these parts as Karl the Viking. The Colonel was a battalion commander with the infamous Widow-makers in the Tiwanaku War."

"How do you know about that?" Karl demanded.

The man paused and focused his stare at Karl before replying, "Because I was there." He then addressed those in the tavern. "They were called the Widow-makers because they killed so many men in their prime that an entire generation of children would grow up without fathers. They were called the Widow-makers because they left a smoking path of destruction behind when whole villages were destroyed, crops ruined, livestock slaughtered. They were called the Widow-makers because they had no problem killing children if they thought it necessary."

Karl saw the faces in the tavern change from respect to shock as jaws dropped, and the once friendly smile slipped away, replaced with grim apprehension. He studied the man, replaying the voice and the words when the epiphany hit. He was surprised they would put the man into the game.

"I know you," Karl mused aloud. "I was there at your court-martial when you were found guilty of desertion and cowardice, not to mention espionage and selling secrets to the enemy. I don't know what name you're using now, but then you were called Kevin, Kevin Bristow." A sneer curled the corner of his lips as he turned to the other patrons, lifting an arm and pointing. "This man was a member of my group in a former life. He was a lieutenant at the time, in charge of

281

a special ops team." He turned back to face his accuser yet his voice carried throughout the room.

"This man traded the lives of his team for money. Then, when he decided he'd had enough, he ran away, like the coward he is –"

"That's a god-damned lie," the assassin bellowed, thrusting his chair back and jumping up.

" – leaving his team heading to an ambush that he knew was about to happen. He ran away."

The mood of the patrons changed once again in favor of Karl and Kevin felt it sway against him.

"He's lying," he yawped.

"Because of you," Karl proceeded, "my best friend was captured, tortured and butchered. I ought to kill you here and now." He took a step forward.

"Stop," the taverner cried out, placing his small pudgy body between them. "Please," he implored. "Not in here. I have a fine establishment. If you must kill each other, do it outside."

Karl and Kevin glared at each other, but neither moved, waiting to see who would blink first. Dieter came up beside Karl followed by the others, fanning out in a semi-circle, ready to pounce. While Raquel and the ranger next to Kevin sized each other up, Annabeth cast a Charm Person spell on the sorcerer whose face abruptly morphed from vigilant antagonist to happy-to-see-you when he caught Annabeth's eye.

Scooting his chair back, the sorcerer ambled over to towards Annabeth, giving her a friendly wave.

"Where the hell are you going?" Kevin burst as he watched Annabeth and his supposed ally join up in friendly conversation.

Ignoring him, the sorcerer introduced himself. "I'm Greg." Not as tall as Karl nor physically impressive, he was nevertheless a handsome man in crimson cape and tailored leather vest and leggings, calf-high boots, and he held a staff topped with a low-glowing orb.

Likewise surprised at Greg's sudden change, Karl activated his screen, discovering the sorcerer was a Level 5.

He ran a quick check on Kevin who was a Level 6 and the other Ranger at Level 5.

Using Annabeth as impetus, Raquel walked over to the Ranger. "I'm Raquel."

"Name's Ron," he cautiously replied, casting a sideward glance at Kevin whose stunned glare was still focused on Greg and Annabeth in animated conversation. Seeing Kevin distracted, he scooted his chair back and stood up, which caused Kevin to shift his attention.

"And what the hell are you doing?"

"I'm talking to Raquel here," Ron explained.

"Sit down," Kevin ordered.

Ron's lips pursed in irritation yet he waffled as he stood there.

"I'd think twice about trusting him," Karl admonished. "Been there, done that, got friends killed. All he cares about is himself. When he feels you're expendable, he'll jettison you like he did all his friends, those who trusted him."

Ron turned to Kevin. "Were you really court-martialed?"

Kevin's nostrils flared as he retorted, "It was all lies. They needed a scapegoat for their crimes."

"So you *were* court-martialed," Ron said with a resigned sigh. He moved away from Kevin who quickly realized he had been deserted by his team.

Curling a lip, he glared at Karl. "You son-of-a-bitch. Don't think I've forgotten what you did to me. You better watch your back." Snapping his head to take in the other two, he barked, "Are you coming with me?"

"I don't think so," Ron replied.

Greg, whose fascination with Annabeth had caused him to miss the exchange between Ron and Kevin, looked up and frowned. "What's going on?"

"I'm not with him anymore," Ron explained, ticking his head at Kevin. "Do what you want, but I'm no longer part of the team."

"You're welcome to join us," Raquel said.

"Thanks," he smiled. "Lemme give it some thought."

"Don't take too long," Raquel warned. "We're leaving in the morning."

"You bastard," Kevin snapped.

"Now you see what he's really like," Karl said.

"Why don't you join us too?" Annabeth said to Greg.

Greg looked back at the fuming Kevin, and with a nonchalant shrug, said, "Yeah sure. Why not?"

Kevin's eyes flared and his jaw clenched. "Don't think you're gonna get away with this," he threatened Karl. Spinning on his heels, he bolted out the door.

"Where's he think he's going?" the taverner mused aloud. "It's gonna be mist time pretty soon and if he wanders too far, he ain't ever gonna find his way back here. And him with a room all paid for." He shook his head and wiped his hands on his apron. Looking back at the newcomers, he grinned. "Now. What can I get you?"

The show over, babble in the tavern resumed to normal levels. Karl and the team scooted two tables together and sat down with their newest team members. A number of patrons wanted to know more of what happened in Westhaven and Karl obliged, the others filling in the parts he forgot or left out. By the time their food and ale were served, the tavern was half-full as many folks left to return home before the mist descended. Those who remained either lived next door or had rooms in the upstairs.

"What did he mean," Ron asked, "when he said he wouldn't forget what you did to him?"

Karl swallowed a bit of meat, followed by a sip of ale. "An ops team is more than a family. You not only depend on one each other, you also know each other's secrets, quirks, and dreams. If one member does less than his or her best, it affects the team. Now multiply that by an entire group made up of numerous teams. The unit is like Easy Company of the 506th after Currahee and on into Europe." He looked at their blank faces and realized they hadn't a clue what he was talking about.

Taking another sip of ale, he said, "Sometimes a man is court-martialed even though his intent was noble. I can't think of an example at the moment, but when that happens, though some will shun him, others understand and offer him solace. When Kevin was court-martialed, it was for the most egregious acts against us. He was worse than a traitor. He let his family get killed. Once word spread of his crimes, not only was he shunned, a bounty was put on his head. He needed to pay for what he did."

"What exactly did he do?" Ron asked.

Karl studied him for only a moment, knowing the man was genuinely interested, but he didn't want to resurrect the pain of reliving the memory. He had managed to push it into the far corners of his mind. Now seeing Kevin again made him remember seeing the body parts of what had once been his best friend. The man had been dismembered and roasted alive. The charred flesh was still smoking when he arrived on the scene.

"Let's just say that he sold out his family. He exchanged the lives of his brothers and sisters for money. Then he sold out his country for more money." He leaned back, shaking his head. "I still can't believe that they put him into this game. Who cares if he had some incurable disease? They should've let nature finish the job."

"Why didn't you kill him when you had the chance?" Greg asked.

"He disappeared and after a while we forgot about him, assuming someone had done the job for us." Looking at the two newcomers, he asked, "How'd you guys link up and how long you been here?"

"Been here about a year," Ron replied.

"A year?" Lana exclaimed.

"Yeah, I know," Ron sheepishly replied.

"What about you?" Raquel asked Greg.

"About the same," he lamely shrugged. "Ron and I were some of the first ones put into the game."

"And you're still on this island?" Annabeth said.

"We were in Marbeck about a month when Kevin showed up," Greg explained. "Spent some time taking out some gnolls –"

"And respawned a bunch of times," Ron added, "before we decided to head down to Abeloft. They wanted us to take out some orcs, but even with the three of us, we figured we didn't stand a chance, so we hightailed it out of there and headed down to Westhaven."

"Spiders?" Lana asked. "Did you see any spiders, big huge things?"

"Naw, didn't see any spiders," Ron replied.

"In a house on the way to Abeloft and another one on the way to Westhaven?"

"We stayed in a house on the way to Abeloft and to Westhaven. Both had maps and everything. Kevin felt the places were creepy so we locked the doors and cranked up a fire. Man it felt like I was in a sauna."

"Goblins? Did you encounter any goblins at the second house?" Lana asked.

"None that I remember," Greg answered.

"That's weird," Lana said to the others. "I figured everyone had to go through the same things in the game, same quests, that sort of thing."

"I don't think it works like that," Greg said. "From what I can figure out, there's lots of quests and ways to level up."

"So you came to Westhaven," Raquel interrupted, redirecting the conversation back to their presence here.

"Yeah," Greg said. "And talk about weird. The lady in charge of the place, I think her name was Gwen or Gwendolyn of something like that. Anyway, she gets the hots for Ron here. He starts acting like a teenager in heat around her."

Raquel and Annabeth slowly turned their heads to give Karl a 'sound-familiar' look.

"Anyway, I can see that she must be doing something to him, so when we finally get him away from her for a minute, we beat feet out of town and ended up here."

"You've been here for almost a year?" Raquel said, her mouth gaping open. "What have you been doing?"

"Mostly keeping out of sight," Ron sighed, "especially when Cyril's army came through. We figured if he found out we were here, he would have sucked us into his army."

"How have you managed to survive all this time?"

"We go out hunting for food and bring it back here. There's plenty of deer and boar and stuff like that around here."

"Ron and I wanted to move on, try some quests, but Kevin said to hold still and wait for more folks to show up, figuring we had the greater chance of success with more players."

"Yeah," Greg agreed, rubbing his neck. "Respawning sucks. I don't want to have to do it again. Hurts like hell."

Raquel narrowed her gaze at Ron. "So you staying here or coming with us?"

"Think I'll come with you guys," he said with a smile.

"We have some rules," she said. "The first is that Karl is the undisputed leader. What he says goes. If you don't agree with that then you stay here."

"I'm OK with that," he nodded.

"The second rule is that we take care of each other. We have each other's backs... no matter what. That said, you fail to be a part of the team, we get rid of you. There's no place for those who care more for themselves than the team."

"I think we get your point," Greg interrupted. He then glanced at each of the others. "I can tell what character everyone is, except for you." He looked pointedly at Elena.

"She's an NPC," Dieter said with a tone that brooked no objection. "She was a serving girl in Abeloft and she's with me now, and a part of the team."

"An NPC?" Ron cocked an eyebrow as his jaw dropped as he turned to Greg. "Why didn't we think of that?"

"I didn't think it was allowed," Greg answered. "What happens when you get to the bridge?"

"Who knows?" Dieter shrugged. "Some thought she wouldn't be allowed to leave the tavern, but here she is."

"Damn." Ron shook his head. "All this time..."

"OK folks," Karl interrupted. "We're leaving first thing in the morning, before the mist is totally gone, so get some sleep. While I think about it, change your bind spots to here so that were not stuck back in Westhaven. Meet here in the morning." He pushed his chair away from the table and stood, Annabeth and Raquel likewise stood, sharing a knowing smile.

"I lost track of whose turn it is," Annabeth said.

"Me too," Raquel replied.

"Whose turn it is to what?" Ron frowned.

"Not your concern." With a maternal smile, Annabeth patted his shoulder. "But you can help. Pick a number between one and one hundred, but don't tell us yet." She looked back at Raquel. "The closest one gets him for the night."

"Agreed," Raquel smirked, looking at a confused Ron then a long suffering Karl who simply rolled his eyes and shook his head.

"You have a number?" Annabeth inquired.

"Yes," Ron replied.

"36," Annabeth said.

"75," Raquel announced.

"57," Ron answered. "Raquel is the closest."

"Oh well," Annabeth shrugged with a light hearted smile then patted Karl's cheek. "I get you tomorrow night."

"C'mon lover boy," Raquel said, grabbing Karl's hand. "Let's find ourselves a room. A girl has needs."

"I'm available," Greg piped up, giving Annabeth a hopeful look.

"Not tonight, Sweetheart," she amiably replied. "Besides, I hardly know you and I'm not that kind of girl... at least not yet," she winked.

"You never told me that Kevin had been court-martialed from the Army," Marc said, his arms folded as he stood before Annika's cubicle, which was decorated with super hero bobble-heads and stickers.

"You never asked," she replied.

"Why would I have to ask for information about an individual in our program?"

"I'm just messin' with ya," Annika grinned. She was a petite woman in her early twenties, with curly blond hair. "It was one of those need-to-know things at the time. We figured we needed an additional player that would further Karl's development."

"We?"

"Jackson and me," she answered, leaning back to look around Marc and gaze into now empty cubicle still filled with Jackson's personal trivia. "Miss that crazy man. Not sure I'd want to spent a life time in a harem game, though a reverse harem sounds appealing." She winked at Marc. "Anyway, after him taking out Ross, looks like Kevin was unnecessary."

"How do you mean?"

"We knew Karl could kill folks under orders. We needed him to be able to kill on his own, without remorse. We tracked down Kevin and threw him in the game, projecting that the two would eventually meet."

"Yeah, but Karl already hates his guts, so where's the character development in that?" Marc pointed out.

"Yeah, I know. I said the same thing, but the higher ups said go with it. Thought it was a good idea at the time. Though if you think about it, Kevin is now primed to assassinate Karl. So it all works out in the end."

Marc thought for a moment. "Say... what if we connected Ross and Kevin? That would make it more interesting."

"We're working on it," she replied with a grin.

Marc started to turn away then turned back with a frown. "How did Kevin know it was Karl? It's not like he looks the same as he did in real life. And Kevin was in the game before Karl."

Annika flashed him a wicked grin. "A little birdie told him that Karl was in the game and on the way."

"Huh?" Marc stared at her. "Is that kosher?"

"Kosher or not, it's gonna add some fireworks."

Karl and the team stood outside the tavern, waiting as the mist dissolved in the morning sun.

"Kevin came back last night," Ron said. "Came in when I was getting in bed."

"How do you know?" Annabeth asked.

"His room is next to mine and when he's really tired, he snores."

"We're going to have to watch our backs," Karl mused out loud. "That means we all need to be aware of our surroundings at all times.

Nodding agreement, Greg asked, "What's the plan."

"We head through Cyril's domain as quickly as we can," Karl replied. "At the same time, we need to get you two leveled up higher before we cross the bridge."

"Yeah. I noticed you all are level 9's," Ron said, impressed. "How'd you manage that?"

"By killing orcs and trolls and waging a war with Cyril," Dieter answered, still unimpressed with the two newest additions to the team.

"Yeah, well," Greg said with an embarrassed grin, "our leader felt it better to lay low than work on improving our skills."

"Should have chosen a better leader," Dieter muttered.

"Let's move out," Karl ordered. "Raquel at point, Ron rear security. Keep an eye out. Stay close."

The mist, though still thick, had dissipated enough to see about ten meters ahead as they slowly followed the road out of town, carefully making their way. Since the two new members had lived in the area a while, they reassured the team that the road was safe for a good distance and when the mist finally lifted, they would be able to make good time by staying on the road.

An hour later, the mist had dissolved enough that Karl decided to check on team members only to discover that Ron was missing.

Grim-faced, he called a halt. "I see only two reasons for Ron's absence. The first is that he decided to go back."

"He wouldn't do that," Greg objected.

"I agree, which means that Kevin, who is an assassin after all, is following us and took out Ron."

"Damn him," Greg spat. "That means he's got it out for me too."

"And the rest of us," Karl reminded him. "Remember, not only is he an assassin, but he was trained in special ops." He turned to Sakura. "My thought is that it'll take an assassin to find another assassin."

Sakura gave him a quick nod of understanding.

"Do what you have to do," Karl advised, "but be careful."

"Take him out?"

"If you can. If not, find out where he is. Perhaps we can set a trap."

"Got it." A moment later she was gone.

"Man," Greg acknowledged, "she's good."

"Let's hope she's good enough to find him," Karl said. "Let's move out. Greg, you take rear security."

"Me?" he squeaked. "What about Kevin?"

"What about him?" Karl challenged. "Now that you know he's tracking us, you'll be more aware."

"But...but..." When he saw them waiting on him, he closed his mouth and moved to the rear.

The road dipped back along the coast then swung away towards the mountains, farm fields stretching on both sides. By midday, they had passed several small hamlets when Karl called a halt. Calling up his screen, he pressed the map button to check on progress.

"Looks like we're almost to Cyril's borders. Don't know who's running the place in his absence, but pay attention. We have to get through there if we're gonna make it to the bridge, so no unusual comments or distractions that call attention to us."

An hour later, the road, overgrown from disuse, led into a forest. Raquel signaled a halt at the edge and Karl came up.

"I'd like to try something," she said. "Now that we're entering a forest, there's a greater likelihood of birds and animals. I'd like to see if I can talk some into scouting for us."

"Go for it," Karl readily agreed. Glancing over his shoulder, he said, "I wonder how Sakura's doing."

"She's fine," Raquel reassured him.

Karl circled his finger in the air indicating the entire group then curled his fingers, signaling to follow.

As they proceeded, Raquel took to scouting the sky, finally spotting a hawk and casting a Charm Animal spell. The hawk descended, landing on her outstretched arm. She then cast two spells in quick succession, Talk to Animal and Compel Animal.

Karl watched in fascination as Raquel talked to the hawk whose head twitched as it listened. Waiting until the raptor was again airborne, he walked over to her.

"What did you tell it?"

"I told her that I wanted her to scout out the road ahead of us. She told me that she'd already scanned the area, looking for food and that the forest is not as wide as we think. Once we get to the other side, there's empty land where Cyril had his army chop down trees to make a sort of no man's land between his domain and the rest."

"The hawk told you this?" Karl knitted his brows in disbelief.

"Well," she smiled, "not in so many words, but she was pretty pissed that Cyril had destroyed so much of the forest. She said the road leads to two checkpoints with guards: one on this side of the forest, the other across the no man's land at Cyril's border. After that the road goes through the forest until the next village. It's a good sized town but most of the homes are abandoned. My guess is that once Cyril closed the borders, businesses probably folded and folks had to move where the jobs were."

Though listening, Karl seemed pensive.

Annabeth peered at him. "What?"

"If we're going to make any progress, I'm beginning to think we need to take the shortest route and avoid towns and cities as places where we might get side-tracked."

"What about the mist, and the orcs and goblins and everything else that goes bump in the night?" Raquel said.

"There is that," he nodded in agreement. "My concern is encountering sorceresses and people like that." He shifted his eyes to glance at Annabeth.

"Don't blame me that every woman wants you," she said with a sweet smile.

Karl rolled his eyes and shook his head. "Still, we're gonna need food and supplies. We'll make the decision after we hit the next town."

Ten minutes later, true to the hawk's words, they came to a guard shack where the forest abruptly ended. Raquel called a halt as soon as she saw the shack. A quick scan and a listen told her it was unoccupied.

"They probably left when Cyril's army came through," Karl softly said. Turning to the others, he motioned for them to stay put as he and Raquel, using the building as cover, made their way forward.

The shack was a small one room affair, with two cots, a pantry, and a stove used for both heating and cooking. A propped shutter covered a wide window allowing Karl to observe the long strip of land that separated the two domains. Trees had been hurriedly cut down and only the splintered stumps remained. Opposite them, about 200 meters away, where the road went into the wide expanse of forest was another guard shack with two seemingly very bored guards sitting on their stools tilted against the side of the building. Studying them a bit more, Karl realized they were asleep.

Folding his arms, he let out a soft sigh. "Wish I knew where Sakura was."

"She knows what she's doing," Raquel replied with calm assurance.

"I don't question that. My concern is that she knows where we're going."

"She'll show up soon enough," Raquel replied.

Karl studied the gap between the two guard shacks. "Let's have some fun," he grinned, exiting the shack and waving the others forward.

They were halfway across the no man's land when he called out, "Look alive over there. We're coming through."

The startled guards bolted upright, upending their stools, momentarily groggy as to the sound of the voice for they both looked behind them only to discover that a group with a large berserker, a beautiful sorceress, a gorgeous ranger, a Viking and the others was already upon them.

"Stop right there," one guard commanded, drawing his sword. He was an older man more used to city life than being out here in the middle of nowhere, pleased that he had been left behind when the army marched, but more than irritated that he had been forced to leave his market stall to guard an entry point that had seen little use.

The other guard was even older with a salt and pepper beard and thinning hair. The bushy eyebrows covered lethargic eyes. Sizing up the group before him, his first inclination was to step aside and wave them through.

"Fine guards you are," Karl chastised. "An entire army could have crept across while you two slept."

"Ain't nuthin happenin' since Cyril left," the older guard lamely explained. "We wuz only takin' a few winks."

"Well you better pay attention. Cyril's army was defeated. Cyril is dead. Orcs and trolls are running wild."

Both guards' mouth gaped wide in shock until the older guard scrunched his eyebrows. "Say... how we know yer tellin' the truth?"

"Because we were there," Karl confidently answered. "After defeating the king, Cyril marched up to Westhaven. That's where we helped defeat him. Last we saw, his head was perched atop a pole outside the city walls. Even now, Queen Gwen is assembling the rest of her armies and is headed this way. If I were you, I'd make sure she knew where your loyalties lie."

"What're we gonna do?" the other guard moaned. "We can't leave our post here, otherwise we're in big trouble." He turned to the other guard. "Leastwise I think we'd be in trouble. Whadda you think Dex?"

"Hard to say, Bron. The way I figure, iff'n Cyril's dead and there ain't much o' his army left, what's it matter? Besides, ain't you got a market stall?"

"The ol' lady's working it while I'm here," Bron replied. "T'aint like we're getting' much action anyway. Still, it'd be nice to sleep in m'own bed."

"I don't think abandoning your post would be wise right now," Karl interrupted. "My recommendation would be that you stay put. In a week or two, this area here is going be humming. My guess is that this guard post will most likely be eliminated."

"Hot damn," the older man said, slapping his thigh. "'Bout time. Mebbe the town'll come back now."

Bron studied Karl and the others. "If'n you all was there, why you here now and where you headin'?"

"We're mercenaries," Karl explained. "We've done our job, got paid and now we're heading south for new adventures. Didn't see the sense of simply hanging around in Westhaven or Durness. Where's the closest town?"

"That'd be Berismo," Dex answered, "straight ahead on this road, 'bout a hour. T'aint much there though. Gotta a couple o' taverns and a smithy and such, but most folks is gone to Hillfurt."

"Hillfurt?" Karl said.

"That's where Cyril and anyone important live. He calls it the capital, but everyone knows Tal Olca's the real capital. Been that way long before my granddaddy's great-granddaddy's granddaddy was born."

Bron suddenly frowned. "You say there's orcs and trolls running crazy?"

"Yes, but we killed a good number of them. They were scattered. Again, my guess is that they will work their ways to their own lands and nurse their wounds for a while, but then they will seek retribution for their stinging defeat. Hopefully by then the kingdom will be united."

"How far is it to the bridge from here?" Annabeth interrupted.

"The bridge over the river afore ya get to Berismo?" Bron frowned, wondering what was so important about a simple wooden span across a river. "T'aint far. You'll come to it right afore ya gets to the main gate."

"No," Annabeth corrected herself. "I mean the bridge to the next island."

"Island?" Dex shook his head in confusion. "Don't know nuthin' 'bout no island."

"You don't?" she replied, surprised.

"Nope," he shrugged. "Lived m'whole life right here in Berismo. Not like I needed t'go anywhere else."

"We understand," Karl interjected. "We'd better get going before it gets dark."

"T'aint far," Bron reassured them, pointing down the road.

"Thank you," Karl replied. "Good luck to you both."

By the time Karl and company were out of earshot, the two guards were excitedly discussing business opportunities when Berismo returned to its former glory.

The road to Berismo was sporadically dotted with small tumbled down farm houses, the forest reclaiming what had once been farmland. Only one of the houses was still occupied as evidenced by the smoke curling out of the chimney. Yet no one appeared nor were there farm animals one would expect.

Berismo turned out to be larger than any of the group expected, for once they passed the edge of the forest, the city spread before them. Though not as a large as Westhaven or Durness, it was the most substantial town since leaving Durness. Yet what had once been a thriving city now resembled a ghost town. The walls surrounding the city, broken in spots, were covered in moss and ivy. The gate was open and a single guard, a frail-looking middle aged man sat outside, beneath the barbican. His attention was absorbed with the book he held in his lap.

So intent was his focus that he didn't see or hear Karl and company until they were almost upon him and Karl cleared his throat. Startled, the man jumped up, clutching his tome.

"Must be a good book," Karl smiled.

"It is," he replied, warily regarding the rest of the team.

"Is the burgomaster in town?"

"Of course. Where else would he be?"

"I wouldn't know," Karl answered. "As is obvious, we're not from here. Where can we find him?"

"He still lives in the middle of the city." He pointed to the open gate. "How did you get past the guards at the border?"

"They let us pass, especially after we told them the news about Cyril." Karl started to walk forward when the man grabbed his arm. Karl felt the earnestness, yet there was a weakness to the grip.

"What's happened?" the man asked.

"Cyril is dead and his army scattered," Raquel answered. "We are here to tell the Burgomaster."

The man's eyes lit up and his head tilted back as he chortled with joy. "Praise the gods my prayers have been answered. C'mon with me. I'll take you there."

"You're glad Cyril is dead?" Annabeth asked as they followed the man into the city proper.

"Who wouldn't be?" he replied as they walked along deserted streets.

Three story houses jammed side-by-side lined the street, their shutters and doors faded. The ever present ivy hid many entrances and windows, the thick vines obscuring the drab stone walls.

"He's responsible for all this," the man said, waving a hand at the surroundings. "This street used to be alive with merchants, farmers driving wagons full of produce, moneylenders, soldiers and more. Families used to live in each of these houses. But when Cyril made it so that we couldn't trade no more with the king, the city just dried up. How can you live in a place when your market is taken away? Berismo used to be the center of trade between the two domains. When trade stopped, just about everyone left to where they could make a living. What stayed behind was those who had no prospects, or else everything they owned was here."

They passed by one house and an older woman emerged. Her grey hair was long, curled in a bun on the back of her head. Her clothing, once fashionable, was tattered and worn. She had been pretty in her prime, but age had claimed her fate and she stared at them.

"You are Karl the Viking," she spoke, her voice rusty from disuse.

Karl abruptly stopped, causing the others to stumble to a halt. "How do you know who I am?" he asked, facing the woman.

"It takes no wisdom to see you are a Viking," she chuckled. "The only Viking I know of is the one called 'Karl.' You have arrived just in time. Come inside."

"We are on our way to see Reyal," the guard explained.

"He can wait," she dismissively replied. "This is more important. Come. Come." She curled her fingers at him as she turned and pushed the door open to her home.

It was dark when they entered and she bustled over to light several candles, placing them at intervals along the wall. The illumination was surprising and the room noticeably brightened. The room itself was sparse, yet meticulously clean. A carpet covered most of the wooden floor. A cooking hearth filled one corner while a single table and chair occupied the middle of the large room. Along the walls, a lone shelf, lined with books, ran the circumference. To the right of the hearth, another door led to what Karl supposed was the bedroom.

She peered intently at him. "You want to know why I asked you inside." She grinned a wide smile, her teeth brilliantly white. "You want to cross a bridge and I can help you."

Karl's interest immediate perked. "You know about the bridge?"

"Of course, dearie," she nodded. "I've been waiting for you."

"You can help us?"

"Naturally," she said, tilting her head. "But you must do something for me in return."

"OK?" Karl raised an eyebrow.

"What Faylen here has not told you is that there is more to why this city has fallen."

"Not that again, Cirissa," he sighed. He turned to Karl, shaking his head. "She believes there's a curse on this city and once the curse is lifted, we'll be the center of trade again." He turned back to her. "There's a rational and logical explanation for our fate, not some sort of mumbo jumbo witchcraft."

"You'll see," she answered him, unaffected by his rudeness. Her attention back on Karl, she asked, "Will you listen to him or me? He won't help you get to the island."

"There is no island," Faylen huffed.

Cirissa winked at Karl. "See what I mean?"

Karl turned to Faylen. "Let's hear what she has to say."

"I thought you wanted to see the burgomaster?' he complained.

"Like she said, he can wait."

"Meaning no disrespect," Faylen said with a shake of his head, "I better get back to my post. She can tell you how to get to the burgomaster." Without waiting for a response, he spun around and headed out the door.

"Pay him no mind," Cirissa said with a flip of her hand then narrowed her gaze at Karl. "Do you wish to get to the bridge?"

"Yes."

"I can help," she nodded with a grin. "But you must help me first."

"You said that already," Annabeth chimed in.

"Just making sure, dearie." She turned to retrieve a book, flipping it open and placed it on the table. The words on the pages were hand written. "I wrote it all down. It begins over 500 years ago."

"Is this really necessary?" Raquel asked. "Can't we skip the history lesson and just get to the facts?"

"Oh," Cirissa admonished with a patronizing stare. "Confident are we? Wants to kill it right away. Impetuous and beautiful."

Raquel rolled her eyes. "This is taking too long."

Cirissa smiled at her then glanced beyond her shoulder. "Welcome lady assassin."

The others spun around to see Sakura in their midst.

"God, I hate when you do that," Annabeth exclaimed.

"The gate guard is dead," Sakura warned. "I couldn't stop him before it was too late."

"He's here?" Karl said, his lips tight.

"Who is here??" Cirissa demanded.

"Another assassin," Karl replied, "out for revenge."

"Damn it all," Greg uttered. "He's got me in his sights."

"And everyone else," Karl reminded him then looked at the rest of the team. "Time to take out an assassin." Turning to Cirissa, he shook his head. "We're gonna have to beg off on your history lesson... at least until we take care of a certain problem."

"I understand," she answered with a slight smile. "Perhaps I can help."

"I'm listening."

She turned to Sakura. "Which way was his direction?"

"Heading towards the center of the city before I lost him," Sakura replied. "He's good."

"He expects you to go to the burgomaster to warn him. Then you must do what he does not expect."

"And what would that be?" Karl asked, beginning to get frustrated both with this silly woman and that they were reacting to Kevin.

"Find him first. Come." She led the way through the other door which was indeed the bedroom. The room was small with a single bed and a dresser. In the wall opposite the bed, a low fire burned in the hearth. Runes covered the front of the mantel.

Cirissa went over to the mantel and fingered several runes in succession causing the fire pit to silently rotate 90°.

"Follow me."

Filing into the gap they entered a large opulent windowless room crammed with tapestries, silver and gold candelabras, dressers, bureaus, music instruments, chinaware, serving sets, silverware chests, and a wide canopy bed covered in embroidered quilts.

Seeing their surprised looks, she smirked, "The other rooms are to keep unwanted visitors away. When they think you don't have anything, they leave you alone. I got all this when they began to leave the city," she proudly explained. "Too much to take with them so they left it. Finders keepers, I always say."

She turned to Raquel. "Well lady ranger, how good are you with the little ones?"

"Little ones, like in children?"

"No," she answered, crossing the room and opening the door to a large wire cage and tenderly lifting out a large rat, nuzzling it as she returned. "These little ones."

"How is a rat going to help us?" Annabeth asked, curling a lip.

Ignoring her, Cirissa held it up to Raquel. "Tell her what you want her to do."

Raquel frowned, shaking her head. "I don't understand what you're telling me."

"If there is one rat, there are plenty more," Cirissa wisely answered. "In truth, there are far more of them than there are of us these days. You want to find your foe, send them to find him."

Raquel's eyes brightened. Invoking a Talk to Animal spell, she gave her instructions. When the rat squeaked in response, Cirissa placed it on the floor and they watched as the rat scurried to a hole in the stone wall and disappeared.

"Give her about an hour," Cirissa said, "then you will know where he is."

Karl twisted his head to look at Greg who abruptly stiffened. "You already know what I'm thinking."

"You wanna use me as bait," he snarled.

"You got it."

"Suppose he kills me before you get him?"

"That's a risk we'll have to take," Dieter calmly answered.

"No, dammit," Greg retorted. "That's a risk *I'll* have to take."

"You're right," Karl assuaged him. "But it's the only way to bring him out into the open."

Greg fumed for a moment then uttered a loud sigh. "Just because it's right doesn't mean I have to like it."

Less than an hour later, the rat returned and informed Raquel that Kevin was backtracking his steps to the front gate, searching for them and the alarm had still not sounded concerning the dead guard at the gate.

"Let him pass all the way to the gate," Karl said, "while we set up farther into the city." Turning to Cirissa, he asked, "Are there buildings where we can get an archer a good shot without being seen?"

"Yes."

"Good." Turning to the others, he said, "Now here's the plan."

Greg bitterly muttered to himself as he pretended to slink along an alleyway in the dull shadows of a late afternoon, knowing it was just a matter of time before Kevin saw him and began tracking him. He was a damned fool in the first place for allowing himself to be taken in by Kevin's smooth arguments. Yeah, they were doing well, but there was always something about the man that he didn't trust. What a way to find out that your partner was only too ready to kill you because you pissed him off.

Believing he heard a noise behind him, Greg jittered to a halt and spun around. The fading sun illuminated half the alley while the other half remained in inky darkness. Chastising himself for being so skittish, he reminded himself that Kevin was an assassin and that he wouldn't hear him.

He caught his breath when he saw a rat scuttle across the alley and disappear into the shadows. Kevin was close. He could feel him. He fears were realized when he turned around, for the assassin stood in front of him.

"At least you have the guts to face me like a man," Greg said, controlling his nervousness, "instead of stabbing me in the back."

"Talk about stabbing someone in the back," Kevin sneered. "You perfected that talent."

"What are you talking about?" Greg replied, wondering where the hell Raquel was with that damned arrow shot.

"Gimme a break, traitor," Kevin retorted. "You know damn well what I'm talking about. Tell me where the others are and I might let you live."

"And then you might not, even if I do tell you," Greg responded. *Any time now Raquel.*

"That's true," Kevin chuckled then quivered as the arrow hit him in the back and emerged out his chest. Blinking in surprise, he dropped his head to stare at the shaft protruding out of his chest then lifted his head to glare at Greg. "You bastard." With a flick of both hands, the knives flew up, one penetrating Greg's throat, the other imbedding into his heart.

As Kevin sank to his knees, he saw the figure emerge from the shadows. Sakura silently walked up to kneel beside him then slit his throat. Ignoring Greg as too far gone, she pulled down the face mask and sucked in the evening air.

A few moments later, Karl and the others appeared just as the two bodies sizzled then vanished. Sakura collected Kevin's blades and potions while Annabeth rummaged through Greg's potions, discovering a small book of spells.

"I ought to feel bad that Greg was killed," Dieter said, "but quite honestly, he was too much of a whiner. Don't see the need for someone we can't trust."

"I agree," Raquel announced walking up.

"Not much we can do about it now," Karl observed. "Let's go thank Cirissa and see what this supposed curse is all about."

Back inside Cirissa's home, they listened as she explained, "The curse began a year after Cyril closed the borders. At first, we ignored Cyril's command and continued trading. The months passed and we prospered as a city. We believed he would turn a blind eye to us because we gave him so much in taxes. Then the soldiers came and cut down the forest between the two domains and by the time they left, Berismo's fortunes had changed. While the farms produced abundance, men began dying of unexplained diseases. Children were born crippled. Mothers died in childbirth."

She flipped a page in her book and continued reading. "When the old burgomaster died, a man well-loved and admired, we learned that Berismo was given a new burgomaster, chosen by Cyril himself. When he arrived, our misfortunes ceased, but by then it was too late. The city was a shell of its former self. Despite his efforts to repopulate the city, word had spread and no one wanted to settle in a place that was cursed. Those who remained worked the farms but they were too few and the farms too many. So farms were abandoned and the fields overgrown as the few farmers left tilled what soil they could."

Pausing, she gazed up at Karl. "I'm telling you this so that you will understand. The curse is not here."

"It's not?" he frowned. "Where is it?"

"It's in Hillfurt, where Cyril once reigned. He has a woman –"

"O God," Annabeth moaned, "not another sorceress."

"Yes," Cirissa replied, bobbing her head. "She cursed this town as punishment for not obeying Cyril's command."

"Why would he allow that when he was getting so much more in taxes?" Dieter asked, her explanation not making sense.

"Well," she hesitated. "There's more."

"Why does that not surprise me," Annabeth mumbled then cocked her head. "She's not a succubus, is she?"

There was a pounding on the door before it was thrust open and two tall guards entered then stood to the side as a diminutive man with airs of authority strode in. He stared imperiously at the group, specifically noting Dieter and Karl then turned a haughty eye to Cirissa.

"The gate guard is dead," he exclaimed, his voice high and reedy, while giving her a disdainful glare.

"So I heard," Cirissa replied, undaunted.

"Why wasn't I immediately notified?" He jammed his fists on his hips.

"Why ask me?" she retorted. "You have guards. Where is your commander? Who checks on your guards? Seems to me your failure lies within you."

"Watch your tongue, woman," he snapped.

"Or what?" she sniffed. "You'll take everything I have? Make me poor? Deprive me of my livelihood?" She folded her arms and stared at him. "Kill me? Go ahead. You do that to everyone you don't like and pretty soon you'll have the entire city to yourself."

"Be silent, crone," he growled, flipping a hand. "Who are these strangers in your house? Were they responsible for my guard's death? I will have the truth from all of you."

From the moment Reyal had entered the home, Annabeth had the urge to toy with him. Deciding now was a good time, she cast an implant idea spell – *Your pants are undone. Turn around and fix them. Do it again... and again.*

Reyal abruptly clamped his mouth shut and turned around, bending his head as he reached to check the front of his trousers. Satisfied they were fine, he spun around, only to realize that his pants might be undone, causing him to spin around again.

After the third time of the burgomaster spinning around, Annabeth's giggling grew and she covered her mouth, looking away as she struggled to contain her laughter.

"What's so funny?" the burgomaster yelled over his shoulder as his hands checked the buttons on the front of his pants.

"Just happy to be here," Annabeth replied with a snort.

With a half-smile, Raquel gave Annabeth an inquisitive glance, wondering why she was laughing.

"The gods damn it," the burgomaster burst. "These damn trousers." Without a word, he stormed out, the guards falling in behind him.

Free to give vent to her amusement, Annabeth laughed out loud then confessed, causing the others to laugh with her, though Cirissa's amusement was the first to fade.

"You are clever and it was good to see him knocked down a notch, but the problem remains."

"Why not just get rid of him? Kill him?" Karl pointed out.

"He was not always like he is now. Reyal was once an honorable and good man," she sighed. "Getting rid of him does not solve the problem. You must eliminate the sorceress who controls him. Kill her and the spell over him is broken."

"So how do we do that?"

She gave him an impatient look. "You must use magic. I see your magic skill is still locked. Why?"

"I haven't the faintest idea," Karl shrugged.

Cirissa frowned and shook her head. "To succeed, you must unlock your magic. You are a Viking. Who is your patron god or goddess?"

Karl gave her a blank stare. "Don't have one."

"What?" she replied, shocked. "You call yourself a Viking and have no patron god?" She flipped a hand at him. "You are no help. How can you expect to defeat a sorceress when you have no magic?"

Karl's not so subtle gaze at Annabeth caused Cirissa to dismissively respond, "You can't always depend on her. Though her powers grow stronger, you will need more than her talents to defeat Mavie."

"Máh-vee?" Annabeth repeated. "That's a pretty name."

"And she's a strikingly beautiful woman," Cirissa agreed with a nod, "with fire and ice in place of a heart." She narrowed her gaze at Karl. "You must unlock your magic if you are to defeat her."

"You've already said that," he replied, frustrated. "How do I do that?"

"You must choose a patron god to help you."

"Like I said," he huffed, "how do I do that?"

Cirissa's frown deepened as she stared at him, her look telling him he was a moron. "Choose one and call upon him or her."

Thinking it a simple process of merely picking a god that closely aligned with his own predilections, Karl activated his screen and scrolled down to the Info tab then pressed the hyperlink. After further scrolling and searching, Karl finally arrived at the page on Nordic gods and goddesses, immediately feeling overwhelmed with all the information.

"This is going to take a while," he complained.

While Karl was occupied finding a patron god, Annabeth turned to Cirissa. "Tell us about Mavie."

Cirissa hesitated, curious at Karl's abstract gaze into the air as he wiggled his finger. "What's he doing?"

"Research," Raquel replied. "Now what about Mavie?"

Cirissa reluctantly turned to face them. "As I said before, she is a strikingly beautiful woman who enchants all with her beauty."

"Is she a succubus?" Annabeth asked with a pained sigh.

"Yes," Cirissa nodded, "just like her step-sisters."

"My God," Annabeth moaned, "not another one. How many freakin' sisters are there?"

"Four that we know of," Cirissa replied. "There are rumors of one more, the result of a liaison with an unknown huntsman. But that is the least of your worries, for not only is Mavie a succubus, she's also a powerful sorceress. That is why Cyril left her to rule the realm while he was trying to unite the kingdom."

"So she's in Hillfurt?" Raquel asked.

"No," Cirissa answered. "She remains in Tal Olca, the old capital. Her power is greatest there."

"Why?"

Cirissa shrugged. "That is what you will have to discover."

Dieter warily regarded her. "How come you know all these things?"

Cirissa flashed a rueful smile. "I once lived in Tal Olca... before I was banished here."

"Banished?" Annabeth's ears perked up.

Cirissa's shoulders slumped then tightened. "I was not always the old woman you see before you. I was once as beautiful as her."

"Her? Mavie?"

"Yes."

"This ought to be good," Raquel said, leaning in to hear the story. "What happened?"

Cirissa turned away. "There wasn't room enough in the realm for two such as Mavie."

Sakura studied Cirissa for a moment before asking, "How old are you?"

Cirissa gazed back over her shoulder at the assassin. "The question you ought to be asking is 'How can we defeat her?' It will take your combined skills to destroy her." She gazed intently at Raquel. "Remember your animal and bird communication skills. Use them to your advantage like you did here."

Turning to Annabeth, she warned, "Do not think your cleverness will work on her. You must be more subtle. Use what you have learned."

"There's a curse on you," Dieter blurted. "Isn't there." It wasn't a question. "We kill Mavie and the curse on you and many others is lifted."

Cirissa slowly nodded and chuckled. "You have a brain in that berserker body. Yes, I have been cursed. Destroy Mavie and I am free. Once free, I can take you to your bridge."

At the mention of 'bridge', Karl's focus diverted. "What do we need to do?"

"Kill Mavie," Annabeth sweetly replied.

"Have you decided?" Cirissa interrupted.

"I think so," he said. "I've been looking at Freya."

"Freya," Cirissa repeated. "An interesting choice, one that should serve you well."

"So who's Freya," Raquel asked.

"Freya's the goddess of love and fertility, and the most beautiful of all the Norse goddesses. She's the patron goddess of crops and birth, sex, battle, sensual pleasure, and matters of love."

"Sex and pleasure?" Annabeth brightened. "I like your choice."

"I figured you would," Karl chuckled. "She also has a thing about music, spring and flowers, and for some reason is particularly fond of elves, though dwarves play into her life... and she's one of the foremost goddesses of the Vanir."

"Vanir?" Raquel said.

"Think of them like the Roman gods and Mount Olympus," he said. "The Vanir gods are into sorcery and magic. What's more interesting though is that Freya is a shape shifter. She has this falcon skin and so she's able to take on the form of a raptor. She also has the power to transform other people into animals."

"So why her as opposed to Thor or Odin?" Dieter asked, causing the others to give him surprised stares. "I've read a little about Norse gods," he sheepishly explained.

"I wanted someone different," Karl replied, "and the shape shifting thing sounded like something maybe I could use."

"Not to mention she's the goddess of sensual pleasure," Sakura teased.

"That's an added bonus," he grinned then looked at Cirissa. "So how do I access my goddess?"

"You need her rune carved on a live oak," Cirissa instructed, "somewhere where you won't be interrupted when she talks with you." She cocked her head and smiled. "I know just the place. Come. You too," she added, pointedly gazing at Lana and Annabeth. "The rest of you stay here and eat what little victuals I have. Or better yet, find some food for us. He'll be hungry when he returns."

She headed for the door and Dieter stepped in front of her. "No one gives us orders except for the Boss here." He jerked a thumb at Karl.

"It's OK, Dieter," Karl soothed. "Go ahead and buy whatever food you can find. Watch yourselves. I shouldn't be too long."

Cirissa led the way through the city gate then along the road back the way that Karl and company had come. Just before the forest encroached on the road, she turned left and followed the forest edge, carefully making her way along a barely perceptible footpath.

The sun was setting by the time she turned into the dim forest, her sure footsteps leading them deeper into the broad strip of forest edging the no–man's land between the two domains.

"Here we are," she announced as they came into a small clearing. In the middle was a tall thick oak with branches that spread wide.

Leading the way to the tree, she slowly caressed the bark, gingerly placing fingers in the grooves and valleys of the hard surface as she haltingly made her way around the tree. She came to a sudden stop.

"Here. Right here is the spot. You can cut away the skin here. Not too large mind you. Only enough to carve the runes of her name."

"Uh," he hesitated. "I don't know how to carve runes."

"Aye," she nodded, "you don't, but they do." She curled her fingers at Annabeth and Lana then turned her attention back to Karl. "No bigger than a hand's breadth. Make it clean."

Karl pulled out his dagger and began carefully removing the outside bark.

"While he's busy," she said to the two women, "do you know runes?"

"Yes," they replied in unison.

"Good, good. Tell me then. Can you spell her name correctly?"

The two women looked at each other. Lana spoke first.

"Her name's 'Freya.' So that would probably be either F-R-E-Y-A or F-R-E J-A."

Cirissa nodded with a smile that just as quickly vanished. "Did you think to check?"

"It's F-R-E-Y-J-A in the old Norse," Annabeth said with a shrug. "I looked it up on the way here."

Cirissa sighed with a grin. "Good. That's right."

"But J and Y are the same symbol," Lana pointed out with just a hint of irritation. "I looked it up too. It also said that Viking age runic inscriptions didn't normally use two identical runes in a row. So it really doesn't matter whether it's a J or a Y, because you would only use one letter."

Annabeth twisted her head to give Lana a look of admiration. "I'm impressed. You wanna carve the tunes?"

"You both will do it, alternating a letter. You," she said to Lana, "will carve the first letter."

"Then what?" Annabeth asked.

"Then we leave him to commune with his goddess."

"We can't watch?" she said, her curiosity obvious.

Instead of answering, Cirissa held a finger to her lips and winked.

"I think that's probably enough," Karl announced, standing back and tilting his head to study the smooth sapwood.

Cirissa ticked her head at Lana to begin carving. Ten minutes later, the runes chiseled into the tree, Annabeth stood back to allow Cirissa to approve her work. With a satisfied nod, she waved for the two women to follow her.

"Wait a minute," Karl called out causing Cirissa to stop and turn around. "What am I supposed to do?"

"Call upon your goddess," she replied with a frown, the answer too obvious.

"How do I do that?"

With a pained sigh and jamming a hand on her hip, she narrowed her gaze at him. "You figure it out. We'll wait for you just down the path a bit." Brooking no further discussion, she spun on her heels and marched away, Lana and Annabeth in a single file behind her.

By now, the sun had disappeared and the last remnants of daylight were rapidly fading. Stalking around the carved portion of the tree, Karl shook his head, running his hands through his hair, struggling to think of what to do. Casting a glance in the direction of the three women, they were already lost in the darkness.

"OK. This is crazy. What the hell am I supposed to do?" He abruptly stopped. "This *is* crazy. I'm talking to myself."

Pausing before the runes, he pressed a hand upon the letters.

How the hell does one call up a goddess? It's not like she's everywhere at once. Suppose she's having dinner somewhere. Does she hear my call and mid-chew jumps up from the table? 'Oh, excuse me. The barbeque is delicious, but some pathetic supplicant has just cried out for my help.' And what if two people call her at the same time? Does she put one of them on hold? 'Hi. This is Freya. I'm busy at the moment. Just leave a message and I'll get back to you as soon as possible.'

Karl snickered at the imaginary scene, tilted his head back and laughed. "Yo, Freya."

"Yes."

"Holy shit," he bellowed, whirling around, his sword halfway out of the scabbard. His shock quickly morphed to awe and his mouth gaped open at the ravishing beauty wrapped in a glimmering aura, hovering midair before him.

Her long flowing blond hair, held back with a garland of flowers, and gossamer dress that did little to hide her voluptuous body, billowed lazily though Karl could feel no wind. Her smile and the intense gaze of sky-blue eyes made him feel she cared for no one but him.

"You called me," she said, her voice warm and melodious.

"Y… yes, I did," he replied, swallowing hard.

"How may I help you?"

"I… I want you to be my goddess, my… uh, patron," he lamely answered.

"You wish to be my loyal devotee?" she said, her eyes bright.

"Yes."

"How wonderful," she smiled, gleefully clapping her hands.

"So," Karl ventured, "how does this work?"

Freya glided closer to him so that she stood an arm's length away. Reaching a hand up, she tenderly pressed a finger to his forehead.

Karl felt an instant sting like an inoculation shot, followed by encompassing warmth.

"There," she cooed. "You are marked as mine."

Karl instinctively touched his forehead.

"You can't see or feel it," she smiled, her laugh enchanting. "But other gods and goddesses can. It tells them that you belong to me."

"Now what?" He felt like an awkward freshman when the prom queen suddenly notices him.

"Now you may call upon me to help you whenever you need help," she replied, leaning in and kissing him.

The universe abruptly exploded inside him and Karl's knees weakened as he struggled to remain standing.

She stood back and demurely gazed at him, an impish smile curling her lips. "You have quite the unbridled passion inside you. I may have to partake of that sometime. In the meantime, as you continue your quests, you may call upon me at any time to help you in time of need."

"What do I do in return?" he asked, catching his breath.

"When the time comes," she answered, holding his gaze with hers, "you will do whatever I ask."

"Like what?"

"That is not yours to wonder," she pointedly replied. "Do I have your unwavering loyalty?"

Karl paused only a moment before answering, "Yes."

"Then I will leave you for now, Karl the Viking. I am pleased you have chosen me." She winked at him. "Tell your sorceress that she may have to share you with your goddess."

In an instant, Karl was alone, the silence of the forest enveloping him, which was then pierced by another woman's voice.

"I heard that," Annabeth loudly complained, striding into the clearing now illuminated by vibrant moonlight. "Who does she think she is?"

"A goddess," Karl chuckled.

"Yeah, well, she better not get any ideas. It was bad enough we had to rescue you from Gwen."

Cirissa led the way back to the city. Once inside her home, she took note of increased amounts of food and ale, as well as the barely concealed anticipation of the group.

"I see you are ready to move on," she observed.

"We saw no sense in delaying," Dieter replied. "Once we can see well enough in the mist in the morning, we'll be moving out. There is extra food and ale for you." He pointed to a separate stack of grains and kegs.

"That was kind of you," she said then beckoned Karl. "Remember, Mavie is dangerous, but now that you have your goddess with you, she can be defeated."

"Yeah," Conrad piped up. "What happened out there?"

"I'll tell you later," Karl said, suddenly tired.

"You said you'd help get us to the bridge," Raquel said to Cirissa. "If we're in Tal Olca, that means we'll have to come back here to get you."

"Use your skills, Ranger," Cirissa huffed. "Send a bird or falcon back to fetch me."

"Oh... yeah," she replied with a weak smile. "I keep forgetting."

"Well it's about time you started remembering," Cirissa chastised. "And that goes for the lot of you. You need to start using your gifts and skills instead of having to be reminded of them. What have you been doing all the time you've been here?"

"Surviving spider attacks, combating goblins, killing orcs and trolls, and saving a kingdom from destruction," Karl shot back. "Other than that we've been goofing off." Turning his back to her, he addressed the group. "Get some sleep. We got a long road ahead of us tomorrow."

"I'm sorry," Cirissa contritely said. "I forgot what it took for you to get here."

"Forget it. We're all tired."

As Karl searched for a place to stretch out, Raquel sidled up to Annabeth. "So? What happened?"

"It was awesome," Annabeth quietly replied. "Well, most of it was." She then explained about the goddess' appearance and the interaction between Karl and the gorgeous Freya.

"She's beautiful?"

"Oh yeah," Annabeth answered with a resigned nod. "And I think she has designs on our Viking."

"Just damn," Raquel groused. "It's getting so you can't share a Viking anymore without someone else wanting to get in on the action."

"And she's a goddess too," Annabeth moaned.

"We'll think of something," Raquel reassured her, "like we did with Gwen."

"What are you two scheming?" Karl asked with a yawn.

"Nothing, Sweetie," Annabeth sweetly replied. "Go to sleep."

Karl and the team were on the road as the mist was thinning. At first, the going was slow, despite the daylight as they couldn't see more than a few meters ahead of them. The pace picked up as the morning progressed and the mist dissipated. By the time the last traces of fog wisped away, they were at a double time, Karl out front.

It felt good to be moving and Karl inhaled the morning air, savoring the bouquet of things growing. Beside him, Raquel loped along with ease. After about an hour at the double time, she looked back and saw some struggling to keep pace. Carole had already climbed into the wagon.

"We may want to slow it down," she suggested.

Karl looked over his shoulder and immediately slowed to a brisk walk, much to the relief of the others. "What's with Carole? I figured she should be back to normal by now."

"She's still suffering from the spider bite," Raquel said.

"I know that," Karl replied. "I just assumed that once you were healed, you were healed. That's what happens when Tina and Kendra use their healing skills. We get immediate healing. Gwen healed Carole but she's still suffering."

Raquel cast him a sideways glance. "Maybe she didn't fully heal her. Maybe she left poison in her on purpose so that it would slow us down."

"That would assume she had designs on me the moment she saw us," Karl countered.

Raquel shook her head and gave him a pitying stare. "Sometimes you are so clueless. I saw through her right away. I just didn't realize the lengths she would go to keep you. I'm surprised she didn't imprison the whole team just so you would stay there." She glanced over her shoulder to where Carole sat next to Tina, vacantly staring at the passing scenery. "I wonder if we should have just let her die and respawn," Raquel quietly said. "She's holding us back."

"Too late now," Karl sighed.

"Maybe we can convince her to stay in Tal Olca. Besides, she's a lore-keeper. What use is that to us when the going gets tough?"

"My my," Karl grinned, "aren't we the hard core soldier."

"I'm just saying," she smiled back.

Annabeth came up between them and slipped an arm in each of their arms. "So what devilish plots are you two up to?"

"Just wondering about Carole," Raquel answered.

"She is pretty puny these days," Annabeth agreed. "Why not just dump her off on the side of the road?"

Karl twisted his head to stare at her, waiting for the punchline. "You're serious."

"Yeah... sort of," she said, letting go and moving around to Karl's other side. "It's obvious she's not going to be an asset. She stayed in the castle the entire time we were there, including the battle. Fortunately she had a safe place to stay. Had Cyril's soldiers broke through and stormed the castle, she'd have been killed. She's still suffering from the poison. And y'know, I don't think Gwen really healed her all that well."

Karl narrowed his gaze at her then switched to Raquel then back to Annabeth. "You two talked about this before now, didn't you."

"Maybe a little," Annabeth innocently smiled then turned serious. "There are some grumblings in the group."

"Like what?"

"A few didn't like what happened to Ross. They're afraid the same could happen to them."

"Names?"

Annabeth spun around so she was walking backwards and keeping pace next to Karl, at the same time surveying the group. "Well, how about I tell you the ones I know we can count on."

"OK," he replied his focus straight ahead.

"There's us three, Dieter and his Elena, Sakura, Lana. Those are the ones I'm sure of."

"Brad?"

Annabeth turned back around and leaned forward to catch Raquel's eye. "He's upset that you won't share."

Karl's jaw tightened. "I told him it wasn't my decision to make."

"We told him the same thing," Raquel said. "I also think he feels he's in the background too much, that no one appreciates him. I have a feeling he's having visions of grandeur and wants a team of his own."

"While you were occupied with her royalness," Annabeth said, "he was working the group for his own designs. I think he succeeded with the elves."

"Conrad and the other dwarves?"

"I think," Raquel answered, "that they wished they had stayed in Marbeck. Now that they are two couples, they have everything they want. Living in Marbeck would have been stress free."

Karl pursed his lips, musing that he was failing as a leader. Half his company was deserting him. But, he rationalized, that meant they were never really part of the team to begin with. With a shrug, he said, "We'll get things settled when we get to Tal Olca. Hopefully the dwarves will come with us. We can use the healers."

"Which is another reason Conrad and Wendell will want to stay," Raquel opined. "They view themselves as unnecessary and hate being reminded of it."

Karl did a quick calculation of who remained. He had himself, a Berserker, a Ranger, a Sorceress, an Assassin, and a Druid, plus an NPC who could cook. The team actually had strong members who wanted to be there. All they needed now was a medic, a healer.

They traveled in silence, each lost in his or her own thoughts. By early afternoon, the scenery changed to undulating hills of large farms. At one point, the road curved close to the sea, and they paused en masse to take in the view, inhaling the salty crispness. Seagulls crested the winds and Karl and a few others crept close to the edge to gaze over the rim to the crashing waves below.

Karl noted a pebbly beach littered with driftwood. Then a shape caught his eye and he realized it was a spar from a ship, the remains of the vessel scattered among the rocks farther out in the water, the ribs of the battered hull barely visible.

His first though was of the injunction that the only way to get to the next island was via the bridge. Someone had built a boat... or was it merely a tease for those wishing to attempt another way?

Deciding that he'd rather trust his future to good solid ground, he turned away only to hear someone say, "Maybe we should hire a boat to get to the next island," followed by a low voiced, "Not sure I'm ready to go anywhere quite yet."

They continued on the main road, which meandered near the coast then inland then back along the coast. By early afternoon, the road consistently stayed away from the coast rising and falling with the rolling hills dotted with forests and small farms.

Calling a midday halt, Karl reminded the group, "We'll steer clear of Hillfurt and head to Tal Olca. I have a feeling we may want to avoid the main road here for fear of being spotted and our presence relayed to those in Hillfurt."

"How far is it to the bridge?" Wendell asked.

"You can figure that out for yourselves," Karl said with a forced smile. "Go ahead and do it now. Also, where is everyone's bind spot?"

"I changed it to Cirissa's place in Berismo," Raquel said. Annabeth and most of the others sounded their agreement while Kendra and Wendell quickly corrected their location to Berismo.

"Looks like we're getting closer to the bridge," Conrad said, staring at his screen. "According to what I can figure out, we could be there in less than three days, barring any interruptions. What say we just bypass the sorceress in Tal Olca and head on to the bridge?"

This was met with resounding support.

Karl held up placating hands. "Part of me agrees with you. It certainly would seem to be the easy way out. The one problem I see is that we don't know what level you have to be to cross. As a pure guess, I'd say we have to be a level 10 to cross."

"Why?" argued Brad.

"When I was put into the game, I asked about the number of islands and was told there were ten. As the highest level is 100, I just divided 100 by ten. It's logical and easy," he shrugged. "If anyone has a better or more logical answer, I'm willing to listen."

"We won't know until we get there," Brad stated. "I asked the same thing and was told that they'd be adding more islands as time goes on. So for all we know, right now a level 5 could work."

"Yeah," several others agreed.

Karl paused before saying, "What's the rush? If it's level 5 or 10, what does it matter as long as we are as high as possible as we continue."

"You're the one who was in such a rush to get to the next island," Brad pointed out.

"Fair enough," Karl agreed. "Team leaders, let's talk."

"Why not talk right now," Brad demanded. "Why do you have to talk to the two team leaders? Why not just let it all out now, to all of us?"

"Because it doesn't work that way," Karl intoned. "But, in this instance I'm going to make an exception. I'm going to Tal Olca. Who else is coming with me?"

Needing no prompting, Dieter, Elena, Annabeth, Raquel, Lana, and Sakura immediately moved behind Karl. After a fleeting moment, Conrad and the other three dwarves followed suit. That left Brad and the three elves, but just as quickly Brad remained by himself as Carole first then the other two meandered over to stand with the others.

With a gruff sigh, Brad frowned and shook his head. "Fine. Have it your way."

"Good. Let's move out." Karl led the way deeper into the hills and forests, taking note of the increasing traffic on the feeder roads to the main road heading to Hillfurt.

As the day wore on, their progress slowed as they kept to the forests, avoiding roads and houses. Through vigilant movement, they managed to avoid discovery. Two hours beyond Hillfurt, Karl called halt at an abandoned house whose foot path was overgrown from disuse.

"We stay here tonight. Sakura and Dieter, take your teams and do a recon around the house while the rest of us check the interior."

While the two teams began a wide sweep of the surrounding forest, Karl led the others into the home. Like so many others, it was a small two room affair. However, unlike the others, a thick layer of dust covered everything. A small table sat in the middle, one ladder back chair to the side. The other chair lay on its side, two of the legs broken, apparently used for firewood. The entrance to the other room gapped open as the door skewed awkwardly, held only by the bottom hinge. When Raquel went to check the room, the door fell off into her hands.

Annabeth checked the fire pit, noting the pitted and rusted cooking pot. Curling her lip, she commented, "Not sure I'd use this, unless you wanted to get ptomaine poisoning." She studied the charred wood in the fire place. "Doesn't look like anyone's been here in a while."

"Let's get a fire going anyway," Karl replied. "I don't want to take any chances." Seeing there were no maps, no potions, and no trinkets, he wasn't sure whether he was disappointed or relieved.

By the time the two teams returned, evening draped the forest and the once roaring fire had settled into smoldering coals. No spiders had bolted out the chimney and the reports from the teams said that all was quiet, nothing out of the ordinary.

"Let's get some sleep," Karl said. "Dieter, your team has first watch then Sakura and we'll take last watch. Double up the watch per usual."

Chapter 9

Karl jolted awake when he felt the firm grip on arm and looked up to see Sakura grimly staring at him.

"Brad's gone," she said. "So are Bruno and Sharyn."

Pushing himself to standing, he stepped over sleeping bodies towards the front door, which was unbolted and slightly ajar.

"That son-of-a-bitch," he growled. "He put us all in danger." Opening the door to peer outside, he knew the mist lay heavily upon the forest yet wanted to see for himself. "Don't know how far they'll get. Can't see squat out there." Still, he noticed that there was just the slightest touch of dawn's light giving a hint of brightness to the mist.

Securing the door, he turned to see Raquel sitting up.

"What's going on?" she asked with a yawn.

"Brad's gone, along with Bruno and Sharyn," Sakura answered.

"When?" Her lips tightened in disgust.

"Don't know," Sakura replied. "I only found out when I woke up and realized I had slept pretty well and suddenly realized that I had overslept and no one was on watch." She glanced over to where Tina snuggled against Wendell, an arm resting on his chest, both soundly asleep.

"Let 'em sleep," Karl said. "I'm awake."

"Me too," Raquel said, standing and stretching.

"Yeah, well, me too." Sakura walked over to the door, checking the bolt. "I notice they decided to leave Carole here." She gazed down at the elf snuggled in a bedroll, lying on her side, head resting on her arm.

"Probably thought she would slow them down," Raquel said.

"Wonder what time they left?" Karl said. "The way I figure it, Dieter had the first watch and then your team picked it up at midnight. I figure it's probably around 0600 right

321

now, which means no one was on watch for at least six hours."

Their answer was provided an hour later when Conrad stirred and saw the three of them in quiet yet concerned conversation.

"What's going on?"

"Did you and Kendra pull watch last night?" Karl asked.

"Of course," he answered, irritated that it was even in doubt.

Sakura folded her arms and frowned at him. "Why didn't you wake me up?"

"Bruno and Sharyn were supposed to," he answered.

"Bruno and Sharyn aren't here," Karl intoned.

"Huh? Where are they?"

"Gone."

Conrad's eyes widened. "Gone? As in no longer here?"

"That's correct."

Conrad blinked for only a moment before realizing what happened. "Not long after Kendra and I took watch, Bruno and Sharyn came over and said they weren't sleepy and said they would take the rest of our watch for us. Not one to turn down an opportunity to get some extra sleep, we said 'sure' and left them to it. I saw Brad come up a bit later. You can ask him."

"Brad's gone too," Raquel stated.

Conrad's mouth slacked open then just as quickly closed. "Why does that not surprise me? I didn't think they would take off," he apologized.

"Of course you didn't" Karl soothed. "No one could have suspected they'd jeopardize the group."

By now, the rest of the team members began stirring and soon discovered Brad and the others' duplicity. Karl noticed that when Carole was informed of their departure, she seemed both disappointed and hurt. He also noted the muted discussions among the dwarves.

"Since we're all awake," Karl said, "and know that three of our team have decided to venture out on their own, understand that under no circumstances will they be allowed back into this group."

"So they left," Conrad sourly stated. "I say good riddance."

"Suppose they went looking for something," Carole asked, hope in her voice.

"Like what?" Conrad answered, cocking an eyebrow in doubt. "And even if they did, they should of told someone."

"So if they came back," Carole stubbornly continued, "they wouldn't be allowed back into the team?"

Karl leveled his gaze at her. "Remember your spider bite? That happened with the door locked. When they left, they left the front door unlocked, which meant anyone or anything could have attacked us while we were sleeping. They put us all in danger. We were lucky this time. We can't count on that the next time."

Deflated, Carole moped a bit as she gathered up her things.

"I'm surprised none of us heard them leave," Raquel observed.

"We were all tired," Karl said. "Besides, we trusted them." Crossing over to the front door, he pulled it open. "Mist will be gone soon. Get ready to move out."

As the day progressed and they encountered more folks on the road, Karl noticed a subdued restraint in the people, as though they were waiting for something unexpected to happen and unsure whether it was for the better. A few gave the strangers a wary eye, but most were friendly enough to give a nod. When Karl asked a merchant how far it was to Tal Olca, the man simply pointed down the road and said, "You'll see it soon enough."

The man was right, for as they crested a rise in the road, they saw the city in the near distance. It reminded Karl of Westhaven for a similar castle crowned the hill in the center of the city, which was surrounded by tall walls. However, unlike Westhaven, part of Tal Olca was built against the cliffs leading down to the sea, the wall spilling over the edges, making an assault from the sea an impossibility.

The main gate was open wide with four guards checking everyone who entered. When Karl and company approached, they were halted by a gruff guard with a scar on his cheek. Giving them a surly stare, he folded his arms and stood in front of them.

"Alright then," he said with an arrogant sneer. "Who might you be?"

"We're travelers just passing through," Karl answered.

"Travelers from where?"

"We've just come from Westhaven."

"Westhaven?" the guard suspiciously replied.

Hearing the town name the other guards waved through the merchants and other visitors, yet bent an ear to the conversation.

"How'd you make it through Cyril's army?" the guard demanded, looking up at Dieter.

"Cyril is dead," Karl said. "His head is stuck on a pike outside the walls of Westhaven. Lady Gwen is now Queen."

The guard's surly demeanor vanished.

"Dead? How?"

"We," Karl motioned to the rest of his team, "helped defeat him. I am Karl the Viking."

The guard's eyes widened. "Karl the Viking? My Lord, I apologize." He bowed with a low grovel, the other guards following suit. "I did not know it was you."

Frowning, Karl wondered how it was that the man knew who he was, yet didn't know that Cyril was dead.

"We need a good place for lodging. I'd appreciate your recommendation."

"M'Lord," the guard said with a hint of nervousness. "I believe she is expecting you in the castle."

"She?"

"Lady Mavie, m'Lord."

"She knows we're here?"

The guard shrugged. "She's a sorceress." He leaned closer, looked quickly around and lowered his voice. "A word, m'Lord?"

"Yes?" Karl bent his head to listen.

"The Lady will not be so willing to yield her place once Gwen arrives to make her claim. There's sure to be a battle. My humble suggestion is that if you don't want to be caught up in the battle between two sisters, you should make haste to depart as soon as you can, though it may be too late once Mavie sees you."

"Then maybe we should simply pass on through."

The guard was about to agree when four more guards, led by a haughty, severely thin sergeant, arrived at the gate. Seeing them, he again shrugged.

"Too late."

"You are Karl the Viking?" the sergeant demanded.

"Who's asking?" Karl retorted, irritated that this bean pole failed to recognize his importance.

Ignoring Karl's response, the sergeant said, "Lady Mavie awaits. You will follow me."

"Perhaps later," Karl said. "Right now we need to find a lodging house."

"You have lodging at the castle," the sergeant not so politely replied.

"Not tonight," Karl replied and motioned for the rest of the group to follow him.

The sergeant stepped in front of him, the four guards fanning out behind him. "You don't seem to understand," he threatened. "You will come with me, now."

Karl sized him up and laughed. "You? You think you and your puny team are going to stop us? We defeated Cyril and his army and you think you are going to stop us?"

The man stiffened and his haughty manner evaporated. "Cyril… is dead?"

"His head suck on a pole on the wall outside Westhaven," Karl said. "A pretty gruesome sight if you ask me. I imagine Gwen is marching on Tal Olca this very moment."

"But… but, what about the orcs and trolls," the sergeant whined.

"Let's just say that neither orcs nor trolls do well in sunlight," Karl snickered.

The sergeant whirled around and pointed to a young guard. "Quick. Tell Lady Mavie the news."

"She probably already knows," the guard at the gate offered.

The sergeant's nervousness increased. "You're right. Why didn't she tell us?" He then looked at Karl with pleading eyes. "My Lord. It would be in the best interest of all concerned if you would allow us to escort you to the castle. If she finds out that we neglected our duties, it would be bad for us and everyone else."

"Fine," Karl nodded. "Lead the way."

They were halfway to the castle when Karl remembered something the gate guard had said. Turning to the sergeant, he asked, "The guard said that Mavie is Gwen's sister. I thought she only had two sisters."

"Lady Mavie is a half-sister," the sergeant answered. "The ladies share the same mother."

"And a succubus," Annabeth mumbled in complaint, loud enough for the sergeant to hear.

"Yes," the sergeant said as though the answer was intuitively obvious, "a very powerful one."

"Just damn," Annabeth groaned.

"As powerful as Kamdyn?" Raquel asked.

The sergeant shrugged. "I don't know. It's not something I have any experience with."

As they entered the castle grounds, Karl felt as though he had been there before then realized the design and layout were the same as Gwen's castle in Westhaven.

"Who is the City Administrator?" Karl asked.

"Lord Merstyn was before Cyril came here. Merstyn's dead and so no one holds that responsibility. Lady Mavie has been ruling the domain and the city."

They were led along the hallways and Karl heard others commenting on the similarity even to the point of the guards outside the suite where Mavie resided.

The door guard knocked on the door and opened it, announcing, "My Lady, Karl the Viking and his team."

Karl led the way in and startled when the Lady, standing by the window, turned to face him, for Lady Mavie looked

326

far too much like Gwen. He felt his passion stir when she smiled at him and effortlessly glided over to stand in front of him.

Annabeth saw the captured look in his eyes. "Damn it all, not again."

Before Mavie had a chance to open her mouth to speak, Annabeth cast an Implant Idea spell; *Karl doesn't interest you.*

Mavie frowned only a moment before turning to Annabeth and smiling. "Don't worry, Little One, I'm not Gwen and I have no designs on your Viking. That was a good try though and I'm impressed you were able to work that on Gwen." She turned to Raquel. "For now, the Viking stays here. The rest of you are free to go."

"Why?" Raquel demanded.

"Because it is what I wish," she coldly replied then softened. "Our new queen has need of him."

"How do you know that?" Annabeth asked, irritated and curious at the same time.

"She told me."

"The birds Ross saw," Raquel blurted.

"Very good," Mavie nodded, impressed. "Putting those Ranger skills to use, I see. I'm surprised you haven't used the birds to scout ahead for you."

"I… I tend to forget I can," Raquel stammered.

"You're a Ranger, albeit a level 1 skills Ranger. Surely you've experimented with your divination skill of talking to animals."

"I… just a bit," she replied, feeling unmasked.

Mavie looked at the group. "So intent on getting to the bridge, you all have neglected developing your own skills. What's so important about crossing a bridge that causes you to disregard your own development? You for instance," she narrowed her gaze at Conrad. "You're a Rogue. Did you use your skills to detect magic or any spells when you entered here?"

"Uh…" he awkwardly answered.

"There is one though," she chuckled, "who had been working on her skills." She turned around and pointed to the couch. "Isn't that true, Assassin Sakura."

Sakura materialized from next to the couch and sauntered over to stand with the others.

"I ask again," Mavie said, turning back to the group. "What's so important about a bridge?"

"That's what I've always said," Wendell interjected. "It's like we're in a rush."

"When did you ever say that?" Annabeth countered.

"Uh… all the time," he lamely answered.

"That's funny. I've never heard you say a word," Raquel riposted.

Wendell reddened, struggling for something clever to say when Conrad spoke up.

"He does have a point though. We really haven't had a chance to work on our skills."

"And where would you work on yours?" Raquel said through tight lips. "Remember what happened in Marbeck? You were lucky when you two only had to spend the one night in jail."

"Yeah, well, we never got the chance in Abeloft," he complained.

"And how would that work?" she asked, knowing the answer. "You two, along with the rest of us, were treated like celebrities. Everyone knew who you were. Just how did you expect to work on your skills?"

"You're being too short-sighted," Mavie intervened with a maternal smile at Raquel. "This handsome Rogue here could have, and should have been working on skills that didn't require him getting into trouble yet would still be useful in the future, like disguises or acrobatics or even escape artist while working in darkness."

"See?" Conrad triumphantly announced.

"Don't you all get it?" Annabeth objected with a loud exclamation. "She's sowing discord among us, getting us to doubt each other."

"On the contrary," Mavie replied, giving Annabeth a wink. "I'm merely pointing out that you all should take time somewhere and hone your skills, long before you cross the bridge."

"She's doing it again," Annabeth huffed.

"But she's right," Wendell said. "We didn't have a chance when we were in Westhaven because of the war. But there's no war now, so why not just park ourselves here and practice our skills?"

Raquel twitched her head to look at Karl who hadn't moved since they entered the room, but simply stared with moon eyes at Mavie. "How about releasing him from whatever spell you have on him?" she crossly demanded.

"Alright," Mavie smirked.

Karl inhaled a deep breath then gazed around the room as though seeing it for the first time before turning to take in his team, immediately noting something was amiss. "What's going on?"

"Wendell wants to stay here," Raquel answered.

Karl stiffened to full height, giving Wendell a stern stare. "This team isn't a democracy. When you signed on, you agreed to follow orders."

"I know, I know," he awkwardly replied. "It's just that... I'm really not sure I'm ready to cross yet. We've been on the go ever since you arrived in Marbeck and I just want to stay put for a bit. It's not that you aren't a great leader," he added. "It's just that I... we can't keep up with you. Why not just stay here for a while to rest and recover. Like you, or someone else said, it's not like we have to cross over right now."

"A wise choice," Mavie nodded.

"She keeps doing it," Annabeth growled. "She's creating discord on purpose."

"Y'know," Karl snarled. "As far as I'm concerned, those who want to stay are more than welcome to stay. As for those who want to move on, we're leaving."

"No," Mavie said, flipping her hand and immobilizing Karl once again. "You're staying, though you," she peered intently at Annabeth, "I suggest you go. She's going to be very cross with you, and anyone else who helped him escape."

329

"How about we just take him with us right now," Raquel threatened.

Instead of anger, Mavie replied with a haughty laugh. "You forget your place and who I am. I'm a succubus. Remember? If I wanted, I could have you all rolling on the floor here in one huge orgy, elves with dwarves, and serving girls with clerics." She stared pointedly at Dieter then relaxed with a chuckle. "Though, in truth, elves and dwarves coupling just doesn't do it for me."

"Why are you doing this," Annabeth demanded, her frustration mounting.

"Because it is in my best interests," Mavie replied with a shrug. "Now if I were you, I'd be making plans to move along. I figure if she's already on the move, she'll be here very soon."

Defeated, Raquel glanced around at the rest of the group then back to Karl, controlling her anger while squelching her feeling of hopelessness.

Annabeth uttered a pained sigh. "Would you release him so that we can at least say goodbye?"

Mavie relented with a sympathetic smile. "Of course." Flipping her hand, Karl's immobility vanished and he blinked and frowned.

"What's going on?"

"We're saying goodbye," Annabeth said.

"Wait a minute." Karl's face tightened. Gazing intently at Mavie he decided to take a gamble. "Cirissa in Berismo sends her regards."

Mavie snorted a laugh as she demurely glided away to sit on the divan. Narrowing her gaze on Karl, she said, "Let me guess. She sent you here to kill me so the curse will be lifted from Berismo." Seeing Karl's undisguised look, she smirked and shook her head. "She's been singing that silly song for years. Works her magic on unsuspecting strangers who come here and attempt to carry out her twisted desires. I've had to eliminate one who got surprisingly close to accomplishing her objective."

Seeing his disbelieving face, she explained, "There is no curse on Berismo. It's a simple result of economics. The town died because Cyril foolishly decided to halt the trade between the two domains."

"If she's so intent on killing you, why not beat her to the punch and eliminate her?" Raquel asked.

Mavie's face softened. "It's not that easy?"

"Why not?" Raquel persisted. "You know where she is and you are certainly more powerful."

"I can't," Mavie slowly replied, "because she's my mother."

"Your mother?" Annabeth's mouth gaped open.

"Yes." Mavie straightened the fabric on her dress. "She's not in her right mind anymore. She thinks her children are out to kill her and to make her penniless. I imagine you've seen the hoard she has hidden in her house."

Karl nodded with a chuckle, remembering the accumulation.

"Still," Raquel said, "why isn't she here so she can be looked after?"

"It's safer to keep her there. My sisters and I have placed a spell so that she cannot leave the town. She knows that. She also knows that should one of us die, the spell weakens. One has already perished because of that imbecile Cyril. One more death and she has enough strength to break the spell. As I am the closest, I am the easier target."

"I always thought she was a little wacko," Conrad said, circling his finger by his ear.

"Now you've being very uncharitable," Mavie chastised. "She is still my mother."

"Even though she wants to kill you," Raquel pointed out.

As Mavie talked about her mother's decent into madness, Karl called up Mavie's stats and uttered a soft whistle. She was more powerful than Gwen.

Lady Mavie, Level 22, sorceress of Tal Olca and spiritual counsellor to Cyril. Sister to Queen Briet and of the royal house of Bale.
Strength: 25 points
Speech: 25 points
Magic: 55 points

Healing: 65 points
Health: 50 points
Mana: 50 points
Combat: 12 points
Leadership: 40 points
Reputation: 35 points

He paused when he noticed the silence. Shutting his screen down, he saw them all staring at him.

"What?"

"She said those who want to go to the bridge can leave whenever we want to and that she would provide an escort to the bridge," Raquel answered. "Those who want to stay here are welcome to do so and that she would see that Gwen leaves them alone."

"Excellent," Karl ticked his head and smiled.

"There's one little problem," Annabeth added.

Letting out a slow breath, he replied, "Yeah. I know. I gotta stay here and wait for Gwen."

"So what do we do?" Annabeth moaned.

"The way I see it," Karl calmly answered, "is that we have a couple of options. The first is that we have to admit the new queen and her sister here are too strong for us to defeat. Isn't that true, Lady Mavie?"

Mavie flashed a confident smile. "Not unless you have some god protecting you."

"Hey," Conrad interrupted. "What about – ouch!" Lifting his leg and rubbing his ankle, he shot Raquel a 'what-was-that-for' look, receiving a cold glare in return.

"You were about to say?" Mavie prompted.

"He was going to say what about using the same method on you that we did on Gwen," Raquel smoothly replied.

"Why not let him answer?" Mavie said, smiling with only her lips.

"That's what I was going to say," Conrad agreed, rubbing his leg a bit more, "but then I realized we did it once and it won't work again."

"What're the other options, Boss?" Dieter asked, torn between staying here with Elena or crossing the bridge and discovering too late that she was unable to cross.

"The other option is that you continue on without me."

"I don't want to do that," Annabeth moped.

Karl cast a glance at Mavie. "Would you mind if I had a private word with my team?"

"Of course not," she pleasantly agreed, standing and gracefully moving to the door. "I'll just be outside."

Once she was gone, Karl beckoned everyone closer, looking each one in the eye. "Those who are going to stay, you might as well leave now. No hard feelings, but I want you to leave now so that what I have to say to the rest will be for their ears only so if she or anyone asks you, you can truthfully say you don't know."

There was a momentary hesitation before Conrad stepped back. Avoiding looking at Raquel and Annabeth, he spoke. "I'm sorry you guys, but I'm not ready to move on yet. I won't speak for the others, but I'm happy right now with me and Kendra sharing a bit of happiness together right here. I'm really sorry."

"No problems, my friend," Karl soothed. "You were hesitant from the beginning yet still were there when we needed you, so go in peace."

Conrad held his hand out to Kendra when Wendell said, "That goes for me and Tina too."

"I understand," Karl said. "You all need to do what's best for you. Anyone else?"

When no one moved, Karl gave the dwarves a warm smile. "I hope to see you again in the future. Good luck to you all."

There were tears in Tina's eyes when she was led to the door. Before she had a chance to change her mind, Wendell ushered her out. As the door swung shut, Karl heard Mavie.

"So you all are staying?"

The closed door clipped off their reply.

Karl turned to the others. "Let's face it; I ain't getting out of here at the moment. Gwen is either going to come in person or will send a sufficient force to compel me to go back."

"We can take them," Dieter argued.

"I'm not so sure," Annabeth countered. "Remember what she said about orgies of elves and dwarves? And with the two of them together, we don't have a chance."

"What about your goddess?" Raquel asked.

"That's pretty much my plan," he nodded. "But if you all hang around, someone's going to get suspicious. So, I think our best course of action is for you to head across the bridge to the first town and wait for me there. Or if you decide to move on, leave word with someone so I'll know."

"We're not leaving without you," Dieter stubbornly stated.

Karl gazed at him and placed a hand on his arm. "Thanks for the support, my friend, but in this instance, if we want to succeed we're gonna have to have some faith. If you stay here, she's gonna suspect we're up to something. We need for her to have her defenses down. The only way we can do that is for you all to head across the bridge. Like I said, head to the first town and hang tight. Relax, enjoy the town. If everything goes right, I'll be there soon enough."

Dieter swallowed and shifted a worried glance at Elena. Karl immediately understood the big man's fear.

"The only way you're going to find out is to do it," Karl soothed. "In fact, why not send her across with someone else while you stay on this side of the bridge. If she can't go across, you'll still be here. If she can cross, then you'll know."

"But if I stay here..." he looked at Karl, his dilemma unspoken.

"How about we worry about that when or if the time comes," Karl reassured him. "In the meantime, you all go ahead and cross over then get a lay out of the land. Raquel is in charge until I get there."

"How long should we wait?" Annabeth asked, not liking leaving Karl behind.

"I leave that to you," he replied.

The door opened and Mavie reentered, exuding a confident smile. "Time's up," she cheerily announced. In smooth graceful steps, she stopped before Raquel and placed a gentle hand on her cheek then behind her head, drawing her forward for a deep kiss.

Annabeth watched in anger as Raquel responded. "Stop it," she snapped. "Leave her alone."

Mavie stepped back, leaving Raquel touching her lips, a puzzled frown creasing her brow. Turning to Annabeth, Mavie grinned with wicked intent. "You're next."

"Oh no you don't." Annabeth started back peddling only to be brought up short, her furious face morphing to serene contentment as she reversed course and walked up to Mavie.

"Why are you doing this?" Karl demanded, his voice rising.

"Because I can," she shot back, "and to remind you to think twice before you try something foolish."

Her eyes staring hungrily at Mavie, Annabeth stood close to her when she abruptly turned to Raquel. Stepping towards her friend, she drew her close and they were soon in a deep passionate kiss, their arms wrapped around each other.

"Stop it," Karl exploded, forcibly trying to separate the two women who shook him off, ignoring him. Turning to Mavie, he angrily pleaded, "I already said I'd stay. Stop this."

"I'm rather enjoying it," Mavie taunted.

Raquel's hands held Annabeth's head as their mouths devoured each other when Karl stepped in between Mavie and the two women.

"I asked you to stop," he seethed. "Keep on and I will ensure Gwen knows about this."

Mavie snorted a derisive laugh. "You think that little witch is a match for me? She'll be more than thankful that I allow her to have you. But," she looked past Karl to see the two women, their bodies pressed against each other, lips locked in deep kiss, "I'll grant you this little boon, this one time. But remember what I can do. Do not try my patience."

As she glided over to sit on the couch, the spell dissolved. Raquel was the first to react. Pulling her head back she stared into Annabeth's still dreamy eyes then snapped her head to look around the room at everyone watching her.

"What the hell?" She stutter stepped backwards, snapping her head to glare at Mavie. "You bitch."

As Raquel folded her arms across her chest, Annabeth's recovery was slower. With a confused frown, she looked at Raquel then everyone else and realization permeated her confusion. Her lips pursed she inhaled a sharp breath.

"That was uncalled for," she huffed, giving Mavie a malevolent glare.

"Oh don't be so melodramatic," Mavie replied, flipping a hand at her. "I was merely tapping into what you both want."

"You don't know what we want," Raquel shot back.

"Apparently neither do you," Mavie snorted.

"Go to hell."

Mavie tilted her head back and barked a laugh. "You should have seen you two," she mocked. "Why I didn't have to do much of anything. Once you two got going, there was no stopping you. I was all set to have you start tearing each other's clothes off if it hadn't been for Mister Spoil-it-all. Pity. That would have been fun to watch."

Instead of responding, Raquel turned to the others. "We're leaving." She then turned to Karl, her face reddening. "If you ever get out of here, you know where to find us."

"I know," he replied with a hint of sadness.

"Don't let us stop you," Mavie interrupted. "Go already."

"Can we at least give him a kiss before we go?" Annabeth begged.

Mavie cocked an eyebrow, studying the young sorceress. Relenting, she said, "A quick one. Then be on your way."

Annabeth turned to Raquel. "You first. Give him a good kiss."

Initially puzzled, Raquel stepped forward and laid a tender hand on his cheek before giving him a deep and passionate kiss.

As their lips pressed together, Annabeth cast an Implant Idea into Karl; *You have to leave Tal Olca immediately. You do not like Gwen or Mavie.*

Karl startled and pulled back from the kiss with Raquel. "We gotta go." He rapidly surveyed the group. "Cmon."

"Not so fast," Mavie called out, waving a hand then was shocked to see it have no effect for Karl was out the door, the rest of the team following behind him. "Come back here," she shouted, chasing after them only to be tripped by Conrad who stepped in front of her as though bending to check the lace on his boots.

"My God, I am so sorry," he apologized, fumbling as he tried to help her up, causing her to stumble again.

"Get out of my way, fool," she snapped.

By the time she was on her feet, Karl and what remained of his team disappeared down the hallway. "Guards! Stop them."

The halls filled with palace guards chasing down Karl and the others.

As Karl and the others worked their way down the hallways, their pace began to slow as they battled more and more guards clogging up the corridor. Finally, surrounded on all sides with no possibility of escape, he commanded a halt.

Facing him was the guard captain, a tall broad-shouldered warrior twirling two falchions. Behind him were dozens more guards. Behind Karl were dozens more who blocked the hallway.

"Let them go," Karl ordered. "It's me she wants. She already said they could go. You are to provide them with an escort to the bridge."

The captain looked beyond Karl's shoulder to a guard behind him. "You, Fergan. Go see what the mistress desires." Then casting a stern look at Karl and the others, he commanded, "Lay down your weapons."

"Can't do that," Karl lightly replied. "If she renigs on her promise, we're going to chop our way out of here and we'll take as many of you as we can. Isn't that so Dieter?"

"Damned right," the berserker growled.

Annabeth smiled at the captain and cast an Implant Idea spell. *You like Karl and the others. You don't want to hurt them. You will let them go.*

"Alright men," the captain ordered those behind him. "Clear a space and let them pass." He stepped aside. "Sorry to have bothered you."

"Are you sure, Cap'n?" a sergeant argued, surprised at the sudden reversal. "I don't think the mistress wants them gone."

Karl was as surprised as the sergeant until he glanced at the smirking Annabeth. "Thanks. Appreciate it. Let's go."

He started forward but stopped when confronted by the sergeant stepping in front of them.

"What are you doing?" the captain demanded, frowning imperially at the sergeant. "I told you to let them go."

When the sergeant refused to back down, Karl spoke up.

"Your captain ordered you to clear the way," he said, hoping they would be gone before the other guard returned. His hopes were dashed when he heard a voice call out.

"The mistress wants the Viking brought back right this minute. The others are commanded to be gone within the hour or their lives are forfeit. She said to tell you to give them an escort to the bridge. Make sure they cross it."

The captain gave Karl a 'sorry-there's-nothing-I-can-do-about-it' shrug. "Will you proceed as the mistress commands?"

"Yes." Glancing around at the others, Karl smiled. "It was a good try. Do like he said. I'll be there as soon as I can."

Raquel grabbed his arm. "Be careful. She's dangerous."

Patting her hand, he nodded. "I'll do my best. Now go." Without further words, he turned and pushed his way through the guards and headed to where a fuming Mavie waited. Passing the door guards, he stepped into her apartment.

"You win," he coldly stated. "I'm here."

Mavie glared at him a moment before flipping a hand at him. "Like I told your friend, don't be so melodramatic. Come, sit beside me."

"I'm fine right here," he replied, crossing his arms.

"I said, come sit beside me." Her face hardened into a scowl when he didn't move. Softening, she tried a different tack. "I'm not going to bite," she cooed and patted the seat next to her.

"I said I'm fine."

Surprise flashed across her face and her scowl turned into a chuckle. "She's good. She's got that Implant Idea spell down quite well. I'll have to remember that. Fortunately the spell doesn't last more than an hour, unless she's given it a boost, but if I remember right, she's still a level 1 sorceress. So..." she merrily sighed, "suit yourself. Soon enough you'll be cavorting cartwheels to my whim."

"What's your point?" Karl responded. "Either way you look at it, you lose."

"How do you figure that?" she snapped then caught herself and relaxed.

"First, Gwen is the queen and you're still... whatever you are here. The way I figure it, that'll last until I tell her that I don't like you and want someone else to rule here. If it goes like I want, you'll be exiled and imprisoned like Kamdyn."

Mavie's eyes bolted wide. "You wouldn't dare."

"Why not? What do I have to lose? I'll be king of Montgrec and you'll be in the way, so I need to ensure you're permanently out of the way." He chuckled as he languidly paced the room. "This actually works out well for me. From your perspective you not only lose your part of the kingdom, but right now at this moment, I am under your control and at any moment I will slip through your fingers and go to Gwen. It really doesn't matter if I like you or not. The fact that I don't like you, especially after what you did to Raquel and Annabeth, means that your tenure here is going to be very short."

He slid his eyes to slyly glance at Mavie whose mouth had gaped open.

"Looks to me like you have an opportunity here," he offered.

"And what would that be?" she asked, beginning to doubt her good fortune.

"Let me go. When Gwen asks what happened, you can say I got away."

Mavie shook her head. "Don't be a fool. She would know the truth." She stood up and began pacing.

Stepping out of her way, Karl watched her as she roamed the room, deep in thought. "What to do, what to do," he said, silently smirking as she pondered her fate. He swept a hand at the room. "All this will soon be a memory."

Pausing to stare at him, she said, "I could kill you and be done with you."

Karl laughed. "That's stupid on at least two levels. First, if you did manage to kill me, my death would be temporary for like a phoenix, I would rise again back in Berismo. What?" he said, seeing fear in her eyes. "You don't know about that part in all players?"

"I don't know what you mean," she said, avoiding his eyes.

"Yes you do," he chided. "You know damned well what I mean, which brings me to my second point. Killing me, which we both know is only temporary, will bring down Gwen's wrath even more. Looks like you lose any way you slice it." He smirked at her.

Resuming her pacing, she puzzled her predicament.

"Looks like Gwen put you in a bad position. I have to give her credit. She's a smart one. Forced you into a corner and you can't get out."

"Be quiet," she snapped. "How can I think with you chattering like that?"

"Merely pointing out the problems you face," he nonchalantly replied, plopping down on the settee and pouring himself a glass of wine. Taking a satisfying gulp, he said, "This is good wine. I guess once you're in exile or isolation, imprisonment or whatever, wine will be a rare luxury."

"Will you shut up?" she barked. Bustling to the door, she yanked it open. "Take him to the guest apartment," she commanded the guards. "Provide him with plenty of food and drink and nothing else. No one is to go in or out without my express permission. Do you understand?"

After they respectfully nodded their understanding, she turned to him. "Go. I will send for you when I want you."

"As you wish," he smiled in reply, dipping his head ever so slightly. "However, though I am your prisoner, you must acknowledge me as your king."

"I will do no such thing," she shot back. "You presume too much."

Karl's smiled widened. "You forget who I am. When I am sitting next to Gwen, ruling this kingdom, you will remember this moment." Slowly walking past her, he lowered his voice and added, "I will ensure you remember this day."

An hour later he was back in Mavie's apartment. She wore a thin translucent burgundy gown that lazily billowed, occasionally clinging to her firm breasts.

"Miss me already?" he taunted, though his eyes raked her luscious body.

She smiled sweetly at him. "Yes I did... your Majesty."

Karl hid his surprise with a chuckle. "Finally accepted our fate, have we?" Suddenly he saw her as a beautiful woman, and his desire to possess her grew. Recognizing what was happening, he struggled to remain in control. "I know what you're doing."

"Do you?" she cooed, gliding over to slide the bolt home, locking the door. Turning to face him, she reached up and slid the strap of her gossamer gown off her shoulder, repeating the action with the other side. The gown slipped down her shoulders and settled to a heap on the floor, leaving her quite naked. Stepping out from the gown, she seductively walked to stand in front of him.

"Why?" he huskily asked.

"Shoosh," she winked, her voice warm and sultry.

Lust raged inside him, yet a glimpse of clarity remained. "She's not going to like this," he pointed out, scooping her up in his arms and carrying her to the bedroom.

"Who says she has to know?" she replied, leaning in to nibble on his earlobe.

341

Karl indolently reclined on his side, his head propped up with his forearm and hand, the fingers of the other hand softly rubbing Mavie's thigh. She sat on her haunches next to and facing him, a hand touching his muscular chest. The blankets of the bed lay in a crumbled heap on the floor.

"I see why Gwen is so obsessed with you," she purred. "You are incredible."

"I do my best to please," he smiled.

Peering intently into his eyes, she leaned down and kissed him. "Suppose I wanted to have you for myself? What would you say to that?"

"I'd say that you're plotting to be queen."

"Would you have a problem with that?"

Karl rolled over onto his back. "It's not a question of my having a problem with it. It's a question of whether you have the forces to back up your ambition. The last time I checked, Gwen has most of the kingdom's army with her."

"I have you," she countered, "and you were responsible for defeating Cyril's army."

"I also had the rest of my team who did far more damage than I did," he pointed out.

"True, true," she nodded. "By the way, Kevin is back in Berismo looking for you."

"Damn. That was fast."

"I can take care of him," she said with a coy smile, "if you want."

Karl smiled knowingly. "In exchange for what?"

"You help me defeat Gwen."

"I need the rest of my team."

"I assumed that," she said, straddling him. "I've already sent someone to fetch them back." She leaned down to kiss him.

Karl's craving blossomed and his focus became more immediate as he crushed her to him.

Sitting at the dinner table in Mavie's dining room, Karl admired the fare set before him, all the while pondering his

342

future. His idea of pitting the sisters against each other seemed to be working. The only problem was that instead of Gwen, he was under Mavie's control and she didn't seem quite as obsessed with him. Karl knew what she expected to happen. He would co-rule with Gwen. With Mavie, he'd be in the way and imprisoned like Kamdyn. His thoughts were interrupted when Mavie pushed back from the table.

"What's taking them so long?" she fussed, standing.

"Who?" Karl asked, refilling her wine glass.

"Your team. They should be back by now." Rapidly striding across the floor, she yanked open the front door to berate the door guards who groveled their apologies but they didn't know where they were.

"Well find out," she commanded, her voice rising. Slamming the door, she traipsed back to the dinner table.

"Give them time," Karl soothed. "They had at least an hour head start and once they made determined to get to the bridge, I'm sure they picked up the pace."

A fleeting grimace passed across her face before she heaved an audible sigh. "I suppose you're right."

"Besides," he added. "It's late and they're likely stopped at some tavern for the night. My guess is that they'll be here not long after the mist goes away." Giving her a winning smile, he silently mused, *though my hope is that they made it across the bridge.*

"By the way," he nonchalantly asked. "How far is it to the bridge?"

"A day and a half of a steady pace," she replied, eyeing him with more than curiosity.

"Ah," he nodded. "Then there's no doubt they'll be back here by tomorrow." Sipping his wine, he peered at her over the rim of his glass. The urge to bed her came and went according to her whims. Right now the urge was absent and he studied the beautiful woman seated opposite him.

Though physically like Gwen, she lacked Gwen's sensual innocence and insatiable desire. There was an edge to Mavie, as though she had something to prove. Who was more dangerous was a curious question, for he imagined a vengeful Gwen would be quite destructive. For Gwen, revenge would be personal. For Mavie, it would just be business. Watching Mavie silently brood reminded him he needed to act if he was going to catch up with the others.

"What were your plans for the sleeping arrangements tonight?" he asked.

She looked up as if suddenly aware that he might want more than she was ready to offer.

Seeing the deer-in-the-headlights look, Karl suppressed a smirk. "I was wondering if you wouldn't mind if I used the guest bedroom. I haven't had a good night's sleep in some time and the only time I get it is if I sleep alone." He again suppressed a chuckle when he saw her relief.

"No," she empathetically answered, "I understand completely."

"Thank you." He pretended to stifle a yawn. "I think I might like a long hot bath."

"Sounds wonderful," she cooed. "Would you like some company?"

Karl felt the stirrings and yielded. "Of course."

Two hours later, Karl was back in the guest apartment, seated in an overstuffed armchair by the window, the bolt to the main door secured. Pulling up his gaming screen, he tapped in a search for his goddess with the subsequent parameter of 'How to summon a God or Goddess.' Scrolling through the list, he stopped at Freyja.

Freyja, a member of the Norse Vanir, is the goddess of love, sex, beauty, fertility, gold, sorcery, war and death. She owns a dwarven made necklace called Brisingamen. She frequently drives a chariot pulled by two cats and can be seen accompanied by a boar called Hildisvini. Her treasured possession, in addition to the necklace, is a cloak of falcon feathers that allow her to shape shift.

To call upon the goddess, one must invoke her name by means of her runes: F-R-E-Y-J-A. Runes must either be carved or drawn inside a circle. Carved runes can only be carved in oak, ivory, or bone. If using a circle, white chalk is required and the circle must be at least three human paces in width.

Once the circle or carving is complete, the summoner will invoke the presence of the God or Goddess with the following words: I call upon the God/Goddess (name of god or goddess), mighty and benevolent ruler (location where god or goddess resides) to come to me from your abode above, now to this place in time and space, appear to me face to face.

Karl changed searches to 'Runes,' soon discovering that the symbols for 'Y' and 'J' were the same. After repeated searches and growing frustration he decided to simply repeat the symbol, wondering how anyone figured out there was a difference.

Hustling over to unbolt the door, he pried it open and poked his head out, grinning amiably at the two guards.

"How about finding me a piece of chalk and string about two meters long."

"M'Lord?" the older guard frowned.

"I need a piece of chalk, white chalk, and a piece of string about two meters long."

"Why?" the younger guard queried.

"An experiment," Karl cryptically answered. "Thanks." He closed the door and began rearranging the living room to allow for a chalk circle. Fifteen minutes later, a polite knock interrupted his sliding a sofa to the wall.

To his delight, the younger guard offered up a large piece of snow white chalk and a wooden bobbin with black thread. The bobbin looked to be made of oak.

Placing a single pedestal side table in the center of the clearing, he broke off a suitable length of thread and loosely secured it to the pedestal. Holding the chalk at the end of the thread and using the pedestal as the center, he drew a large circle on the floor. Removing the pedestal out of the way, he kneeled and called up his gaming screen.

Imitating the runes on the screen, he wrote down the letters F-R-E-Y-J-A. Double checking the bolt of the door, he returned to the circle and stood just outside the edge.

"I call upon the Goddess Freya, mighty and benevolent ruler in Vanir, to come to me from your abode above, now to this place in time and space, appear to me face to face."

Silence lasted only a moment before a sensual voice said, "Now that's a lot better than 'Yo, Freya.' You've even drawn a summoning circle. How quaint."

Freya materialized within the circle. As before, her long flowing blond hair was held back with a garland of flowers. She smiled at him, the intense gaze of sky-blue eyes making him feel no one else in the world existed. Her diaphanous dress, billowing in the windless room, accentuated her curvaceous body and Karl was momentarily distracted.

"Try to stay focused," she teased before glancing down at the runes. "You've done quite well, though to be honest, for all future correspondence, you can skip the 'J' in my name. A simple F-R-E-Y-A is sufficient."

"Yes, Mam."

Hovering within the circle, she slowly looked around the room before returning her attention to him. "What can I do for you?"

"I'm in a bit of a fix," he began.

"Yes, I know. So many women so little time." She smiled impishly at him.

"That's just it," he acknowledged. "Gwen wants me to stay with her in Durness while Mavie wants me here with her. Regardless of who wins, I'm still held captive here."

"What do you want me to do about it?"

Karl blinked in surprise. "I… I thought I could call on you and you would fix it."

"So what is it exactly you want to happen?"

"I want them to let me go."

Freya shook her head with disappointment. "You don't need my help to do that. Call me when you really need me."

Her body began fading when Karl called out, "Wait. What do I do?"

Rematerializing, she huffed, "Use your brains. You're too much the gentleman. Think about it."

Without further word, she disappeared, leaving Karl both irritated and confused.

"I'm too much of a gentleman?" he frowned. "What the hell does that mean?" As he dropped to his knees to begin cleaning up the chalk mark, it dawned on him and he smacked his forehead with the palm of his hand.

Chapter 10

At breakfast the next morning, Karl marched into Mavie's apartment looking like he'd slept hard, hair wild on one side and matted on the other. Scratching his crotch as he approached the table, he slid out the chair and flopped down, loudly smacking his lips.

"Hey," he called out. "Someone gimme an ale."

Seeing Mavie's mouth slack open in unconcealed disgust, he turned his head towards the door so she wouldn't see him struggling to control his laughter.

"Did you sleep well?" she asked, attempting to make light morning conversation.

"Slept like a prince after a night with the harem," he grinned, winking at her then barked at the door. "Where the hell's my beer?"

"Do you mean ale?" Mavie asked.

"Ale, beer, same damned thing," he grumbled, looking over the fare on the table. Noting the portions of eggs and sausage on Mavie's plate, he curled a lip. "You might wanna slow down on them calories if you know what I mean. That stuff'll go to your hips and butt and you're at the point where you gotta start watching what you eat. Mebbe a carrot or stick of celery might be better."

She sat stunned as he reached over the table and jabbed a fork into one of the sausage links, sticking an end in his mouth and chewing noisily.

A male servant came in holding a tray with a stein of ale. Placing the stein in front of Karl, he was about to turn away when Karl grabbed his arm

"Not so fast. Hold tight there just a moment."

Lifting the mug up, he tilted his head back and drained the entire contents in several gulps, slapping the stein down on the table with a loud, "Oh yeah. That's what I'm talkin' about." What followed was a long loud belch that echoed out the door and into the hallway. "You can bring me another. No wait. I don't wanna see your ugly mug. Send someone good looking with nice big boobs and a small tight ass."

"That's enough," Mavie snapped.

"What's a matter with you?" he said with an arrogant frown.

"What's the matter with me?" she shot back. "You're acting like a common uncouth lout."

"Oh, mighty high falutin' words," he sneered, stabbing the other sausage on her plate.

"What's got into you? Where's the gentleman from the past several days?"

"Him?" he replied, still chewing. "I was getting tired of having to act like some hoity-toity mind-my-manners guy. You can't imagine what a pain in the ass it is pretending to be someone else. Figured if I was gonna stay here, I might as well act my normal self. Say, they got any more them sausages in the kitchen?" He looked back up at the servant. "Have a hot chick bring me some sausages when she brings me my beer, or ale. You know, whatever."

"Yes, m'Lord," he replied, shifting a pained inquiring glance at Mavie who replied with a curt nod.

The servant gone, Mavie turned a cold glare at Karl. "Why are you acting like this?"

"Haven't the faintest idea what you're talking about," he answered then burped. Leaning back, he surveyed Mavie's apartment with a thoughtful nod. "Yup. Staying here's gonna be just fine. Didn't really care for Durness all that much, though the food was better." Placing his elbows on the table, he grinned at her. "So. What're we gonna do with Gwen once we kick her ass off the throne?"

"I... I haven't decided yet," she answered, studying him.

"Well," he said, leaning back and propping an arm on the back of the chair and once again looking around the apartment. "If I'm gonna rule with you here, we're gonna have to make some changes. Like this place for instance."

"What's wrong with this place?" she demanded, bristling.

"It's got too much of the girly touch," he complained. "It's all soft and cuddly and lacks a man's presence. First, we need to repaint the walls in a forest green and then add more natural wood to the trim, sort of give it a man-cave feeling. Then we put a mace or two on the walls, along with a bunch of swords and some halberds, and mebbe a bunch of animal heads. Then we find some artist to do a tapestry of an orgy. Probably wanna hang that in the bedroom," he winked.

"I'll do no such thing," she snapped.

Ignoring her, Karl continued. "Then we'll need two thrones, imposing things that will show who's boss around here, set up high on a platform, which means we'll need a throne room. I figure we can temporarily use one of the rooms towards the main doors until we find a more suitable place. Might have to knock out a wall or two and raise the ceiling."

A servant girl entered carrying an ale and a plate of sausages. She was a buxom lass with narrow hips and long auburn hair done in a braid. Her blouse, though demurely buttoned was more than snug over her large breasts.

Karl's eyes brightened with delight. "Now that's what I'm talkin' about. Come over here you young filly." Waiting for her to place the ale and food on the table, he grabbed her and sat her on his lap. Giving Mavie a lascivious stare, he winked while ticking his head at the girl. "You're a succubus. What say we have a little threesome."

Mavie thrust back from the table and bolted up to standing, an arm outstretched pointing at the door. "Out," she bellowed, glaring at the girl who leaped off Karl's lap and raced out the room.

Leaning heavily on the table, Mavie gave him a withering look. "Let's get one thing straight. I rule this domain and when I rule the kingdom, you will learn your place."

Unfazed, Karl noisily chewed on a sausage chasing it with deep swallows of ale. "Dream on little girl. You may be a succubus, but you ain't ruling a damned thing without me and my friends who, by the way, will expect some reward for their help. I figure since I'll be king we'll give them a part of the kingdom to run, either here or Westhaven."

"Like hell, I will," she fumed.

A knock on the door elicited a loud and angry "What?" from Mavie.

The door opened and a guard cautiously poked his head in. "M'Lady. A messenger from Queen Gwen has arrived."

"Tell him to wait," she snapped, knowing full well why he was here. "No, tell him I'll be right there." Flashing a fierce stare at Karl, she said, "I'm not finished with you."

"Of course not," he flippantly replied. "We still got a date in the bedroom with that servant girl who was just in here. Y'know, I never did get her name."

Gritting her teeth, Mavie whirled around and stormed out.

For two days, Gwen's messenger was kept waiting for Mavie's final answer. For two days, Karl made life odious in the castle, so odious that Mavie refused to share her bedroom or meals with him, forcing him to happily seek companionship with the servants who were at first wary of his advances until Mavie gave the 'go ahead.' After that, Karl never lacked for partners willing to share his meals and especially his bed.

It was after two days that Mavie's messengers returned with the fated news.

"They're gone, m'Lady," one man said. He was a trim fit man, tired from the rush to get back. "They've crossed the bridge.

"Damn," she exploded. "You were supposed to stop them."

"I did my best, m'Lady," he nervously answered. "They had a head start and barely paused to sleep. They were across the bridge by several hours by the time I got there."

"Damn it, damn it, damn it," she fumed, pacing the floor in angry strides. Storming to the door, she commanded the guard to "Get Gwen's messenger." Whirling around to her own messenger who wearily wobbled after the long ride, she yelled, "Get ready to leave. Now get out of here."

So it was that Karl found himself on the road back to Durness, escorted by six of Mavie's finest warriors as well as the poor messenger who had been placed in charge of the escort. Not wanting to appear too subservient, Mavie specifically chose an ox and wagon as the means of delivery, horses being much too quick.

With a wide grin, Karl stretched out in the back, hands interlaced on his stomach, head propped on a bedroll. His grin split wider as he remembered their parting words."

"You're sending me back?" he had blurted, surprised. "What about you wanting to rule the kingdom?"

"I changed my mind," she dismissively answered.

Karl stared at her then shook his head. "Where's my team?"

"There not here," she crisply replied.

Karl stared at her for a moment then sniffed in disdain. "They crossed the bridge and now you realize you can't do squat without them. So now you're sending me back like some peace offering."

"What I do is my business," she exclaimed then narrowed her eyes at him. "But you want the truth? I'll give you the truth. You're boring, uncouth, crude and quite honestly the worst lover I've ever had."

"Well don't sugar-coat it," Karl yawned. "Tell me how you really feel."

Titters erupted from the waiting guards that just as quickly vanished under her harsh glare.

"Don't forget what I said about what's gonna happen when I become king," he said as a not so subtle threat.

Mavie sniffed in derision. "After a week with you, Gwen will be begging me to take you back." Turning to the messenger, she added, "I hold you responsible for his safe return to Gwen. If anything happens, your head will roll."

"Yes, m'Lady," he replied with a hard swallow.

"Go," she commanded. "He's wasted my time too much already."

Now riding in the wagon heading for the first stop towards Hillfurt, Karl chuckled. His plan was working well so far. All he had to do now was figure out how to escape from his guards who, unfortunately, were well trained and quite alert... and all armed with crossbows and swords.

Mavie had initially contemplated shackling him, but when he pointed out that Gwen would hardly want her lover shackled like some common criminal, she wavered. He then gave his word that he would be good and nothing would happen and she relented. Of course, he had his fingers crossed behind his back. It was juvenile, but for some reason he found it appropriately absurd considering he was being sent to another woman like a peace offering.

Despite the early start, the slow pace made the day drag and Karl alternated between sleeping in the cart and walking along with some of the guards who were reticent to engage in conversation. The one individual willing to talk was the original messenger whom Karl convinced to sleep in the cart after the sergeant of the guard nodded his assent.

By late morning, the man awoke, refreshed to see Karl contentedly strolling by the cart.

"Thank you," he said, sitting up and stretching.

"No problem. You needed the rest. It's not like we're in any danger and I've already promised to be good." Karl flashed a winning smile. "What's your name?"

"Nervel," he answered, pushing himself over the side of the wagon to walk beside Karl.

"Sorry she made you come along," Karl said.

"Me too. This is baby-sitting and nothing more."

"I've already given my word," Karl pointed out. "You all could just let me go on by myself."

Nervel frowned at him then laughed when he saw Karl's innocent look. "It's *my* head, remember?"

"Ah, I had forgotten about that." He then looked around at the six guards who repositioned themselves every so often, yet always in a circle surrounding Karl.

"I didn't," Nervel soberly replied.

"I guess you wouldn't. So tell me, you're sure that my team got across the bridge?"

"Quite sure," Nervel replied. "The last guard at the checkpoint not too far from the gate told me."

"There's a gate at the bridge?"

"Of course," he frowned as though the response was obvious. "No one is allowed to cross unless they know the password."

"There's a password?" Karl startled.

"Naturally. And if you don't know the password, the gods help you because the land giant guarding the bridge will rip you apart."

"Land giant?" Karl cocked an apprehensive eyebrow.

"Yup. Biggest, nastiest piece of work you'd ever want to see. Don't recommend pissing him off."

"Um... do you know the password?"

"Of course not," Nervel sniffed then leaned in closer and whispered, "but I know what it is."

Karl cocked an eyebrow at him. "You don't know the password, but you know what it is. That doesn't make any sense."

"What I meant is that while I don't *know* the password, I know what it is."

"You're still not making any sense."

Letting out a sigh of frustration, Nervel leaned closer and whispered, "The password is the name of the island on the other side of the bridge."

Karl blinked at the revelation. All this time, his gaming map only filled with the present island. As far as he knew, there had never been a name listed for the next island. He was about to call up his screen when he realized the others could see what he was doing. Deciding there was a reason the name was kept secret, he simply nodded and settled back to light conversation, though pleased his team had made it across, at the same time wondering how they figured out the password."

Thinking of Raquel and Annabeth caused him to ponder how Conrad and the others were faring. Since their parting, he hadn't seen them though he had heard they had moved on, back towards Durness. While part of him understood their desire to live a carefree life, he wished either Tina or Kendra had stayed. The team needed a medic.

That evening after they stopped to make camp in an abandoned house, Karl settled into a corner and pulled up his screen. Pressing the map icon, he saw that they were not far from Hillfurt. Scrolling the map to the corner, he looked to where the bridge ended at the partial edge of another island. The two word name for the island was initially crisp, but quickly disappeared before Karl had a chance to focus on it.

Closing down the screen, he surmised that the name would reappear once he got close to the bridge. If he was going to catch up with the team, he needed to escape... very soon.

They were half a day's journey from Berismo when they stopped for the night at an abandoned cabin tucked at the edge of the forest at the end of a long unused path off the main road. Karl silently chuckled once inside, noting the cabin had the same look as all the other small houses in the game, down to the table and chairs in the center of the front room and the bed in the back room. Even the scratches in the window frames looked the same.

Nervel had quickly inspected the place and pronounced it suitable before commanding a fire built in the fireplace.

"Spiders?" Karl asked when two guards returned with armloads of branches.

"Not anymore," Nervel said. "The last of the chimney spiders were run off a long time ago. Still, old habits run deep and one never knows if they might not return. Better safe than sorry."

"No arguments from me." Karl glanced around the front room then ambled to the back room where he checked the shutters to the windows.

"Thinking of going somewhere?" Nervel wondered aloud, stepping into the room.

"The last time I was in a place like this we were attacked by goblins," Karl informed him. "Like you, I like to be prepared."

"You won't find any goblins in these parts," Nervel told him, "nor orcs or trolls or anything else that goes bump in the night. Nothing much happens in these parts except for the occasional highwayman and they keep to the lesser traveled trails."

The sergeant of the guards, a tall man with a scar across his collar bone, stepped in the room. "I think we have trouble."

"What?" Nervel frowned.

"Egan went for a piss and hasn't returned."

"So send someone to look for him," Nervel impatiently replied.

"I did that already," the man huffed. "He's gone too."

"What?" Nervel stormed across the room, Karl and the sergeant of the guard following. Yanking open the front door, he saw the four remaining guards probing the forest areas close to the cabin. "Well?"

"Nothing," a guard called back.

"They can't just disappear," Nervel groused.

"And they wouldn't just take off," the sergeant stated. "I know them. They're good professional soldiers."

When Nervel looked up he noticed there were three guards. "What the hell? Where's Caulrun? He was there just a moment ago." He pointed to a crop of trees twenty paces from the rear of the cabin.

As the remaining three hurried over to inspect, two stumbled and fell in succession, impaled by arrows through the throat. Not waiting to see if they were dead, the last guard bolted straight for the front door only to be hit from behind, an arrow protruding out his chest. Glassy eyed, he stumbled across the threshold as Nervel and Karl dragged him in while the sergeant slammed the door closed and bolted it.

"Hallo in the cabin," a voice called out.

Karl quickened as he recognized it. "Hello Kevin. What brings you here?"

"You do."

"And why is that?"

"You know why. That's twice you've destroyed me. It's my turn now."

"What happened to you was your own fault," Karl called back.

"Who is he?" Nervel hoarsely whispered.

"An old acquaintance who wants to kill me," Karl calmly replied.

"Why?"

"Long story," Karl shrugged, glancing down at the now dead guard whose blood was pooling beneath his body.

"You in the cabin," Kevin called out. "I've no beef with you. Give me the Viking and you're free to go."

"Like the rest of my squad that you killed?" the sergeant shot back.

"An unfortunate consequence," Kevin said. "I had to whittle down the odds. As a soldier, I'm sure you can understand that."

"Be careful," Karl quietly warned Nervel. "He's an assassin and he's good."

"Dammit," the sergeant muttered.

"I can't," Nervel called back. "I'm responsible for escorting him to Queen Gwen."

"I'm afraid that mission has changed," Kevin answered.

"How so? Gwen is still queen, is she not?"

"Oh, she's still queen," Kevin said, "But your Viking friend will never get there. So do yourself a favor and turn him over to me so you can save your own lives."

"Then you do not know either Gwen or Mavie," Nervel retorted. "We do as you ask and we condemn ourselves. Why not let us deliver him to Gwen and then you can do as you wish?"

"Sorry," Kevin said. "Can't do that. And I know that you're thinking. You'll wait for the mist and escape. I wouldn't do that if I were you. I've set traps all around the cabin. It would be a pity to fall into one of them."

"He's bluffing," Karl softly cautioned, "otherwise we'd have seen them. Still, while we're in here, he has the advantage and the time to set new traps."

"What do we do?" the sergeant growled. "I'll be damned if I stay in here like some quaking new recruit afraid of battle."

"It's not a question of being afraid," Karl countered. "It's a question of eliminating the problem. He has the advantage because he knows where we are, but we don't know where he is." He tilted his head back to stare at the ceiling. "Douse the fire."

"Why?" the sergeant asked.

"The roof," Karl answered. "It's thatch. One of us gets on top of the roof and finds out where he is." He focused on the sergeant. "You've got a crossbow and can get a good shot from up there. Once you know where he is, we can create a diversion down here for you to get off a shot."

Liking the idea, he briskly nodded and went over to the dying fire, kicking and spreading the embers, crushing some under the heel of his boots.

"So?" Kevin said. "Will you give him to me?"

"Haven't decided yet," Nervel answered. "Don't see how this works to my advantage. Either way I'm a dead man. At least here and now I have a slight chance of success."

"How you figure that?" Kevin demanded, his irritation mounting.

"Good, good," Karl whispered. "He's getting mad. Keep it up."

"There's three of us," Nervel pointed out, "and only one of you. Now that we know there's just you, we do have a certain advantage."

By now the fire was out and the sergeant positioned the table in the back bedroom.

"Keep him talking," Karl urged as he went to help the sergeant.

"You forget I'm an assassin," Kevin retorted.

"Even assassins make mistakes," Nervel said. "You still haven't told us why you want him."

"Ask him."

"I did. He said it was a long story. So why don't you tell me your side, or at least give me some justification for what you ask."

There was a pause before Kevin replied, "He killed me not long ago."

"Killed you?" Nervel snorted a laugh. "If he killed you, how is it that you are here now talking to us?"

"I... I am like him and some others. Though we can be killed, we do not die."

"Now you are making no sense," Nervel said, glancing back to see the sergeant worming his way up through the roof. Once through, Karl handed him the crossbow.

"It's hard to explain," Kevin said.

"Go ahead and try," Nervel answered. "We've got all night."

"Ask the Viking to explain it," Kevin snapped. "Also ask him what he did to me."

Karl came up to stand beside Nervel by the door. "That's because you're a coward," he called out. "You were a coward before and have proven to be a coward once again by killing innocent men who were sent to escort me to Durness. Your beef was with me, yet you had no qualms about killing five innocent men though they had nothing to do with your perverted concept of revenge."

"It couldn't be helped," Kevin replied, his tone apologetic.

"That's your excuse?" Karl sniffed in disdain. "It couldn't be helped? Why don't you tell them why you were branded a coward, Kevin. We'd all like to hear that tale."

"Go to hell, Karl."

"By the way, did you kill Brad and the others as they came through here?"

"Why would I do that? They had no part in what you did to me."

Karl was about to reply when Kevin burst a loud, "God damn it," followed by the sergeant exclaiming, "Got him."

Nervel jerked the door open just as the sergeant's body rolled off the roof. Kevin stood in the near distance, a crossbow bolt in his thigh. He had already notched another arrow and let it fly, hitting Nervel in the stomach.

Karl leaped over the crumbling Nervel and slammed a fist into Kevin before he had a chance to notch another arrow. From then on the fight was lopsided as Karl pummeled Kevin to a bloody pulp.

As Kevin lay broken and bleeding, Karl returned to the dying Nervel and withdrew the man's sword. Kneeling beside him, he gazed down at the man and knew there was nothing he could do for him, nothing that would ease the pain of his life slipping away.

Off to the side, the sergeant lay bent and still, a single arrow through his heart.

Within that small span of time of Karl attending to the fallen men, Kevin had struggled and groped his way to the small pile of weapons where he grabbed a one-handed crossbow. When Karl stood and turned, he fired.

Karl felt the impact into his chest, the pain exponentially exploding throughout his body. Despite the pain, he staggered over to the prostrate Kevin. While his health bar dwindled into the red, Karl used the last of his strength and raised the sword then plunged it into Kevin's heart. Sinking to his knees, he collapsed on top of his nemesis.

Darkness swirled the periphery of his mind and eyes before engulfing him and casting him into a vortex of electric impulses and static jolts of excruciating pain. The minutes of his agony felt like hours until in a final burst, the pain fled and he stood, quite naked, in the bedroom of the guest apartment in Mavie's castle.

Gulping a breath like a man surfacing for air after too long under water, he wobbled as he numbly glanced around, thankful it was night and that hopefully no one was in the room. He let his eyes adjust to the darkness, feeling his strength returning and saw in the moonlight filtering in through the tall windows that the bed was made. For some reason he couldn't explain, he flicked on his game screen, reassuring himself that his level remained the same, though he was now without any clothing, weapons, potions, or coins.

But he was alive, and that was what counted. He was also closer to the bridge, so there was that to be thankful for. Now all he had to do was get there.

Pleased to have remembered to make this apartment his bind spot, he navigated around the furniture in the dark, passing from the bedroom to the large room that served as living and dining rooms. Light from the hallway slipped in under the front door.

Pausing before the door, he twisted his head and pressed an ear close to the door, focusing on the sounds in the hallway. Satisfied, he twisted the door knob and slowly pried open the door, blinking in the light spilling through the crack. No door guards told him that no guests were assigned to the apartment, which meant he was safe for the night.

Through the slit in the door, he watched and waited for the right person to pass, though traffic was sparse this time of night. At one point, a passing man servant noticed the door ajar and paused to check, pushing it open as Karl ducked behind it. The servant swung the door wide enough to peep inside, decided nothing was amiss and closed the door.

Karl waited until silence once again ruled the hallway before cracking the door open again. An oppressive quiet seemed to stretch as no one ventured in the corridor for a quite a while and he found his attention wandering. He shook his head, chastising himself to focus. Then he heard footsteps and his senses sharpened.

A pretty young woman with long blond hair tied in a ponytail passed by. She wore a forest green servant's dress though without the inner blouse, which meant she was off duty, for no woman servant would parade around the castle with bare shoulders. Karl recognized her.

Louder than a whisper but not normal tone, he called out, "Gillien."

She stopped and abruptly turned around then frowned when she saw no one behind her.

"Over here." Standing to the side of the door, he opened it wider so she saw only his head.

"M'Lord," she brightened with surprised pleasure.

"Shhh, not so loud. C'mere." He curled a finger at her.

"I thought you were gone, m'Lord," she said, walking up.

"I was," he replied, opening the door wider for her to enter.

"Why are you hiding in the dark?' she asked, passing by him and striking a match to light a taper.

When she heard Karl close and lock the door, she turned. "Oh... my... Lord," she blurted, her eyes raking over his

362

muscular body, before settling below his waist. Jamming the taper in a holder, she began unlacing her dress. "Gimme just a minute. Had I known you were already prepared, I –"

"Slow down," Karl interrupted with a smile. "It's not what you think, at least not yet," he hastily added, seeing her disappointment.

"Does m'Lady know you are back?" she asked, her eyes momentarily lifting to his face then dropping again.

"No, and I want to keep it that way." He repositioned to stand behind a high back chair so that her focus would be on his face and the urgency of what he said. "There's a reason I'm as you see me now," he began, his mind racing to come up with a plausible story. "I was on my way to Durness when we were attacked by an evil witch. I was able to fight her off, but in the last minute, she cast a spell and sent me here."

"An evil witch?" Gillen breathed with terrified delight. "O my God that had to have been scary."

"It was," he replied. "The problem is that I am as you see me. I have no clothing, no weapons, no money, nothing. I need your help. If I am to resume my journey to Durness, I obviously can't go like this."

"Of course, my Lord," she said with enthusiasm. "But why not simply ask m'Lady for what you need?"

"I can't because it would endanger those who were supposed to escort me to Durness. You don't know it, but Mavie charged Nervel and the others with my safety. Me showing up here, now, would mean, in her eyes, that they failed, and that means they would pay with their lives. They're good men and I don't want that to happen to them. It wasn't their fault."

Gillen's eyes filled with admiration and respect. "You are such a good man, m'Lord. All of us know what you did and why you did it to get away from her."

"What do you mean?" he said, fearing he was not the consummate actor he thought he was.

"My Lord," she answered with a knowing smile as she moved closer to him. "When you were with her, you were inconsiderate and rude, but once you left her, you were back

to normal, kind and caring. Even us girls who got to share
your bed with you all said how sweet you were, how gentle
and what an incredible lover you were, how large... uh, I
mean, how much you cared for us."

"Then you'll help me?"

"Of course, m'Lord." She reached up a hand and gently
placed it on his shoulder, her eyes focused on his face before
slipping down to his chest, wishing he hadn't pressed closer
to the chair.

"Good. The first thing I need is clothing. Do you think
you can get something for me tonight?"

"I have a cousin your size," she cheerily replied. "I'll be
back in no time."

As she headed towards the door, he added, "See if you
can get me a short sword or something."

She skidded to a halt. "I don't know how I'm going to
do that, m'Lord," she pouted. "Servants don't normally carry
weapons."

Karl nodded in understanding then smiled. "Just the
clothes for tonight and hopefully you're free for the rest of
the night."

Gillien perked up. "I am at your service, m'Lord."

Gillien was true to her word and she returned less than an
hour later, slipping into the apartment, a pile of neatly folded
clothes in her arms.

"I know they're not exactly Viking clothing, but it's the
best I could do," she apologized, laying the clothing on the
bed. She stepped to the side admiring the view as Karl came
up and inspected the clothes.

"These are excellent," Karl said, holding up the trousers,
pleased for he determined that not looking like a Viking
might be an advantage in his escape, though the trousers
seemed a little large in the waist.

Seeing his focus, Gillien gamely shrugged. "He's not
put together quite as good as you are."

"These will be fine." He turned and stepped closer to her
then gave her an impish grin. "Well, I've got clothes thanks
to you. What else do I need this evening?" he innocently
asked, unlacing her dress.

Gillien was up early and out the apartment door before most in the castle was awake, heading down to the kitchen, which was just beginning to hum with breakfast preparation. By the time she returned, Karl was dressed and standing behind the door.

"Anyone ask you why you wanted food so early?" Karl said, closing and locking the door behind her.

"Not really, m'Lord," she answered with a smile as she placed a small block of cheese, sliced cold meats, fresh bread, and a large mug of ale on the dining table. "Sometimes I'm up early and so it's not unusual for me to go to the kitchen to get something to eat. But I was able to get this," she proudly announced, placing a large kitchen knife next to the ale mug.

"Well done," he complimented, lifting up and inspecting the blade while nibbling on a slice of meat. The knife was sharp and sturdy, something that would last until he found a better blade or a sword. "This will do nicely." He leaned over and kissed her on the forehead.

Blushing at the praise, she handed him the mug of ale.

"We're sharing this meal," he reminded her, taking a sip then handing the mug to her. "It's not like you can go again to the kitchen for another breakfast. Besides, you've managed to get enough food for two."

Gillien stared at him with reverence. "See? That's just what I mean. Anyone else would've eaten everything and not even worried about me. But not you. That's why we all knew you were tricking the Lady."

"Let's hope I can trick her enough so that she doesn't know I'm here," he said, rolling his eyes. "Now I have one more favor to ask."

"Anything, m'Lord."

"I'll need money, just enough to get me to Durness. Is that possible without you getting into trouble?"

"I have some you can have," she replied with a bashful half-smile.

"I can't take your money," Karl said, shaking his head. "It's hard enough to come by for servants."

"I really don't mind," she said with a shrug. "I figure you can owe me and once you're king, you'll have all the money you need so no one will notice if you pay me back."

The way she said it seemed to imply that she didn't want to be paid back, as though being owed somehow gave her leverage. Karl silently rued her innocence, at the same time wondering how he was going to pay her back.

"Are you sure?" he asked.

"Of course, m'Lord. I'll go get it now if you wish." She made to leave but Karl stopped her.

"I don't need it quite yet. I don't want to rush off without a plan. For instance, when would be the best time for me to leave the castle without being noticed?"

Gillien frowned as she pondered the question. "Early morning would be the best because no one's up except the kitchen staff."

"The city gates are still closed," Karl pointed out, "but I could hang out in the shadows until the gates open." He grinned at Gillien. "Guess I'll have to spend another night here."

"I'd be happy to keep you company, m'Lord," she said with a virtuous smile.

"I was hoping you'd say that." He gave her a not so subtle look of desire as he took in the lovely woman before him. While not the experienced lover like Raquel or Annabeth... or Gwen and Mavie for that matter, Gillien had an enthusiastic innocence about her that more than made up for her lack of experience. The fact that she also had a beautiful body added to the enjoyment. Pity he couldn't take her with him.

What am I saying? Good God, that's the last thing I need. Focus, Karl. Get your ass across the bridge. That's the mission.

"I'll be back at lunch time," she said.

"Be careful," he warned. "We don't want someone to inadvertently see you."

"I'll be careful, m'Lord." She pressed her body against his, luxuriating in his strength and raw sensuality.

"You better go before I drag you to the bedroom," he said with a chuckle.

Momentarily torn between taking him up on his offer and suffering the verbal abuse of her supervisor or delaying the sweet promise until a safer time, she chose responsibility.

"I'll be back as soon as I can."

"That's my girl," he smiled, giving her a playful swat on the butt.

She was back in the early afternoon, slipping into the apartment and unloading a meat and cheese sandwich and a pitcher of ale.

"I can't stay long, but I thought you might be hungry. I also brought this." She placed a small leather bag of coins on the table. "There's fourteen gold in there. That should last you until you get to Durness."

"That's more than enough," he said with heartfelt gratitude, grabbing her hand and pulling her into him to deliver a deep kiss.

Starry eyed as she caught her breath, she said, "I've got more if you need it."

"No. This is plenty. You have done so much for me. I will not forget this." He held the sandwich up to her. "Have you eaten yet?"

"I had a snack a little while ago," she lied as her stomach gave a loud grumble.

"Silly girl," he admonished as he split the sandwich in half. "You need to eat too. Here. Take a drink."

"I've got to get back, m'Lord, before they miss me."

He held on to her, lifting the sandwich up to her mouth. "At least take a bite."

Obeying, she took a large bite and soon finished her half the sandwich.

"Now some ale. Then go on."

"Yes, m'Lord," she answered, swallowing two gulps.

Karl escorted her to the door, giving her a quick kiss before opening it for her. It was as she closed the door that he heard a haughty woman's voice.

"What are you doing there?"

"I was just checking, Miss," Karl heard Gillien reply.

"Why?" the voice demanded, sounding close, like they were on the other side of the door.

"I heard one of the servants say the door was open a little bit earlier and I came by to check to make sure nothing was amiss."

"Well?"

"I looked around, Miss, and there was nothing out of place."

The door handle twisted and the door began to open when Karl realized his half of the sandwich and mug of ale were still on the table. He was about to reach around the door and grab whoever it was when he heard Gillien.

"You're looking different today, Miss. Have you done something different with your hair? You have such pretty hair and it looks good."

The door paused then closed. Karl raced silently over and retrieved the sandwich and ale then retraced his steps back to the door.

"No. It's like I always wear it," the voice haughty replied though flattered.

"Well, I've always liked your hair. It's such a pretty brown, soft and full."

"That's enough about my hair," the woman replied with a slight chuckle. "Go on about your work."

"Yes, Miss."

There was a pause and the door opened again. Karl tucked behind it, holding his breath. After a few moments, he heard a "Humpf," and the door closed. It wasn't until he heard the footsteps soften then disappear that he let out an exhale of relief. He glanced at the open door to the bedroom, thankful that Gillien was conscientious enough to make the bed after the night of pleasure.

It was well after the dinner hour when Gillien returned with a tray laden with roasted pork, hot bread, some green vegetables that Karl didn't recognize and a pitcher of ale.

"How did you manage to get all this without anyone noticing?" Karl asked, impressed.

"It's late and most everyone's in their rooms, relaxing. Those still on duty are preoccupied with what they're doing." Setting the tray down, she poured him a mug of cold ale.

It was then he noticed the bag on her shoulder. "What's in the bag?" he asked, taking a satisfying swig of ale.

"Some of my clothes and things," she nonchalantly replied, setting it down on a chair then turning her attention to prepare his plate.

"Seems an awful lot of stuff for one evening," he frowned.

"Oh," she said, arranging several slices of pork, "I'm coming with you."

"What?" he sputtered, choking on ale.

"I said I'm coming with you. There," she smiled as she slid the plate towards him. "Enjoy."

"But... but, what about your job here?" he argued, his mind racing.

"They won't miss me. I'm just a junior level maid though thank the gods not a scullery maid. You haven't tasted your food yet. Sit. Eat."

"Let's talk about this," he countered.

"Sit." She pointed to the chair.

Sliding the chair out, he obeyed, as she refilled his mug. Deciding honesty was probably his best course of action, he said, "Listen. I'm not going back to Durness."

"I know," she answered, smiling sweetly at him. "You're going to the bridge."

"How... how did you know that?" he said, his frown deepening.

"It doesn't take a genius to figure that out," she grinned at him. "All your friends have crossed the bridge. Why would you not go be with your friends?"

"But... but..." He put his fork down and leveled his gaze at her. "OK. Let's be realistic about this. My team and I are mercenaries. We fight. We kill. We are in constant danger. How do you see yourself fitting into that?"

She scooted a chair back and plopped down, reaching for a piece of pork and tearing it in two. "Elena isn't a warrior and she's with you."

He was about to say 'it's not the same,' but realized the argument wasn't valid. "What skills can you bring to the team?"

"I can cook, perhaps not as well as Elena, but I can sew and mend and I know some healing arts. Why don't you want to take me? Are you disappointed with me?" Her lower lip protruded as she pouted.

"No," he exclaimed, "not in the least. It's your safety I'm worried about. We get into some pretty severe scrapes and I and the others won't always be around to protect you."

"Elena's still with you," she pointed out.

Damn. I knew we should have left her back where we found her. How can I get rid of this woman without jeopardizing my escape? How do I tell her that I don't want her with me? He then thought of how her presence would settle with Raquel and Annabeth... *about as much as Gwen and Mavie did.*

"Let me think about it," he said, taking a slow sip of ale.

Felix stood at the window in his office, cursing the weather gods. For more than ten days in a row, the wind and temps were down to comfortable levels and the sun blazed brightly across clear blue skies... and he was stuck inside his office, vicariously swinging his five iron with the rare golfer across the river.

The door opened and Scott walked in. "You wanted to see me?"

"Yes," he said, not turning as he watched a sole golfer playout from the fairway. It was a good hit. *Probably a six or seven iron.* "Take a seat."

Wondering why the display of authority, Scott sat down in one of the overstuffed chairs facing Felix's desk.

Turning, Felix stared at him a moment before saying, "I understand we have an NPC who wants to go with Karl."

"Yes," Scott said with a weak smile. "Her name's Gillien."

"I know," Felix said, cutting him off. "She's a maid at the castle in Tal Olca, and she intends to accompany Karl on his trip across the bridge. Your thoughts?"

"Uh," Scott hesitated.

"I remind you that your recommendation was to let nonessential NPCs cross the bridge. I agreed to allow Elena to cross. Tell me what the benefits of allowing this NPC to cross, especially, as I understand it, Karl does not desire her to cross."

"Uh, hmmm." Scott pondered the wisdom of letting Gillien cross. "The way I see it is that it has two possible benefits. This Gillien could be a distraction and thus we could see how Karl deals with unwanted distractions. Or," he quickly stated, seeing the undisguised disapproval in Felix's eyes, "we let her cross, place her in a town somewhere and have her act as a sort of quest aid for future bridge crossers."

"Or we leave well enough alone," Felix flatly stated. "I saw a benefit with Elena crossing as Dieter had formed a bond with the character. Karl has no inclination for this woman other than to relieve sexual urges. Therefore the woman stays on the island."

"But –"

"No 'buts'," Felix interrupted. "The woman does not cross. Is that clear?"

"Suppose Karl tells her the password to cross?" Scott objected.

Felix narrowed his gaze at him. "I repeat. She does not cross. Kill her if you have to. Let her respawn back at the castle. I don't care what you do with her, but she does not cross."

"I understand," Scott said. "What if Karl tells her the password?"

Felix huffed and rolled his eyes. "Puh-lease. You're the designer. Fix it."

"Yes, Sir."

Dawn had yet to appear when Karl stood at the door to the apartment, Gillien behind him. He was tired. They were both tired. After finally agreeing to allow her to accompany him, they had adjourned to a wild session in the bedroom. Though exhausted, they were both too keyed-up to sleep, preoccupied with thoughts of the journey to the bridge.

Now, their adrenaline pumping, they hesitated one last time at the door.

"Ready?" Karl asked.

"Yes," she replied, eyes wide with excitement.

"You're sure no one other than the guards are up."

"Yes."

"And you know the way once we get outside the castle?" Karl knew that not only would the mist be heavy, it would also be dark.

"Yes."

"Then let's do it." Opening the door, he led the way down the dimly lit hallway. Gillien carried the previous evening's left overs on the tray.

Turning the corner, they came to the first set of guards outside Mavie's quarters.

"You're up early," one of the guards said, quizzically looking at Karl.

"Yeah," Gillien replied with a sigh, rolling her eyes. "I forgot to clean up last night and figured I'd better get it done before I get in trouble."

The guard flashed an understanding smile thought studying Karl. "Say, aren't you –"

"I am," Karl acknowledged. "Do you know Nervel?"

"Yes," the one guard said. "He's a friend of mine."

"Then you know he was charged with escorting me to Durness. We were attacked on the way there by sorcery and I ended up here again. I don't know who or why we were attacked, but," he ticked his head at the door, "I don't want her to know I was here, otherwise it would get Nervel and the others in trouble. I'm heading back out to try and catch up with him. I would consider it a favor if you would keep my presence here to yourselves."

"Of course, m'Lord," the guard readily agreed. "You have our word."

"Good. Also, this wonderful lady was kind enough to feed me. I'd also appreciate it if you kept her involvement likewise a secret."

"Of course, m'Lord. We understand."

"When I get to Durness, I will be sure to remember your actions and your professionalism. And I don't need to remind you that Gwen is now your queen, which makes me..." He left it unfinished, silently chuckling at their response for both immediately straightened to full height and bowed.

"One more thing," Karl said with a regal tone. "I am without a weapon. The sorceress who attacked us flung me here, defenseless. I do not wish to deprive warriors like yourself of a weapon, but would consider it a kindness if you could procure me a suitable sword so that I can properly defend myself as I work my way to find Nervel and the others."

"Take mine, m'Lord," the younger guard said, holding his sword out.

Karl gazed at him with approval. "You are a fine warrior. However, how would you explain to your sergeant or captain that you are on watch without a sword. No, I will not put you in that position. You are already protecting me and I do not want to get you into more trouble should someone untrustworthy relay my presence here. Is there another means of procuring me a sword?"

"The armory," the older guard said.

"But it's locked," the younger guard said.

"I know where the keys are," the older man said with a grin, touching his finger to his nose.

"Excellent," Karl praised. "How soon can you be back here?"

"In no time at all, m'Lord."

"Good. Be quick about you then. I'll stay here with your compatriot until you return."

The older guard hustled down the hallway, returning not more than five minutes later, breathless, but holding a new sharp sword.

"Perfect," Karl lauded. He twirled the sword, feeling its balance. "This will do just fine. I am in your debt, gentlemen." Placing a finger to his lips, he whispered, "Remember, I was not here."

Both guards placed a fist over their hearts and bowed. "We swear we will keep your secret."

"I won't forget this," Karl said as he led Gillien away.

It wasn't until after Karl and Gillien disappeared around another corner that the one guard turned to the other, giving him a confident grin that abruptly disappeared. "He didn't ask our names."

"Aw, don't worry about that," the other replied. "We been here enough that he knows who we are."

"Yeah," the first one perked up. "When he's king, we're gonna be in for some good stuff."

Karl and Gillen raced down the remaining hallways, stopping only twice more to relay the same story with the same results. After the last set of guards, Gillien jettisoned the tray when they emerged into the shrouded courtyard. The faint illumination of dawn rimmed the mist.

"Take my hand," Gillien said, holding out her hand then feeling Karl's strong grip. Creeping slowly, Gillien led the way, cautiously venturing along the cobbled streets. A few times they bumped into parked wagons, but for the most part arrived at the closed main gate without incident.

Karl found a spot close to the gate and leaned back against the wall, sliding down to sit on the ground. Gillien sat next to him, wrapping a thin blanket around them both.

Chapter 11

The gate guard startled when Karl and Gillien emerged from the shadows and plowed through the entrance. The guard puzzled for only a moment thinking he had seen the tall man somewhere, but quickly forgot him when the normal merchant traffic began building.

The pace was quick as they sought to put the castle and city far behind them. So quick in fact that twice Karl had to slow down for Gillien to catch up. Finally, after two hours' forced march, Karl slowed and turned around, walking backwards. The city was far enough away to be but a tiny display in the distance.

"We can slow down now," he said. He observed that she was perspiring then thought with admiration that she hadn't complained once during their flight. "You doing OK?"

"I'm fine," she cheerily replied, wiping the sweat from her forehead. "How long is it until we get to the bridge?"

"Day after tomorrow," Karl assured her.

Gillien's eyes lit up. "This is so exciting. We snuck out of the castle and the city and no one is the wiser. You are so clever." She hugged his arm. "I wonder what life on the other side of the bridge is like. Do you think they're like us?"

"I would think so," Karl replied, resuming the march, but at a slower pace.

Gillien slipped a hand into his. "This is going to be so much fun. I'm going to make you so happy that those other two women on the team will be so jealous. But I don't want to make them angry. You'll explain everything won't you?"

"Explain what?" Karl said, his attention focused on the terrain and getting them safely to the bridge. Yet most of his thoughts dwelt with what to do with her. Should he take her with him? Did he really want that headache? Was there a benefit to having her along? What were the downsides? And what were the likely repercussions gonna be with Annabeth and Raquel?

"That you and I are together, that you don't need anyone else. They'll understand."

"Understand what?" he asked, realizing that he was missing out on part of a discussion where he was a prime participant.

"About us."

"What about us?"

"That we're together," she dreamily answered, "that we're united in a holy bond that even demons and angels can't break."

Karl's eyelids fluttered as he suddenly understood her meaning. "Let's not get carried away here," he admonished. "Maybe you need to go back. We don't know how dangerous this all could be."

"Oh no you don't," she laughed. "You're just testing me, seeing if I really mean it." She stepped quickly in front of him and wrapped her arms around him, squeezing him with all her might. "You're the best. You're always caring about me. You don't need to worry. You can sleep with those other women sometimes. I won't be jealous. They're the ones who are gonna be jealous when they see how much in love we are."

"Love?" Karl sputtered, prying her away. "Who said anything about love?"

"Oh don't be such a silly," she smirked knowingly at him. "Men. You're all alike, afraid to say how you really feel. That's OK though, because I know deep inside what you really feel." She slid around to his side and pulled him forward. "C'mon, Mister I'm-afraid-to-show-my-feelings. We got a bridge to cross."

For the next day and a half, Gillien smothered Karl with her devotion and attention while Karl worked through various schemes on how to get rid of her. Unfortunately, none came in time for the forest swooped in upon the road and Karl knew they were getting close.

He relaxed, closed his eyes and inhaled the scent of the sea. He knew they were not far from the bridge and was about to tell Gillien when he opened his eyes and saw the half rotted corpse of a man to the side of the road. Shifting a glance at Gillien, he saw her shock and horror. She pointed beyond the corpse to another set of bones.

Karl followed her gaze and counted another six bodies in various forms of decay, leading up to a gap in the trees. The farthest body had been reduced to skeleton, the carrion birds having long ago torn and ripped the flesh from its body.

Cautiously proceeding, they stepped over and around bodies until they emerged from the forest into a clearing. Directly in front of them was the granite archway of the bridge leading across the sea to the next island. Yet their focus latched on to a silent creature in the middle of the gate, sitting on a wide chair made of dark marble with shimmering veins that moved like snakes. It wore an iron helmet with pointed horns. The creature lifted its head to look up as soon as they entered the clearing. A glowing like the fire in smithy's forge pulsed behind the eye slits in the helmet.

Karl activated the gaming screens and his shoulders slumped when he read the stats: *Hill Giant, Level 40*. He didn't bother reading the rest of the stats. What did it matter? If he was wrong, he would be respawning back in the guest apartment in Mavie's castle, which meant another painful journey back to a naked resurrection... which meant he would still be stuck on this damned island.

The giant ponderously pushed himself to standing, his mighty hands resting on the pommel of his great longsword. Thick vaporous clouds swirled behind him then twined around the sword morphing into angry asps that slithered and hissed.

Strewn around his feet and throughout the clearing were more bodies and bones of those who were not allowed to pass. Vultures plucked and fought, rose briefly then resumed their feast on a body at the edge of the clearing.

The giant stood three times Karl's height and at least twice his width, spreading himself across the gate. With a sneer, he stared down at the Viking and his smaller partner.

377

"What business have you here?" he asked, his voice a deep growl.

"We wish to cross the bridge," Karl replied.

"No one may pass without the key." He held his cudgel ready.

Momentarily flummoxed, Karl blurted, "The key? I know the password. No one said anything about a key."

The giant snarled at him. "Do you have the key?"

Karl hesitated and pulled up his gaming screen again.

To cross any bridge in Bridge Quest, a player must know the password for the next island. Clues to passwords are provided on each island during various quests and/or by NPCs. Once a player crosses a bridge, it is expressly forbidden that he or she return to the previous island. Any player attempting to return to a previous island will die and respawn at the entrance to the current island. Further, a player may NOT give, share or otherwise provide the password to a NPC, regardless of circumstances.

"Do you have the key?" the giant growled louder.

Karl looked at the giant then at the intimidated Gillien who had attached herself to him by tightly wrapping her arms around his left arm. She stared up at him, her eyes pleading for safety.

"Do you have the key?" the giant asked one last time. Grasping the handle of his broadsword, the giant took a step closer and pointed the tip at them.

Twisting his head to focusing on Gillien, Karl pleaded, "Go back."

"No," she cried. "I want to be with you."

"It's too dangerous. If I'm wrong, we're both dead."

"It doesn't matter," she melodramatically answered, "as long as I am with you."

Unable to extricate himself from her delusional devotion, Karl pondered telling her the wrong password, fully knowing the giant would beat her to a bloody and gruesome death. Could he live with that? Would her death be permanent? The rules said he wasn't allowed to tell the password to a

NPC. Yet it didn't say what would happen if he did. But what about Elena?

He quickly glanced around at the bodies strewn about, yet couldn't identify any of his team. Though relieved, it didn't help. Then he remembered that Nervel said they had all crossed, which meant that Elena had crossed too.

"I ask one last time before I destroy you, like all the others who came here thinking they could pass," the giant snarled. "Do you have the key?"

"Yes," Karl answered, gazing at Gillien, accepting that he would not allow her to be hurt. Not because he loved her, which he didn't, but because it was the right thing to do, regardless of what the game rules said.

Leaning down, he whispered in her ear, "The password is 'Innis Torr.' Do you understand? 'Innis Torr.' It's the name of the next island."

Gillien nodded and softly repeated the two words. Her eyes brimmed with devotion as she reached up and gently touched his cheek. "Thank you."

A large raven, black as agate, wretched and mean, settled on the left shoulder of the giant who then addressed the two bridge crossers.

"You will tell the bird the key. If he likes you, you may cross. If not... you die."

The bird flew up and circled around Karl, waiting for him to stretch out his arm. When it landed, Karl was surprised how light it was.

"The key, the key," the bird chirped, cocking its head side to side.

A swirl of wind immediately surrounded Karl, effectively separating him from Gillien.

"The key, the key," the bird repeated.

"Innis Torr," Karl said.

The swirling wind evaporated as the raven flew up and cawed, "Friend, friend."

"You may pass," the giant grunted. When Gillen made to accompany Karl, the giant held out a threatening palm. "Not you."

"M'Lord," she wailed at Karl. "Save me."

"Tell the raven what I told you," he reassured her. "I'll wait for you just past the gate."

"I'm scared."

"Of course you are," he said, hugging her. "Wait 'til I get past, then it will be your turn. It will all be OK. You'll see."

Unhooking himself from her clinging grasp, he cautiously made his way past the giant who stepped aside. Once past him, the giant stepped back into position, effectively blocking Karl from witnessing Gillien's trial. He took several backwards steps onto the bridge, all the while trying to seeing what was happening, yet he heard and saw nothing until the giant stepped to the side and Gillien came racing past him, leaping into Karl's arms.

"O my God, O my God," she exclaimed. "It worked. I'm here with you. Thank the gods, I am with you. I love you, I love you, I love you." She smothered Karl in kisses until he finally pushed her away.

"OK," he chuckled, "I get it. C'mon. Let's find where the rest of the team is." He turned and started across the bridge, Gillien happily skipping beside him, both hands holding his left hand.

The bridge was constructed of roughhewn stones, thick and heavy. As the bridge curved up and over the ocean span, Karl could not see what was at the other end, yet he could hear the cacophony below them where the sea churned, foamed, and roared. He paused to peer over the side, blinking in surprise at how high above the water they stood. He then craned his neck to see the jagged cliffs in the far distance, descending straight down to the crags and rocks littered with debris.

The island before them, thick with forest, filled the vista.

"Where do you think they might be?" Gillien merrily chatted. "This is so exciting. I've never been anywhere outside Tal Olca in my entire life. This is such an adventure. I wish my parents could see me now. My father always said that if you put your mind to it, you can do anything. Do you think your two women friends will mind it that I've taken you away from them?"

Karl silently moaned, wondering how much more of her jabber he could take when he was jerked to a stop. Twisting his head to frown at her, he saw the startled look in her eyes. He stepped back and turned to face her.

"I don't feel so good," she said with strained breath.

Karl heard it before he saw it, a faint static crackling emanating from Gillien, followed by her body beginning to fade and dissipate.

She gaped at him with terrified and imploring eyes, as she sobbed, "My Lord."

"O God, no," were the last words he heard before she vanished.

Karl remained rooted, stunned, suddenly realizing that he may have killed her. His next thought was of Elena. Had the same thing happened to her? He sucked in a deep breath remembering the injunction: *a player may NOT give, share or otherwise provide the password to a NPC, regardless of circumstances.*

He then thought of Dieter and how he must be crushed not to have Elena with him. Accepting that he could not change what had happened and justifying the emotion that Gillien was a NPC, a made up character in a game and not a real person, he pushed his angst into the far recesses of his mind, out of the way where they couldn't bother him. Then he turned and headed to Innis Torr. It was time to catch up with the rest of his team.

OTHER BOOKS

I write GameLit, Space Opera, Steampunk, Dystopian, Literary, Romance, and even poetry, and you can find my books in numerous eBook stores. You can check out my website for more information about my books, upcoming projects, and events I'll be attending where you can visit with me and even get signed books.

Thank you for choosing to read this story! If you enjoyed it, I'd appreciate your feedback in the form of a review.

Thanks for reading!

-pdmac

WEBSITE: www.pdmac-author.com

FACEBOOK: www.facebook.com/pdmacauthor/

The Wyvern Master Chronicles

The Sixth Kingdom
A Spy in the Court
Raising the Dead
Wizard King

Bridge Quest: A GameLit Adventure Series

Bridge Quest
Orc's Bane
Lord of Innis Torr

Steampunk Western: Tombstone Trilogy:

Fool's Gold

An Ounce of Lead

The Devil's Disciple (Coming soon)

Viking Time Travel Romance

Beyond Her Touch

A Dystopian Novel

Rebirth of Angels

A Time Travel Novella

Ctrl Z: The Do Over Stone

Poetry

a young man no more